Paper Tigers

Paper Tigers

Lou Aguilar

Deeds Publishing | Atlanta

Published by Deeds Publishing in Athens, GA
www.deedspublishing.com

Printed in The United States of America

Library of Congress Cataloging-in-Publications data is available upon request.

978-1-947309-55-5

Books are available in quantity for promotional or premium use. For information, email info@deedspublishing.com.

First Edition, 2018

10 9 8 7 6 5 4 3 2 1

To Jim and Aman,
Their friendship made me a better writer and better man.
Wish they'd stuck around to read this book. Perhaps they will
where they went.

Part One
The New Man Test

1

Nick Jarrett stood on the north end of Franklin Park looking across K Street at the Washington Post Building. The iconic masthead spanned the twelve-story white façade as if in defiance of the internet forces besieging it. With newspapers dying all over, the Post had lost much of its muscle, but it still packed a mean punch. Nick hoped to leave a mark of his own someday, so five months out of the University of Wyoming, on a cold, bright mid-October Monday morning, he was ready to start his first day as a Washington Post copyboy — now politically corrected into "copyaide."

A red torpedo entered his right periphery. It became a dynamic young woman in a maroon coat striding toward the building entrance. Even from across the street, Nick could discern her striking beauty: august face mopped by thick black hair, fierce eyes, round hips, and firm legs powering grey slacks. Nick dashed across the street to reach the glass door ahead of the girl. He opened it, and held it open for her. She frowned for a second, gave him a curt nod, and went inside. Nick admired her backside all the way to the security desk, where she spoke to the black female guard in a refined, breathy voice.

"Hello. I'm Laura London—new copyaide."

Nick smiled. Some political correctness was all right by him.

"Newsroom, seventh floor."

"Thank you."

Laura proceeded toward the elevators.

"Same deal," Nick said to the guard.

"Follow her."

"My pleasure."

He joined Laura at the elevator row. She barely looked at him despite her piercing brown eyes. He smiled at her anyway.

"Fellow copyaide," he said, tapping his chest. "Where you from?"

"Boston."

"Spenser."

"Is that your name?"

"No, a Boston private detective created by Robert Parker," said Nick. "I'm a mystery buff. I like to match each city with its resident sleuth."

"Detroit."

"Amos Walker."

"Bombay."

"Sartaj Singh."

"Where does V. I. Warshawski live?"

"Beats me. She's for girls."

"Oh, forgive me," said Laura. "I suppose all your heroes guzzle scotch, talk tough, and have women jumping into bed with them."

"Not all of them...Some prefer bourbon."

An elevator door slid open. Nick kept it from closing.

"Thanks," Laura said, stepping into the elevator. "That door's much too heavy for me."

Nick pressed seven on the floor indicator. Laura peered at him with some interest. He stood two inches taller than her. He had a ruggedly handsome face with hazel eyes and dark brown hair under a blue-grey Irish tweed cap, and a sturdy upright frame, evident even through his black faux leather aviator jacket. The elevator started to ascend.

"So, who's your home sleuth — Wyatt Earp?"

"My town's too small," said Nick. "Medicine Bow, Wyoming."

"Do women vote there?"

"Sure, after they've made supper … It's not so bad. Nice place to raise kids."

"But not their consciousness."

"We can always use a new schoolmarm."

"Sorry, I'm needed in the twenty-first century," said Laura.

The elevator door opened on a massive, high-tech, grey-and-black newsroom abuzz with activity. Editors and reporters sat behind desktop monitors in cubicle clusters marked "Metro Desk," "National Desk," "Foreign Desk," "Financial Desk," and more. On the far side of the beehive, a glass wall separated the two executive editors' offices and the conference room. Laura gaped.

"Don't get too excited," Nick said, and tilted his head right. "The mailroom's that way."

He and Laura walked right from the elevator. They hung their coats at the far end of a hall-long closet, Nick admiring his new colleague's perky chest in a violet button blouse. They passed through a doorless opening into the copyaide station.

It was a reverse L-shaped room, with an entrance at each end of the long bar, the far door closed. The short bar went left from the newsroom entrance into a narrow annex, dead-ending five yards in. Mail slots covered the three walls above a waist-high counter. The long bar was dominated by a high metal block table, a plastic crate full of envelopes at its base. The right wall had mail slots and supply cupboards. The left side opened on a small alcove with a beverage, snack, and coffee machine. In the back left corner perched a widescreen television, running CNN on mute. An analog wall clock above the door indicated nine o'clock.

Five other copyaides stood around the table, appraising Nick and Laura. Nick mentally classified them Philip Marlowe-style: dark-garbed Brooder with earbuds on, buxom short-skirted Hot Blonde, handsome blueblood Preppie, gregarious black Jock, comely redhead Amazon in designer jeans. On the tabletop before them lay a disemboweled Washington Post newspaper. Preppie and Jock resumed scanning the Sports section, Hot Blonde the Style page. Beside her, Amazon studied Laura, until Hot Blonde's Southern country accent distracted her.

"Isn't this the saddest thing you ever saw?" Hot Blonde said, indicating the Fashion page.

"Sure is," said Amazon, glancing over Hot Blonde's shoulder. "Fashion models send women a dangerous message. Be impossibly skinny just so men will find you attractive."

"I meant her Gucci pumps," said Hot Blonde.

"They should've benched Thompson in the second half," said Preppie, indicating the Sports section.

"You don't pull your star forward for missing a few rebounds," Jock said. "It demoralizes the team."

"Oh please. They're grown men. Make that overgrown men. They can take it."

Laura said, "Did you know the Women's Basketball Team at Old Dominion won more games than the men's? And when their coach demanded equal pay, they fired her."

"Probably for being dumb," said Nick.

Laura glared at Nick. All other eyes focused on the two newcomers.

"Dumb?" Laura said challengingly.

"Yeah. That coach was lucky to have a job. Chick teams are a luxury for any college, and a deficit. It's guy sports that rake in the dough."

"I'd rather watch men play," said Hot Blonde.

The other copyaides turned to Laura as if spectating a tennis match, Amazon the most intently.

"So, it's all about money?" Laura asked Nick.

"You bet. If that lady was coaching the men's team, she'd deserve equal pay."

"More," Jock said. "I'd like to see a woman giving LeBron shit."

He mimicked a shrill female voice. "You'd best make that next foul shot, baldy!"

Laura fixated on Nick.

"Do you have a problem with strong women?"

"No. I like Lara Croft—the Angelina Jolie incarnation of course."

All the other copyaides chuckled except Sarah. The office door right of the newsroom entrance opened. Copyaide Supervisor Susan Machado stepped out, joined by a bulldoggish, middle-aged, white-haired black man. The matronly Latina had interviewed everyone in the room over the past summer, among a hundred recent college graduates. She smiled at her young flock and spoke.

"Ladies and gentlemen, welcome to the Washington Post. I know you've all come from great schools, and will one day be fine journalists. But here and now I expect you to stack mail, answer phones, and be good little gophers. As far as more glamorous work goes ... I'll leave that to our Metro Desk Editor, Mr. Frank Russell."

Everyone turned to her companion.

"I got bad news and good news, "Russell said. "Bad news is the Post no longer promotes copyaides into reporters. That is unless you come up with an earthshaking scoop. The good news for you guys is we let go a dozen reporters in the downturn. So some charitable editors like me will let you write soft features for them — off the clock naturally. When you got enough clips with your byline in the Post, another news service might hire you."

"The Alaska Seal Times," Preppie whispered to Nick.

"Everglades Gazette," Nick whispered back.

The two of them grinned, bonding.

"You'll be issued press cards, so you can be our eyes and ears around the city," said Russell. "My advice is, be on the lookout for potential stories. Good luck."

He exited to the newsroom, leaving Susan to address the copyaides.

"Okay, kids. Introduce yourselves to the rest of us, stating what desk you'd prefer to assist on."

Brooder said, "Warren Jones — rock and roll."

"The Style Music Desk covers all music," Susan said.

"I don't do rap," said Warren.

Hot Blonde said, "Tammy Perkins — Style."

Preppie said, "Hugh Sinclair the Third — Financial."

Jock said, "Mike Carter — Sports."

Amazon said, "Sarah Woronov — Editorial."

"Laura London — Metro or National."

"Nick Jarrett — Metro or National."

Laura sighed.

"Great," said Susan. "Stop by the Photo Desk sometime today to get your press card picture taken."

She indicated the mail crates on the floor.

"Mr. Carter, start the ball."

Mike hoisted the full crate over the tabletop, and spilled its contents. The copyaides began sorting mail.

2

Shortly before noon, Nick, Laura, Mike, and Sarah were the only copyaides in the station. Nick stacked envelopes while softly whistling the theme from *Laura*, his second-favorite film noir. Laura grabbed a stack, and began inserting each envelope into the appropriate mailbox. Nick's unchanging melody finally got to her.

"Don't you know any other tunes?"

"Can't get this one out of my head," said Nick.

"What is it?"

"Some old movie theme."

Laura looked askance at Nick.

Mike and Sarah took their stacks into the annex. Mike's six-feet-two made it easy for him to reach the highest slots. The five inches shorter Sarah had a more difficult time with one envelope slated for the top row. Mike offered to take it. Sarah shook her head, and grabbed the stool. She climbed onto it, so that her shapely blue-jeaned butt was directly in Mike's face. Staring at it, he missed the slot entirely with his own envelope, crumpling it against the divider.

On his way to the supply room, Hugh Sinclair the Third paused near the Financial Desk. Two male journalists, one sitting and one standing, were focused on the sitter's computer screen. Hugh moved closer to the pair, and looked at the same screen. After a moment, both men turned inquisitively to him. Hugh gave them a sheepish smile, and continued to the Foreign Desk. Making sure that no superior was watching him, he took out his cellphone.

"Hey, dad," he whispered. "Sell Petrocorp."

The Style section was a mini version of the newsroom, with more casually dressed denizens functioning at a calmer pace. Tammy Perkins slunk through it on the way to the Fashion and Food Desk. The Fashion Editor—a thin, shaggy-haired, thirtyish male with a pearl earring—sat at his computer, scrolling photos of the Milan Fall Fashion Week. Tammy appeared beside him. Mocking the price of the Giorgetti gown on screen, she got his attention. She gave him a flirtatious smile, and introduced herself as a copyaide. The Fashion Editor smiled politely, and refocused on the screen. Tammy brooded for a moment, then noticed the desk photo of a buff young man under the inscription: *To my darling husband, Eric.* Tammy nodded, and stood by till the Fashion Editor turned to her once more.

Deeper in the Style section, Warren Jones approached the Music Desk, the iPod Touch playing in his ears. Music Editor Rick Masetti sat in his cubicle, grimacing at the sound from his Bose headset. He was a heavy man in his mid-fifties, wearing a Navajo design sweater and his grey hair in a ponytail. Seeing Warren move closer, he lowered the headset to around his neck.

"Dude, whatever you're listening to has to be better than this shit."

"'Shout'," said Warren, removing his earphones.

"Ah, Tears for Fears," Masetti said fondly.

"Scandroid."

"Sacrilege."

"Hey, Reagan's no longer President."

"And I lament that every day. I'm Rick Masetti. So you think you know music?"

"Try me," Warren said.

Laura got the noon Internal Mail run. Approaching the Investigative Desk with her tray box, she recognized the grey head of Todd Armstrong, iconic reporter and now sexagenarian chief of Investigative. He was on the phone giving one of his people a hard time.

"Don't tell me how many of her aides are denying it! I know the First Lady was at that séance! Talk to someone else who was there—even if it's Eleanor effing Roosevelt!"

He hung up, and came face to beautiful face with Laura London.

"Hello," said Armstrong, softening instantly. "Who might you be?"

"Laura London."

"One of Susan's drones, eh? I'm Todd Arms—"

"I know who you are, Mr. Armstrong. You're a legend."

"I'm too young to be a legend, or Mr. Armstrong. Call me Todd. Where'd you graduate from, Laura?"

"Mount Holyoake."

"Great school. I've spoken there twice. Journalism major?"

"English Lit."

"Good for you. Have to learn what to read to know how to write."

"I've read all your pieces."

"Smart girl," Armstrong said, then a thought crossed his face. "Hey, what are you doing tonight?"

"Excuse me?"

"I've got this White House Press Dinner thing. I need a gorgeous yet sophisticated date who can blend in with the In crowd. You'll do."

"Oh," said Laura, stupefied. "I can't, Mr. Arms—Todd. I have a significant other."

"Lot of bigwigs will be there. Don't you want a career?"

"Of course I do, but..."

"Tell you what," said Armstrong. "Think about it, and let me know by three."

"I will, Todd."

Laura moved away in a daze. She reentered the copyaide station to find Nick and Sarah finishing up the mail, Nick still softly whistling the same melody. Hugh came in, pushing the box-laden supply cart. He unloaded a box of printer paper, and turned to the whistling Nick.

"'Laura's Theme'," he said.

Nick felt Laura's eyes boring into him. He feigned surprise.

"Is that what that is?"

"We used to play it in my frat house at Tulane," said Hugh. "The Nat King Cole version. Sorority girls always fell for...I mean, appreciated it."

"Uh, I'll go see if there's more mail," Nick said.

He hurried out the newsroom doorway. Hugh followed with a roll of fax paper. Sarah looked at Laura.

"You know, that could be construed as sexual harassment."

"Difficult to prove," said Laura. "He was just whistling."

"Maybe...Hey, Laura?"

"Yes, Sarah."

"Let me watch your back in here."

"Thank you. I'll do the same for you."

"I doubt that'll be an issue. Just so you know, I'm into women."

"I envy you," said Laura.

Sarah smiled, and took a stack of envelopes into the annex. Laura pursed her lips, and began softly whistling *Laura's Theme*.

3

The Washington Post cafeteria was a large, clean buffet operation on the second floor, lunch served by two efficient black women. Nick stood at the counter, receiving his hamburger, fries and Coke platter. He bore his tray into the crowded dining area, where he spotted Laura's lovely profile. She sat alone at a two-seat table, nibbling on a tuna salad, engrossed in a familiar paperback edition of *The Great Gatsby*. Nick thought about joining her, but decided she would prefer the reflections of Nick Carraway to his own. Tammy's voice from his right distracted him.

"Hey, Nick. Join us."

She sat with Warren Jones at a four-place table, looking far more inviting than the Brooder. Nick sat down with the pair.

"I was just congratulating Warren on getting the Music Desk," Tammy said.

"Hey, that's fantastic, Warren," said Nick.

"Thanks. Would love to interview some living legends — Springsteen, Jagger, Bono ..."

"Elvis," said Nick.

His table companions looked at him.

"I know he's out there," Nick said.

He cast a wistful glance at Laura. Tammy caught it and frowned. Nick turned to her.

"How 'bout you, Tammy? Any luck with the Fashion Desk?"

"I had a small setback. The editor's gay."

"Small?"

"He's still a man," Tammy said, with an impish smile.

"And all men like Marilyn Monroe."

"Why, thank you, Nick," Tammy said. "Meantime, it's back to the mailroom for me."

She stood up, then so did Warren.

"I'll walk you up," he said.

"You got half your lunch hour left."

"I, uh, need to go over my new duties."

"See you up there, Nick," Tammy said huskily.

She walked away with Warren at her side. Nick turned to Laura, still reading and nibbling her food. Before he could think twice, he took up his tray and moved to her table. Laura peered up at him over her book.

"May I join you?" Nick asked.

"Why would you want to?"

"We work together. Even the Berlin Wall came down."

"Don't expect any unification," Laura said, with a slight nod at the other chair.

She lay down her book as Nick took a seat. He indicated the paperback.

"*The Great Gatsby*. One of my favorites."

"That's odd. It's not a mystery.

"It kind of is. Who is Jay Gatsby? Where did he come from?"

"He's a stalker," Laura said.

"What?"

"The whole book is about male sexual obsession."

"Wow," said Nick. "One of the great American love stories, deconstructed to a feminist nutshell."

"I'm here to help."

"So how's your first day going?"

"Oh, you know…sort mail, deliver mail, get invited to the White House press dinner by Todd Armstrong, sort more mail…"

Nick's jaw fell. "What? You mean like a date?"

"That was Todd's word for it."

"Todd," said Nick. "Well, it's one way to get close to the President. Used to be the internship program."

Laura smirked.

"Are you going?"

"I don't know," said Laura. "Todd Armstrong's a hero of mine—besides being someone who can jumpstart my career. On the other hand, it goes against my principles."

"And," she added with a smile. "My boyfriend would balk."

"What does he do?" asked Nick, feeling oddly jealous.

"He's a Legislative Aide to Wayne Hawthorne."

"Oh God."

"You have a problem with the Senator from Connecticut?" Laura asked.

"You want my top ten?"

"Make it two. And don't count the Potomac Stripper incident. That was four years ago."

"Okay," said Nick. "Blocking the best Supreme Court nominee we had in years. Voting against every weapon system since the catapult."

"Someone has to hold back the right-wing hordes."

"That was my third objection."

Laura shook her head. "Why are you here, Montana?"

"Wyoming."

"All those red states look alike to me."

"Stop lights to progressive insanity," said Nick. "But I was a History major so I..."

"Live in the past?"

"No...I learn from it—unlike your crew. And I want to chronicle history as it's happening. What's your reason?"

"Journalism give voice to the voiceless," said Laura. "And mine shall be heard."

"Through a left-wing speaker. You need stereo for balance."

"The right one's just primitive noise—made by cavemen like you, Nick."

"Me hurt. But why a newspaper? With your face and...form, you'd be a natural for television news."

"Now there's a sexist remark. I don't want to be gaped at. I want to be read."

"I read you."

Laura grunted.

"Boy," she said. "You must really miss Teddy Roosevelt. I'm surprised you came here straight out of school, instead of the military."

"I did both. I'm in the Wyoming National Guard. My unit could be called up to Afghanistan any day now."

"Oh," Laura said, with a concerned expression. "Why'd you do a stupid thing like that for?"

"Family tradition. My older brother's over there now, with the Marines. I may join up when he takes over the family ranch next year. Dad didn't want both of us in harm's way. He lost his father in Vietnam."

That evening, Nick and Laura handled the last crate of mail. They'd exchanged few words since after lunch, but none of them snippy. Nick twice spied Laura looking enigmatically at him across the mail table. Her expression made his heart beat faster. He believed she could crack it with little effort. To diffuse her power over him, he looked back at her with forced nonchalance. But circling close behind her at one point, he caught a whiff of her perfume, and stifled a gasp. He'd always thought perfume a female extravagance, like jewelry. But the sweet scent of it on Laura's neck captivated another of his senses. It took him a moment to see the envelope she held up, strewn with exotic stamps, addressed in cursive lettering to the Foreign Desk.

"You were aghast at the amount of ground mail we get," she said. "This one's from Mombasa."

"Kenya. Their snail mail's probably faster than their internet."

"I had a farm in Africa," Laura said.

"No, you did not."

"It's the first line in 'Out of Africa'. Have you read it, Nick?"

"Uh uh. I saw the movie. Meryl Streep with another accent. Lots of flying over trees. I kept waiting for Tarzan to show up."

"The book is wonderful. By Karen Blixen. Pen name Isak Dinesen. You've got to read it."

"I will," said Nick, delighted by Laura wanting to share something special to her with him.

"Karen loved Kenya."

"And Robert Redford."

"He was nothing like Denys Finch Hatton, the Englishman

who wooed her. But she did run a coffee plantation in Kenya, all by herself. Can you believe that, back then and there?"

"Well, Kenya was part of the British Empire," Nick said. "They kept their colonies safe."

"For white people."

"True. The Mau Mau fared much worse."

"The land she describes was a paradise of flora and fauna," said Laura. "I love elephants. I should like to see one in the veld, before men exterminate them all."

Her poignancy touched Nick.

"I'm sure you will," he said.

"And to be loved the way Karen was."

"That wouldn't be difficult," said Nick.

Laura looked at him with her bright brown eyes.

"Nick. You're so endearing. If only you could..."

She shut up when Hugh walked in through the open doorway. Nick longed to know what she had been about to say.

4

Nick walked east on the Duke Ellington Bridge, above the night shrouded treetops of Rock Creek Park. The glowing round streetlamps gave the bridge a Parisian winter appearance, making Nick feel like Inspector Maigret. As a fledgling journalist, he minimized cellphone usage on his walks, preferring to soak in the sights and sounds of the city for a potential story.

He had a yen for Ethiopian food, and the Adams Morgan neighborhood offered the best. What it lacked was a subway stop, so Nick took the long, brisk stroll from Woodley Park station a mile west on Connecticut Avenue. Although he enjoyed lone walks, tonight he would have preferred some company, specifically one beauteous brunette Brahmin.

Nick had thought he'd loved two girls in his life, one in high school, the other during his upper-class years at the University of Wyoming. Neither had made his pulse race the way Laura London now did. He finally understood a line from *The Godfather*, which he watched every time it ran on cable. Like Michael Corleone, he'd been "hit by the Thunderbolt."

He did a search for "Corleone" and "thunderbolt" on his smartphone. The answer came up, "What Sicilians call a powerful, almost dangerous longing in a man for a particular woman." Nick half expected Laura's picture to appear beneath it instead of the actress who played Apollonia. Not being a Mafioso, he would have to win Laura the old-fashioned way, with his charm. Certainly not his politics.

Nick's mind was not the only one on Laura London that night. Sarah Woronov also thought of her while jogging south on Buckman Road in Old Town Alexandria. She wore a grey sweatshirt, green sweat pants, Nike running shoes, wool gloves, and her auburn hair in a ponytail behind earbuds playing EDM. The final stretch of her three-mile run passed small old houses, with enough streetlight for safety. Additional security came from her athletic body, evident in her powerful strides.

She realized she would have to seduce Laura. She'd done it before—turned straight women into insatiable lovers, her current roommate being the latest. Allison had been easy to convert, having been taught at George Mason University that heterosexuality was akin to white privilege. Of course it helped to be attractive, which Sarah knew she was, to both sexes. But Laura's high sophistication would be a challenge. In the Trojan War against men, Laura was Athena to her Artemis. Sarah wanted her to be her Aphrodite too.

She made a left on Aspen Drive, and slowed to a cooldown walk, feeling the sweat on her body. Near the end of the block, she turned right toward a one-level brick house. She took a single key out of the mailbox, unlocked the front door, and went inside.

Allison smiled sweetly at her from the loveseat in the living room. She looked quite cute with her short brown hair, pink sweater, and long denim skirt. She put aside her Kindle to give Sarah her full attention. Sarah barely acknowledged her while removing her gloves and sweatshirt. In a moistened gold tank-top, she bent down to touch her toes.

"How was your run?"

"All right," said Sarah, her face almost at her knees.

"Hope it made you hungry."

"Why do you say that?"

"We're going to Tim and Nancy's, remember? To celebrate your new job at the Post?"

Sarah straightened up.

"I forgot…I don't really feel like going out tonight. Would you mind if I stay home?"

"You mean if *we* stay home, don't you?"

"No, you should go," said Sarah. "Thank Tim and Nancy for me."

She put her hands on her waist, her right leg three feet back, and stretched the leg by bending her left knee.

"I don't want to go without you," Allison said, getting nervous.

"I really think you should, Allison."

"What are you trying to say?"

"We should start spending more time apart," said Sarah.

She switched legs to begin stretching her left leg.

"I don't understand," Allison said, now anxious.

Sarah ceased her stretching.

"The new job is pretty intense. I need to focus on it for a while."

"Who is she?!" blurted Allison, her lips quivering.

Sarah looked at her.

"Someone I'd like to get to know better. It'll be easier if I'm single."

"You fucking bitch!" cried Allison.

"Guilty," Sarah said. "I'm sorry."

Mike Carter left the Anacostia Metro Station carrying his battered Howard University gym bag. He walked north on Shannon Road, once again surveying his home turf. The two-story, tri-columned, gable-roofed wooden houses perfectly reflected the neighborhood's fluctuant state. More than half of them had well-tended facades and small lawns. The rest appeared decrepit, foreboding. The latter number had increased in the last decade, Mike knew. It used to be one out of three.

He remembered his childhood thrill, in fact the whole community's, at the election of the first black President. But the hope he'd placed in him—for a better, safer environment and racial healing—had eroded over eight years of the man's standard liberal agenda. Mike could name two offenses that affected him personally. He had eliminated the DC private school voucher program, right before Mike's kid sister and brother could access it, trapping them in their inept school. He backed the racist anti-police protest movement, born of a lie, which resulted in less aggressive policing, fewer local businesses, and more crime on the streets.

Two years earlier, Mike had almost left Anacostia for greener pastures, and taken his family with him. As the star quarterback at Howard, he'd been wooed by New Orleans and Denver—until a Duke rush busted his left leg and NFL future. The university ty terminated his football scholarship. Fortunately for him, he'd paid attention to scholastics, and gotten a college loan his senior year. He had covered sports for the Howard Hilltop, including his former team. Now he hoped to go pro as a sportswriter.

One block from his home, Mike stopped before an ominous sight. A male figure, his face obscured by a black hoodie, stood on one of the unlit porches, accepting paper money from two preteen boys. Mike recognized one of them as a friend of his little brother's. He glared at the hooded man, who looked back at him with his hidden face. Rick's friend turned to Mike, and scurried off the porch with his companion, away from Mike. Mike resumed the walk home, shaking his head.

The Carter house complimented the neighborhood. It had bright white wood panels and two healthy potted shrubs on the porch. Mike went inside. The small living room was neat and clean, despite the cheap threadbare furniture. Mike's siblings, Rick, a lanky twelve, and Alice, fifteen and blossoming too fast, sat on the couch in their school uniforms. A *Big Bang Theory* re-run played on the old TV. They both turned to Mike, Rick only for a moment before refocusing on the show.

"Hey, bro," Alice chirped. "How was the Washington Post?"

"Good," Mike said. "Lotsa smart folks."

"Now there's one more," said Rita Carter, emerging from the kitchen, an apron around her plump waist. "Hi, baby."

She looked up proudly at her much taller son. Mike gave her a kiss on the forehead.

"Dinner's almost ready," Rita said.

"You're a life saver, mom, 'cause I'm starving to death."

"Alice, please set the table."

"All right, mom."

Alice went into the kitchen behind Rita. Mike took her place on the couch beside his brother, eyes still on the TV. Mike grabbed the remote, and muted the sound.

"Hey!" said Rick.

"You still hanging with Dwayne Walker?"

"Not so much this year."

"Yeah? How come?"

"He don't wanna do nothin' after school no more."

"Doesn't want to do anything anymore," said Mike.

"Come on, man."

"Trust me, Rick, you'll thank me later. But it's good you're seeing less of Dwayne. 'cause where he's heading you don't wanna go."

Mike unmuted the television on a raucous laugh track.

Thirty miles north of Anacostia lies its antithesis — Potomac, Maryland, an ultra-affluent community of colonial-style homes on large landscaped gardens. One of the medium-size houses was a broad, redbrick, two-story structure with white marble columns belonging to Mr. and Mrs. Hugh Sinclair, Junior. Hugh Sinclair the Third parked his black 2016 Subaru sports car in the driveway outside the left-end garage. He walked to the front door, and used his key to unlock it — an after-dark requirement, even with people inside.

Hugh hung his double-breasted cashmere coat in the foyer closet. He moved past the white staircase, and turned right into the archway. He stepped aside for the exiting Hortense, carrying an empty drinks tray. The forty-something Haitian maid warmly greeted Hugh.

"Bonsoir, Monsieur Hugh."

"Bonsoir, Hortense. My parents ..."

Hugh pantomimed taking a drink. Hortense grinned.

"Boissons, oui."

"Good," said Hugh. "They'll be in bonne humeur."

He entered the living room to soft jazz coming from over the fireplace. His parents sat behind open laptops, his mother on the sofa, white wine in hand, wearing a blue wool dress and designer glasses under short grey hair. Hugh Junior sat in his favorite armchair, a martini glass in the armrest slot, a tailored grey suit hiding his expanded stomach.

"Hi, darling," Helen Sinclair said with a smile, prompting her husband to look up at Hugh. "Well?"

"The place is great, mom. There's an incredible energy there. You can just feel it."

"The Post brought a President down once," said Hugh Junior. "Let's hope they can do it again. This one's killing our medical malpractice profits with his damn healthcare reform."

"I'll see what I can do, dad," said Hugh.

Helen snickered slightly. Her husband turned to her, and saw her typing on her laptop.

Nick made a right off Biltmore Street onto Columbia Road. He walked between twin rows of brightly painted antique buildings with cheerful Third World restaurants at street level. His destination, *The Red Sea*, was two blocks down on Kalorama Street. He never got that far. Three diminutive Hispanic men in tight black pants and puffy gold shirts dashed past him, carrying a guitar case, horn case, and flute case. They ducked into the side street just ahead of Nick. Something told him to follow them. He ran up to the side street, and looked right.

Thirty yards down, they stood before the door of an indistinct restaurant. Nick couldn't see the name of it, only Guitar Man pulling open the door, which closed fast behind the trio. Nick approached the restaurant, getting close enough to read the name, *El Caribe*. A sign on the door said, *Cerrado los Lunes*. Nick was about to move away, when he heard a sirenic voice belting out a heartfelt ballad in Spanish, accompanied by guitar and flute. Hoping to see the siren's face, Nick opened the door, and went inside.

He moved past the vacant hostess stand to a wooden post. Leaning against it, he had a good view of the restaurant. It was a compact, low-lighted place. Posters of old Caribbean lighthouses lined the wood-panel walls. Impecunious Hispanics of both sexes and all ages over twenty sat with their backs to him, drinking coffee, tea, or soda. Everyone fixated on the makeshift stage at the far end.

On it stood a short, thirty-something woman in a flowery dress, singing sweetly into a foot microphone, accompanied by the three musicians behind her. The wistful tone of her song enthralled the audience, and Nick, who had learned some Spanish from his family ranch's Mexican foreman, La Candela. Nick tried to translate the song in his head, while snapping pictures of the stage show with his phone.

Lejos de mi tierra / Far from my land
Recordaba su belleza, / I recalled its beauty,
Pedacito de cielo / A piece of heaven
Nacido del mar / Born of the sea

Mas a volverla a ver / Oh to see it again
Mis mas lindos recuerdos / My loveliest memories
Se volvieron sombras / Became shadows
Ante la realidad. / Against the reality.
Una claridad de estrellas / A clarity of stars
Iluminaba la bahia. / Illuminated the bay,
Y una briza de manana / And a morning breeze
El mar de plata mecia. / Rippled the silver sea.
Olor de tierra y de flores / The scent of land and flowers
Un gallo rompe a cantar, / A cock breaks into song,
Y se olle el suave murmullo / And you hear the soft murmur
De un palmar. / Of the swaying palms.
Detras las negras Colinas /Behind the black hills
Ya nace el sol encendido, / Now comes the blazing sun,
Manchndo con rallos de oro / Marking with golden rays
El campo en la oscuridad. / The countryside in the dark.

The woman concluded her song to vigorous applause. She gave a grateful wave and moved off the stage. The trio began a lively Brazilian tune that seemed to uplift the crowd after the siren's melancholia. Nick took more pictures of the troupe, and felt a finger tapping his upper back. He turned to see a Latino priest, two inches shorter than himself, with a monkish bald spot.

"I'm sorry, senor," said the priest in a thick accent. "The restaurant is closed."

"I'd like to see it when it's open," Nick said, pointing at the clearly full house.

"This is a private coffee house for my parishioners. The restaurant owner donates the space every Monday night."

"For a hell of a show. Sorry, Father. But those musicians are amazing. And that singer ..."

"Yes, we have some talented artists among our immigrants. The coffee house gives them a chance to perform, and the rest some free entertainment, other than television."

Nick felt a jolt of electricity.

"You know, Father, this could make a good story."

"What do you mean?" the priest asked suspiciously.

Nick took out his wallet and showed him his Washington Post press card.

"I see ..." said the priest. "You would use only the names I provide?"

Nick understood his concern for illegal aliens.

"I promise."

"Ta bien. I'm Father Juan Ramirez. My parish is more than the church. It is a bridge linking different peoples who share the same language and faith, not necessarily the same ..."

Nick, frisking himself, interrupted Ramirez's speech.

"Can I borrow a pen, Father?"

Nick took an Uber to his vintage brownstone four-story apartment building on Connecticut Avenue, right below Chevy Chase Circle on the Maryland border. Approaching the entrance, he again silently thanked the friend of a college friend who grandfathered him into the rent-controlled building he could never have afforded on a copyboy's salary.

He entered his third-floor studio unit, flicking the light switch by the door. It illuminated the cozy "living room" from the door to the rear window, and the pine furniture set in between—sofa, loveseat, armchair, coffee table—and the small oak desk at the window. Four framed film noir posters hung on the opposite walls, in order of movie preference—*Double Indemnity*, *Laura*, *Gumshoe*, *The Blue Dahlia*. A low bookshelf, full of paperback mysteries and classics, stood against the right wall, with an Alexa device on top.

To the door's left, two white shutter portals were open on a spacious walkthrough closet. The closet doubled as Nick's bedroom, thanks to the large futon mattress on the floor, its head several spare feet beneath his hanging clothes. The bathroom entrance was at the right end of the closet, near the foot of the futon. To the right of the front door—past a red-and-black Cervelo racing bike—a two-seat dinette table gave the illusion of a corner dining room.

Nick threw his flight jacket on the back of the window-facing sofa. He walked to the illusory dining room, then left into the small, narrow kitchen. He took a Dos Equis Dark out of the refrigerator. Returning to the den, he sat down on the sofa with his feet on the coffee table. He turned to the Alexa cone, only one song on his mind.

"Alexa, play 'Theme from Laura'."

"'Theme from Laura'," said Alexa. "By John Williams and the Boston Pop Orchestra."

As Nick Raskin's sublime piano music score began to play, Nick took a welcome sip of beer. His cellphone buzzed an incoming text. He read the message, from his mother in Medicine Bow (two hours earlier by Mountain Standard Time): *Hi, darling. Dad and I want to hear all about your first day at work. Any nice copy girls? Call us. Love, mom.*

Nick looked up at the *Laura* poster, focusing on Gene Tierney's exquisite face.

"Maybe not so nice," he said, toasting Gene with the beer bottle.

Laura London raised the middle window in her Capitol Hill row house living room and blew a plume of smoke into the frosty night. Gazing down one story at the lamp lit "E" Street, she took a second drag on her cigarette, and watched a ski-capped bicyclist rush by the house.

She wondered how the White House press dinner was progressing without her. She would have worn her black silk slit dress. Then with the sexist President ogling her, she would have lauded the historical candidate he beat. Probably not but she could dream, even if her last dream had been crushed on Election Night. Instead of the first woman President, they were stuck with a swaggering alpha male—like Nick Jarrett. Picturing Nick, she tried to smirk, but had to dissolve a smile instead. She breathed in more smoke, and heard Phil's voice behind her.

"Laura."

She quickly extinguished the cigarette on the window sill, ready to toss it out. Only she couldn't bring herself to litter. She lay the cigarette butt in the window rail, and closed the window, hoping Phil wouldn't spot the evidence. She turned to her partner of two years. Phil Cartwright looked as attractive today as when they met at a mutual friend's Boston wedding. He had the same lean frame, bushy brown hair, and magnetic intensity, although the lines on his forehead had deepened since the election. He held five pages of printout in his right hand.

"What are you doing?"

"Just taking some air," Laura said.

"Unseasonably cold air. A sure sign of climate change. Yet the deniers are in charge of the government."

"And we're in political Siberia," Laura said sadly.

Phil nodded in assent.

"Are we eating anytime soon?" he asked.

"Of course, sweetheart. I was waiting for you to finish your labor. All done?"

Phil proudly raised the printout sheets. "I crunched the Senator's speech down to its essence. Still a bit long, but he'll hit all the right notes. The union crowd should eat it up."

"I'm sure they will," said Laura.

Phil moved to Laura and took her in his arms. He gave her a fervent kiss, then withdrew before she could respond, a grimace on his face.

"You've been smoking."

"Just one."

"We made a pact, Laura. To personally oppose the tobacco lobby."

"I had a rough first day."

"We're fighting an almost trillion-dollar industry—and its Republican lackeys. All we have to go on is our own resolve."

"Should I wash my mouth out with soap?"

Phil smiled, softening. "Maybe later."

He went in for a second kiss, which Laura sensuously returned.

"Now what was so hard about today?" Phil asked when they broke off the kiss.

"Another copyaide was getting on my nerves. Talk about a cigarette ad. He's like the goddamn Marlboro Man."

"It's pathetic some deluded women ever saw him as a sex symbol," said Phil.

Laura cast down her eyes.

"Forget it, honey," said Phil. "Soon his type will be as extinct as he is."

Laura's face took on a malevolent smile.

5

Just before ten the next morning, Nick and Hugh worked alone in the copyaide station. Nick tried to concentrate on Hugh's humorous account of a sexual encounter, but could only picture Laura enjoying one — at the hands of Todd Armstrong.

"So we're both down to our underwear, and my Swedish doll starts talking up her homegrown lovers. I hear Sven did this, Olaf did that, and Igmar did both at the same time. Naturally I'm thinking, 'How can I compete with those Vikings?'"

I could handle fair competition, Nick thought, but a legendary journalist is a bit much.

"Now comes my turn to 'Ride the Valkyrie.' So I say to myself, 'Remember the Alamo!' and I go for it. Well I'm proud to say, the red, white and blue came through with flying colors."

Nick chuckled, then glanced up at the clock above the back door. If she walked in now, he thought, her face would reveal all.

"Clock watcher," Hugh said.

"What? Sorry, it's just, we could use another hand."

"Yeah. I know whose—and where you want it. Easy, boy. Miss London will be marching in here any minute."

"Have you noticed her eyes, Hugh? They're like laser beams, the way they bore right into you."

"I'll tell you what," said Hugh. "There's chemistry between you two. It may blow you up, but it's there. My own motto is, 'Don't fish where you swim.'"

"That's silly. Work has always been a good place to hook up. Just like school was."

"Oh yeah? Then why are several companies banning office relationships?"

"They're virtue signaling," said Nick. "Ever since a bunch of liberal celebrities got caught harassing babes, the media's been trying to throw us normal guys into that net. They brand any male advance as predatory. 'No means no!' If no always meant no, I'm still a virgin."

"You're saving yourself," said Laura, walking into the station. "I'm proud of you, Nick. Most men are sluts."

Her outfit, flared black trousers and a red button shirt, worked for Nick.

"Don't you worry, Nick. The right mail-order bride will come along."

Nick smiled.

"Good morning, Miss London," Hugh said. "You look lovely today."

"Save the crap for Tammy," said Laura. "Where is Tammy?"

"She got the Fashion Desk," Nick said.

"By flirting no doubt."

"You have no idea," Nick said.

"Well, Sarah got Editorial the correct way."

"Male bashing," said Nick.

"Three up, and three of us to go," Hugh said.

He left on the internal mail run. Laura joined Nick in the mail sorting. He glanced at her nearby face, avoiding the deep brown eyes so she couldn't penetrate his mask of indifference.

"How was the White House press dinner?" Nick asked.

"I didn't go."

Nick exhaled, unaware he'd been holding his breath.

"Really," he said, extremely relieved. "How come?"

"I rebuffed Todd Armstrong. Bad career move. Now I'll be a copyaide forever."

"You heard Russell. Write something for the paper."

"I can't come up with a story idea," said Laura. "Between gophering here all day, and nursemaiding Phil at night."

"What's the matter with Phil?"

"Senator Hawthorne is very high maintenance. The Republican juggernaut is wearing him down. Phil has to placate him. Which means I have to soothe Phil."

"And who comforts you?"

"No one, Nick, I'm Joan of Arc."

"You hear voices in your head? That explains everything."

Nick took the next internal mail run, concluding at the Metro Desk. He stood beside Frank Russell's cubicle. Russell, scanning copy on his monitor, took a while to notice him.

"You waiting for a tip, kid? Here's one. Bust ass and don't screw up. How's that?"

"Inspiring enough to do a story for you."

"Say, you don't waste any time."

"My byline's Nick Jarrett."

"Pretty sure of yourself, huh? Okay, kid, whatcha got?"

"Father Juan Ramirez, Latino refugee angel."

"Talk faster, kid. I'm on deadline."

"Every Monday night, Ramirez holds a special coffee house for his flock. I was there last night. There was singing, dancing, a good time had by all. It's a nice twist on the scared immigrant cliché."

Russell rubbed his chin.

"Hmm," he said. "Tough interviews. A lot of 'em don't speak English."

"I got some good quotes."

Russell looked impressed. "Can you have it in by three today?"

"Piece of cake."

"You'd better write as good as you talk," said Russell.

The newsroom was half empty during the noon-till-two lunch hours. Nick sat in a vacant Metro Desk cubicle, typing a story from his notes on *El Caribe* napkins. Hugh and Mike stopped near him on their way to the elevator.

"Hey, check out the new reporter," Mike said.

"They're getting younger every day," said Hugh.

"Maybe he can give us some pointers."

"Beat it, peons, I'm on deadline," said Nick.

"Woah, talk about the media elite," said Hugh.

"You coming to lunch?" Mike asked.

"Can't," said Nick. "But bring me back an apple pie."

Mike and Hugh snickered, and continued to the elevator.

Frank Russell retuned from lunch to find Nick pacing near his cubicle. The Metro Editor uploaded Nick's story and began to read. Nick continued pacing behind him. Laura, at the end of the two o'clock mail run, noticed the nervously pacing Nick.

Her curiosity piqued, she moved into eavesdropping range of the Metro Desk. Russell turned from his computer to Nick, who instantly quit pacing.

"Did you CQ the names?" Russell said.

"Yes, sir. Some of them need Spanish accent marks. I don't know how to do that in our system."

"Mark 'em on a printout. Then fill out a photo assignment form. We'll run this Saturday."

Nick beamed. "Will do."

He started to walk away.

"Hey, Jarrett."

Nick halted.

"You not only talk. You can write too."

Nick smiled and walked away. Laura smirked. She moved into an empty cubicle on the Foreign Desk. It took her a minute to access Nick's story in the editing cue: *A REFUGEE OASIS by Nick Jarrett, Special to the Washington Post*. Laura began reading it aloud, cynically at first.

"Every Monday night in Adam's Morgan, El Caribe Restaurant turns away paying customers—to welcome poor immigrants with distant loved ones and thoughts of home."

Laura paused, unable to maintain her smugness. She resumed reading, still aloud yet with more sincere interest.

"For three hours, once a week, El Caribe is a coffee-warm oasis, where patrons enjoy the best of their homeland, without fearing the worst."

Laura softened more. She read the rest of the piece in silence, with respect for the material. Upon entering the copyaide station, she found Nick all alone, slotting mail. She studied him in silence for a while.

"I'm impressed, Nick," she said, alerting him to her presence.

"It's all in the wrist," Nick said, and pantomimed flicking envelopes like playing cards.

"I meant your refugee coffee house story."

"Oh," said Nick.

He was secretly delighted that Laura had shown enough interest in him to find and read his unpublished story, and liked it.

"It's sweet—and sensitive," said Laura.

"No need to insult me."

"Oh, right. You'd rather be known as a rogue and a bounder."

"Ow, such language."

"Seriously, where'd you learn to write like that? Montana U?"

"Raymond Chandler," said Nick. "His every line's a lesson in style."

"And misogyny."

"Untrue. The man totally respected women." Nick added in a Bogart-like tone, 'She was a blonde to make a bishop kick a hole in a stained-glass window.'"

Laura palmed her forehead.

6

Nick was the only white person in the Howard University gym, a fact of no concern to him or the nearly twenty collegians of both sexes exercising on a Thursday night. He stood beside the Smith Machine watching Mike Carter bench press two-hundred-twenty pounds ten times. Nick had seldom pumped iron. Working on his father's cattle ranch, he grew up very fit. He'd kept in good shape through college, doing push-ups, pull-ups, dips, and then in combat training with the National Guard. But when Mike had talked up his lifting regimen at lunch that day, it drew Nick's interest, and he'd accompanied Mike to his alma mater's gym.

Nick's eyes strayed from Mike to one of the stationary bicycles, on which rode a comely coed in a green sports bra and gold shorts, her strong dark legs pumping smoothly on the pedals.

"What would Laura London say?" asked Mike, sitting up on the bench, breathing hard.

"That I'm an equal opportunity sexist," said Nick.

Mike chuckled, and got off the bench.

"Your turn."

"Uh," said Nick. "Can't I just do isometrics?"

He pressed his palms together with pretend extreme pressure.

"You wanted to come," Mike said. "Still not sure why. You're in decent shape."

"There's an east wind coming," Nick said.

"Huh?"

"Sherlock Holmes, 'His Last Bow'. His warning against the dark forces that threatened Great Britain, and this country. They're massing again, this time on the inside. I want to be ready for 'em."

"Yeah, well, paranoia's a good motivator," Mike said. "Get your ass on the bench."

Nick lay down on the bench with his chest under the bar. Mike pulled out the weights pin, and stuck it in the hundred fifty-pound slot.

"Let's start with eight reps. Grab the bar."

Nick did so, his hands ten inches apart.

"Breathe in deep and hold it in," said Mike.

Nick obeyed.

"Breathe out."

Nick exhaled.

"Okay, do it again—this time lifting the bar when you breathe out...Ready?...Go."

Nick inhaled, then exhaled while pushing up the bar. It resisted him but he lifted it.

"Good," said Mike. "Seven more. Breathe in—bar down, breathe out—bar up."

Nick made four herculean lifts. By the sixth one, the weight

seemed to have tripled and his arms shook from the strain. Not
wanting Mike to think him a weenie, he managed to lift the bar.
He failed to notice Mike no longer watching him but instead
the coed on the bike machine. On the seventh lift, Nick gave up,
then followed Mike's gaze.

"Headline, Washington Post. Copyboy crushed by massive
weight. Trainer questioned."

"Long as it's not by my girlfriend," Mike said with a grin.

"I won't rat you out when I meet her tonight."

"Then you might survive your workout. Six more reps. Go."

Nick groaned, but lay down on the bench, taking hold of the
weight bar.

Forty minutes later, freshly showered, gym bags in hand,
they walked out into the cold starry night. Two hoodied youths
approached the entrance. One of them halted, staring at Mike.
The other did also.

"Mike Carter," said the taller of the two.

Mike looked at him without recognition.

"Ike Johnson. I was in high school your last year on the team.
Saw you go down for good against Duke. Heard your leg snap.
The whole stadium did."

"Not me," Mike said. "Passed out like a pussy."

The younger jocks laughed.

"I'll be trying out next year," Ike said.

"Great," said Mike. "Slam Duke for me."

"I will, man. Good luck."

The two students went into the gym. Mike looked nostalgic
for a moment. He walked on beside Nick through the mostly
red-brick campus.

"That wasn't quite true, was it?" asked Nick.

"Hell, no. I felt that motherfucker. Still do after ten leg lifts. But you know what hurts most? Never knowing how good I would'a been in the pros."

"You stayed in college after losing that scholarship. Now you're a Washington Post sportswriter—almost. You're kicking ass—just like you would've in the NFL."

"You know," Mike said, "Leg feels better already."

"Wish my arms did. They're like rubber."

"Good sign. Same time Saturday?"

"Better make it next week," said Nick, wiggling his arms.

They laughed. Exiting the Howard campus, they crossed Georgia Avenue at Florida Street. A red light stymied three long lines of northbound traffic headed for Silver Spring, Maryland, and the fewer southbound cars. Nick and Mike turned left on the sidewalk. They walked past several locked storefronts, Mike telling Nick about the girl he was about to meet.

"Nat was the second cheerleader I slept with my junior year, when I was an a-hole jock. Took me a while to realize her fine legs also carried a sharp brain and a good heart."

"That's a one-two punch to singlehood," said Nick.

"Yeah. Sticking with me after I broke down was proof of one. Helping me keep my grades up so I could graduate clinched the deal."

"Now you're in a post-college relationship."

"And I got a tough decision to make," said Mike. "End it now and absorb the shock, or run with it, taking lesser but continuous hits."

"Never heard a football metaphor for love before," said Nick. "Real romantic, Mike."

"Either way, I don't see us making it to the end zone."

"Why not? She refusing to bake quesadillas for the game Sunday?

"Nothing that crazy," Mike said with a smile.

"Good. All else can be worked out."

"'Cept for our money differences."

"What's the problem? Your girl's gonna be a lawyer, right?"

"Yeah, pulling in six figures from some DC power firm. While I'm the only black face in Smallville, South Dakota, covering peewee ice hockey."

"They got law firms in Smallville."

"Nat won't be down with that. She grew up poorer than me. Making lots of dough is high on her agen..."

A long claxon blast drowned out Mike. He and Nick turned to the source of it. On the opposite side of Georgia Avenue, some twenty yards down, a grizzled man in a wheelchair was attempting to cross the street, absent any traffic light. He had grey skin, an orange hunter's cap, an old Army camouflage jacket, and two stumps for legs. The cars in the first northbound lane had stopped for him, none too obligingly, given the cacophony of claxon sounds. The man clearly wished to advance to the next lane but his wheelchair was in a blind spot, too low for SUV drivers to see, despite the good street lighting.

Nick and Mike stood on the sidewalk watching his effort with concern. A Metro Bus rumbled past them. It stopped for three women half a block ahead, directly across the street from Wheelchair Man.

"He's trying to catch that bus," Nick said.

"He ain't gonna make it."

"You stop the bus—I'll get killed!" declared Nick.

He darted into the street, dodging lethally fast cars in the first three lanes. Mike ran toward the bus as the last woman climbed aboard. The bus began to pull away. Mike caught up to it on the run, and pounded on the door until it came to a stop.

Nick reached the street's center yellow line then had to pause for the ceaseless northbound traffic. He stepped into the first lane, right in front of an oncoming SUV, desperately signaling it to halt. The SUV braked five feet away from Nick. The car behind it also stopped, and naturally began to honk. Nick pushed his luck into the middle lane, making the same halt gesture to a fast-coming dark car. It stopped well short of him.

He spun to Wheelchair Man, who looked up at him. Nick gave him a National Guard military salute. The man seemed to shudder slightly, then returned the salute Army style. He pushed his wheelchair across the southbound lanes. He went around the front of the waiting bus to the already lowered wheelchair lift. Mike stood beside it. Wheelchair Man backed his chair onto the lift. As it rose, he nodded once to Mike, who nodded back. Nick joined Mike in time to watch the bus pull away.

"General MacArthur was wrong," said Nick.

"About what?"

"Old soldiers. They don't just fade away. Some end up like that." Nick pointed at the disappearing bus. "We can't let 'em, Mike. Not a single one of them."

Mike nodded somberly. He and Nick turned around, and walked back six storefronts to Tiko's Coffee House.

Toasty heat and soft jazz welcomed them, less so the oblong African masks glaring from the two side walls. The all black young patrons crowding the place didn't look up from their laptops, tablets, and books, except for one stunner sitting alone at a four-chair table. Maintaining that status must have been a challenge with her looks, Nick thought. She had luxurious hair and full lips, and wore a white wool sweater, partly hidden by an open textbook with the words "Energy" and "Law" on the cover. A paper coffee cup stood on the table. She brightened at the new arrivals, primarily Mike.

"Hey, Nat," Mike said.

"Hey."

Mike bent down and kissed Natalie lightly on the lips. She responded with greater fervor, until he broke it off. Nick noted the body politics.

"Nick—Natalie."

Natalie gave Nick a radiant smile then her hand.

"I've heard a lot about you, Nick. You're the great copyaide hope."

"I'm glad you said 'copyaide'," Nick said, his eyes darting around the coffee shop.

Natalie and Mike laughed.

"Coffee?" Mike asked.

"No thanks. Too close to my bedtime."

"Try the vanilla chai latte," said Natalie, tapping her coffee cup. "It'll help you sleep."

"Might also bar me from Wyoming but okay. One of those, Mike."

He took out a five-dollar bill. Mike waved it off, and went to the end counter, behind a couple in line. Nick sat down across from Natalie. She looked curiously at him, as if contemplating just how personal to get.

"Mike's doing all right," said Nick. "He's up for a slot on the Sports Desk."

"Yeah, he's really hoping for that," Natalie said, with little enthusiasm.

"Your cheerleading's a little creaky."

Natalie smiled sadly. "What else did he tell you?"

"That love might not conquer all," said Nick.

Natalie took a sip of her tea, as if the taste had become bitter.

"If Mike gets that promotion, I want to be happy for him," she said. "But I can't help thinking it'll be one more step away from me."

"Maybe he'll find a job right here in DC—writing a sports blog or something."

Natalie looked dubiously at Nick.

"Yeah," said Nick, agreeing with her look. "Wouldn't even pay the electric bill."

"I'd be happy to pay *our* bill."

"That's too high a price for some guys."

"Like you?"

"And Mike."

"So true, dammit."

"There is Option B," said Nick.

"Follow my heart?"

Nick shrugged.

"Then my law school loan would follow *me*," said Natalie. "It's no way to start a family, Nick. Trust me. I've been there."

"So I heard."

Mike returned with two hot beverages. He handed one to Nick and sat down. Natalie put her right hand over Mike's left, brushing it gently. They looked inquiringly at one another. Nick grabbed his vanilla chai latte and stood up.

"I'll have this to go," he said. "See you at work, Mike. Great meeting you, Natalie."

"You too, Nick. And thank you."

"For what?" Mike asked.

"Being your friend," said Natalie.

Nick hurried out the door, a new idea gnawing at him. He looked down Georgia Avenue along Wheelchair Man's bus route. The man had a tale to tell, of war and adversity, and he'd let him get away. He had to try to find him. But how?

"Come on, Jarrett, you've read enough gumshoe books," Nick said aloud. "What would Marlowe do?"

He turned to the southbound traffic while pulling out his cellphone. A quick search revealed the next Metro Bus would be by in nine minutes. It appeared right on schedule, and Nick got on board. The bus was nearly empty, except for a tired woman with two grocery bags on the seat beside her, a sleeping man, and the fortyish black female driver. Nick showed her his Post ID.

"Hello. Nick Jarrett, Washington Post."

"Don't read it."

"I hope to change that."

"Change my fare count first. Two dollars."

Nick tapped his month-good Metro Pass against the meter probe.

"Tell me—you ever pick up a guy in a wheelchair missing both legs?"

"Sarge."

"Sarge," Nick repeated.

"Maybe twice a week, round this time."

"Where you drop him off?"

"Morrison Street, one mile down."

"And he answers to 'Sarge'."

"I call 'im that," said the bus driver. "Have ever since one night last summer."

"What happened that night?"

"Couple'a punks didn't like waiting on the wheelchair lift. One says to 'im, 'Hey, pop, why you taking the bus? You got your own set of wheels.' The other fool laughed. Man looked right at 'em and said, 'Assholes call me Sergeant.'"

Nick whistled. "What'd they do?" he asked.

"Didn't do nothin'. I kicked their punk asses off my bus."

"Good for you," Nick said, meaning it. "Does Sarge ever talk to you about himself?"

"Like how he lost his legs?"

Nick nodded.

"Nah, he mostly plays with his cellphone the whole ride. Some kind of baseball app."

"Please tell me your name and age," said Nick.

"Cherise Wilson, forty-six. Next stop, Morrison. You want out?"

Nick looked out the door pane at the dark, ominous neighborhood.

"Uh, not tonight," he said. "What's the nearest subway stop?"

7

Sarah Woronov burst into the copyaide station through the rear doorway to find Laura there, and Nick.

"Laura, guess what!" she declared.

"Hello … Sarah," said Nick.

"Nick," Sarah said dismissively.

"Congrats on Editorial."

"Thank you," Sarah said.

"What's up, Sarah?" Laura asked.

"Lowenstein just handed me two tickets to the Signa Barashi concert tonight."

"Wow. Who're you going with?"

"You, if you're free."

"I'm liberated. What time?"

"Who's Signa Barashi?" Nick asked.

Sarah and Laura looked at him as if he'd asked who Oprah Winfrey was.

"An Indian folk singer, decrying her country's patriarchal order," Laura said.

"More power to her," said Nick.

Both women looked suspiciously at him.

"Are you being sarcastic?" Sarah asked.

"Not at all," said Nick. "The Third World's pretty rough on women."

"Why, Nick," Sarah said, "I'm pleasantly surprised at you."

"Unlike the spoiled cry-babes we got in this country," said Nick.

Sarah seemed to shake off a tick, and went out the way she came. Laura glowered.

"Nice going, Nick."

"Hey, it was nothing personal."

"Ever hear of sisterhood?"

"Sure," said Nick, adding in a movie trailer voice. "Beyonce Knowles *is* Sister Hood!"

Laura took up a stack of envelopes, shaking her head, and moved to the annex.

Walking into the Style section on his way to the Music Desk, Nick instantly felt the lower energy. He looked left at the Fashion and Food Desk. His eyes rested on Tammy Perkins, sitting at her cubicle in a short green Scotch dress with brown tights. A nice, smart, desirable girl who clearly liked him, Nick thought. What more could a guy want? He sighed at the answer, and the purpose of his Style visit. Tammy looked up from her computer monitor, and slowed Nick down.

"Hi, Nick."

"Hey, beautiful. How's the fashion life?"

"Just fine. Short skirts are in this winter, thank goodness."

"You got legs for all seasons."

"Charmer," Tammy said with a smile.

Warren sat at the Music Desk, appreciating what came through his headphones—an innovative new goth band, No Quarter. He saw Nick approaching. Warren liked Nick but resented the way Tammy did. Yes, Nick was taller, handsomer than him—but his own feelings for Tammy were realer. He knew Nick wanted someone else, and whom. Nick stopped before him, speaking inaudibly. Warren took off the headphones.

"What?"

"I said…"

Nick silently moved his lips.

"Funny," Warren said, with the hint of a smile.

"Tell me something, Warren. You guys covering the Signa Barashi concert tonight?"

"It's not on the assignment sheet," Warren said, adding in surprise, "Why, you want it?"

"Hell no. But another copyaide does."

"I'll talk to Masetti."

Nick and Laura finished the last mail crate at a little past five. Nick got ready to leave, knowing Laura had another hour of work left, when Rick Masetti blew into the copyaide station.

"Which one of you wants to cover the Barashi concert?"

Laura's mouth fell open, but no sound came out.

Nick pointed at her. "She does."

"I think we ought to do it," Masetti said, looking at Laura. "You done concert reviews before?"

Laura's mouth remained agape.

"She has," said Nick.

"Good. Have it in my system by midnight, or we won't be able to use it."

Laura's eyes widened anxiously.

"She will," said Nick.

Masetti departed. Nick watched him leave, and felt Laura's hand gripping his upper arm, her brown eyes drilling into him.

"Nick! What have you done to me?! I've never done a concert review in my life! On deadline, no less!"

"Piece of cake."

"You have to help me! Right here — tonight!"

"What happened to Joan of Arc?"

"You got me into this, and by God you'll get me out of it, or I'll break your arm!"

"Okay," said Nick. "Meet me at the Post Pub after the show. I'll come up with you."

Laura unhanded his arm. Nick started for the door, hiding his pleasure from her.

"Hey, Nick."

He turned to her. She gave him a dazzling smile.

"Thank you."

Nick exited the copyaide station, and grinned.

8

On the ground floor of the Washington Post building, left of the main K Street entrance, was the Post Pub. The dim, dark wood interior had a subtle Irish nuance, left over from a harder drinking age of newspapermen. Iconic Post front pages decorated the side walls in chronological order, among them: *Kennedy Orders Blockade of Cuba as Reds Build Nuclear Bases There*, *President Kennedy Shot Dead*, *'The Eagle Has Landed'—Two Men Walk on the Moon*, *Nixon Denies Role in Cover-up*, *Nixon Resigns*. A quarter full at just before seven, the Pub's present clientele included Nick, Hugh, Mike, Warren, and Tammy at the single long table, half a pitcher of beer in their glass mugs. Hugh raised his.

"To Nick Jarrett. The first one of us to get a story in the Post."

Everyone else raised their mugs.

"Let's kill him," said Mike.

The copyaides laughed, and drank.

"It's just a fluff piece," Nick said. "They're holding it a week so they can add photo art."

"Photo art," said Tammy. "Wow, Nick. You're a real journalist now."

"Remind me when I'm slinging mail," said Nick.

"You're about to have some serious competition," Warren said. "Laura London. And it's your own fault."

"Oh?" said Tammy.

"Nick got Laura a concert review."

Tammy frowned.

"I should've covered that dothead concert," said Hugh. "And met some hot chicks in the bargain."

"And if you thought they were angry before..." said Mike.

"Too bad you don't look like Laura or Nick would've set you up," Warren said.

"Come on, guys, she was going to it anyway," said Nick. "It was good timing."

"And campaigning," Hugh said.

Tammy looked soulfully at Nick. "You sweet on Laura, Nick?"

"She's all right."

"She's kinda cold to me," said Tammy. "So's that Sarah. Her being a lezzie, you'd think she'd go for me."

"They hate you 'cause you're beautiful," said Warren.

"Bless your heart. But so are they."

"The difference is you work it," said Nick.

"Does that bother you?"

"No. I think it's honest. If you got it, flaunt it."

"So, what is it about Laura?" Tammy asked. "What's she got that I ain't got?"

"Passion, I think," said Nick. "Flaming, if misguided, passion."

Tammy pouted, and turned to Warren.

"I need a ride home," she said. "You going anywhere near Georgetown?"

"I'd take you to Baltimore," Warren said.

"Thank you, Warren."

Tammy stood up and grabbed her black down coat with brown faux fur. "See y'all tomorrow."

"Better yet, we'll see you," said Hugh.

"Both eyes on the road, Warren," said Mike.

Warren waved him off, and left with Tammy. Nick pointed at the closing front door.

"You see, Hugh? You *can* fish where you swim."

"Yeah," Hugh said solemnly. "And her hook'll cut pretty deep."

Mike picked up his Howard U gym bag off the floor and rose to his feet.

"I'm outta here."

"And out of the copyaide station on Monday," said Hugh.

"Good job getting the Sports Desk, Mike," Nick said.

"Thanks. I'll be covering high school soccer to start."

"Next year, college soccer," said Hugh.

"It's a fine GOALLLL!" Nick said.

Mike and Hugh chuckled.

"I'll drop you at the subway station," Hugh said, standing up. He turned to Nick. "Good luck with Miss London."

Nick nodded. He took a swig of beer as his friends headed out the door.

Warren was too nervous to focus on the Vogue magazine on his lap, or David Bowie's final album, *Blackstar*, on the stereo. He sat on a polyester sofa in the femininely decorated living room of Tammy's shared Georgetown row house. His hostess was in the kitchen, pouring wine. She'd invited him in for a drink, and though he expected nothing more, he couldn't stop fantasizing about her.

Tammy was more beautiful than any woman he'd ever known, let alone been with, and certainly his last girlfriend. He recalled the sting of seeing Sandy's recent Facebook post. How content she looked on the Great Falls hike beside the bearded IT hipster she left him for, had slept with even before then. He longed to post one of himself and Tammy, with the words *in a relationship*. Sandy would seethe at it, not because she wanted him back, but because he'd found someone hotter, and cooler, than her.

Tammy entered from the kitchen with an open bottle of Merlot and two wineglasses. She placed them on the coffee table and sat down next to Warren, her shapely left leg touching his right. He could feel the contact even through his jeans, grateful for the magazine on his groin. Tammy poured the wine into both glasses and handed him one. They clinked. Tammy leaned back on the sofa, and looked pensively at Warren. Nonplussed, he pointed to the air and began to talk fast.

"You know, when this album came out a few years ago, I thought Bowie was back—to being the weird genius he used to be. I didn't realize till he died a month later that he was saying goodbye. Which makes it even more creepy. Twenty-sixteen was a brutal year for music. We lost five icons—Bowie, Prince, Glenn Frey, Leon Russell, and George Michael. Okay, maybe George wasn't in the same league as the other guys, but he did make a significant contribu..."

"Stop talking," Tammy said.

Warren shut up, crestfallen. Tammy looked at him for a tortuous half minute. He knew he'd blown his only chance with her, if he ever had one. At last, Tammy seemed to come to a decision. She took hold of his wineglass and placed it on the coffee table, along with her own. She moved her gorgeous face toward his adoring one, and pressed her lips against his. Warren reeled with pleasure, praying she felt something too. Tammy stood up, and held out her hand to him. He took it, throwing off the Vogue with his free hand. Tammy led him to the foot of the staircase, then up the steps to heaven.

Nick was on his fifth beer, watching CNN. A talking head was blasting the President's Supreme Court nominee as if she intended to outlaw Hispanics, when Laura appeared beside him.

"Here it is, Nick—the most important moment in my professional career, and what are you doing? Getting drunk!"

"I'm an old-school newspaperman."

"They used to write the story first."

"Piece of cake," said Nick.

He stood up, felt dizzy, and grabbed a chair back for support.

"Whoops," he said.

"I'm doomed," said Laura.

They entered the newsroom, joining the sparse nightside staff that sat ready for any late-breaking news event. Laura commandeered a vacant Metro Desk cubicle, and laid her reporter's notepad by the computer keyboard. Nick pulled a chair from the adjacent cubicle and sat down close to Laura. Her subtle yet delicious perfume combined with his beer buzz, making it hard for him to concentrate.

"What now, Nick?" Laura asked, wiggling her fingers over the keyboard.

"Answer five questions...In your piece...Five questions...Is it hot in here?"

"Is that one of them?"

"No...Who is Signa what's-her-name—and why should we give a damn? Answer both of those in your lede."

Laura thought for a moment, then began to type, the words appearing on the screen.

In her native India, Signa Barashi is considered a revolutionary. But you would never know this from her slight 28-year-old frame and soft, high voice.

Nick leaned closer to the monitor, his shoulder near Laura's.

"Not bad," he said. "Now describe the atmosphere at the concert. Where was it? How was it? Be opinionated, Laura. I know that's hard for you."

Laura typed again, encouraged.

Both were in commanding evidence last night.

"Tuesday night," said Nick.

Laura made the correction on keyboard and screen.

Tuesday night at the Bayou, where Signa performed...

"Last name only," Nick said. "This ain't the gossip page."

Laura typed.

...where Barashi performed six songs on sitar.

"You're doing great. How big a crowd? What type of people?"

Laura smiled, gaining confidence, appreciating Nick's proximity for more than his guidance. She typed.

...before a full house of mostly women.

"Okay, start reviewing."

Laura typed.

All her song lyrics were in English. And though "My Father's Dream"' assails the Indian tradition of arranged marriages, it affected the American women in the audience.

"There's a stretch."

"Critic's discretion," Laura said, smiling.

She resumed typing. Nick alternated between watching her copy and her profile. She caught him looking at her, but smiled back. He made a few more suggestions, which she inserted. She ended in a flourish of typing. Nick read the full review while Laura squirmed.

"Well, kid," he said. "You won't be needing me anymore. You're good. Real good. Send it on."

Laura pushed the send button on the keyboard. She turned to Nick with a heart-pounding smile, and brought her incredible face close to his. His chest tightened. He averted her eyes.

"You're quite the coach, Nick Jarrett."

"I just called the plays. You had all the moves."

"I'm not moving now," Laura said, her lips semi-pursed.

"True," said Nick. "I guess it's up to me then."

He brought his mouth closer to Laura's. Just before their lips touched, she withdrew hers, frustrating him and, he thought, herself. He looked at Laura. She appeared furtive.

"Will you wait with me outside until I get a cab?" she asked.

"Maybe we can share one."

"Where are *you* going?"

"Your place or mine?"

"I live with someone."

"I live alone."

"Get used to it, Nick," Laura said, although without her usual bite.

They walked out of the newsroom, Laura texting a message on her cellphone. Three minutes later, they stood in their coats outside the Post entrance, physically close to one another. It was bitter cold, with minimal traffic and no cabs in sight. They both knew something had changed between them. Laura raised the back of her fist to the night sky, intriguing Nick.

"Woman confronting God, Nick."

"Right," said Nick. "Pardon me while I move out of lightning range."

"It's an aluminum sculpture I made in Sculpture one-o-one—'Woman Confronting God.'"

"Were you going for an N.E.A. grant?"

Laura smiled, and hugged herself for warmth.

"Want my coat?" Nick asked.

"No thanks."

"You sure? Made in Wyoming—warm, tough, durable."

"Too rugged for me."

"Only on the outside. Inside's real cuddly."

"I have another coat at home," said Laura.

Her meaning stung Nick. He scanned two approaching headlights. Laura looked at him.

"You really think I'm a good writer?"

"Yeah," said Nick.

The unmarked car went by.

"I heard that once before you know," said Laura. "From my Creative Writing professor at Mount Holyoake. He's a great author. His work used to move me to tears. He told me mine was good enough to publish, and would I have a drink with him after class to discuss it. Three martinis later, he asked me to sleep with him. I probably would have—only I was already involved with my Poetry professor."

"Poetic justice."

"Hey, affairs with professors were a status symbol at my school—they being the only men on campus. Last year, a friend of mine had one, with the very same Fiction teacher. Do you know what this brilliant, wonderful artist told her about me? 'Sure, I remember Laura. She had the best ass of any student in my class.'"

Laura looked at Nick for sympathy. He reflected for a moment before speaking.

"But that doesn't mean he lied to you. I mean, you do have a nice, ah, posterior. 'Beauty is truth and truth beauty...'"

"'That's all ye know on Earth, and all you need to know,'" said Laura.

Her eyes bore into Nick's. He looked away.

"Why can't you look at me, Nick?"

"It's difficult for me."

"You're not so tough, are you?"

"It comes and goes," said Nick.

New headlights approached them, on a silver BMW. It stopped hard in front of them. Phil Cartwright got out, in a navy-blue suit. He circled the car toward them, glaring at Nick. Nick neutrally returned the look. Laura tensed.

"Phil, what are you doing here?"

"Picking you up," Phil said, scowling at Nick. "Unless you have other plans."

"Of course not, honey. This is Nick. Nick, Phil."

Nick gave Phil a mini-wave, which seemed to annoy him more.

"Are you working late too?" Phil inquired of Nick.

"Just helping Laura out."

"Oh? And who asked you to do that?"

Nick glanced at Laura, now standing behind Phil, pleadingly shaking her head.

"I volunteered," Nick said.

"Maybe you should mind your own business."

"That's good advice," said Nick.

Laura nodded to Nick. Phil smugly turned to her.

"Door's unlocked," he said.

She climbed into the BMW's front passenger seat, Phil behind the wheel. Nick watched the car pull away. On the road, Laura stared guiltily out the windshield. She knew Nick had backed down because of her, and that it went against his grain.

"Was that your Marlboro Man?" Phil asked.

"Yes."

"Like I said, a phony image. Let me know if he keeps bothering you."

"You didn't just come from our place."

"From the Senator's," Phil said somberly.

"This late?"

"I'd say just in time."

"Oh no," Laura said in alarm. "He's drinking again."

"He was bombed."

"The old fool. He'll ruin everything."

"He almost did tonight," said Phil. "He had a call girl there—a thousand-dollar whore. And was refusing to pay her. Said he never got it up for her."

"Where are his wife and daughter?"

"Concorde till Sunday."

"What did you do?"

"Called the whore's madam. She said not to worry. The Senator always makes good once he's sober."

"Good God, Phil. Have we cast our hopes on the Titanic?"

"No! Hawthorne's our last best hope to restart the progressive agenda. He could be the next Vice-President — if the Religious Right doesn't crucify him first."

"You'll save him, babe."

"Promise you'll help me, Laura," Phil said, no longer cocky.

Laura sighed.

"Yes, Phil. Don't I always?"

9

Nick worked solo in the copyaide station, emptying the first crate of mail. He sorted the envelopes faster than usual, trying to outpace his irritation. Entering the station, Mike instantly noticed Nick's altered state.

"Hey, Pony Express, slow it down. We get too efficient on mail, Susan'll keep us both here."

"What of it," Nick said in his Bogart impression. "I'm gonna die in the mailroom. It's a good spot for it."

"What's eating you, man? Fact that Laura got her byline in the paper first? I'm sure she thanked you for it. What were you expecting, gratitude sex?"

"For starters."

"You screwed up. You gave your main rival a leg up."

"It's a nice leg."

"Damn, boy. In a war between the sexes, you'd be blown away."

"Not a bad way to go," said Nick.

Hugh's singing voice was heard approaching from the elevator area.

"Oh-ho the Wells Fargo Wagon is a-comin' down the street, oh

please let it be for me. Oh-ho the Wells Fargo Wagon is a-comin' down the street, I wish, I wish I could know what it could be…"

Hugh entered pulling the supply cart laden with reporter-editor equipment. On the double-A batteries box lay a Post newspaper open on the Style page.

"Morning, guys. Did you see Laura's piece in the paper today? Damn fine writing I say."

Nick grimaced, amusing Mike. Susan Machado's office door opened. The Copyaide Supervisor came out holding the same Style page.

"Where's that angel, Miss London? I want to compliment her on her excellent concert review."

Nick snorted. Sarah entered from the Editorial side, also wielding the Style page, and looking around the room.

"We read it!" Nick said.

"Laura's not in yet?" she asked.

"She's picking up her Pulitzer Prize," said Nick.

"Why, Nick. You're looking a bit green this morning."

Laura walked in through the open doorway. Everyone burst into applause except Nick. He picked up the internal mail tray, and started for the back door. Laura smiled graciously at her audience, but got serious seeing Nick leave.

He returned eighteen minutes later, coming through the rear door with the empty mail tray. He was about to address Hugh, when he spotted Laura near the newsroom doorway in an intimate conversation with Todd Armstrong.

"Todd Armstrong," Hugh whispered. "Looks like Laura's moving up the food chain."

"Why not," Nick whispered back. "She already took a bite out of me."

Armstrong put a friendly hand on Laura's shoulder and said something clearly encouraging, to which she smilingly responded. When the famous reporter moved away, Laura stepped into the mailroom. She placed herself across the table from Nick, with Hugh at the table's end. The three sorted mail in silence, Laura and Nick barely looking at each other. Hugh, feeling the tension, glanced from one side of the table to the other.

"Seen any good movies lately?" he asked.

"Yeah," Nick said. "'Double Indemnity'."

"I've heard of it," said Hugh. "Film noir, right?"

"Right. Barbara Stanwyck seduces Fred McMurray into helping her do something drastic, then double-crosses him."

"How does it end?" Laura asked.

"They shoot each other."

"Well," Hugh said, then mimicked a cable news host. "When we come back…extra-terrestrials. Do they exist? Laura London…"

"Yes," said Laura. "And they're male."

An hour later, Nick sat at a two-chair table in the cafeteria, finishing a roast beef sandwich. Laura appeared before him, a bowl of steamed vegetables and iced tea on her tray. She nodded questioningly at the chair in front of him.

"May I?"

"Why would you want to?"

"To apologize for not defending you to Phil last night."

"That's okay," said Nick, pleasantly surprised. "I could see he's the jealous type."

He indicated the chair. Laura took it. For the first time since he met her, she looked unsure of herself.

"To be perfectly honest, Nick, he has some reason to be."

"Why? You cheating on him with Ted Armstrong?"

"No. But I would have been more forthright with Phil ... if I didn't like you so much."

Nick mis-swallowed his lemonade, and had to cough it down.

"Why'd you have to say a thing like that for?!" he blurted.

"To torment you, Nick, to torment you," Laura said with a fetching smile. "But since we're never going to be lovers, I'd like us to be friends."

"Friends, eh? You wanna go fishing with me? Play some golf, watch football, maybe do a little hunting?"

"None of the above."

"Huh. Then I should hang out with you and Sarah. Groove to Signa what's her name. Bash men ... No? Just what kind of friends do you want us to be, Laura?"

"You're not saying what I think you're saying? That men and women can't be platonic."

"Sure they can," said Nick. "If there's no attraction between them. But you're too damn cute."

"So are you, Nick. If I wasn't with Phil, things might be different. But as you know ... "

"Phil's no friend of mine."

"So?"

"So romancing you wouldn't violate the Code."

"I'm afraid to ask," said Laura. "The Code?"

"A friend's girlfriend is off limits."

"And the rest are fair game."

"That's right," said Nick.

"What about a friend's ex-girlfriend?"

"If she dumped him, the Code applies. If he dumped her, she's doable."

"What if your friend's girlfriend prefers you?"

"The Code," Nick said.

"What if she's not officially his girlfriend, just someone he lusts after."

"If he's staked his claim to her…the Code."

"Staked his claim to her," Laura said incredulously. "What if your friend is a lesbian?"

"Hmm…That could be a loophole."

"Incredible," said Laura. "I came here to apologize to you—and now I feel insulted. But I still have to make amends for last night—by inviting you to our soiree Friday."

"Me? At your and Phil's love nest?"

"He's throwing a party to celebrate my writing debut in the Post. I finally told him how much you helped me. And he said to be sure to invite you. That's the kind of gallantry he has. Naturally, if you'd feel awkward…"

"I'll be there."

"As my friend?"

"As your co-worker," said Nick. "For the time being."

Laura's brown eyes bore into him. He looked back at them, this time without flinching. They stood up simultaneously, and walked out together. In the elevator car, with Laura next to him, Nick pressed seven on the floor indicator. Just before the doors shut, a thin wrist parted them. Nancy Shea, the Managing Editor's assistant, stepped into the elevator. A small woman with bright red hair, she looked from Nick to Laura. Both smiled politely at her.

"Are you two dating?" Nancy asked.

Laura looked surprised, Nick less so.

"No," Laura said.

Nick shrugged.

"I'm sorry," said Nancy. "It just seemed like ... Never mind."

She stepped out into the newsroom. Laura looked curiously at Nick. He glanced around the elevator car.

"Must be a time machine," he said. "I read science-fiction too."

Laura took in a deep breath, and let it out. She exited the elevator.

10

Nick and Laura worked the afternoon mostly in silence, without Hugh intruding upon it. He was assisting on the Financial Desk for the day. Nick handed Laura a small stack of envelopes slated for the annex. Laura started toward it just as Warren came in through the open doorway.

"Hi, Laura."

"Hey, Warren," Laura said. "What brings you back to the Pit of Despair?"

Warren pointed past her to Nick. "Him."

"Please limit the male bonding to three minutes," said Laura, slipping past Warren.

Nick watched Laura disappear into the annex as Warren joined him.

"Earth to Nick."

"I like it here," Nick said, turning to Warren. "Feeling nostalgic? Grab some mail."

"No thanks," Warren said, then added in a whisper. "How's it going with...?"

He nodded at the annex wing.

"We're in a state of armed neutrality," Nick said in an equally low voice. "You're way ahead with your babe."

"I still can't believe it," Warren said at his normal volume, with a semi-smile that for him amounted to a grin. "Anyway, thought you might be interested in the concert I'm covering tonight."

"Elvis?"

"Sorry ... Roddy Baker."

"Roddy's great," said Nick. "Colorado man. Caught a couple of his shows in Laramie."

"Definitely an up and coming country star."

"Bit outside your music forte, isn't he?"

"Yeah, but Masetti wants the interview."

"So you want my insight as a country-western hand," Nick said, tugging on an imaginary tie.

"Nah, I got a Southern peach for that. And she's a lot prettier than you."

Nick mock moped.

"But I got an extra pass for you and a date," said Warren, nodding toward the annex.

"I think she's had her fill of patriotic good ole boys. But I'll show up."

"I'll leave your name at the door."

"Thanks, Warren."

Nick took an Uber from his place to the Bullpen, a broad one-story building on River Road, two miles inside Maryland. He wore the western outfit his mother made him pack for Washington—blue flannel shirt over a black t-shirt, brown corduroy pants and cowboy boots. He'd drawn a line at the Stetson hat. He gave his name to the burly doorman, who checked his cellphone, and let him through.

He entered a large orange-wood hall featuring a railed dance corral, to the sound of Roddy Baker singing, *"You can't judge a pickup by its hood / She might be bad, but she sure looks good."* Within the corral, two dozen young to middle-aged couples in western dress twirled with graceful arm and leg work. On the raised stage, brown mustached thirty-something Roddy Baker stood before his four-man band, making vocal love to a wand microphone. Several pretty women near the rail appeared to be taking this to heart.

It reminded Nick of a Saturday night in Laramie two years ago with Jenny Stewart, his college girlfriend. She had wanted marriage and kids. So did he—eventually. He just hadn't been sure about Jenny. Given how he now felt about Laura, he knew he'd made the right decision for both of them.

Every booth along the left wall was taken, the next to last one by Warren and Tammy, sitting side by side on one end of it. Warren wore blue jeans and a black sweater. Tammy resembled a country music video chorus girl in a low-cut yellow blouse, denim miniskirt, and black boots. Her sensuous glow may have been enhanced by the whiskey no longer in in her glass. Warren held a bottle of Budweiser, his phone on the table before him. Nick sat down across from the pair.

"Nick," Tammy said with a welcoming smile.

"How'd you guys finagle a booth in this crowd?"

"The power of the press," Warren said.

"The power of Tammy's looks more like," said Nick.

Tammy smiled. A slow, low song began.

"Baker said he'll talk to me after this set," Warren said.

"How's he doing?" asked Nick.

"He's fine," gushed Tammy.

"Pretty basic formula," Warren said. "Simple beat, juvenile lyrics, and a lot of alpha male posturing. Works for this hayseed crowd."

"I must be a hick then, 'cause I love it," said Tammy.

Warren choked down a throat full of beer. "I didn't mean you, Tammy."

A cowgirl waitress appeared beside Nick. He pointed to Tammy's whiskey glass then himself. The waitress nodded and withdrew. Warren was still trying to mollify his girlfriend.

"Takes special people to rise above their limited backgrounds. You did."

"Oh, so now you're knocking my folks," said Tammy.

"No," Warren said tensely. "They just have some regressive views in West Virginia."

"Like clinging to their God and guns," Nick said.

Warren looked accusingly at him.

"I agree with 'em," said Tammy. "I'm like every girl in here. I wanna have fun with boys, and someday marry me a good one. Keep a home, raise some kids, while my husband works hard to support us. What's so damn hayseed about that?"

"Nothing?" Warren said, making it sound like a question.

Tammy looked inquisitively at Nick.

"Search me," said Nick. "I love how feminists want women to do men's work while knocking the one labor they can do that men can't."

"Now that's an inequality I support," Warren said.

"It's silly," Tammy said. "Most men are nice guys, like you two. Looking for love, not to oppress us gals. Why, I been proposed to more times than I been propositioned. Sure, there're creeps out there. I get hit on by my share of 'em. But I don't go crying to the world about it. I just smack 'em down."

"They probably enjoy that," Nick said.

"I mean, who made Laura London and Sarah the spokes-women for our gender?"

"Hollywood," Nick said.

Warren and Tammy looked at him.

"In every movie or TV show now, the girls are just as macho as the boys, if not more so. You got anorexic starlets beating up two hundred-pound guys. Female sensuality and sensitivity are out. You never see a housewife or a femme fatale on screen anymore. Even Wonder Woman now wears a suit of armor. The most famous sex symbol of all time now looks like every chick on *Game of Thrones*. Guess they're afraid her old costume might perk up preteen boys…like it has some in the past."

He cleared his throat. Tammy chuckled.

"But it's contra-nature," said Nick. "Little girls still wanna be Disney princesses not Amazon princesses."

"That's right," said Tammy. "Our power ain't in our muscles but in our feminine charms."

She put one hand behind her head in a cliche cheesecake pose and looked stirringly hot. Nick smiled. Warren gawked.

"That's what artists have been trying to capture since the Stone Age," said Nick. "Like the smile on the Mona Lisa. It's why Jennifer Lawrence and Jessica Chastain will be forgotten in three years, but Monroe, Hayworth, Novak never. They were goddesses, not the feminist fantasy of one. Lefties may deny that for a while with the help of metrosexual men, but nature will out. I just refuse to wait that long."

"But you're in love with Laura," Tammy said solemnly.

"The irony hasn't escaped me," said Nick.

"Or her," Warren said. "Mike said she's digging you."

"My grave maybe," said Nick.

The cowgirl waitress brought his whiskey. Another fast song started, Roddy singing, *When the whistle blows on Friday, I don't hang out with the guys / I fly home like a rocket to the fire in your eyes.* The couples in the corral began to dance, most of them quite well. Tammy watched them for a moment, then looked inquiringly at Warren, who shook his head in regret.

"May a backwoodsman dance with your girl?" Nick asked Warren.

Tammy beamed. Warren nodded with little enthusiasm. Nick led Tammy toward the corral, and through the gap in it. They found a maneuverable space between dancers and faced each other a foot apart. Nick moved his right hand under Tammy's left arm and cupped her shoulder blade. Tammy placed her left hand just above his bicep. Their free hands clasped at shoulder height.

Nick began dancing Tammy backward counterclockwise, her legs gracefully retreating. Whenever he spun her, she twirled with ease. They danced the rest of the song as if they had together many times before, exchanging smiles, their chests never touching. The song and dance ended. A romantic slow tune began. Tammy looked desirously at Nick.

"This isn't my dance," Nick said.

"It could be," said Tammy.

"You're spoken for. And I'm...unspoken for."

Nick got home just after midnight. He took a shower and went to bed, actually the futon mattress in his walkthrough closet. He opened his laptop, and resumed watching his current fall-asleep movie, *His Kind of Woman*, an unsung film noir that Vincent Price steals from Robert Mitchum and, shockingly, Jane Russell.

The scene on screen showed Jane constantly sniping at Price, whose mistress she is, for not leaving his wife. Nick was almost asleep when he heard Price's retort. *If you used that needle to sew with, you'd be a happier woman.* His eyes popped open. The line would have been biting in 1951, but today, incredibly offensive to feminists. Nick smiled. He knew just who to use it on.

11

"What are you doing after work?" Hugh asked Nick.

They were alone in the copyaide station, Laura being away on a mail run.

"Finishing the new Stephen Hunter book," said Nick. "You know he used to be the movie critic here? Now he's a bestselling thriller novelist. One of the best. There's hope for us all. You?"

"I'm invited to a modern art exhibit in Dupont Circle," Hugh said haughtily. "And I wish to share the cultural experience with you."

"No thanks. The only modern art I like is in comic books. I'm surprised you're into it."

"I'm a man of great depth."

"Right, you sink pretty low."

"Seriously, come with me. We'll pop in for a bit, then I'll drive you home."

"I don't think so, Hugh."

"Open bar."

"Say…maybe those squiggly lines will start making sense to me. All right, I'm in."

"In where," Laura London said, entering the station, "The Playboy Club?"

"They closed down years ago," said Nick.

"So did your mind, Nick."

Nick smiled, withholding his return fire.

"Jarrett!"

Frank Russell walked into the station looking typically gruff.

"Boy Scout Fall Jamboree. Going on right now in Occoquan Park. My Virginia stringer is sick. Get your ass over there. You can catch a ride with our photog, Ned O'Rourke."

Nick gestured at the mail table. "What about…?"

"I cleared it with Susan. I'm sure this pretty miss can hold the fort without you."

Laura grimaced. Russell left the room. Nick unlocked the supply cabinet, and extracted a notebook computer, digital audio recorder, earphones, and a twin AA-battery packet.

"Woah," said Hugh. "An actual story assignment. You're a star, dude."

Nick placed the equipment on the table, then worked on opening the stubborn battery packet. Laura stared at him, her grimace now a smirk.

"Boy Scout Jamboree," she said. "That's perfect for you, Nick. A male-exclusive cabal of young men behaving like primitives. You'll blend right in."

"If you used that needle to sew with, you'd be a happier woman," said Nick.

Laura's jaw dropped. Nick had never seen that literary cliché occur in real life. Even Hugh looked shocked. Nick finished inserting the two batteries into the audio recorder.

"See you guys in a few," he said, then walked out to the newsroom.

As a top Democratic leader, Wayne Hawthorne had a covetable office in the Russell Senate Office Building of the Capitol. Phil Cartwright looked down at the Senator from Connecticut over his grand dark antique desk. Despite his near six-foot height and puffy grey hair, Hawthorne appeared smaller today, slumped in the brown leather chair. When Phil joined his staff three years ago, that chair had seemed a throne. Now Hawthorne squirmed like it was a toilet seat. He took off his owl glasses and laid them on the document in front of him.

"Perfectly worded as usual, Phil."

"Thank you, sir."

"And a complete waste of our time, like my current term," Hawthorne said.

"There's a chance your rider might pass, sir. The Senators from Alaska and Maine are on the fence about the proposed bill."

"Those two bitches are traitors to their sex. Sure, they'll occasionally throw us a bone—but only when their right-wing Republican masters get too scary even for them."

"This may be one of those instances," said Phil. "Mandating an ultrasound for any woman who wants an abortion is a violation of their reproductive rights."

"I agree with you, son. But you know what that pompous nutcase from Texas will say." Hawthorne continued in a bad

Texan drawl. "'How's it a violation? They can still choose to kill their babies afterward—heartbeat, pain, and all.'"

"And he'd be right," Hawthorne added in his normal voice. "The new ultrasound machines can detect a fart from a fetus. Hell, even science is getting to be anti-woman."

"That's what's so clever about your rider, sir. It doesn't prohibit the examination, merely delays it till the last trimester, when termination is already illegal."

Hawthorne rubbed the bridge of his nose with thumb and forefinger.

"That's the type of legerdemain we're reduced to in this miserable time," he said. "How'd it happen, Phil? We had it all—the House, the Senate, the White House. We were about to get the Supreme Court, along with the first woman President. It was going to be a progressive century, with the GOP as dead as their hero, Reagan. Then in four hours on election night, goddamn Armageddon. A loudmouth pig and his party of swine in charge of the whole pen, while we're left wallowing in the mud."

Phil had heard the same lament too many times. He knew the answer but couldn't voice it, even to his liberal boss. Speaking the truth had cost their standard bearer the Presidency. But she had been right. Middle America was indeed a breadbasket of racist, misogynistic, homophobic, xenophopic, superstitious, gun-loving deplorables. Like Laura's cowboy admirer, Nick.

The thought of Nick Jarrett made Phil smirk. Did he actually believe Laura could feel anything for him other than contempt for his anachronistic machismo? Phil half hoped Jarrett would come to his soiree for Laura tomorrow night, so that their friends could have fun pricking such a retrograde specimen. Yet somehow they had to win back fools like him before the next election. And the best chance to do that now sat before him, pulling a vodka flask from the middle right hand drawer of his desk.

"Senator," Phil said urgently. "You have to be on the floor in twenty minutes, giving a great speech, one that will provide cover for any wavering Republicans."

"All the more reason I need this," Hawthorne said, taking a swig from the flask. "It's all right, Phil. One sip will do for now."

He recapped the flask. Phil watched him replace it in the drawer. At that moment, he could have used a shot from it himself.

Laura had been right about Nick having a blast at the Boy Scouts Jamboree. He ran with a tomahawk through the cypress woods at Occoquan Regional Park, amid a dozen hatchet-wielding boys in green camouflage coats and caps. Black scoutmaster Tom Newell easily kept up with them, being just a decade older than his troop. But Post photographer Ned O'Rourke fell well behind, due to his hefty fifty-plus condition more than his Nikon D4 camera, brown ski jacket, and Redskins cap. A gray sky peered through the treetops, threatening snow or sleet.

"Brody!" Newell shouted, "Get out of Kalbacher's blood circle!"

The short kid running in front of Nick moved farther right from a gangly fellow Scout's axe range.

"Here!" cried a boy from somewhere ahead and to the right.

The Scouts veered in that direction, Nick among them, toward a natural gulley. Four boys ahead of Nick leapt over the gulley. Then so did Nick, mentally thanking the Wyoming National Guard obstacle course. They came upon the lead Scout by a fallen tree branch, dry yet undecayed, with numerous smaller branches emanating from it. The other boys stopped, and looked inquiringly at their Scoutmaster.

"Looks good," Newell said. "Hit it."

The Scouts began vigorously hacking at the tree branch with their tomahawks. Some attacked it standing up, others on their knees, but all with their legs apart. Nick watched them chop, until Scoutmaster Newell came up beside him, pointing at the branch.

"You said you wanted the full experience."

"Wouldn't that be cheating?" asked Nick.

"Not if the judges don't see it."

"In that case," Nick said, raising his hatchet barbarian style. "Ayee!"

He joined the Scouts in the branch chopping, one foot before the other.

"Spread those legs, Trooper Jarrett, or you'll be limping home."

Nick parted his legs, now grasping why the Scouts did so. Ned O'Rourke appeared with his camera, huffing. He took multiple shots of the branch chopping boys, and a couple of Nick.

"Okay, that's enough kindling," Newell said. "Go, go, go!"

The Scouts scooped up bundles of wood like footballs, and took off running in the direction they came, Nick and Newell behind them. O'Rourke took a deep breath, and hurried after the group.

They ran out of the woods into a grass clearing encircled by the forest on three sides. At the treeless end, near a row of food-laden picnic tables, stood a line of parents, mostly mothers, excitedly spectating the campfire-building contest. Another troop was already in the clearing, around a circle of rocks, their kindle propped up teepee style within the circle. They cheered a muscular boy who was down on his knees scraping two flint stones together, supervised by a martial forty-something Scoutmaster.

Two more rock circles lay to the right some ten yards apart. Nick's troop swarmed the farthest one, and hastily stood up their kindle in the teepee formation. Their fire-starter champion, Anderson, a hardy Nordic kid, began rubbing two flint stones, encouraged by his mates. A third troop rushed out of the forest, kindling wood underarms, and toward the middle rock circle. Parents snapped away with their cellphone cameras, O'Rourke on his more sophisticated Nikon.

Anderson got the campfire going in two minutes, a minute after the first troop did. The third troop abandoned its effort. Everyone applauded when the winning troop, with its dozen happy boys, was awarded the campfire medal. Nick interviewed eight Scouts, the three Scoutmasters, and several proud mothers, who gushed into his digital recorder.

Before heading back to the Post, Nick and O'Rourke sat down for the picnic-style lunch. Nick enjoyed the boisterous camaraderie among the Scouts at his table, and their innocence. They were still oblivious to the insipid sexual politics that would soon be crammed down their throats. It was his bad luck to be stuck on the poster girl for that movement, Laura London. He also noticed some subtle glances being cast his way by a pair of pretty moms across the table.

"Been a long time since I've seen kids having this much fun," Nick said between hot dog bites. "Without a Gameboy or phone in hand."

"Funny," said O'Rourke, chewing on a cheeseburger. "To me you look like you're the Gameboy age yourself."

"I've always been the geezer of my group," said Nick. "Preferring books and old movies, mostly the hardboiled kind. I blame my father. He forced his love of them on my brother and me. Although Scott liked samurai films. He used to make me fight him with bamboo sticks — like Kato and Inspector Clouseau."

"My wife's a TCM addict," said O'Rourke. "I catch it with her sometimes, when I'm not playing video games myself."

Nick smiled.

"Funny thing about those old films," O'Rourke said. "You know what they had that today's movies and TV shows don't? Nice people."

"True. Men and women seemed to like each other more back then."

"You married, Nick?"

"No ... Although watching these boys, I can see the appeal."

"Girlfriend?"

"Not yet. But I got one in mind. And I've learned one lesson from being here today."

"What's that?"

"Be prepared," said Nick.

During the fifty-minute ride back to DC, Nick, in the passenger seat, wrote the story on the Post notebook computer. He kept replaying the comments on the digital recorder, into his headset. O'Rourke, driving, nodded at Nick's electronic support.

"That ain't the way Clark Gable would'a done it."

Nick grinned.

12

Alex's Subaru pulled out of the Washington Post parking lot into K Street and an early night rain. Nick, in the shotgun seat, watched the wipers smoothly sweeping away the icy drops. He unzipped his flight jacket to enjoy the quick-acting heat.

"Nice ride, Hugh."

"Gets me around."

"So who's this artist guy we're seeing?"

"I don't know him, but he paints a lot of fruit."

"And you like that," said Nick.

"Not particularly."

"Then why are we … Oh, I get it. You're after some chick."

Hugh made a left turn on 13th Street.

"She's beautiful," he said.

"I'm happy for you. But why drag me into it?"

"As my date," said Hugh.

"What?!"

Hugh kept his eyes on the road ahead.

"Spill it, Hugh."

"I've been working on this babe for a month," Hugh said. "She's a limey actress with the Folger Shakespeare Company. I had to sit through 'King Lear' three times to get in good with her."

"That's a tragedy," said Nick.

"No kidding. I almost gouged *my* eyes out. And she's not even the star of the show. But at least I got to talk to her backstage the last time."

Hugh made a left turn on I Street.

"Pray continue," Nick said, imitating Basil Rathbone as Sherlock Holmes.

"She emailed me to say she'd be at this art show tonight. Probably thinks I can promote it in the Post."

"Wonder how she got that idea."

"I may have had something to do with it," Hugh said, smiling. "But it's my best shot at her. My problem is another actor who's always buzzing around her. Total queer, but best friends with Margaret and her lawyer fiance in London. I need you to distract him for ten minutes while I put the moves on Margaret. It'll help if he thinks we're a couple—so that it's safe to leave her alone with me."

"Good plan. Except for one little flaw. I'm not gay!"

"But you're attractive," Hugh said, and cleared his throat, adding, "to those who lean that way. Come on, Nick, do it for romance. 'Nothing can come of nothing.'"

"That's from King Lear, you bastard."

Hugh smiled, and made a right on Nineteenth Street.

"All right," Nick said, pulling out his cellphone. "Guess I'd better figure out what LGBQET stands for."

"You're off to a bad start," said Hugh.

They entered the Commeroz Gallery, a few storefronts south of Dupont Circle. It had a surprisingly spacious interior, crowded with flagrant sophisticates holding champagne glasses in various stages of consumption. Their hairdos, eyewear, makeup, beards, and fashionable attire seemed more on display than the spotlighted artwork. The paintings depicted various fruit in Dali-esque settings, only with a space age bent.

Hugh was admiring a livelier work of art—a long-haired, busty brunette in a pink double-breasted jacket over a long yellow skirt. She stood before the painting of a gold peach atop a leafless tree trunk, talking with a thin, handsome blonde male, clearly older than his look. Hugh tapped Nick on the shoulder and nodded in their direction. Nick sighed. Hugh approached the pair. Nick moved behind him, close enough to overhear the conversation.

"Hello, Margaret," Hugh said with a rakish smile.

Margaret beamed at him while the blonde man looked on suspiciously.

"Hugh," she said in a lilting English accent. "How good of you to come. Simon, you remember Hugh."

"How could I not," said Simon, in a similar accent but less friendly tone. "After multiple attendances of our show. You must be quite the Shakespeare aficionado."

"Oh yes," Hugh said flamboyantly. "I adore *King Lear*...in particular the character of Regan. I always thought her deliciously evil. But not until Miss Scott's turn did I find her so erotic."

A few feet behind Hugh, Nick rolled his eyes.

"Thank you, kind sir," said Margaret, smiling.

"Erotic," Simon said in challenge. "What exactly do you mean by that?"

"Yes," said Nick, intruding on the group. "I'd like to know the answer to that one."

Hugh squirmed showily.

"Oh hello, Nick," he said with false anxiety. "I was just complimenting Margaret on her performance in King Lear."

"You've been doing a lot of that lately," Nick said coldly. "At the most inopportune times."

Margaret looked disappointed, Simon more relaxed, while appreciating Nick.

"You mustn't blame your—companion," said Simon. "Margaret is a brilliant Regan." He switched to a booming Shakespearean tone. "Heed the Earl of Kent!"

"Oh wow," Nick said, looking closely at Simon. "I'm sorry, I should've recognized you. You're amazing as Kent."

"Thank you," Simon said, gleaming.

"What brings you to this exhibit?" asked Nick with profound interest.

"Margaret and I are friends of the artist. He's also from the U.K."

"I'd like to meet him," Nick said, indicating the peach painting. "These are lovely."

"I'll be happy to introduce you—Nick."

"Could you introduce me to some of his paintings first? So I'll know what to say to him."

"Of course," said Simon.

Nick pointed to a painting on the far wall—a green apple orbiting a watermelon planet against a purple backdrop.

"Let's start with that one."

Simon led Nick to the distant painting. Margaret looked petulantly at Hugh.

"You tricked me," she said.

"Tricked you. Me? However so?"

"You made me believe you liked me."

"I do like you, Margaret. Very much."

"I meant in a different way."

"Oh, I see," Hugh said, moving close to Margaret. "Well, extraordinary women do affect me in that way. I had a hunch you might be one of them."

"But you're not sure."

"Well, it would require further exploration," Hugh said, caressing Margaret's cheek.

"Of what sort?" asked Margaret, enjoying Hugh's strokes.

"This sort," said Hugh.

He moved his mouth to Margaret's and gave her a forceful kiss, to which she eagerly responded. Nick observed the kiss over Simon's shoulder with widening eyes. Simon noticed his expression, and began to turn around. Nick clutched his arm, and spun him toward the painting.

"Tell me something. That apple. Is it orbiting the melon or just hovering above it?"

"Ah. That all depends on your perspective."

"Impressive," said Nick, seeing Hugh lead Margaret by the hand toward the exit. "Very impressive."

Simon turned to where their friends had been, and were no longer. Comprehension crossed his face. He looked accusingly at Nick, as if hurt by his deception more than Margaret's disloyalty. Nick felt guilty.

"It was his idea," he said.

"You aren't really gay, are you?"

"Only in the Shakespearean sense," said Nick.

"'My gay apparel for an almsman's gown,'" Simon said sadly. "I understudied David Tennant for Richard the Third."

"Must have taken a lot of ugly makeup."

"Why thank you, Nick. Are you sure you aren't…"

"Sorry," said Nick, then on a sudden thought, "But maybe I can make it up to you."

Simon looked hopefully at him.

"Not that way," Nick said. "With a story in the Washington Post. An English thespian at the Folger. Compare and contrast your DC theatre experience with Bard country."

"All the world's a stage," said Simon, brightening.

13

The soiree for Laura was less festive than most previous cocktail parties at the Capitol Hill row house. It had the same offerings—hors d'oeuvres of bruschetta with assorted toppings and broiled shrimp vermouth—plus an open bar. It had the same music—classic soft rock. And by nine o'clock, it had many of the same guests—three dozen successful people from their early twenties to late thirties. Yet a pall hung over the event—radiation from the bomb that struck Washington on the last Presidential Election Day, which had hit this group particularly hard.

Laura did her part to raise spirits, starting with the black silk sleeveless dress she would have worn to the White House Press Dinner as Todd Armstrong's date. She floated between guests like a beautiful dark fairy. Even the gender-neutrality advocate in the group admired her.

Another set of eyes focused on Sarah. She had on a green V-neck dress that hugged her physique the way Taylor Rushnel desired to. The Freedom from Religion attorney couldn't stop staring at Sarah through the glasses below his straggly brown hair. Rushnel had been put off by most of the women in his orbit, still railing against the current Administration, like his significant other, Maria. But the Amazonian beauty before him appeared a worthy companion for a progressive rising star like himself. To his surprise, he appeared to have no visible competition for her, as she kept eying their lovely hostess, Laura.

Laura approached Phil, who was conversing with Greg and Ann Bates, the executive couple from Planned Parenthood.

"There you are, Laura," Ann said. "Glad you still have time for us little people."

"Getting smaller every day under this regime," Greg said. "Like our budget."

"Be comforted," said Laura. "We'll stop the fascist pigs from defunding reproductive services, while I have a voice."

"You certainly do now, as the new queen of the Post," Greg said.

"I sure hope so, Greg."

"We need a young Maureen Dowd," Ann said. "She's getting mushy in her old age."

"You're right," Phil said. "Dowd barely criticized the Catholic zealot nominated for the Supreme Court."

"Christ, if she gets through," said Taylor Rushnel, joining the group, "We lose the Court for thirty years."

Everyone sulked at the thought.

"I don't know what we can do about it with the Grim Old Party in charge," Greg said.

"We can win the White House back next year," said Laura. "Make Hawthorne Vice President."

"Phil?" inquired Ann.

"I'm working on it," Phil said.

"Much too hard," said Laura, stroking his arm, "As I can attest."

Everyone chuckled. In the lightened mood, Taylor spoke quietly in Laura's ear.

"Could you introduce me to that gorgeous woman near the door?"

Laura glanced that way, and saw Sarah gazing at her over a glass of white wine.

"Of course, Taylor. Come with me."

She led Taylor to where Sarah stood. Sarah smiled at Laura, ignoring her companion until Laura indicated him.

"Sarah, this is Taylor Rushnel, super lawyer with the Freedom from Religion Foundation."

"I bring salvation," Taylor said. "From having to hear 'Merry Christmas' every time you buy a coffee in December."

"That'll make it a happy holiday," said Sarah, extending her hand to him. "I'm Sarah."

Laura left them in mid-handshake.

"Are you here with anybody?" Taylor asked.

"Laura," said Sarah.

"Ha. Lucky for me she has a date."

"Yes, isn't it."

The doorbell chimed.

"Excuse me," Sarah said.

She stepped away from Taylor to open the door. Her face dropped on seeing the person in the vestibule.

"Nick."

"Sarah, baby," Nick said. "You didn't have to get dolled up just for me."

He stepped inside. Laura gulped at the sight of him. He wore his aviator's jacket over olive green khaki slacks and grey desert boots, and was clearly failing to amuse Sarah.

"All right, I'll dance with you, but no groping," said Nick.

Sarah moved away from him, back to Taylor. Laura cast an apprehensive glance at Phil beside her, and saw him smugly eying Nick. She went to welcome her coworker as a proper hostess.

"Hello, Nick. I'm so glad you could make it."

"With you—anytime," said Nick.

Laura sighed. "Let me take your coat."

"Why stop there?"

Nick took off his aviator coat and surrendered it to Laura, who hung it in the closet by the door. This gave her a moment to think. She'd grown rather fond of Nick, having seen past his boorish trappings to the sensitive boy infatuated with her. She'd wanted him to meet her group so he would see for himself why he had no chance with her. Or did *she* need the reminder? She suddenly felt bad for Nick. These people would pick him apart, leaving the carcass for Phil to skewer. But Nick wouldn't go down without a fight, she knew. He'd land some blows. Either way, one of the two men closest to her would probably get hurt tonight. Laura gulped at her sudden admission. She'd just equated her lover of three years with Nick Jarrett.

"Oh no," she said into the closet.

Forming a polite smile, Laura turned to Nick, who was appraising the elegant living room. She tried to ignore how dashing he looked in a white Irish Fisherman's crewneck sweater.

"Nice place you got here," Nick said.

"Thank you. Just a stone's throw from the Capitol."

"That explains the decrease in Republicans."

"Not fast enough," Laura said. "They're still doing serious damage."

She led Nick back to her little group, too aware of Phil's predatory expression, and Ann's curious one.

"You remember Phil."

"Sure, your knight in shining BMW," Nick said, amiably extending his hand.

"Sorry I was rude to you last time," said Phil, shaking Nick's hand. "I'd had a rough night."

"Give her my number."

Phil withdrew his hand from Nick's.

"Greg, Ann," said Laura. "My colleague, Nick."

"Oh, are you a copy-aide too?" Ann asked.

"No, I'm the real thing," Nick said, and shook hands with the couple.

"Ann and Greg work for Planned Parenthood," said Laura, gauging Nick's reaction.

"Oh."

"That sounded like disapproval," Greg said.

"Sorry," said Nick.

"For disapproving?

"For sounding like it at the wrong occasion."

"*Do* you disapprove of our organization?" Greg asked.

"If you really want to know ... yes," Nick said.

"We help to keep abortion legal and safe," Ann said.

"Not so safe for the babies being snuffed," said Nick.

"A fetus isn't a baby," Ann said.

"Whatever helps you sleep at night," said Nick.

Laura saw Phil grit his teeth, and could sense his more than ideological disdain for Nick. This was personal, she knew, and she was the cause.

"You sound like one of those Christian lunatics," Greg said with a piteous smile.

"You're half right," said Nick.

Everyone but Laura looked at him as if he'd grown a third eye.

"Wait," Ann said. "You didn't vote for—"

"Grab yourself a drink at the bar, Nick," said Laura, interrupting Ann before things got any tenser. "There's plenty of Scotch."

"You trying to get me drunk?" Nick asked with a smile.

He headed toward the bar, and crossed paths with Taylor Rushnel, carrying two full red wineglasses to Sarah. Taylor handed her one, and was rewarded by a smile.

"Tell me, Sara," he said. "How do you keep in such amazing shape?"

"I run four miles three times a week."

"I run too," said Taylor. "Would you like to pair up sometime?"

"I prefer running alone. It's a mental thing with me."

"I get it," said Taylor. "Well, how about dinner then? There's a new Portuguese seafood restaurant in Georgetown that serves a delicious calama..."

Sarah placed a firm hand on his shoulder. "No offense, Taylor, but you're not my type."

"Okay," said Taylor, deflated. "Might I ask who is?"

Sarah cast a meaningful look at Laura, who was anxiously watching Nick pour himself a Scotch at the bar. Taylor finally got it.

"Oh," he said. "Well, of course I respect that. And you, for sharing it with me. If you ever change your mind…About dinner I mean—just dinner—I'd enjoy talking with you."

Nick approached the pair, full Scotch glass in hand, and dramatically addressed Sarah.

"I leave you alone for five minutes and you're all over another man! Didn't last night mean anything to you?!"

Taylor looked at Sarah in confusion.

"Pay no attention to him, Taylor," she said. "Nick's a sexist throwback."

"She meant sexy throwback," Nick said to Taylor with a wink.

"How do you view lesbian relationships?" Taylor asked, clearly to impress Sarah.

"Preferably on Cinemax," said Nick. "In HD."

Taylor reeled in shock. Sarah shook her head. Nick moved away. He rejoined Phil and Laura's circle in the middle of an intense discussion.

"That's outrageous," Laura said. "Where'd you see that?"

"It was on Channel Five like two nights ago," said Greg. "DC taxi drivers routinely bypass African-Americans to pick up white passengers."

"Utterly unacceptable," Laura said.

"And punishable," said Phil. "Washington's a federal city. Which means, Congress can revoke cab licenses merely on the suspicion of racism."

"Not racism," Nick said.

Everyone turned to him.

"What would you call it?" Phil asked challengingly.

"Capitalism," said Nick. "I asked a couple of cab drivers

about that story. They said the reason they prefer white passengers is because blacks tend to tip less."

"That is racism," Phil said condescendingly.

"I doubt it," said Nick. "Both cabbies I spoke to were black."

"Ha," Ann said.

Phil bristled. Sarah and Taylor joined the group, Sarah practically pushing Taylor.

"He passed the test," Sarah said to Laura.

"I'm proud of you, Taylor," Laura said.

"What test?" Ann asked.

"The New Man Test," said Laura. "How a man responds to changing norms — such as being turned down by a lesbian."

"Some test," Nick said. "Now scoring with a lesbian — that's the Real Man Test."

Laura stifled a groan.

"What do you believe a woman finds attractive in a man, Nick?" Ann asked.

"Chemistry aside? Sense of humor, protective instincts, and enough money to take care of her."

"Why not bearskins?" Laura said.

"Sorry?"

"Women east of the Mississippi and west of the Rockies don't need men to support them, Nick. They can work and look after themselves."

"And who'll raise their kids?"

"Child care," Greg said. "Employer or government — someone will pay for it."

"Yeah, the kid," said Nick.

"That's an archaic notion," Laura said.

"Tell me that after you have one," said Nick.

A tense silence followed. Nick tried to lighten the mood.

"Okay, no more politics for me," he said. "How 'bout the Redskins game Sunday? If the offensive line can give Cousins just a little more protection, he'd throw fewer intercep...tions."

Nick stopped, aware of the hostile stares around him.

"What now?" he asked.

"We don't use the name of that team," Phil said. "In fact, we're pressuring the owner to change it."

"Oh man."

"It's offensive to Native Americans," said Greg.

"How?" asked Nick.

"It disparages the color of their skin," said Taylor.

"Have any of you ever met an Indian?" Nick asked.

No one spoke for a moment, then Phil did.

"What's your point?"

"There's a lot of 'em where I come from. Cheyenne's named after one tribe. Proud people. And guess what. Indian skin's no different from yours and mine. Name comes from the berry juices they used for war paint. So 'redskin's about as insulting to an Indian as 'redcoat' is to an Englishman. For some Indians, it's a compliment."

Everyone stared at Nick, Phil dismissively. An image crossed Nick's mind, of a black man in a wheelchair saluting him on Georgia Avenue.

"If you really want to be offended by the NFL," he said. "Try millionaire players taking a knee during the National Anthem, when better men than they, of every race, *lost* their knees or a lot more, fighting for our country, and their right to whine about it."

"Those athletes have a point," said Phil, losing his temper.

"America betrayed African-Americans when it voted in this bunch of Nazis."

"Who follow the Constitution, not *Mein Kampf*," said Nick.

"All reactionaries are paper tigers," Phil said.

"Mao Zedong," said Nick. "Boy, have you guys found a role model."

"That's it, Jarrett!" exclaimed Phil.

Laura had dreaded the explosion yet been powerless to stop it. Phil moved his face close to Nick's. Nick looked calmly back at him. All party chatter ceased as everyone observed the confrontation.

"We've had enough of your cowboy lore!" said Phil. "Time for you to 'vamoose'!"

"Phil," Laura said soothingly, to no effect.

"This townhouse ain't big enough for the two of us!" said Phil. "So git!"

"You wanna back off," said Nick. "Then I'll go."

"I said now, varmint. It's way past high noon."

Laura could see Nick trying to constrain himself, but Phil kept pushing him.

"Phil, please," Laura said. "He's leaving."

Phil was too deep into his clever intimidation to desist. He failed to see his target exhaling softly, as from a decision made.

"We don't like your kind around here," said Phil.

"You forgot one," said Nick.

"What's that, cowboy?"

"Happy trails."

Nick fired a right jab at Phil's jaw, knocking him to the carpet on his back. Phil's eyes remained open but unfocused. Laura knelt down and cradled his head. She looked angrily up at Nick.

Nick went to the coat closet and retrieved his flight jacket, then walked out the door.

14

Nick sat on the sofa, the laptop on his lap, typing furiously between swigs of Dos Equis Dark. The words came quickly to him with the events of the past hour still fresh in his mind.

The New Man Test

by Nick Jarrett

Last night I got thrown out of my first Washington party. I had some political differences with the host, a legislative aide to a powerful Democratic senator. But instead of debating me intellectually, he became churlish and hysterical in the face of opposing thought. He was backed up by a feminist chorus line, which included the lovely hostess. He passed the New Man Test.

I learned about this test at the same party. It's a new standard to measure a man's abandonment of traditional male behavior. Basically, the wimpier he acts, the higher he scores. Contrary to progressive doctrine, women haven't gotten stronger, they've made men weaker. It's the wrong way to achieve "gender equality"....

He sent the finished piece to Rick Spencer, the lone conservative opinionist at the Post, who'd taken a liking to him. While rereading his piece, Nick heard a knock at the door behind him. Outside visitors having to call for admittance, he guessed it was his pretty neighbor, Kelly, a Houlihan's waitress who sometimes dropped in for a beer. She could be just the right company for tonight, thought Nick. He laid the open laptop on the coffee table and stood up with the beer bottle. He opened the door, and blinked twice. Laura London stood in the hallway looking like the Masque of the Red Death in her scarlet coat.

"I must be dreaming," said Nick.

"Or drunk again," Laura said, glancing at his beer bottle.

"How'd you know where I live?"

"The copyaide directory. Another tenant let me in."

"A man I hope."

"What difference does that make?"

"He'll be able to describe you after you shoot me," Nick said, and switched to his film noir voice. "She looked like a million bucks. And that was only for one night with her."

"Are you going to let me in?"

Nick stepped aside for Laura, and shut the door behind her. She paused in front of it, surveying the apartment. Her eyes went to the *Laura* poster.

"Film noir posters, pulp novels, pine furniture. You're a walking cliché, Nick."

"I also own a pistol — in Wyoming," said Nick. "Is the party over?"

"Thanks to you. How could you hit Phil?"

"Someone gets in my face, they better be wearing lipstick."

"You should've left when he told you to."

"I like leaving to be my idea," said Nick. "How is Phil?"

"He's furious at me. Blames me for your presence there. I had to leave our house, to spend the night at Sarah's. Why'd you do it, Nick? Act like such a jerk?"

"I was trying to fit in with your crowd."

Laura took off her coat and practically shoved it into Nick. She stepped around his sofa and sat down in it.

"You want a beer?" asked Nick.

"No. Just you out of my orbit."

"So you beamed up here to tell me that."

"Yes," said Laura. "And that whatever you think will happen between us, never will."

"I'll turn off the video camera."

He sat down on the sofa, a foot away from Laura, draping her coat on the armrest.

"It's obvious we can't be friends," she said. "It's hard enough being coworkers. And that's all we'll ever be, Nick. Get it through your head. You represent everything I loathe in a man."

"The voice of reason?"

"We will not get involved. Is that clear?"

"And sharp," Nick said, wincing as from a sting.

Laura noticed his look of pain, and softened.

"It could never work out, Nick. You oppose all that I stand for."

Nick shrugged.

"I like *you*," he said.

"You don't get it. What I stand for *is* me. Maybe *you* can love someone you vehemently disagree with. Not me. I have to fight for my beliefs. And it's an uphill battle."

"I'm against women in combat," said Nick.

"What?"

"I'm pro-life, pro-death, and pro-God. I choke up at the "Star Spangled Banner." I think housewives should be role models, and marriage only between a man and a woman. But right now, none of those mean a damn. The only thing worth fighting for is you."

Laura stared at him, her brown eyes less penetrative than normal, actually opaque.

"Kiss me, Nick," she said.

"What?...You just said it couldn't happen. You made a great case for it. Even I the Jury was ready to pack it..."

"Nick," said Laura. "You think too much."

Nick took hold of Laura's sleeveless arms and pressed his mouth against hers. Her pliant yet forceful lips responded. Her tongue began doing wild, wonderful things inside his mouth. The resultant bliss surpassed any previous, deeper sexual encounter he'd ever had. Laura seemed equally in the spirit, letting out a long, soft moan.

"My God," she said, gasping breath.

"You're not so bad yourself," said Nick.

Laura laughed. Nick pushed her back onto the sofa cushion, feeling her luscious legs against his groin. He kissed her again, hard. She reciprocated while writhing beneath him. Somehow, he found the willpower to desist. He looked down at her gorgeous face.

"I can't believe I'm asking this," said Nick. "But are you sure?"

"No...But I want to."

"That's good enough for me."

Nick got ready to kiss Laura again. She glimpsed at his open laptop on the coffee table, the words too small for her to read, including the title in bold, *The New Man Test*.

"What are you writing?"

"Oh that," said Nick, suppressing a moment of panic. "Just a story idea."

He sprang to his feet and shut the laptop. He turned to Laura with desire, the same look on her face. He put his arms beneath her legs and behind her back, and lifted her off the sofa. He carried her toward his walkthrough closet.

"Nick, where are you taking me?" asked Laura, palpably excited.

"To my cave — woman."

Nick pulled open the double shutter doors to enter his closet-bedroom. He eased Laura onto the futon mattress, her head on the pillow beneath the hanging clothes. She trembled in anticipation as he straddled her legs, and slipped the straps of her cocktail dress from her shoulders. He pulled the dress down, and off, revealing her black silk bra and panties. He unstrapped and removed the bra, and let out a small gasp. Laura's exquisite face and bare breasts forever replaced the Gene Tierney *Laura* portrait as the go to picture in his mind.

"Jesus, Laura! You're beyond beautiful."

"That's not an accomplishment."

"It's a hell of a start," said Nick.

He yanked off his sweater and the long-sleeve pullover underneath. Laura looked up admiringly at his bare torso. He lay down on her left and took off his pants, stripping down to his azure briefs. Laura's expression of approval turned to longing. Nick began gently stroking her full breasts, back, and buttocks. Laura squirmed with pleasure.

"I'm supposed to be at Sarah's," she said.

"Anything she can do I can do better."

"Sexist."

"That's me," said Nick.

He kissed her mouth. Laura more than reciprocated. His sexual probing became more invasive yet nonetheless welcome.

"I want you, Laura — body and soul."

"You're the devil."

"And preparing to re-enter heaven," said Nick.

Which he did.

Sarah Woronov tossed her cellphone on the sofa cushion beside her. It bounced off and fell to the floor. She didn't care, after the depressing text from Laura. *I won't make it tonight. Explain later.* The perfect storm that had made Laura leave her own party, and would have brought her into her arms, had ended somewhere else. Sarah longed to know where. Maybe an old boyfriend, she sulked.

She had planned her seduction of Laura as a change in partners not principles. Sisterhood was the key to winning Laura, her own incestuous variant on it. A rival other than Phil would require a new strategy on her part. She knew any lover Laura chose would have to be ideologically like-minded. Or would he?

She pictured Nick Jarrett at the party earlier. He was so blatantly in love with Laura. And it seemed she kind of liked him. But the way she'd looked at him when he hit Phil would have closed that book for good. Sarah picked up her cellphone and went to bed.

15

Sunlight filtered into the closet-bedroom through the slits in the shutter doors. Nick stirred awake. His first thought was of the wonderful dream he'd had of making love to Laura. It seemed so real yet too fantastic to be true. But someone lay atop his right arm under the covers, hand on his chest, breathing softly in his ear. Has to be Kelly the waitress, he thought. He turned his head to the right, and saw Laura's beautiful face an inch from his own, her eyes lightly closed under long lashes. It became the happiest moment of his life. He watched her brown eyes blink open, look uncertainly at him for a moment, then widen in apprehension.

"Good morning," he said.

"God," said Laura. "What have I done?"

"Trusted your instincts. They steered you right."

"To Atilla the Hun."

Nick sighed. To his relief, Laura smiled.

"But I have to admit," she said. "It was a tender ravishing."

"That's because I'm *your* captive."

"My. You're good, Nick."

"There's more where that came from. 'Come live with me and be my love, and we will all the pleasures prove.'"

"Marlowe," said Laura.

"Christopher, not Philip, in your honor. But I'm serious, Laura. Move in with me."

"You're mad."

"About you."

"I can't, Nick," said Laura. "Phil needs me."

"Let the nanny state he's pushing for take care of him."

Laura scowled.

"And I'll take care of you," said Nick.

"I'm self-contained."

"But not self-satisfied."

He gave Laura a lusty kiss, to which she vigorously responded, but then broke it off.

"I have to go."

"Back to Phil," said Nick.

"He'll be wondering where I am. As you're by now aware, he has a temper."

"Has he ever hit you?" Nick asked intently.

Laura remained silent for a moment, then spoke in a low voice. "Once. 'Bout a year ago. After a fundraiser. When he thought I'd been too friendly with one of Hawthorne's Silicon Valley donors."

Nick grimaced.

"He begged me to forgive him right away. And it never happened again. But..."

"But?" said Nick.

"I've seen the same look on his face a few times since."

"He ever does more than look — that punch I gave him will seem like a love tap."

Laura kissed him. He responded. Their kissing intensified.

"We'd better stop," said Laura, showing little inclination to do so.

"Why?"

"I have to go."

"You have to come first," said Nick.

They became more intimate, their bodies now in sync. Laura's cellphone buzzed on the futon. She read the name on the screen and looked pleadingly at Nick. He reluctantly withdrew from her. Laura answered the phone.

"Hi, Phil," she said, breathing hard. "Oh, um…I've been working out."

"With a partner," Nick whispered.

Laura looked reproachfully at him.

"I'm still at Sarah's."

Nick clucked. Laura mouthed the word "please" at him.

"We can talk about it when I get home…See you in an hour…I love you too."

Nick winced. Laura hung up, looking guiltily at him.

"Why didn't you tell him the truth? You're in my bed and out of his — for good."

"He couldn't handle it," said Laura. "I'm not sure I can."

"You're gonna have to, and soon. This is it, Laura. The black bird."

"The black bird?"

"The stuff that dreams are made of," Nick said.

"I know. That's what scares me."

"You know what scares me? If I live to be a hundred, I'll never love a girl as much as I love you."

Laura smiled sweetly at Nick.

"Give me the rest of the weekend to sort this out. And how to tell Phil. All right?"

"All right," said Nick. "Bring a packed suitcase to work Monday. So you won't have to go back to your place."

Laura looked melancholic.

"What's wrong, kid?" asked Nick.

"You are — for me."

"I'm the rightest guy you'll ever know. So don't go breaking my heart."

"Bah. One couldn't break your heart with a sledgehammer."

Laura grabbed her underwear and dress, and stood up on the futon. Nick watched the most perfect ass at Mount Holyoake, circa two years ago, head into his bathroom. Soon, the shower started. Nick lay back on the pillow, a happy man.

16

Laura walked into her house to see Phil on his cellphone headset in the living room. He wore his blue-grey power suit and held a mug of coffee. She noted the purplish bruise mark on his jaw, the souvenir from Nick. Phil gave her a curt nod.

"They'll be there, Senator. All three cable networks — CNN, MSNBC and Fox ... Not sure who from Fox. One of their blonde bimbos. They're all the same — right-wing sluts ... You'll be great, sir. I've been promoting your appearance... See you there."

Phil hung up, and faced Laura.

"Hey ... How was Sarah's?"

"All right. We didn't talk much. Just went to our respective beds — couch in my case."

"Where does she live again?"

"Old Town Alexandria."

"Oh right," Phil said, trying to appear nonchalant. "Apartment? House? Townhouse?"

Laura tensed for a moment. She had a quick thought and took out her cellphone.

"Just a second," she said. "Let me reply to this text."

"From who?"

"Mother."

Laura found the photo Sarah texted of her home, its Alexandria address, and the message — *Looking forward to our girls' night in*. Laura pretended to respond to it, then looked at Phil.

"Sorry, what did you ask me?"

"Sara's place — townhouse or apartment?"

"It's a small blue house. What is this, Phil? You don't trust me?"

"Of course I do, honey," Phil said more softly.

"You're the one who went berserk last night. Accused me of siding with Nick. That's why I left, remember?"

"You're right. I'm sorry. But your cowboy friend got to me. I take enough crap from Hawthorne's backward enemies. I didn't need one in our home."

"Yes, Nick was a brute last night," Laura said, fondly recalling her time on his futon.

"He caught me by surprise last night. Otherwise I would've kicked his ass."

Most unlikely, Laura thought, then felt guilty for her machismo comparison. Damn you, Nick Jarrett.

"How's the jaw?" asked Laura.

"Why don't you kiss it and make it better."

"Phil, we need to talk."

"What about?

"Us."

Phil frowned. "Can it wait till tonight? Hawthorne's leading a Resistance rally on the Mall at noon. You should come to it."

"All right, I will."

"Sarah too."

"I'll call her."

"Good," Phil said. "I love you, Laura."

"I know," said Laura.

17

The farther east Nick walked on Morrison Street from Georgia Avenue, the gloomier it seemed, even on a bright sunny Sunday afternoon. Shuttered storefronts lined the supposedly commercial street, with few people in sight. None of this darkened Nick's mood. With Laura as his girl, Calcutta would resemble Oz. He wore his aviator coat, blue jeans, RayBan sunglasses and no cap. The only open business he saw was Ben's Liquor, half a block ahead on his left. Deeming it the social center of the neighborhood, he approached the place.

It was a surprisingly neat little shop doubling as a convenience store. The sole occupants were two fiftyish black men conversing on each side of the counter. The man before it held a brown bag with a large beer bottleneck sticking out. Both shut up when Nick came in, perhaps surprised by a white face. He made it a friendly one while showing his press card.

"Gentlemen, I wonder if you can help me. I'm with the Washington Post and ..."

"You guys suck!" said Bag Man.

Nick looked at him.

"Picking Georgetown over Howard by four," said Bag Man. "That's messed up, man."

"Hey, I'm not on the Sports Desk," Nick said, adding, "But my friend, Mike Carter, is."

"Mike Carter," said the man behind the counter. "I remember him. Kid was good. Got a bad break against Duke."

"Screwed me," said Bag Man. "I lost fifty bucks on that game."

"I'll reprimand him for you," said Nick.

The man behind the counter smiled.

"I'm Spike," he said. "Nathan Detroit here is Roscoe. Whacha need?"

"I'm looking for the Sergeant," said Nick.

Both men frowned.

"Whatcha want with him?" Roscoe asked.

"And how do you know 'im?" asked Spike.

"We met three nights ago," said Nick. "I'd like to do a story on him. Anything you guys can tell me about him?"

"Not much," Spike said. "Man keeps to himself. First showed up here a year back. Wheels in here every Monday, and always gets the same thing, bottle of Jim Beam Apple."

"Apple?"

"A snort a day keeps the doctor away," Roscoe said.

"Know where he lives?"

"The Morrison, two blocks down," said Spike, thumbing eastward.

"Don't buzz the wrong guy over there," Roscoe said. "You might get shot."

"I might have to — not knowing his real name. I doubt he's listed under Sergeant."

"There's a faded nametag on his Army coat," said Spike. "J. Wallace."

"Thanks," said Nick.

The Morrison was a cubic three-floor brownstone on the right side of the street. Nick climbed the two steps to the entrance, noting the absence of a wheelchair ramp. There was an old-style intercom system left of the door, a button next to each tenant's last name. Nick pushed the one for *Wallace — 108*. Half a minute elapsed with no response. Then a gruff voice came through the intercom.

"Yeah."

"Sergeant Wallace? My name's Nick Jarrett. I helped you catch a bus the other night."

There was another long pause, then, "Right. Thanks."

Silence ensued. Nick went for broke.

"I'm in the service myself—well, National Guard. And work at the Washington Post. I'm supposed to come up with interesting stories. Got a hunch you might have one."

"You mean be one."

"Yeah," said Nick, feeling rapacious.

Another half a minute passed. Nick prepared to make a tactical withdrawal, when the door lock buzzed. He walked on a dingy carpet through a dim hall with hard-to-see door numbers. Number 108 was the last door on the right, next to the exit. Nick knocked on it.

"Wait," said the voice from inside.

Nick did. He could hear a toilet flushing, followed by a faucet spray. What it must be like, he reflected, struggling to do the commonest things most people did without a thought. He already had second thoughts about the story, and his ability to do it justice. One conviction kept him going. Any man who'd fought for his country, and at such great cost, deserved better. The door opened inwardly to reveal Wallace in his wheelchair and Army camouflage coat.

"You want a story, Guardsman? Come with me."

Wallace rolled out to the hall, pulling the room door shut. He continued to the rear exit door, with Nick behind him. Wallace pushed the cross bar to open the door. Before Nick could reach him, he dipped out of sight. Nick caught the closing door and looked down. Next to some black steel steps, a tin ramp descended to a grey alleyway. At the bottom of the ramp, Wallace sat in his wheelchair, apparently waiting for him. Nick joined him. They went rightward in the alley, Nick on Wallace's left, the man's muscular arms and wheels moving in fast tandem.

"No offense, sir," Nick said. "But would you like me to push you?"

"'Sir' is for brass. Call me Sarge."

"Sarge."

Wallace stopped the wheelchair.

"All right, Guardsman. I'll pretend you're the motor I can't afford for this thing."

Nick clutched the two short pole handles behind the backrest and began pushing the wheelchair forward. They turned right at the side street, then left on Morrison. Approaching Georgia Avenue, Wallace spoke again.

"You know what a V-bed is, Guardsman?"

"No, Sarge," said Nick.

"Short for Vehicle-Borne Improvised Explosive Device. It's a Jihadi favorite. They pack the back seat of a car with these fuckers, and cover 'em with plastic bags full of nails, screws, ball bearings, whatever'll cause the most projectile damage."

"One moment, Sarge."

Nick stopped pushing the wheelchair. He took a digital recorder out of his coat pocket and turned it on, but then couldn't figure how to carry it while handling the wheelchair. Wallace turned around, and understood his dilemma.

"Gimme that thing," he said.

He took the recorder from Nick's hand and laid it between his thigh stumps. Nick resumed pushing the wheelchair, and Wallace his story.

"The one advantage we got is that the lethal junk weighs down the back of a vehicle. You gotta watch for cars riding high in the front, low in the rear. If eight or nine cars down the line, you see one with the trunk lower than the rest of it, your 'fuck me' meter better go off."

They passed Ben's Liquor Store across the street. Roscoe stood in the doorway, staring at them. Nick waved to him. Roscoe raised his beer bag in a toast.

"So our intelligence boys came up with a brilliant counter to the V-bed...the TCP."

"I know that one," said Nick. "Traffic Control Point."

"Fancy name for some low concrete barriers arranged like a maze. But any vehicle entering the TCP has to slow down and snake its way through it, making it harder for Jihadis to reach a target and blow it up."

They came to Georgia Avenue near the northbound bus stop on the left, where Nick had gotten off. Wallace signaled Nick to stop pushing. While awaiting the bus, he continued to talk.

"TCP guard duty is a nightmare for a bunch of reasons. In

Afghanistan, the worst two are heat and boredom. They fuck with your mind as much as your body. Soldier brains melt down as they search cars and question drivers for twelve hours at a stretch. By hour four, they start to lose focus. Go from scanning for threats to treating their TCP like a tollbooth. Talk drifts from suspicious cars to what chicks they banged in high school. I'd drive around from point to point, busting their balls, trying to save their butts."

A Metro Bus stopped before them. Nick climbed aboard. He sat up front, right behind the sideways seat that doubled as the wheelchair berth. The bus driver left his chair, and folded back the seat. Retaking his chair, he started lowering the wheelchair lift. Nick recalled Cherise Wilson's story about the two punks on the bus who had mocked Wallace. He scanned the dozen passenger faces, and saw no menacing ones. Wallace backed his wheelchair into the berth, locking it. The bus resumed its journey.

"I had just one last inspection left that evening," Wallace said. "It was cooling down fast, with one helluva desert sunset. Like a postcard I'll never forget. I joined Private Tim Rawlins on his final round, supervising him. He was young, born and bred here in DC. We noticed the sixth car in line had a slightly sunken ass. Could'a been anything besides a bomb. I stood right behind Rawlins as he leaned in to question the driver. Saw him look at the back seat and freeze. There's an S-O-P rule on how to respond to a threat. Jump over the T-barrier and drop. It's why they're only three-feet high. Tim could'a made it. He had just enough time. But he didn't. He yelled, "V-bed!," and shoved me back over the T-barrier. The blast erased him. Took only my legs."

Nick felt a clasp in his gut. Wallace shut off the digital recorder and handed it back to him. They rode in silence for another minute.

"Where we going?" Nick asked.

"To get you your story."

"I thought this was it."

"Nope," said Sergeant Wallace. "That was only the intro."

That evening on his sofa, cold beer within reach, Nick began to write the story.

Army Sergeant John Wallace lost more than his legs in Afghanistan. He lost the will to live. Only one thing kept him from, in his words, "blowing his brains out." It was the debt he owed Private Timothy Rawlins. Rawlins sacrificed his life shielding Wallace from an ISIS car bomb outside of Kamdesh. He left behind a fiancee, Ann Feder, now 31, and her son, Bobby, 10, with little means of support. After two tours of duty fighting terrorists in the Middle East, there was one force Rawlins couldn't beat—the Department of Veterans Affairs.

The VA requires that a soldier be married in order to remunerate his dependents. Rawlins had planned to wed Ann and adopt Bobby at the end of his latest tour. He died two months short of it. Wallace learned of the SNAFU when he first visited the Feders in their modest Pleasant Plains apartment. He went there to personally describe Rawlins' heroic death to his loved ones. Divorced since 1997, Wallace has not seen his own son or daughter in seven years. That evening, he made a life decision.

"The way I saw it, I had a choice," Wallace said. "Shoot myself like

I'd intended, and save the VA a budget-busting four grand a month, or stay alive, and use that dough to help a good kid grow up safe."

The next day, he signed a form putting all his future disability payments into a trust for Bobby Feder. Bobby's now in St. Patrick's Catholic School, earning high grades in Math and Science, and playing on the basketball team. Wallace, meanwhile, is subsisting on his Army pension, which won't even pay for a motorized wheelchair. But he says he's happy with the deal, and enjoys having dinner at the Feders' home twice a week. His bus trips there and back are not without their challenges however...

Nick went on to describe the bus incident as told to him by Cherise Wilson. He detailed the V-bed attack that cost Wallace his legs and Rawlins his life. When done, Nick emailed the unassigned story to Frank Russell on the Post Metro Desk. Tomorrow he would learn its fate.

18

"You did it!" Hugh exclaimed, just above a whisper. "You banged Laura London!"

He stood next to Nick at the back end of the mail table, a low stack of envelopes untouched before them. The clock above their heads read 9:18.

"Nothing so crude," said Nick in the same low voice. "I consummated our relationship."

"Your relationship was hostile."

"It was a little shaky."

"Like the San Andreas Fault."

"Well the Earth did move for both of us," said Nick. "And the only reason I'm telling you this is so you'll know we're a couple now."

"You fished where you swim, and caught a beautiful mermaid. Now you just have to keep her on dry land while her sisters try to pull her back into the sea."

"Their siren song versus my…harpoon," said Nick.

Susan Machado stepped out of her office, frowning at Nick.

"You're in trouble, Mr. Jarrett."

"What'd I do?" said Nick.

"You apparently wrote a great story. Now Frank Russell wants to see you—leaving me a copyaide short."

"I'm sorry, Susan. I promise to focus on this job for a while."

"Too late," Susan said. "Serves me right for hiring smart, ambitious youngsters. From now on I'll stick to slackers—like Mr. Sinclair."

"Hey," Hugh said.

Nick and Susan laughed.

"Go on, Nick," Susan said. "Oh, I forgot. You're to meet Frank in Henley's office."

"Yikes," Hugh said. "The Managing Editor."

"He'll probably spike the story," Nick said.

"Better it than you," said Susan. "I've seen him chop some heads in there."

Nick put a protective hand around his neck, and exited to the newsroom.

The path to the glass wall demarking the two main editors' offices, and the conference room, led between twin reception desks facing each other. Nick approached the right desk, where sat Nancy Shea, her tall red hair bent over a Post crossword puzzle. She looked up at him through gold-rimmed reading glasses.

"Hello, Nick."

"Hi, Nancy."

Nick pointed past her to the Managing Editor's transparent office.

"Good thing you can see inside there," he said. "They can't hide my corpse."

Nancy smiled. "You'll be all right. How's your lovely non-girlfriend?"

"No longer non."

"I knew it," Nancy said. "I felt the aura between you two in the elevator. Go on in."

Nick walked past her desk into the Managing Editor's office. The wood-paneled left wall separated it from the Executive Editor's office. A large window took up the entire back section, offering a splendid view of the National Geographic Museum. On the right wall hung six color pictures of Jeff Henley shaking hands with every President since Reagan, each subsequent one with less hair on Henley. The now semi-bald Henley, in a grey suit and dotted gold tie, sat behind a large walnut desk on the left, facing two tan leather armchairs. Frank Russell occupied the right chair, holding a full coffee mug.

"Gentlemen," Nick said.

"Have a seat, Nick," Henley said.

Nick sat down in the vacant left chair. Russell nodded at him.

"Would you like some coffee?" asked Henley.

"No, thank you, sir."

"Frank showed me your story on that wounded Army sergeant. Very moving. We're running it tomorrow."

"That's great. He's quite a man."

"And on the strength of it, I'd like to talk to you about a story idea we're kicking around."

"I play soccer," said Nick.

Henley and Russell smiled.

"Told you he's a wise guy," Russell said.

"You may or may not know," said Henley, "That Alice Lassiter is supposed to give a speech at Daniel Carroll University Wednesday night."

"That should be pretty eventful," said Nick.

"Could be violent," Russell said.

"Sure," said Nick. "The university's an unsafe space for the chief promoter of the Pentagon's transgender ban."

"How do you feel about that?" Henley asked.

"Feel, sir? I don't. I *think* the military's the wrong place for social experimenting. Detracts from their main job—to kill people and break things. Takes some hard men to do that—like my jarhead brother."

"Well," said Henley. "That's certainly the traditionalist view."

"The issue's moved closer to home," Russell said. "Maryland House of Representatives."

"The Transgender Bathroom Bill," Nick said.

"It would allow any man to use the ladies' room," said Henley. "If he identifies as a woman. Lassiter has been the bill's strongest critic. Now the Governor said he's going to veto it."

"Making Lassiter even more popular on a university campus," Nick said. "Who invited her to Daniel Carroll?"

"The Young Conservatives for Freedom," Russell said.

"Those radicals," said Nick.

"Whatever happens on Wednesday, we'd like to get the inside story on it," Henley said.

"Want me to cover the speech?" asked Nick, feeling lofty.

"No, we got actual reporters for that," Russell said.

Nick deflated.

"Frank is right, Nick," Henley said. "Blunt, but right. Every news service will have bland quotes by students slamming Lassiter. We want to go deeper than that. What we need is an inside journo. Someone young enough to blend in with the students, who can define the opposition to her. For instance, is it generic or external? Is faculty involved? How far are they willing to go? Will the campus police step in or stand down?"

"The job calls for an undercover punk," Russell said. "Naturally, I thought of you."

"Thank you, uhm, I think."

"You'd have to live on campus for the next two days, leading to the speech," Henley said. "Attend classes. Befriend the protesters."

"Even sleep with 'em," said Russell. "Anything to get the story."

"Is this something you're willing to do?" asked Henley.

"You bet," Nick said, then had a reservation. "Only... Never mind."

"No, tell us your concern," Henley said.

"Well, there's one group I'll have a hard time getting in with. Who has a special grudge against Lassiter."

"Feminists," said Henley. "We thought of that, but couldn't come up with a good approach to them."

"Might I make a suggestion?" said Nick.

Laura's fork stopped an inch above her tuna casserole. She looked at Nick over his roast beef sandwich, coleslaw, and Coke. They were sitting at their now usual cafeteria table.

"Are you joking?"

"Nope," said Nick. "We're going back to school—Daniel Carroll University, for two days."

"Oh my," Laura said, laying down her fork. "A feature story in the Post. That's incredible."

"My name goes first."

"Of course, sweetheart. You're bringing me in on this."

Nick basked in the glow of Laura's first ever term of endearment for him.

"What'd Susan have to say about our desertion?" Laura asked.

"She's not happy. Neither are Mike and Warren. They gotta leave their cushy jobs to cover us back in the copyaide station."

"Who cares? This will give me the chance to skewer Alice Lassiter."

"She's a brilliant scholar."

"She's a horror."

"Laura, I'm ashamed of you. She's no looker, but that's a bit harsh."

"I didn't mean her physical appear..."

Laura stopped, seeing Nick's smile. She mirrored it.

"Conservative humor," Laura said. "It'll take me some getting used to."

"I'm serious about some things though—mainly you. Did you bring your suitcase?"

"No. I didn't have time to pack. I was at a Resistance rally with Phil all day, and a Hawthorne fundraiser till midnight."

"Where'd you sleep last night?"

"In my bed," said Laura.

"Oh," Nick said sourly.

"Phil slept on the couch."

Nick brightened.

"I told him I needed some space," Laura said.

Nick sighed.

"I know, an embarrassing cliché," said Laura.

"Why didn't you just tell him the truth?"

"I couldn't, Nick," Laura said almost apologetically. "Not yet. Phil would die. He'd sooner see me turn prostitute."

"Well, I'm buying your services for tonight," said Nick.

"I think we can work out a price, sailor."

They both laughed.

"Where are we staying at the university?" Laura asked.

"You — in the local chapter of Tammy Perkins's sorority, Eta Gamma Omega."

"Me — in that Dixie Barbie's sorority? I'll go mad."

"Not in front of the sisters or you'll blow our cover ... I'll be close by, in Hugh's frat house, Delta Tau Epsilon. Think of that. I can serenade you in public."

Nick began to croon.

"Laura is the face in the misty light,
Footsteps that you hear down the hall.
The laugh that floats on a summer night
That you can never quite recall."

Laura groaned.

Part Two

Back To School

19

Nick entered his apartment carrying a Vincenzo's Pizza box and bag. He flicked the light switch with his elbow, and placed the food on the dinette table. Returning to the quasi-living room, he removed his flight jacket and Irish cap. Uncharacteristically, he hung up both in the walkthrough closet over the head of the futon mattress.

"Alexa," he said. "Play the soundtrack to 'Body Heat'."

"Soundtrack to 'Body Heat'," said Alexa. "By the John Barry Orchestra."

John Barry's sultry jazz score commenced on the unit, inspiring Nick. The overtly carnal eighties homage to *Double Indemnity* was his fifth favorite film noir. He could have resisted committing murder for Barbara Stanwyck. Kathleen Turner would have taken more willpower.

In the narrow kitchen, he took down two wineglasses from the rightmost cupboard, and put them on the counter near a recorked bottle of *Anko Malbec*. The adjacent cupboard yielded two dinner plates and a salad bowl. He opened the middle drawer but didn't find what he sought. From the next one, he took out two stiff green placemats and four napkins. Then he did something he hadn't done in his two months' residency in his apartment. He set the table.

While pouring Greek salad into the bowl, he had a jolt of foreboding. Here he was, a fast-rising star at the Washington Post, the woman he loved on her way over to spend the night, and countless more. It was all too wonderful. For the second time that night, he thought of Fred MacMurray in *Double Indemnity*, his Chandler-written narration right after he'd executed the perfect crime. *"Nothing had slipped, nothing had been overlooked. There was nothing to give us away. And yet, Keyes, as I was walking the street to the drugstore, suddenly it came to me that everything would go wrong."*

The knocking on the door soothed him. He opened it on a breathtaking Laura London, holding a full *Barnes & Noble* tote bag.

"I pushed your buttons," she said.

"As only you can," said Nick, letting her in.

"Your entry code — ten-six-six."

"Battle of Hastings."

"I should have known," said Laura. "The barbarians won."

"But intermarriage tamed them."

"Let's not get ahead of ourselves."

"You're right," said Nick. "One step at a time."

He pulled Laura toward him and gave her a fervent kiss. She dropped her tote bag to return it full force. Nick helped her out of her maroon coat, and hung it in the closet next to his. He led her to the dinette table, and pulled out the chair for her. She gracefully sat down. Nick filled the two wineglasses and took his seat as Laura examined the wine label.

"Argentina," she said.

"My dad took me there on a bull-buying trip before college. Got me hooked on their wine."

Laura waited for Nick to make a move, but only his lips did, his hands under the table, eyes looking nowhere in particular. Laura was intrigued. After half a minute, Nick smiled and passed her the Greek salad bowl.

"Were you praying?" Laura asked.

"Yeah," Nick said somewhat defensively.

"I've never seen anyone our age do that without parents around."

"Well, I got a lot to be thankful for."

"Like this pizza you shot."

"And a greater marvel," said Nick. "You."

Laura melted slightly. "Nick, you're such an enigma. So tough and yet so sweet."

"One's no good without the other," Nick said. "Salud."

He clinked wineglasses with Laura. They sipped the wine.

"Delicioso," said Laura.

They began to dine.

"Where did you tell Phil you'll be the next few days—and nights?" Nick asked.

"At my new friend Tammy Perkins's house. It's half true."

"Right, her sorority house."

"I said Tammy's a lonely wallflower in need of womanly support."

Nick chuckled. "You better hope he never meets her."

Over the rest of the meal, they learned more about each other. Laura's late father, Paul London, wrote for National Geographic. He suffered a fatal heart attack in the Australian Outback four years earlier.

"Your father was a Hemingway-esque figure," said Nick. "The type of guy you disparage."

"Dad was always amused by my feminism," Laura said fondly. "He considered it a passing fancy till the right boy showed up. Made it his running joke on me. He'd bring me back a native doll from every country in the world he traveled to. I'd come home from college ready to fight for womankind, and there'd be a new exotic girly doll in my bedroom. Drove me crazy. But now, whenever I visit mom in Boston, I really miss seeing new dolls."

"And you still have the old ones."

"Every last one."

"I think I would've liked your dad," said Nick.

"I hate to admit it, Nick, but he would've liked you. You're more like him than my older brother, Kyle."

"What does he do?"

"Nothing. He dropped out of Amherst right after dad died. He's been living in mom's basement all this time, trying to find himself."

"He needs to get lost first."

"There's something in what you say."

They finished the pizza.

"Ice cream?" asked Nick.

"No, thank you, Nick," Laura said.

"How about a movie? I got some good ones."

"Any starring Jessica Chastain or Ann Hathaway?"

"I'm all out," said Nick.

"Any with a still-breathing star?"

"Uh, Kathleen Turner?"

"Don't tell me—'Body Heat'."

"It's what we've been listening to the whole dinner."

"Subtle, Nick. Music to seduce me by."

"An old fantasy of mine."

"It's working for me," Laura said.

Nick grinned. They stood up, and headed to the closet bedroom.

20

As exciting as the night had been for Nick, the morning appeared more auspicious. Being the start, he hoped, of a permanent ritual. It began the moment he opened his eyes at six-forty-seven. Laura lay asleep against his right shoulder, her beautiful face trustingly close to his, lined with strands of black hair. He breathed in the faint trace of her entrancing perfume. Gingerly, he lifted the comforter from himself, and rolled left away from her. He rose to his feet, trying not to shake the futon mattress and awaken Sleeping Beauty.

From the compact dresser in the right back corner, he took out his grey briefs, white running socks, long-sleeve azure T-shirt, and black denims. He carried the whole wardrobe into the bathroom, silently pulling the door behind him. After a vigorous warm shower, he came out dressed from the closet bedroom and quietly closed the shutter doors.

He washed last night's dinner dishes in the kitchen sink, redeploying them for breakfast service. He filled the coffeemaker, toaster, and two glasses of grapefruit juice, then began cooking four scrambled eggs. Setting the dinette table for the second time ever, he heard Laura's phone alarm start chirping in the closet. The sound of the shower soon followed.

He was putting down the two hot coffee mugs when she exited the closet bedroom, her hair tussled and moist. She had on a dark green nylon pullover with a broad gold stripe across the chest, containing blue diamond shapes, and an olive knee-length wool skirt over grey tights. Watching her approach, Nick's chest tightened. He would never get used to this.

"Good morning," Laura said.

"Just got better," said Nick with an appreciative smile.

Laura took in the table layout. "You made breakfast."

"Yes, I thought I'd launch our partnership in style."

Laura sat down in the same chair she occupied the night before. Ritual, Nick thought contentedly, and sat down himself. Laura took a bite of her eggs and made an approving face.

"Hmm. Very good, Nick."

"Thanks. I learned to cook for twenty ranch hands at a time."

"All men?"

"Sure. Ranching's not for girls. Unlike journalism, where you can more than hold your own."

"Now that has to be the ultimate backhanded compliment," Laura said. "Speaking of our nascent career—is there anything about the Lassiter protest in today's Post?"

"Haven't checked yet."

"Do you get it delivered?"

"That's one tradition I abandoned."

"Discard a few more and there may be hope for you."

"It's too convenient to read online," said Nick. "The only reason men still buy the news-*paper* is so they can hide in plain sight from their wives."

"I take it back, Nick. There is no hope for you."

Nick smiled.

"So if I move in with you, you'll resume getting the print version."

"No, for two reasons," said Nick. "First—even our fights will be fun."

Laura smiled. Nick scooped up some egg with his toast and bit into it.

"What's the second reason?"

"I'll never get tired of looking at you," said Nick.

Laura's brown eyes twinkled. They quickly finished their food. Nick carried the empty plates and his half-full coffee mug to the sink. Laura took out her cellphone and began scanning the Post online. Nick glanced at her from his dishwashing station.

"Anything on the protest?"

"Not that I can see."

"So I guess it's up to us," said Nick.

The northbound Red Line train flew past the Rockville Pike morning rush hour traffic on its lower left between White Flint and Shady Grove stations. The bright sunlight at the train window and the nice heat inside made it seem warmer than the thirty-six degree day. In the middle left double-seat of their compartment, Nick and Laura had their coats off and phone screens on. Nick was reading a *Salon* magazine essay by Alice Lassiter, but Laura's posture—knees against the seatback in front of her, skirt hiked to mid-thigh—kept distracting him.

"You know," he said. "Daniel Carroll isn't an all-girl school like your alma mater."

"Women, Nick. And what's your point?"

"Your student body will be a lot more distracting."

"It did all right at Holyoake," said Laura.

Nick opened his mouth to explore her titillating remark but held back. He refocused on his phone screen, now distracting Laura.

"You're still reading Alice Lassiter's agitprop?"

"She's right on target."

"Her target being the LGBT community," Laura said.

"She has total empathy for gays, being a lesbian herself."

"She says there's no such thing as transgender."

"She's right, technically," said Nick. "And science backs her up. That's the Unholy Grail for your side, isn't it? That we're all gonna drown from melted icebergs in five years."

"You're exaggerating."

"Maybe. But unlike climate change, genetic science *is* settled. Chromosomes determine gender, not sexual discomfort. Cutting off his pecker won't make an X-Y into a X-X. And grafting one won't enable a double-X to lug a ninety-pound battle pack through the Afghan desert. That's why Lassiter is against the bathroom bill. She thinks it's anti-woman to have a guy walk in on a naked chick just because he's feeling pretty that day. Yet she's willing to compromise. If you're minus a dick, you can use the little girl's room. But you gotta walk the walk in there . . . For that, progressives want to burn her at the stake. Next they'll be banning pregnant women as offensive to gay couples."

"She doesn't allow for people's feelings," said Laura, prickled.

"Feelings," Nick snorted. "Feelings are reactive not proactive. We can't keep them from getting hurt. How we respond to that is what makes us who we are."

"I should've known you're a Nietzschean."

"Minus the whole 'God is dead' thing. I'm prepared for the worst—unlike college snowflakes with their 'trigger warnings' and microagressions in the face of opposing thought. 'Cause when the real threat comes, there'll be no 'safe space' for them to hide."

"I'd say it's on the way," said Laura. "And me alongside it."

The computerized male voice chimed in, "Next station stop, Shady Grove. Last stop on the Red Line. Exit on the left."

"Showtime, baby," said Nick, adjusting his imaginary tie.

They stood up and donned their coats.

21

They emerged from the Shady Grove Metrorail station into its vast parking lot. The surrounding neighborhood seemed pleasantly generic, with modern townhouses everywhere. In the bus zone, they mounted a waiting Daniel Carroll University shuttlebus along with seven other young people. The bus transported them two miles north, past medium homes and gardens, and one mile east to the old-fashioned small college town of Clifton, then a quarter mile north, up a hill, to the university's West Gate.

Daniel Carroll University was a semi-bucolic campus with well interspersed, predominantly orange-brick buildings. Nick and Laura walked north on the main footpath, Nick checking the university map on his cellphone.

"Greek housing's on the far end."

"Ancient Greek," said Laura. "They probably still have toga parties."

"Toga!" Nick exclaimed, channeling John Belushi in *Animal House*.

"God," said Laura. "One of us has come home."

Just ahead on the left stood the Administration Building, a four-story structure with a protruding gold metal entrance. Before it was a broad lawn quadrangle dominated by a statue of Daniel Carroll triumphantly waving the original Constitution in his right hand. About two dozen students of both genders — the women unglamorous, the males unmanly — walked around the statue bearing stick signs, many of them with unflattering pictures of Alice Lassiter. Nick and Laura stopped to observe them, Nick again checking the campus map.

"This area's known as the Quad. Short for 'quadrangle'."

"It appears to be Ground Zero for the protest," Laura said.

"Makes sense," said Nick, pointing to the statue. "Daniel Carroll was Maryland's Founding Father, an original signer. But he didn't get much historical respect over the years."

"He still doesn't."

Nick pointed at the Constitution in Daniel Carroll's hand.

"I'm surprised they haven't ripped that document from his hand," he said. "Good thing he never owned slaves or his whole statue would've been toppled by now."

A thin youth with long thin brown hair and facial fuzz that would never become a real beard upheld his sign: *Alice Lassiter = Malice Vomiter!*

"Poetry lives," Nick said.

"On life support."

A girl with round glasses and short hair displayed her sign: *Ban Hate! Ban Lassiter!*

"Ban speech," Nick said.

"You're right for once. They should let her speak then debunk her to her face."

"Much too 'triggering' for these snowflakes."

"I might help out the poor dears," said Laura.

"Don't become the story, Laura. Let's go check into our campus digs."

They walked past the Administration Building toward Fraternity Row. It was a semicircle of white colonial-style houses with three pillars apiece. They came up on the right end, and stopped before the third house.

"Eta Gamma Omega," said Nick, glancing at his campus map. "Your new sisters await."

"The Stepford Girls."

"You can learn some new recipes, spice up our meals at home."

"Hope you like the taste of bitter almonds."

"Preferably without the cyanide," said Nick.

They both smiled.

"You remember the greeting Tammy taught you?" asked Nick.

"I think so."

"And remember, Laura, be perky."

Laura did a quick silly hand dance. Nick smiled affectionately.

"Kiss for luck," he said.

Laura moved her lips toward Nick's, but instead put her right forefinger to his mouth.

"We can't," said Laura.

"Why?"

"Because, I haven't been pinned yet."

"Stickler," said Nick.

Laura blew him a kiss and approached the sorority house. Nick watched her press the doorbell, then proceeded toward

Delta Tau Epsilon, five houses to the left. The sorority house door opened for Laura, held by a pretty girl with long brown hair covering parts of a grey-white paisley blouse. She looked approvingly at Laura.

"Hello."

Laura made a victory sign with each hand, crossed them—left sign vertical, right one horizontal—and spun the cross to make the left sign horizontal, right one vertical, then clasped the left sign in her right hand. The sorority girl smiled.

"You must be Laura. I'm Ellen. Come in, sister."

She led Laura into a long grey-carpeted living room. Two rows of three white sofas faced each other, throw cushions all over them. Four attractive, modestly skirted young women—two brunettes, one busty blonde, one black—occupied the middle sofas. A fifth girl—studious, auburn-haired and quite lovely—sat on the farthest left sofa with a large paperback textbook on her lap, *The Contemporary Jane Austen*. Laura recognized the cover painting of *Pride and Prejudice*—Elizabeth Bennet rejecting Guy Darcy's first proposal. All five sisters looked up from their cellphones, laptop, and book at Laura. Ellen addressed them.

"Girls, this is our sister Laura from UNC. She'll be staying with us for a couple of days."

"Hi, Laura," said the seated females.

Ellen introduced them. "Jenny, Cathy, Liz, Trina, Caroline."

"You're here to write about that lezzy speaker for the UNC paper," said Liz the blonde.

"Alice Lassiter," Laura said.

"The whole school's freaking out over her," said Cathy. "A lot of icky people are upset."

"Freaks and geeks," said Jenny, one of the brunettes. "Of both sexes."

"And all the ones in between," Liz said.

The sorority girls giggled. Ellen pointed to the farthest sofa on the right.

"Just throw your bag on that last sofa. 'Fraid it's got to be your bed, since we have no rooms to spare. There are two bathrooms in the hall upstairs."

"Sofa's fine, thanks," said Laura, approaching it.

"You can use my room to change," said Caroline, the Jane Austen reader, shyly admiring Laura.

"Thank you," said Laura. "I'm sorry to be such a golem."

"What's a golem?" asked Cathy.

"A kind of Jewish Frankenstein," Caroline said.

"Are you Jewish, Laura?" Liz asked.

"Would it matter if I were?" Laura said, suddenly guarded.

"It sure would," said Jenny. "A-E-Phi gets all the pretty Jewish girls. They're totally snarky to us. Having one in our house would show them."

"I'm sorry," said Laura, relieved and guilty over her assumption. "I'm a double-WASP."

"Who cares about other sororities," said Cathy. "How are the frat boys at UNC?"

"Yes, Laura, give us your report," said Trina, the black girl, patting a spot beside her on the sofa.

Laura gathered her thoughts while sitting down next to Trina.

"They're, uhm, very nice."

"As in polite or in the sack?" Liz asked.

"Lizzy!" said Ellen.

The sorority girls giggled.

"Are you dating one of them?" Cathy asked.

"Sort of," Laura said nervously.

"From which house?" Jenny asked.

"Uhm …" Laura panicked, unable to recall a single fraternity name, and mixing up the Greek words. Which the hell one was Nick in? It came to her before the sisters got suspicious.

"Delta Tau Epsilon."

"Ooh, some of them here are dreamy," Cathy said.

"Mine's a real dreamboat," said Laura, trying not to roll her eyes.

"Awww," said everyone except Ellen and Caroline.

"So is Caroline's Delta House boyfriend, Peter," Jenny said.

"He's not my boyfriend," Caroline said defensively.

"Not for lack of trying," Cathy said. "You're at the Hangout every night he's there."

"I like his singing," Caroline said.

"And you want to make him scream," said Liz.

The sorority girls giggled. Caroline blushed. Trina sniffed the air near Laura's neck.

"Are you wearing Flowerbomb?"

"Why yes," Laura said.

"Smells wonderful on you."

"Thanks," said Laura. "I found it blends nicely with my natural body fray... fragrance."

She suddenly realized she was discussing cosmetics. I've been possessed, she thought. This sorority house is haunted.

"Let Laura settle in," Ellen said. "I'm sure she has a lot of work to do for her big story. Maybe we can all do something fun tonight."

The image of a pillow fight in underwear popped into Laura's head.

"The Hangout," Liz said.

"Is Peter performing there tonight?" Jenny asked Caroline.

Caroline nodded.

"Come with us, Laura," Cathy said.

"I'll look forward to it," said Laura, and meant it, much to her surprise.

22

Nick bonded quickly with the Delta Tau Epsilons. He hadn't belonged to a fraternity at the University of Wyoming, but he and his two best college friends outdid any frat boy in taking full advantage of young manhood. They had given little thought to race or religion, but plenty to the opposite gender, in the most politically incorrect form. Their approach had been mostly rewarded, other than a few romantic disappointments, which they got as well as gave.

He sat in the inelegant, color-discordant Delta House lounge with four frat brothers: stocky brown-haired Irishman Sean, Woody Allen-ish Ben, Chinese-American Lee, typing on his laptop, and shag-haired blonde pretty boy Peter, softly strumming an electric guitar. All except Peter held a coffee mug bearing the Delta Tau Epsilon insignia. Only Lee's mug had a teabag in it, which he periodically dipped. Nick felt at ease with his hosts, and decided to come clean.

"Guys, I want to be honest with you," he said. "I'm here under false pretenses. I'm not a Delta. I'm not even a student. But I *am* a reporter, at least on this story."

"For who?" Sean asked.

"The Washington Post," said Lee.

Nick turned to him in surprise.

"How'd you know?" he asked.

"Lee knows everything," Peter said.

"He's going to be a spy," Sean said.

"For Red China," Ben said.

Lee shook his head.

"CIA," he said.

"Sure, that's what they'll think," said Ben. "Until our nuclear subs go missing."

"Seriously, how'd you know?" Nick asked.

"I checked our national membership list," said Lee. "You're not on it. But Hugh Sinclair is—the guy who referred you to us. He's also on Facebook—Tulane alumnus, now a copyaide at the Washington Post."

"The science of deduction," Nick said. "A real-life demonstration of it. I won't mind being kicked out of here now."

"We'll take a house vote on it," Sean said, then added smiling, "at the end of the week."

"Thank you," said Nick.

"Just give our frat a fair shake in the Post," Sean said. "We're getting hammered by the snowflakes as patriarchal creeps."

"I know the feeling," said Nick.

"They call our house a hostile environment, just 'cause we like to sleep with girls."

"Without the use of handcuffs," Peter said.

"Speak for yourself, Peter," said Ben.

Everyone laughed. Ben became more serious.

"They're gonna be ugly tomorrow."

"The girls?" asked Nick.

"Them too," Ben said. "But I meant the protests. Never seen it this bad. Even worse than last year when we invited the Vice-President."

"Hold on," Nick said. "*We*? Are you a Young Conservative for Freedom?"

"Yes," Ben said somberly. "I'm a Jew among Jews."

"You're a prophet to me. I have to interview one of you guys for my story."

"Can you give him a fake name?" asked Peter.

"Sorry," said Nick.

"Great," Ben said. "No girlfriend my senior year either. My only regret is that I have but one love life to give for my country.

"That's a new twist on Nathan Hale," Nick said, smiling.

"Benedict Arnold would get more dates on this campus," said Ben.

Everyone laughed. Peter played the first few chords of *Yankee Doodle Dandy*. Ben stood up, lifting his book bag off the floor.

"Speaking of American history," he said. "I've got to get to my Financial Accounting class."

"How is that American history?" Lee asked.

"When was the last time we had financial accounting in Washington?"

"It's history all right," Nick said. "Mind if I walk with you?"

"As long as you don't cramp my style with the ladies."

"He can only help you, Ben," said Peter.

"Good luck on your gig tonight at the Hangout," Ben said to Peter.

"What time?" Nick asked.

"We start at eight," Peter said.

"I'll try to catch some of it."

"Thanks, dude," said Peter.

Nick and Ben walked on the path to the campus, Nick cueing Ben on his digital recorder.

"Interview with Ben Fisher. Senior, Daniel Carroll University, member of the Young Conservatives for Freedom. This group invited Alice Lassiter to speak on campus Wednesday, October nineteenth…Are you expecting violence tomorrow?"

"'Fraid so," Ben said. "The Guevarans like to put on a show."

"The Guevarans," said Nick. "As in Che Guevara?"

"Did you see *The Motorcycle Diaries*?" Ben said. "Che was a romantic idealist."

"He was a bloodthirsty butcher," said Nick.

"What's truth got to do with it? Today he's a progressive hero. The Guevarans are in all the best schools. Wolves among sheep, ready to pounce on right-wingers like Alice Lassiter. Funny, though. They always seem to show up in bigger crowds than their student presence."

"Could some be outside agitators?"

"I'd say so."

"What does the Administration say?"

"To us, two words — 'disinvite Lassiter.'"

"Seriously?" asked Nick.

A small squirrel scampered up the tree trunk just ahead of them.

"President Harris had us in her office last week," Ben said.

"Waxed about free speech for five minutes. Then said the campus cops can't guarantee Alice Lassiter's safety, and told us to rescind our invitation."

"So the media pressure would be off the university," said Nick.

"Right. Naturally we refused."

They paused to watch a shapely coed jog by them, not out of concern for her cold bare legs. When she disappeared from view, they resumed walking, and Ben talking.

"We gave Harris no choice but to cancel Lassiter's speech herself, which she did."

"Causing the very firestorm she hoped to avoid," said Nick.

"And Alice Lassiter stoked it, by vowing to come anyway. Leaving three possible scenarios for tomorrow. One, the cops physically stop her from setting foot on campus."

"And make your school a national disgrace, scaring off alumni dough," said Nick.

"Two, Alice gives a rousing speech, hushing her critics and rallying the students to conservative enlightenment."

"Unlikely."

"Three…"

"All hell breaks loose," said Nick.

"Most likely."

They stopped before a long two-story building marked *School of Economics*. Ben pointed at it.

"Should be called School of Keynesian Economics, to hear my professors rail against capitalism."

"Give the Left more time," Nick said.

Ben prepared to head inside.

"Where would I find a prominent Guevaran?" Nick asked.

"Teaching Social Justice. Professor Evan Ballard."

"There's a Social Justice class?"

"There's a Social Justice major."

"Must be a big demand for malcontents," said Nick.

23

Nick waited for Laura in front of the Social Studies Building. Intense-looking students streamed past him and up the four steps into the structure. A plump Asian girl gave him a suspicious look, he imagined for excess heterosexuality. He gave her his most dazzling smile, and she scowled all the way up the steps. He saw Laura approaching, the picture of a beautiful coed, down to the green backpack straps over her red-coated chest. He took a deep breath before she greeted him.

"Hi."

"Backpack's a nice touch," said Nick.

"Yes, the girls thought it would help me blend in."

"Girls?"

"Women. They're charming enough in their doll house, oblivious to the torments yet to befall them."

"Like their kids not making the soccer team," said Nick.

Laura smirked.

"Your text said you've got something on the protest," she said.

"Possibly one of its leaders — Doctor Evan Ballard. Here."

Nick pulled two slips of paper from his right coat pocket and gave one to Laura. She glanced at it.

"What's this?"

"Permission to audit Ballard's next class — Political Culture in Comparative Perspective."

"Sounds tedious."

"And you call yourself a progressive."

"I'd rather just occupy the Administration Building," Laura said. "How'd you get these? We're ringers."

"Chinese Intelligence."

"What?"

Nick put a finger to his lips. "Just be glad he's on our side."

The Social Studies auditorium was a descending theater-style classroom with two row sections facing the narrow stage below. Grunge-fashioned students filled half the seats. Nick and Laura sat alone in the penultimate right row beside the aisle. Their clean-cut attractiveness stuck out in this group, but most eyes were on the stage, commanded by Doctor Evan Ballard.

He was a distinguished-looking plump man in his late fifties, with long, wiry black hair and a trim beard. He wore a gold V-neck sweater, blue jeans, and a headset mic. His voice sounded smooth, yet forceful, over the sound system.

"They think they've won. They think they hold all the levers of power. So their Clown Prince in the White House can do anything he wants. Build a wall to keep out immigrants. Spread oil pipelines across the land. Exit the International Climate Accord. Convert the military into a universal death machine..."

"They all sound good to me," Nick whispered to Laura.

"Wait for it," Laura whispered back.

"But there's one lever they do not control. And never will. The most powerful one of all... We, the people!"

Laura elbowed Nick on the shoulder. Nick groaned.

"We have the numbers. More of us voted for the losing candidate than the Electoral College winner ..."

"In communist California," whispered Nick.

"We have the culture—thanks to academia and the media..."

"Not all of us," Nick whispered.

"All we lack is the organization. And that's where you young people come in. You must better channel your energies to defeat the forces of darkness now occupying our government ..."

Laura nodded enthusiastically. Nick shook his head.

"You must be like Gandalf at the Bridge of Khaaddum—shouting at the right-wing horror, 'You shall not pass!'"

"*Lord of the Rings*," whispered Nick. "Fantasy these snowflakes can relate to."

"And the next beast you'll confront is Alice Lassiter—the purveyor of hate against the transgendered. She plans to speak on our campus tomorrow night. But she shall not pass!"

Ballard raised a fist.

"Say it with me! She shall not pass! She shall not pass!"

The students took up the chant, with increasing fervor.

"She shall not pass! She shall not pass!"

"She shall not pass!" Laura said, pumping her fist with the others. "She shall not pass!"

Nick looked reproachfully at her. She winked at him. Ballard waved the crowd to silence.

"No, Alice Lassiter shall not pass. But the Transgender Bathroom Bill will. Because the Governor won't dare veto it once we teach his oracle a lesson. That offensive speech is not protected speech."

"It actually is," Nick whispered.

Laura nodded.

"You all have your homework for tomorrow night. Assemble at the Quad by five o'clock. There you'll be shown how to stop Lassiter from entering our campus, let alone speak here, despite all the Young Conservative Brownshirts with her … Yes, Flint."

He addressed a semi-attractive short-haired brunette in the second row, wearing a shapeless blue shirt and torn jeans, one hand raised.

"There aren't enough of us to manage that," said Flint.

"Don't worry," Ballard said. "Tomorrow night there will be."

Nick and Laura exchanged more curious looks. A student with a man bun raised his hand. Ballard called on him.

"Yes, Kyle."

"What if the campus cops pig out on us? Do we push back?"

"Don't worry about the Campus Police," said Ballard. "They will do nothing."

Nick and Laura exchanged curious looks.

"That's all for now, people. Good luck tomorrow. I'll see you here Thursday, the day after Armageddon."

The students rose from their chairs. Flint and two homely females walked down to Professor Ballard, engaging him in conversation. Nick and Laura remained sitting.

"Prof seems to have some inside dope on the protest," Nick said.

"That he's reluctant to share with the rest of us."

"Would help to get it out of him."

"Without blowing our cover," said Laura. "Got any devious ideas?"

Nick looked at Ballard, then at Laura, again at Ballard, then lingeringly at Laura.

"Nick, why are you looking at me like that?"

"Affairs with professors were a status symbol at your school."

"Yes, that's what I..." Laura said, then balked. "Now wait a minute! You don't mean...!"

"It's Mata Hari time."

"You're crazy. I'm a hardcore feminist.

"So is he. That's the beauty of it. You speak the same language. But you've got one big advantage."

"What?"

"You're beautiful."

"That shouldn't matter," said Laura.

"Oh, but it does. In the real world, Laura, there are no New Men, there are only men. And most don't stand a chance against a girl like you. Neither do those three groupies down there."

Laura looked accusingly at Nick. "What about us? How can you ask me to do this?"

"You think I want you turning on some old hippie?" said Nick. "We got a story to write, and that's one sure way to get it, that's all. But you're right. We'll come up with another."

Laura looked somber.

"We're out of time," she said.

"I know."

"All right, I'll do it."

Nick suddenly felt uneasy. "Look, just harpoon 'im so he'll spill the goods, then pull out, er, get out."

"Remember, Nick, this was your idea," said Laura.

She stood up, leaving her coat and backpack on the adjacent seat. She slinked down the aisle toward the stage. Nick watched her backside. Her gold cashmere sweater seemed suddenly clingier, her black wool skirt tighter, her very physique more curvaceous. How did women do that? he wondered. And why did some deny it? If men had that power, most of them would have a harem. Nick remained in his high rear seat, observing the show below.

Evan Ballard entertained his three female fans and some lascivious thoughts about their leader, Flint. Intellectually, he knew he should regard her as no different from his male students. But heterosexual desire always arose, as did opportunity. He was fifty-seven, divorced, and surrounded every day by nubile young women who in any other profession would have nothing to do with him. Who viewed sleeping with him as a kind of progressive initiation. So every semester he took the comeliest of them under his wing and bedsheet. This time it would be Flint, presently harping about some local burrito stand. She was attractive enough for him, if not what his more sexist students would call a "hottie." Then he saw someone who more than fit that term.

She descended toward him like an angel but with a face and body from a steamier plane. She stopped behind the three young women, looking at him with remarkable brown eyes. He tried to refocus on the trio in front of him and whatever Flint was on about.

"So what should we do about it?" Flint asked.

"About what? I'm sorry."

"The burrito stand. It's owned and operated by two non-Hispanic white women. That's cultural appropriation!"

"Certainly sounds like it," said Ballard, casting a quick glance at Laura's sublime face.

"Do you want to come with us and see it?"

"After the Lassiter event, Flint. That takes precedence."

He glanced again at Laura. She blinked prettily.

"We'll make you proud tomorrow, Professor," said the girl on Flint's left.

"I'm sure you will."

Ballard shot another glance over Flint's shoulder. Flint caught it and turned around. Seeing Laura, she frowned. Everyone else stared at Laura, Ballard now unguardedly. Laura addressed him in a slightly husky voice.

"Can you help me, Professor?"

"I'll do my best," Ballard said, then addressed his original audience. "Let's shut down that burrito stand next week, all right?"

The three women withdrew, Flint giving Laura a hostile look. Laura posed desirably in front of Ballard. He tried for professional aloofness with little success.

"Are you in my class, Ms ...?"

"London. Laura. No, Professor, but I'd like to be ... in your class."

"Right, I would have noticed you," said Ballard, then realizing the implication of that statement quickly added, "I try to remember all my students' faces."

"I hope you'll be seeing a lot more of mine."

"It'll be a pleasure ... to have you among my victims, er students."

They both smiled, Ballard somewhat nervously.

"What can I do for you, Laura?"

"I'm interested in Social Justice. And you gave me goose bumps — I mean your lecture."

"Why, thank you."

"But my boyfriend, he ..."

Ballard raised his right hand, interrupting Laura.

"Significant other," he said. "We strive to use gender-neutral terms."

"I'm sorry. Anyway, he's been blaming my new interest for the problems we're having."

"Problems?" Ballard asked, a bit too hopefully.

"Like political ones. But they're spilling into every other area, even ... our bedroom."

"I see," said Ballard, trying to hide his prurient interest. "Your friend sounds like a classic phallocrat."

"He sure is," said Laura, her voice quivering. "This Alice Lassiter protest could be the last straw. Nick says if I join in it tomorrow, we're done. I know she's evil, Professor. I just need to know that stopping her will be worth the consequences for me. If you could explain that to me, clearly and patiently, I can make the best decision. Listening to you just now, I knew you were the perfect man, ah, person for me."

"That's very flattering," Ballard said, trying to contain his excitement. "But also rather weighty. To think that my advice could have such critical effect on your future. It's a great responsibility, requiring much more time and effort than I could normally spare any student."

"I understand, Professor. I'm just so desperate. I'll do anything for more inspiration."

"Hmm," said Ballard. "Well, I happen to be reasonably free

tonight. If you want to come to my house, around six, I may be able to assist you with your dilemma."

"Oh, thank you, Professor. I'll be there for sure."

"What's your phone number?" Ballard asked, taking out his cellphone. "To text you my address."

"Two-oh-two, five-nine-seven, three-one-four-one."

In his high row seat, Nick witnessed the entire phone number routine, then Laura beam at Ballard until he went out the right front exit. She turned to Nick. He gave her two thumbs up. Laura scowled.

24

The University Police station was a wide one-story building beside the main parking lot. Nick chose not to jaywalk from the two cop cars in the last row, and took the marked crosswalk to the station's left entrance. Inside, a short hallway cornered right into a broader corridor. Before the turn was a door marked "Office." Looked pleasanter than "Cell," Nick thought, preparing to fib to the police chief. He entered the office.

Four aluminum yellowish desks faced him, two on each side of a middle aisle ending at an inner officer. Three short-haired musclemen in bronze police uniforms manned the desks behind sleek desktop computer screens. None of them wore sidearms. Only the nearest man on the right, a very dark black, addressed him in an African accent.

"Can we help you?"

"I'm Nick Jarrett with the Daily Bobcat. Here to see Chief Bosco about the Lassiter protest."

The young policeman pressed a key on his desk phone and spoke into the receiver.

"Chief. There is a student reporter here. Wants to talk to you about the protest tomorrow night...Okay." He looked up at Nick. "Go on back."

Nick walked past the desks to the back office, with *Chief Tracy Bosco* imprinted on the door. Nick opened it, and momentarily froze. A heavy yet pretty woman on either side of thirty sat behind a wooden desk and an open laptop. She wore her brown hair in a bun, no makeup, and the same bronze police uniform as the men, only with a prominent badge on the more prominent chest. Nick stifled his surprise, aware that a real student reporter would know the top cop was a woman, and ignore her good looks like a future New Man.

"Have a seat," Chief Bosco said, indicating one of two plastic visitor's chairs.

Nick complied. Chief Bosco studied him.

"The Bobcat, eh. You a Journalism student?"

"No, I just like writing for the paper," said Nick.

"What's your major?"

"History."

"And what's your view on Alice Lassiter?"

"I was going to ask you that," said Nick. "After my third degree."

Chief Bosco almost smiled.

"Old habits," she said. "Okay, shoot."

"I can't, this is a gun-free campus — and a nuclear-free zone. When DC gets hit, we'll be much safer here."

Chief Bosco smiled. "Guess you don't go with the flow at this school."

"I try to keep to the right of it," said Nick, returning the smile.

"Ask away."

Nick took out his Post digital recorder. He turned it on and laid it on the desk.

"What's your view on Alice Lassiter?" he inquired.

"It's irrelevant," Chief Bosco said.

"Are you going to let her come on campus tomorrow?"

"Good question," said Chief Bosco, shifting her eyes to the closed door. "Can we make this off the record till I say different?"

"Sure."

"I've been ordered to keep her out."

"By President Harris," said Nick. "Because you can't guarantee her safety."

"That's the official statement."

"What's the fact?"

"They don't want her here. The faculty and Administration. They agree with the kiddies."

"Lassiter's evil."

"And we take the heat."

"Of course," Nick said. "Make it about security and not freedom of speech, the Administration comes off smelling like a rose."

"My team like dogshh-doo."

"This is a public university," said Nick. "You've got no legal ground to stop Lassiter from speaking here. Under the First Amendment, you're obligated to protect her, in spite of Harris's order."

"That's why I'm off the record."

"*Can* you protect her?"

"From the snowflakes? Easy. My team could swat 'em like flies. But they'll probably have reinforcements."

"The Guevarans," said Nick.

Chief Bosco looked impressed. "So you know about them."

"I hope to learn a lot more."

"They wear masks to hinder that, and us, from finding out who they are, or where they come from. They rush in out of nowhere, riot, and melt away."

"The Heckler's Veto," Nick said.

"Yeah."

"So what are you gonna do, Chief?"

Chief Bosco solemnly tapped her badge. "You know, before I put on this toy badge, I wore a real one — patrol officer, Chicago PD."

"Rough town," said Nick.

"You know it?"

"Just vicariously, through Mike Kelly, private eye. First book, *The Chicago Way*."

"Think the Austin way," said Chief Bosco. "My first year on the job, me and my partner respond to a call there. Man had crashed his car into a drug store. He was big and gone on crack. Juan and me pull him out of the car. Guy punches Juan, dazing him. I try to cuff him. He knocks me to the sidewalk like a rag doll, starts kicking the crap out of me. Would'a killed me, if Juan hadn't put three slugs in him. I lay in the hospital for a week, with a concussion and five broken ribs, while they took concrete bits out of my face. The whole time, all I kept thinking was — an unarmed man was dead 'cause I couldn't pull my weight."

"Maybe not on the streets," Nick said. "But I read women cops are needed to help domestic violence victims, and for the brainier detective work."

"They offered me DV, but I'd had it," said Chief Bosco. "I got out of the hospital and quit the force. Thought I'd never put on a uniform again. Then I heard about this job."

"Now you pound the university beat."

"Where the hardest thing I gotta do is bust a hockey player for nude jogging."

"Till tomorrow night."

"Yeah," said Chief Bosco. "I do the right thing tomorrow—I lose my job. I do the other—I'm not fit to be in it. But if I do my badge proud—you can put me on the record, 'cause I won't be wearing it no more."

"You got it, Chief," said Nick.

25

By late afternoon, the number of protesters on the Quad had tripled since the morning. Close to sixty students marched counterclockwise around the Daniel Carroll sculpture. Daniel appeared crosser than he did before, the Constitution in his hand a little heavier.

Nick scanned the group for one particular protester. He saw her scarlet coat and superb shape come around Daniel, bearing a sign that read, *Stop Hate! Stop Lassiter!* Behind Laura walked a skinny kid with a goatee and a sign—*Trigger warning: Lassiter*. And after Goatee came the semi-pretty girl from Ballard's class, Flint, with her two sidekicks. Goatee kept eying Laura's ass, Nick saw. Nick moved to Laura's right, and began speaking in her ear as they marched.

"About your hot date with the Prof tonigh…"

"Act angry," Laura whispered.

"What?"

"Teacher's pet, two persons back, watching me like a hawk."

"Flint."

"She thinks I'm a false progressive who's using Ballard for my own ends."

"She's way off," said Nick. "You're a real progressive using Ballard for your own ends."

"Us cozying up would be all the proof she needs. Now be the sexist jerk I know you are."

"Bitch!" Nick said, loud enough for those nearest them to hear.

The couple in front of them tensed but didn't turn around. Goatee's eyes widened. Behind him, Flint perked up her ears.

"I told you not to join this stupid protest!"

"It's who I am now, you big phallist!" snarled Laura.

"I'll take that as a compliment," whispered Nick.

"You've held me back long enough with your toxic masculinity!" Laura declared. "That's all over!"

"Right on, sister!" said the girl in front, turning to face Laura. Her partner gulped.

"You're worse than Lassiter!" Laura said. "At least she likes women! You just objectify them—and me!"

Nick looked aghast.

"What *about* tonight?" Laura whispered.

Nick stared blankly at her.

"Nick."

"Right," whispered Nick, refocusing. "We need to know Ballard's connection to the Guevarans. And what they have planned for tomorrow."

"I know that."

Nick grabbed Laura's right hand in his left and slipped a small black hard drive into it.

"Stick that into Ballard's computer for seven minutes," he whispered, still looking angry.

"Seven!" Laura whispered. "How will he not see it?"

"You'll think of something," Nick whispered uneasily.

Laura yanked her hand away from Nick's, dropping the hard drive in her coat pocket.

"You're an asshole, Nick!" she cried. "Get out of my life!"

"If that's how you feel about it!" shouted Nick. "Enjoy your loser friends!"

He stormed out of sight. Goatee moved his head closer to the back of Laura's.

"You rule, Laura," he said.

The couple in front of Laura raised their fists in solidarity. Behind Goatee, Flint frowned.

26

Laura left the protest at four o'clock, hurrying toward Eta Gamma Omega to prepare for her assignation with Doctor Ballard. She tried to downplay her feigned argument with Nick but couldn't, knowing how readily the barbs had come to her, and how appropriate they sounded. Someday soon those thoughts would resurface. For now, however, she and Nick were on the same page, literally. So she had to charm Professor Ballard, even though she agreed with him politically and disagreed with Nick vehemently.

She hadn't brought any alluring clothes, never imagining her imminent turn as a seductress. She owned two dresses suitable for the role, but lacked the time to go home to get them, not to mention a rational explanation to Phil for grabbing her slinkiest outfits. She would have to buy one at a local dress shop and charge it to her almost maxed out credit card. Fortunately, she happened to be staying in the ideal habitat to get shopping advice—a sorority fashion house.

She climbed the staircase to the hallway, and knocked on

Caroline's door. Caroline opened it, looking lovely in a yellow skirt and pink cashmere sweater. She smiled welcomingly.

"Hi, Laura.

"Hey, Caroline. Do you have a minute?"

"Of course," said Caroline, pulling back the door.

Laura entered a white-walled bedroom with a single queen-size bed under a gold-striped bedcover. Over the headboard hung a poster of Ryan Gosling and Emma Stone dancing romantically in *La La Land*. A light study desk with rolling chair stood against the far wall next to the closet. Caroline closed the door.

"What's up?"

"I've got a date in two hours," Laura said.

"Wow. That was fast. Sit down."

Laura did so on the right edge of the bed. Caroline rolled the desk chair in front of her and sat down.

"Who's the lucky boy?" she asked.

"Man. He's a professor."

"Laura," Caroline said in mock reproach.

"I need to knock him out fast. And a fawning student from his mind."

"That shouldn't be a problem for you."

"Thanks," said Laura. "But I didn't bring a sexy dress with me, so I've got to hurry up and buy one. What's a good dress shop around here?"

"No need for that. Liz has plenty of slut-wear she can loan you."

"I can't ask Liz to loan me her ..."

"She'll love it," said Caroline. "Hang on."

She took out her cellphone and started texting. Laura looked around the bedroom, pausing on the *La La Land* poster. She'd found the film pleasant enough. Phil had thought it pointless in a pointed age. Caroline put down her cellphone.

"She'll come model for you in a minute."

"Great," Laura said, and nodded at the *La La Land* poster. "Ryan Gosling played a pianist in that movie."

"Yeah."

"And Jenny said you're liking a musician — Peter something."

"Noyce," Caroline said softly. "He's a Delta, same as your UNC friend."

"Life imitating art?"

"I hope not. Ryan and Emma don't end up together."

"Right. How far along are you with Peter?"

"I'm in the running," said Caroline. "Trouble is, too many runners."

"Take the inside track."

"He's a pretty boy. I don't have your self-confidence."

"Some of it is an act," said Laura. "But you're naturally cool. Use that."

Caroline smiled. "Thank you, Laura. Now I have more confidence too."

"Let's see how you do tonight at the Hangout."

"You still coming? With your professor date?"

"Without him."

"Are you really going to cheat on your boyfriend?"

"Yes, but only for ten minutes," said Laura.

"What?"

There was light knocking at the door.

"Come in, Liz," said Caroline.

The door swung open to reveal Liz, busting out of a purple halter-top, plunging-neck dress, knee length except for the almost waist high slit on the right leg. Spike-heel shoes accentuated the maneater look. Liz sashayed past her staring housemates and stopped at the foot of the bed. She twirled to expose the backless aspect of the dress. She turned to the bed with her hands on her waist and a smile on her face.

Laura cursed Nick Jarrett for the next words out of her mouth.

"I'll take it."

27

Nick paced the frat house lounge like a prisoner on death row, continuously crossing Lee on the sofa, focused on his laptop. Ten minutes before Laura's scheduled tryst with Ballard, the sheer folly of it overwhelmed him. What if ideological seduction trumped sexual seduction? What if Laura went too far to stop? What if Ballard didn't let her stop? And what if she handled everything adroitly and came out with a great story? The way she got it would gnaw at her feminist conscience. She'd naturally blame him for making her the femme fatale in a scheme right out of one of his mysteries. Their love story would be short-lived. And he had long-range plans for it. His earlier fake argument with Laura now seemed a preview of coming detractions.

"Idiot!" Nick said.

"My IQ is a hundred-fifty-three," said Lee, looking up from his laptop.

"Not you, Lee, me and my stupid idea."

"You mean turning your girlfriend into a sexual agent to get guarded information from a source?"

"Yeah."

"Standard operating procedure," said Lee.

"In Alfred Hitchcock movies."

"And my future firm. That's why I'm helping you, as an exercise. And because Ben said you're exposing the Guevarans, who are Enemies of the State."

"Have you already been accepted by the Company?" Nick asked.

"Recruited right here on campus. And if that gets out, I'll have to kill you."

"Sure. You're behind enemy lines—at an American university. Can't risk being outed."

"If you're gay, Nick," Peter said, entering with a notebook computer and water bottle, "I'm turning in my gay-dar."

"He's not," Lee said. "Nick has a girlfriend problem."

"Who doesn't," said Peter, sitting down in the armchair.

"But his is just one girl," said Lee.

"That *is* a problem."

"One girl isn't the problem, Peter," said Lee. "One girl's the source of it."

"Really? That'd be a slump for me."

"How many you got?" asked Nick.

"I'm down to three chicks."

"Down to?"

"And one of 'em's even demanding I dump the other two."

"How narrow minded of her," said Nick.

"Caroline Forrest," Lee said. "You should see her, Nick. Most guys would give their right nut for her. But Peter wants her on the groupie plan."

"She is awesome," said Peter. "Maybe she'd settle for me dropping Nina and keeping Kim?"

"Doubt it," Lee said.

"Will Caroline be at your gig?" asked Nick.

"Probably, with some of her Eta Gamma Omega sisters."

"Hey, my girlfriend's staying at that sorority tonight," said Nick.

"You hope," Lee said.

Nick cringed, and resumed pacing.

"You know," said Lee, "if that SJW professor gets wise to what your girlfriend's up to—he might sic his Guevaran friends on her. And they play rough."

Nick froze.

"My God," he said. "I didn't think of that."

He took out his cellphone and tapped out a number. After five rings, the voicemail reply came on. Nick left a frantic message.

"Laura, pull out. Abort the mission. Call me back right away."

He hung up, looking worried.

28

Caroline drove Laura the mile-plus from campus to a piney residential road mixing large modern houses and Tudor-style homes. Their interior lights gleamed in the cold darkness. Over her scanty dress, Laura wore a trim white faux-fur coat, also from the Liz collection. She kept fingering the tiny memory stick in its right pocket. A red mini-purse, Liz's, lay beside her, containing her muted cellphone and wallet.

The silver Dodge Challenger stopped before a two-story, twin-gabled, white-and-brown Tudor that seemed too big for its lawn. A blue marble walkway led to the front door, illuminated by a globe lamp. In the cozy heat of the car, Laura and Caroline appraised Evan Ballard's house.

"Daniel Carroll must pay its faculty pretty well," Laura said.

"Not that well. Your professor's rich. Could make up for your age difference, like Colonel Brandon and Marianne Dashwood."

"I have my John Willoughby to contend with."

"Willoughby was a dashing scoundrel."

"That's Nick," said Laura. "I haven't yet come to my sense and sensibility."

Caroline smiled.

"Call me when you're out of there," she said. "I'll come get you. And you can meet *my* John Willoughby, Peter Noyce."

"Thanks, Caroline. See you in a bit."

Laura got out of the car, and traveled up the walkway in Liz's spike heels, damning the sexist male invention. She rang the front doorbell and struck a provocative pose. It had a staggering effect on Ballard the moment he opened the door. Laura added to it in her huskier tone.

"Hello, Professor. I'm here for my arisal."

Ballard stared at Laura for three seconds without realizing it then caught himself.

"Ah yes. Come in, Ms. London."

Laura heard Caroline's car pulling away behind her. She stepped into a cream-walled foyer on a medieval tapestry carpet, unicorn included. An arched mirror hung on the right wall above a grey-cushioned walnut bench. Indian sitar music emanated from deeper inside. More subtle than *Body Heat*, Laura thought. Ballard closed the door behind her. Laura hoped he didn't lock it.

"May I take your coat?"

Laura placed her purse on the bench and took off her coat, giving Ballard the full view of her naked back. Staring at it, he didn't notice Laura clutching a small object in her right fist. She turned around with coat in hand, and saw Ballard gape, first, at her breasts—their inner sides on display in the plunging front—then at her right thigh, unleashed by the high slit. This time his mask of indifference took longer to reform. As Ballard laid her coat over the purse, Laura wondered where on her dress to hide the memory stick. And how the hell did Nick's Bond Women manage it in the movies? She had no choice but to keep holding the device.

"Pardon the immodest dress," she said. "I'm supposed to go to a concert tonight — if there's time. This is much more important to me."

"It's all right," said Ballard, trying to look at the dress rather than what protruded from it. "I think we'll be most comfortable in the study. Shall we?"

He led Laura past a stairwell on the right, then alongside the wall of a Persian-style living room. Laura took in the sumptuous golden carpet and plush orange sofa and chairs. A stone fireplace took up much of the right corner beyond a pair of brown French doors.

"What a beautiful home you have," said Laura.

"Thank you. It's a refuge."

"From what, Professor?"

"Injustice and tyranny," Ballard said, with a touch of drama. "Both all too prevalent in our nation today. They depress me no end."

He glanced at Laura. His rueful delivery seemed to have affected her as he hoped.

"At least you're fighting them," she said. "You're making a difference, unlike me. Look at me ..."

Ballard did. Laura smoothed down her dress at the hips, the memory stick hidden between right thumb and forefinger.

"I've been a party girl since high school. I need your advice on how to better service the cause."

"I'll do my best," Ballard said delightedly.

He pulled the right French door. It opened on a rectangular study, both side walls covered with books above chest level. The left wall had a built-in cabinet beneath the bookshelves, the right wall a black leather couch. An antique desk looked out the large rear window, the outside view partially blocked by a large desktop monitor. The screen saver showed exotic marine life in motion.

"Have a seat, Laura," Ballard said, indicating the couch.

Laura sat down, her legs crossed to show off the bare right one, ending in a spike-heel shoe. Long accustomed to androgynous Social Justice Warrior fashion, Ballard felt deliriously base, like he was watching pornography for the first time in years. Briefly he tried to reconcile his belief in gender indistinction with the tingling in his groin, then had to acknowledge the reality. He lusted after this exquisite young goddess like a common laborer. But unlike one of those, he would use his superior intellect to possess her.

"My goodness," Laura said. "I've never seen so many books outside a library."

"Yes, these are *my* teachers," said Ballard with a sweeping gesture of the shelves.

Laura rolled her eyes but quit before Ballard turned back to her.

"And only half of them by dead white males," he said.

"I'd rather have you as my teacher," said Laura. "You're very much alive. And more receptive to my desire—to improve."

Ballard felt overwarm in his sweater.

"Your passion is enticing," he said.

"Thank you, Professor."

"Please, call me Evan."

"Evan," Laura said with an enticing smile.

"How about a glass of wine?"

"Please. I need to relax. I'm way too stimulated right now."

"Be right back," said Ballard, exiting the room.

Laura sprang to her feet and rushed the desk. Scanning the left side of the computer base, she found the USB portal. She inserted the memory stick into it. The black device contrasted with the grey shell of the computer, but its tiny size concealed it, unless one really looked at the machine. She had to make certain Ballard wouldn't do so for seven minutes, and then remove the gadget without him noticing. But returning to the couch, she felt a chill down her spine. Turning to the computer, she realized all was lost.

The screen saver image was gone, replaced by the icon menu on a Venice backdrop—a gondola approaching a canal foot-bridge. The instant Ballard came back, he'd see Venice instead of the swimming fish, and would realize she touched the computer. He would then spot the memory stick jutting out of it. Her only hope was to delay his reentrance into the study until the screen saver recomposed. But what if it was set for five minutes, or ten?

Laura dashed to the doorway, and leaned her back against the left side of it, provocatively blocking the study entrance. Whatever happened next, she thought, she'd have to resign in shame from the National Organization for Women.

29

For the fifth time in three minutes, Nick grabbed his cellphone off the sofa and checked it for a message from Laura. He sat next to Peter, who was studying Astronomy on his notebook, and across from Lee, still at his laptop. Nick didn't dare send Laura another text, in case her phone was in Ballard's sight. He sprang up from the sofa.

"I'm going to go get her," he said.

"Just barge into Ballard's place?" Lee asked.

"If I have to."

"I can't let you do that."

Peter looked up at Lee then Nick.

"Why not?" asked Nick.

"That drive stick I gave you is top secret equipment," said Lee. "You get arrested, it'll be in Ballard's possession, then the Guevarans'. I'll be in trouble with my future employer."

"I'm going, Lee."

Lee placed his laptop on the sofa and stood up in front of

Nick. He adopted a karate stance, making some exuberant flat hand gestures.

"You'll never be a field agent with those moves," said Nick, taking a step toward Lee.

"Guys, come on," Peter said with concern.

Lee's laptop pinged. Lee glanced at it.

"It's in!" he declared.

He retook his couch seat and laid the computer on his lap. Nick sat down on Lee's left. Looking at the screen, he got the shock of his life.

"Woah!" said Lee.

In the upper right frame was Laura London—more an erotic fantasy of her—flattering a skimpy purple dress that revealed much of her breasts, most of her back, and all of her right leg. She stood in a study doorway pushing her spine against the right door jamb. It was the hottest view of Laura Nick had ever had, and he'd seen her naked in the flesh. The trouble was that Lee could see her too. Nick wanted to slam the laptop on his fingers.

"How the hell ...?!"

"I meant to tell you," said Lee. "The drive stick activates the computer camera."

Peter darted to Lee's couch and sat down on Lee's right, staring at the laptop screen.

"Holy shit!" he exclaimed. "Is that your babe?! She could be on the Playboy Channel!"

"Hey!" snapped Nick.

"Sorry, dude, but she's smoking hot!"

"You did tell her to distract Ballard," said Lee.

"A heart attack'll do it," said Peter. "And might be worth it for him."

"Laura is not a sex object," said Nick. "She's a strong, intelligent woman."

"But can she dance?" asked Peter. "If she can I want her ..."

Nick glared at Peter.

"For our next music video."

"What's she doing?" Nick asked. "And where the hell is Ballard?"

"I don't know, unless ..." said Lee, tapping several laptop keys. "Her USB insertion scrambled the screen saver. She's trying to keep Ballard from noticing that."

"How long before the screen saver comes back?" Nick asked anxiously.

"Six minutes."

"Awesome," said Peter. "She'll be putting on a nice long show."

"Shut up, Peter," Nick said.

"I may be able to accelerate the process," said Lee, typing rapidly on the keyboard.

Laura kept looking out the door and at the computer screen, the damn gondola still in the same spot.

"Merda!" she said, a bit too loudly.

The curse came through on Lee's laptop speaker, heard by Lee, Nick, and Peter.

"She speaks Italian too," Nick said.

"Did you say something, Laura?" Ballard said loudly from farther back in the house.

Laura quickly scanned the bookshelves. She focused on *A Room of One's Own* by Virginia Woolf, one of her literary idols.

"I said, 'Heard that'," Laura answered. "The quote by Virginia Woolf. 'It is far harder to kill a phantom than a reality.'"

"Woolf was right," Ballard said, his voice closer. "But Alice Lassiter is no phantom. She's a witch."

Laura looked at the unchanged computer screen and groaned. She raised her right knee and began sensuously extending and folding her lower leg, grateful that her mother couldn't see the current application of her preteen ballet class.

Watching Laura on the laptop screen, Nick's eyes widened.

"She can dance," said Peter.

Ballard approached the study bearing an open bottle of French red and two wineglasses. Seeing Laura's sensuous leg action, he froze in his tracks.

"Excuse me, Evan," Laura said. "I got this awful leg cramp from my run today. This motion helps reduce the pain. I'll stop now."

"No, please," Ballard said, transfixed. "By all means, complete your therapy."

"I'm gonna need some after this," said Peter.

Laura spun her lower leg in small circles, casting glances at the desktop screen. Ballard ogled her.

As did Peter, watching her on Lee's laptop. Nick cringed.

"How long till the screen saver?" he demanded.

Getting no response, he noticed Lee staring at Laura on the screen, his hands motionless.

"Lee!"

"Sorry," Lee said, and resumed typing.

"Got it!" he said.

Laura saw the swimming fish reappear on the computer screen. She ceased her leg moves, and smiled at Ballard.

"Ooh. That feels much better. Thank you, Evan."

"My pleasure," said Ballard, his truest words of the night.

Laura retreated from the doorway, clearing the approach for Ballard. He stood the bottle and glasses on the lamp table and poured the wine. Laura sat down on the couch, her right leg draped over her left, appearing just inside the camera frame's left end.

"She'll definitely get an 'A' from him," Peter said.

Nick scowled.

"Four minutes to full download," said Lee, watching a blue line slowly fill a blank slate on his laptop screen.

Ballard handed Laura a full wineglass and sat down snugly against her left leg. She didn't remove it. They clinked glasses.

"I attended the Quad demonstration today," Laura said.

"So I heard," said Ballard. "And that you had a conflict with your ... significant other."

"He's insignificant to me now," said Laura.

Nick winced.

"Burn, dude," said Peter.

"Excellent," Ballard said. "He was keeping you from your higher calling — as an angel of the Resistance."

"An angel? Me?"

"Yes, Laura. You have a transcendental beauty that's quite rare in our movement. What you need is a mentor who can help you harness it, so that others will be drawn to your light."

"That's ridiculous," said Nick. "No real woman would fall for that bullsh..."

"Wow!" Laura gushed. "You really think I could lead people to social justice?"

"Absolutely — with my help."

"That old dude's smooth," said Peter.

"Three minutes," Lee said.

"Where do we start?" asked Laura.

"Right here and now," said Ballard. "First, by dispelling your insecurities."

He took Laura's glass from her hand and put it on the lamp table, then moved his face closer to hers.

Nick seethed.

Laura gently blocked Ballard's nearing chest with her hands.

"Wait," she said. "Can we talk a bit first?"

"You see?" Nick said. "She's playing him."

"There's no time left for talk," said Ballard. "Alice Lassiter's coming in tomorrow. You can help me galvanize the protest. But we need to be a team, Laura. One mind, one…body."

He again leaned into Laura, and met with the same gentle resistance.

"I was expecting a more intellectual approach," Laura said.

"Of course. But for that I must be free of sexual tension, which you engender in me."

"Good line," said Peter.

Nick smirked.

"Help me help you, Laura," Ballard said. "And together we will save our country."

"It's just too soon for me right now," said Laura. "Nick was so mean to me, so cruel…"

Peter and Lee turned accusingly to Nick.

"She's improvising," he said.

"It's going to take me a while to trust any man," said Laura.

"Two minutes," said Lee, his eyes back on the laptop screen.

"At least until tomorrow night, if the protest goes well," said Laura, stroking Ballard's cheek. "Can you wait that long?"

"I couldn't," Peter said.

Nick fumed.

"I'm really excited about this, Evan," Laura said. "Are you planning something big?"

Ballard's frustration lessened at her touch and challenge.

"There may be a surprise in store for Ms. Lassiter, and the Young Conservatives."

"Tell me," Laura said.

"It's a secret. But I have instructions for our troops tomorrow. I'll print one out for you."

Ballard started to get up.

"Computer printout . . ." Laura balked, "Evan, wait!"

She pulled Ballard back down on the couch beside her.

"There's no hurry."

She pressed her palms against Ballard's temples and gave him a deep, delightful kiss.

"Woah!" exclaimed Peter.

Nick felt nauseous.

"One minute," said Lee.

It became the longest minute of Nick's life, watching Laura kiss Ballard every second. He cursed himself for concocting the scheme, and Laura for going through with it. He wanted to look away but couldn't, feeling his companions' lewd eyes riveted on the screen. He also feared for Laura, wondering how she would extract the memory stick without Ballard catching her.

"Done," Lee said.

Laura pulled away from Ballard and stood up.

"I can't trust myself with you a moment longer," she said.

She started backing toward the desk, leaving Ballard in a swoon.

Nick, Lee, and Peter watched Laura's shapely butt coming at them on the screen, Peter's mouth wide open.

"Shut up, Peter," Nick said.

Peter closed his mouth.

"You're a much better kisser than Nick," Laura said, still backing toward the desk.

Lee and Peter turned to Nick. He shook his head.

"Acting," he said.

"Let's see how tomorrow goes," said Laura, "and we'll take it from — oh."

She bumped into the desk chair. It rolled into the desk. Laura stumbled with it, hands shooting to the keyboard for support. The screen saver vanished, replaced by the Venice backdrop, the gondola no closer to the footbridge.

"You made me unsteady," Laura said, straightening up.

"Are you okay?" Ballard asked with concern.

"I think so. Let me check."

Laura spun the desk chair so that it faced Ballard. She placed her right spike heel on the seat, and began rubbing the thigh with her right hand. Ballard fixated on Laura's luscious leg, oblivious to her left hand groping the computer side. She plucked out the memory stick.

The video frame on Lee's laptop went dark.

"Man!" said Peter.

Laura put her foot down on the floor.

"I have to go," she said. "See you tomorrow, Evan."

She rushed past Ballard and out of the study, leaving him frustrated, and not intellectually. In the foyer, Laura grabbed her purse and coat, and thrust the memory stick in the coat's right pocket. She hurried out to the street, adrenaline pumping. She'd accomplished her Mission Impossible by simple sexual roleplaying, and had found it exciting.

Approaching the cross street, she phoned Caroline. As she stood on the street corner waiting for her ride, one question beset her. Had she just validated Nick's contention about a woman's greatest power being her sex appeal? She had been his 'girlfriend' just two days. One more week with Nick and she'd be joining the NRA.

30

The Hangout was a big grey cement room masquerading as a student music club. A glass counter to the right of the entrance sold bottled coffee, juice, water, and—post an ID check by the young Arab barista—beer. Lounge chairs took up the front area, filled by students reading, talking, or typing. The rest was standing space only, ending at an elevated floor that served as the stage. Some eighty collegians stood near it, the slight majority of them female. They watched Peter Noyce in tight black T-shirt and blue jeans singing *It's My Life* into a wand microphone, backed by a long-haired electric guitarist and a black keyboardist. The group was billed as the Persuaders.

Knowing Peter to be a total hound, Nick was pleasantly surprised by the soulful tone he gave the classic oldie, his third song in an all-Eighties hit list. Smart play, thought Nick, weaned on his father's favorite show, *Miami Vice*, and believing that decade's songs had more melody, poetry, and clarity than any from the last three. Certainly the screen stars were manlier—Don Johnson, Bruce Willis, Mel Gibson, Schwarzenegger and Stallone—and nothing like the weepy Damon-Clooney-Gosling types of his own time. How many times did he, Scott, and their dad watch *Die Hard, Lethal Weapon, Predator, Rocky 3* and *4, First Blood* and *Rambo 2, 3* and *4*?

Nick stood between his new friends, Lee and Ben, a bottle of Budweiser in hand, waiting for Laura. He had needed the entire hour to suppress his distaste at what he saw her do, what he had essentially made her do. Laura had tried to warn him. Love was a thrill not a thriller. Its real-life consequences hurt. He knew Laura would be expecting his inquiry about her time with Ballard, never suspecting that he had actually observed it, and, worse, with two other voyeurs. He hoped she would admit what she did so he could trust her in the future and make this episode the sordid past.

She appeared with five pretty girls in similar attire to hers: green knee-length skirt, brown tights, and gold cashmere sweater. Nick relaxed. Compared to the last outfit he'd seen Laura in, this one was practically a burka. As they made eye contact, Laura gave him a slight nod. Nick turned to Lee, and caught him staring fascinatedly at Laura.

"You've never seen her before," Nick reminded him.

"Oh right," said Lee, softening his look. "I'll try to remember that."

Laura's group joined them, delighting Ben. The six women smiled at Nick, Liz sultrily. Laura introduced them.

"Nick, this is Liz, Jenny, Cathy, Trina, Caroline."

"My pleasure," said Nick.

"And Laura's," Liz said suggestively. "For now."

Ben stepped in front of the girls.

"Hi. Ben Fisher—millionaire…well, in two more years."

"Then target of the Revolution," said Laura with a smile. "I'm Laura."

"You would be," Ben said, smiling back at her.

"How will you make your fortune?" Trina asked.

"By cornering the beauty market," said Ben. "Beginning with your lovely self."

Trina laughed.

"Just for that, your beer's on me," Ben said, and started toward the entrance.

"This is Lee," Nick said, pointing him out to the group.

"I know Lee," said Caroline with a smile.

"As a friend of a friend," Lee said, and nodded at the stage.

"Not so much," said Caroline, glancing wistfully at Peter.

Laura approached Lee, who stared at her in awe. She took it as professional approval of her mission success. As they shook hands, Laura slipped the memory stick into his.

"I have to go," Lee announced to the group.

"So soon?" asked Caroline.

"Homework. Nice meeting you guys."

Lee started for the door. On stage, Peter began a rousing version of *Melt with You*. The sorority sisters gathered closer together, Liz pulling Laura into their circle. They began to eagerly question Laura, who appeared to be enjoying herself. Observing her in her new social circle, Nick smiled. They were a nicer bunch than Sarah Woronov and Laura's Capitol Hill coven, he thought. He watched Ben rejoin the women with two beers, one for Trina.

"Hello, Nick," said a female voice on his right.

He turned his head to face Caroline's auburn hair, deep green eyes, cute nose, and full lips, and instantly understood their disruptive effect on Peter's wild life plans.

"Caroline Forrest," said Nick.

"I've heard a lot about you."

"Same here."

"You're good for her," said Caroline, casting a glance at Laura.

"How can you tell?"

"The way you're looking at me—appreciatively yet detachedly."

"Guess you're used to more aggressive stares," said Nick.

"From boys who aren't in love with someone else. Or in your case I might've returned the look."

"Only you're in love yourself," said Nick, nodding at the stage.

"Less reciprocally than you and Laura."

"Don't be so sure."

Caroline looked hopeful. "Did Peter mention me to you?"

"He offered to cut down his love life to two girls—you and 'Kim'."

"That's as romantic as he gets," Caroline said with a wan smile.

"Whoever 'Kim' is, I'm sure she can't hold a candle to you."

"Thank you, Nick. But she has one big advantage over me. She's sleeping with him."

"Aha. And you're not."

"I haven't yet…with anybody."

Nick gulped down his beer.

"I'm sorry," he said, looking at Caroline. "Been a long time since I've met one."

"It's a spiritual thing—saving myself for the right man. I just hope I end up happier than Jane Austen."

"You will, Caroline," said Nick. "You're prettier."

Caroline smiled, and moved toward the stage. She ran into Laura, on her way back to Nick. They had a brief friendly exchange, then Laura joined Nick.

"You looked mighty chummy with Caroline," she said.

"She's quite a girl. Did you know she's a ..."

"Yes. I suppose you approve of that."

"I respect it," said Nick.

"You know, I could always follow suit, retroactively. Save myself for marriage."

"Now let's not go that far," said Nick.

They exchanged smiles.

"Nice to see there's a limit to your conservatism," Laura said.

"You're a bad influence on me."

Nick spotted a student couple vacating two adjacent chairs near the entrance.

"Step into my office," he said, directing Laura toward the furnished area.

They sat down in the lounge section, Nick tensing about the subject he had to broach. Peter began a low-voiced rendition of *Under the Milky Way Tonight*.

"Good job with Ballard," he said.

"Yes, I thought I was quite resourceful," said Laura.

"How far'd you have to go?"

"Oh, to what the kids would call 'first base'."

"You're pretty casual about it," said Nick, irritated.

"It didn't mean anything. And you've no right to sulk. You put me there."

"That I did. And I'm sorry ... Would you have let him get to second base?"

"That, Nick Jarrett, is something you'll never know."

"Fair enough. I won't bring it up again."

They listened to Peter for a little while.

"He's very good," said Laura. "If you like that fluffy music."

"What music do you like?"

"It may surprise you ... Gospel."

Nick looked at Laura in surprise.

"I know, I'm an agnostic," she said. "But glorious black voices singing soulfully to God really gets to me. No preaching, Nick."

"No need to. Sounds like you're on the right path."

"How do I get back on the left one?"

They chuckled.

"So what now, Chief?" said Laura.

"Let's see what Lee turns up and go from there. Tonight we must keep up appearances, as a loving college couple. Come back to the frat house with me."

"I'd like to. But I promised Caroline I'd hold her hand to-night. Sorority sisterhood."

"Bring her with you."

"Hmm. But what if Peter takes home another woman? It would crush Caroline."

"We'll have to make sure he doesn't," said Nick.

"Are we playing Cupid?"

"Why not. After all—if you and I could get together ..."

"Anything is possible," said Laura. "I'll see what I can do."

She got up, and returned to the standing area. Nick moved to the bar to buy another beer. On his way back to the music crowd, he saw Laura at the back of it, huddling like a quarter-back with her sisters, minus Caroline. Ben stood off to one side, hoping to recapture Trina's interest.

"What's the most popular sorority on campus?" Laura asked.

"Alpha Phi Gamma," answered Jenny and Trina in unison.

"They're beyond stuck up," said Liz.

"We're about to join it," said Laura.

The four sisters looked at her.

Nick continued toward the stage. Caroline stood in the third row, totally engrossed in Peter's touching version of *If You Leave*. Nick took a spot next to her.

A striking, voluptuous, muddy blonde approached the stage crowd. She had on a blue flannel miniskirt, high black stockings and an orange sweater, unbuttoned to display her expansive cleavage. As she bypassed the sorority group, Liz pointed her out to Laura.

"That's her. Kim Heller, Caroline's rival for Peter.

"She's definitely the rival type," said Laura. "All right, sisters, we're on."

Jenny started for the entrance. Laura turned to the other three young women, upsweeping her palms. Cathy, Liz, and Trina assumed haughty poses and expressions. Laura nodded in approval, then waded into the crowd behind Kim Heller. Nearing the stage, Kim passed Caroline and Nick on her right. Caroline stiffened.

"Kim Heller," she said loud enough for Nick to hear above Peter's singing.

Kim tapped the back of a geek in the front row, so he would make room for her on his left. Getting an eyeful of Kim, the boy almost shoved his mousy date into the girl on her right. Kim placed her hands on her waist as if willing Peter to notice her. He did, and winked at her in mid-song. Caroline saw the wink, and buried her face in Nick's left shoulder. He placed a comforting hand on her back.

Laura came up behind Kim. She turned to Nick, and smirked at him holding Caroline. Nick made a "What can I do?" face. Laura pointed to Kim Heller's back. Nick nodded, indicating he knew who she was. Laura tapped the back of the nerd on Kim's right. Seeing Laura, he again pushed his date right into the next girl, making space for Laura on his left.

As Laura emerged in the front row, Peter's eyes widened in admiring recognition. An irritated Kim turned to check out Peter's new person of interest, the beautiful brunette on her right. Laura smiled at her. Kim became less annoyed yet no less curious. Laura shouted in her ear to be heard over the music and song.

"Kim Heller?!"

"Yeah?!" said Kim, shouting back.

"Laura London, Alpha Phi Gamma!"

"Wow, you guys rule!" Kim exclaimed. "How do you know me?!"

"We've been following you on Facebook, and we like what we see. We want you to join our sorority!"

"Really?!"

"Yes! We love the way you help the women at our school—by proving their boyfriends unworthy of them!"

"You get it!" exclaimed Kim. "Thank you! Boys dump their girlfriends for me—then I dump *them*! I'm like the avenger of women! Except they hate me too!"

"You're Alpha Phi material all right! Come with me if you want to join!"

"Now?!" Kim asked, glancing at Peter.

"Now or never! It's a rush!"

"Okay!"

Kim caught Peter's eye, and put an imaginary phone to her ear. He nodded. She blew him a kiss, and followed Laura to the rear of the crowd. Nick watched them go by and gently turned Caroline's face to the front row, so she could see her nemesis was gone. Laura and Kim reached the emptier floor space, where stood the sorority sisters, still acting pompous.

"What's playing at the Opera House this week?" asked Cathy.

"'The King and I'," said Trina. "It got a mahvelous review in the Post."

"Let's attend."

"Tickets are a hundred dollars each," said Trina.

"Our boyfriends will pay for them," Liz said. "Or be our ex-boyfriends."

"Tee hee," said Cathy.

Kim looked impressed.

"Sisters, this is Kim," Laura said.

"Hello, Kim," said Trina and Cathy.

"Hi," said Kim.

"You look positively charming," said Cathy.

"Are you ready for your initiation?" asked Liz.

"Yes," said Kim.

"Your phone please," Trina said, sticking out her hand.

"Oh," Kim said, hesitating. "Do I have to?"

"It's a secret ritual," said Liz. "There must be no contact with the outside world."

Kim reluctantly handed Trina her cellphone. Trina took ahold of Kim's left hand, Cathy her right.

"Come, future sister," Liz said. "Your destiny awaits."

She glanced at Laura, who down-waved her palm, telling

Liz to tone it down. The sisters escorted Kim out the front door. And into Jenny's waiting Honda Civic. Laura smiled, knowing Kim would be a Missing Person until midnight. Ben joined her as Peter sang *Don't Dream It's Over*.

"Thanks a lot, Laura," said Ben. "You got rid of my potential girlfriend too."

"You're not a millionaire yet," Laura said smiling.

The Persuaders went backstage for a twenty-minute break, replaced by recorded techno music. Nick leaped onto the stage, and took the same side exit as the band.

Caroline joined Laura and Ben in the sitting area. Ben gave up his chair for Caroline, earning a sweet smile from her.

Nick followed a dim hallway to the only open door on the right. He entered a small room with two old brown armchairs facing a frayed yellow couch. An antique refrigerator stood near the door. The guitarist and keyboardist slumped on the couch, Peter in the right chair, all three drinking bottled Budweiser.

"Nick," said Peter. "What brings you back here? You wanna join the band?"

"With my voice, I'd end it," Nick said, and nodded at Peter's bandmates. "You guys are terrific."

The keyboardist smiled. The guitarist raised his beer.

"Perry, Ron — Nick Jarrett."

Nick gave them his trademark mini-wave.

"Grab a beer," said Peter, indicating the refrigerator.

Nick did, and sat down in the chair a few feet from Peter's.

"Let's talk about Caroline Forrest," he said.

"She's awesome," said Peter.

"What are your intentions toward her?"

Peter gulped too much beer.

"Intentions?" said Ron.

"Toward her," said Perry. "Who talks like that?"

"Nick's a history expert," said Peter. "What about Caroline?"

"She's your date for tonight," said Nick. "Kim Heller's out."

"It'll end just like our first date—and last. With her telling me to fuck off."

"You probably deserved it."

"Maybe," said Peter.

"All right, what happened?"

"She showed up at our first gig here. Said I was awesome. She was a total hottie so I asked her out. Put her through my 'sure thing' routine. First—dinner at Krokovia with plenty of wine ..."

"She's underage," said Nick.

"The waiter there's a Delta-Stu. You met him at the house."

"Oh yeah."

"Then back to the frat for the usual bullshit talk and high school makeout session, before going up to my room for the real deal."

"And?"

"We never got upstairs. Caroline prolonged our talk, challenging me. Asked me questions about my Astronomy major. I told her it was my fallback plan, in case of a music career fail."

"Dude!" said Ron.

"Sorry, Ron," Peter said, and continued rather fondly. "Anyway, she brought out my inner nerd. I mentioned how a trip to Mars could be a distinct possibility for me. She compared me to her British hero, some explorer—Richard something. He found the source of the Nile ..."

"Richard Burton," said Nick.

"Grandma loves him," Perry said. "And some old movie queen he married—Cleopatra."

"No, Perry," said Ron.

"I gotta admit, she kind of pumped me up," said Peter. "We finally started making out. Got real hot and heavy. But when I asked her up to my room, she shot me down. And instead of throwing her fine ass out—I said I'd call her, like a loser."

"But you didn't, did you?"

"I meant to. More willing chicks kept changing my mind. Though a part of me kind of regretted it."

"A nobler part, Peter," said Nick. "That rises above instant gratification to the man you ought to be—in two years, ten years, life. A bright, beautiful, supportive girl like Caroline can put you on that path, and be worth the delayed pleasure."

"That's what I'm afraid of," said Peter.

31

Nick and Laura felt like parents, walking side by side on the Clifton Main Street sidewalk a few feet behind Peter and Caroline. Despite their own "modern" relationship, they understood the eternal dynamic at work on the pair ahead. The womanizer and the virgin — he seeking short-term enjoyment, she long-term commitment. For once, Nick and Laura were on the same side — Caroline's, spurring Nick to a decision that had been germinating for some time.

"They seem to be getting on," said Laura, indicating Caroline and Peter.

"Since you had her competition kidnapped."

"Not for nothing is Cupid an impish god."

They passed the last of the small shops catering to students, a pharmacy. Caroline hugged her shoulders against the cold breeze challenging her black down coat. Peter, in a blue ski pullover, thrust a hand across her back to her left shoulder, pulling her against him.

"Her coat is warmer than his is," Nick said.

"That old trick never fails," said Laura.

"Yeah, she's pretty expert for a choirgirl."

"It's how she'll make church wife," said Laura. "For that's her goal. And tonight, she'll either be closer to realizing it, or become arm candy for a man, like so many women."

"You're more than that to me, Laura."

"I know."

"You're Swiss chocolate."

Laura laughed. Nick became serious.

"You said something tonight that got me thinking."

"That you're a right-wing retrograde?"

"No. About there being a limit to my conservatism, because we're sleeping together."

"And I offered to constrain myself until marriage," said Laura.

"Will you?"

"Stop sleeping with you?"

"No, the other thing," said Nick.

Laura clutched Nick's left arm, halting him, and spun him around to face her.

"Marry you?!"

"Yeah."

Twenty feet ahead, Peter looked back and stopped, and so did Caroline.

"You guys go on," said Nick. "We'll see you at the frat."

The student couple continued toward campus.

"Are you serious?" Laura asked.

"Completely. I love you, Laura. I know I'm never going to find another girl like you. And I'll do my best to make you happy. I promise you — even our fights will be fun."

"You may be right about that part."

"So what do you say?"

"It's not an entirely disagreeable prospect."

"Is that a yes?"

"Let me think about it, Nick."

"Sure...For how long?"

"A few days."

"Okay," said Nick. "Er, can we still make love while you're thinking?"

Laura placed her hands on his temples and pulled his face to hers. She gave him a long, lusty kiss. They resumed walking, Laura with her arm through Nick's.

"You like my last name?" Nick asked.

"Jarrett? Very much."

"Then you won't mind taking it on."

"Get this straight, Nick. If and when I marry, I'll keep my own name."

"Laura's fine."

Laura snorted. They continued on in silence, past an Office Depot, Laura lost in thought.

"Laura Jarrett..." she said to herself, and smiled.

Peter enjoyed the way Caroline felt against his shoulder, as if under his protection. It went against his predatory instincts. They were on the main campus walkway, approaching Fraternity Row. He sensed she might put out tonight if he pressed her, but Nick's little talk gave him pause. It would be like spoiling something precious, he thought.

They entered the Delta House den, discarding their coats. Two fraternity brothers occupied the sofas—Sean, adding a straight line to the architectural plan on his notebook, and scruffy Eric, reading an Advanced Filmmaking textbook. Seeing the new arrivals, they both stood up and left the room, as if by agreement. Peter and Caroline sat down on the right sofa, their legs touching. She looked vulnerably at him. He kissed her without using his tongue. She responded with hers. Their physical contact intensified, as much on her part as his.

"Take me to your room," said Caroline.

Peter pulled back his head and looked intently at her. He saw tears in her eyes.

"No," he said softly.

"Don't you want me?"

"More than anything."

"Then why?"

"Caroline, listen to me. I'm a total jerk to chicks. Have been ever since high school. They've made it pretty easy for me. But you didn't. I want to be a better guy with you."

"I don't want to lose you," said Caroline.

"We go upstairs now, you probably will."

"If we don't?"

"There's no guarantee, but we might have a chance," said Peter. "You're worth getting to know over a long, long time. And I'd like to try it the old-fashioned way for once."

"Oh, Peter," said Caroline, the tears flowing freely.

He kissed her tenderly on the lips. She threw her arms around his neck. A coatless Nick and Laura came in to witness the chaste embrace. Caroline stood up, and hugged Laura.

"Aren't boys wonderful?" said Caroline.

"They're little angels," Laura said, adding softly. "Fallen ones."

"Let's go home, Laura," Caroline said.

"Hey, now, not so fast," said Nick, seeing his salacious plans for the night dissolving.

"What's wrong, Nick?" asked Caroline.

"Yes, Nick, whatever's the matter?" said Laura with a mischievous smile.

Nick looked from Laura to a happy Caroline.

"Nothing," he said. "Nothing at all."

"Good night, boys," said Laura.

The women left the den. Nick plopped down on the sofa next to Peter.

"You had to pick tonight to go noble," said Nick.

"There are some old magazines in the library," said Peter.

They both slunk in the couch. Lee came bounding into the den.

"I thought I heard your voice," he said to Nick. "I managed to crack Ballard's computer data. I know who's behind the Guevarans. And what they got planned for tomorrow night."

Nick sprang to his feet and hurried up the stairs behind Lee.

32

The door to Lee's room was locked for maximum security. Lee sat at his black metal desk facing his open laptop and rear window. Nick looked over his shoulder at the screen, on which shone the website homepage of *The Tomorrow Students Society*. A large picture showed a half dozen multicultural collegians gazing raptly skyward at the overhead quote: *"This is the time for bold measures. This is the country, and you are the generation."* — *Bono*.

"So Bono's behind all this," Nick said.

"No," said Lee. "Someone who could book U-2 for breakfast. The Tomorrow Students Society is his money line to the Guevaranas. Almost a hundred million dollars last year, distributed among nineteen universities."

"Including Daniel Carroll."

"Yes, unfortunately, three million. Half a million of it went to Evan Ballard as Executive Consultant to the Society."

"That's a lot of money for an old playbook—divide and conquer," said Nick. "Pit blacks against whites, women against men, poor against rich, gays against straights, atheists against Christians—to form a voter base of nominal victims. Trouble is, once you start down that road, where does it end? Blondes versus redheads? By then it won't matter, 'cause the whole country'll be a wreck."

"There is racism, Nick. I've encountered it as an Asian-American."

"Sure there's racism, where there's freedom of stupidity. Only it's individual not institutional. Cops aren't out gunning for black people like the race baiters claim. They just wanna go home at night to their wives and kids. But there'll always be idiots obsessing on an arbitrary thing like skin color. The truth is, I got more in common with most black, Asian, Latin, and Arab men than I do with any white woman."

"So sexism is your argument against racism," said Lee.

"Original, ain't it?" Nick said with a smile. "Don't keep me in suspense, Lee. Who's behind the big curtain?"

Lee clicked on a laptop key. On the screen appeared a Fortune magazine cover photo of a sixtyish man with windswept thin grey-hair, thick eyebrows, and olive skin in a white silk shirt open down to the third button. He leaned against the guardrail of a yacht, the deep blue Aegean Sea and a tall Greek island in the background.

"Of course," said Nick. "Gregory Lanos."

"Billionaire funder of far-left policies, and politicians, like the most recent Presidential loser."

"Lanos helped turn his native Greece into a socialist dump. Now he wants to do the same to our side of the pond."

"The last election must have set him back," said Lee.

"Progressives are like vampires," said Nick. "They keep coming, sucking the traditional lifestream of this country. The universities fell long ago, followed by the movies, and the press."

"You're the press."

"I'm the ghost in the machine," said Nick.

There was a knock at the door.

"Looks like they found you," Lee said.

Nick opened the door on Ben Fisher.

"Is this a private insurrection or can anybody join?" Ben said.

Nick relocked the door behind him. Ben looked at the laptop screen.

"Gregory Lanos," he said. "Guevarans?"

"Yep," said Nick.

"Did you find out who they are?"

"Where they are—or will be tomorrow," said Lee.

He tapped another laptop key. A yellow webpage appeared, with big letters proclaiming, *The Sports Bowl*, above the smaller words, *Website under construction*.

"The Sports Bowl," said Nick. "I used to buy running shoes from them. They closed down like a year ago."

"Two," said Lee. "The one here in Clifton did. But the building's still there."

"Who's paying for the real estate?" Nick asked.

"The mother ship—the Olympic Group," said Ben. "They took a Chapter Eleven bankruptcy. Means they can maintain the store shell for five years while paying off their debts."

"And what is the Olympic Group?" asked Nick.

"A mysterious Eastern European consortium," Ben said.

"Bet you twenty drachmas Lanos is in the mix," said Nick.

"No bet," Ben said.

"What makes you think the Guevarans will be dropping by the Sports Bowl?" Nick asked.

"The local store's first supply order in two years," said Lee, hitting another key.

On the screen popped up a very short Sports Bowl inventory list. The cursor defined each line item as Lee read it.

"Thirty baseball bats."

"Winter baseball," Nick said. "Perfectly normal."

"Thirty ski masks."

"It's colder on the slopes this year," said Ben.

"Delivery set for between three and five PM tomorrow," said Lee.

"Guevaran time," said Nick. "I'll be one of them."

"They'll kill you," said Ben. "Or mess you up bad."

"Yeah, if they bust me, it'll be thirty against one," Nick said. "But you said yourself, Ben, that's more than there are at this school. So some will be coming in from off campus—like me."

He tapped his chest.

"You may get your Pulitzer Prize," said Ben. "Posthumously."

33

"It's too dangerous, Nick," said Laura, sticking a plastic spoon in her vanilla yogurt.

"You're worried about me."

"Of course I am. If anything should happen to you...I lose the story and go back to the copyaide station."

"How thoughtful," said Nick.

They were having breakfast at the Bobcat Cove, a pleasant bistro in the Theater Arts Building near the center of campus. It was half full of artsy students at nine-thirty in the morning. Nick feasted on pancakes with bacon and coffee. Laura partook of sliced peaches, yogurt, and cinnamon tea with honey. Nick had just appraised her on the Lanos-Sports Bowl-Guevaran connection and his intent to infiltrate it.

"It'll make our story, finding out who those guys are," Nick said.

"But at what cost? Your life?"

"I'll be all right, baby. Chief Bosco will know where I am, and with who."

"Oh right, the beauteous campus police commander," said Laura. "You're putting your fate in the hands of a woman?"

"I already have…yours."

Laura smiled, touched.

"Why don't your girl's troopers just arrest everyone inside the Sports Bowl?"

"On what charge? Trying out baseball bats and ski masks? Cops can't do a thing till the damage is done…even if it's on me."

"You'll probably survive it. You're so hard headed, a bat would break first."

Nick smiled.

"So what are you going to do between now and four?" Laura asked.

"Work out. In case I have to fight or flee. You?"

"Protest in the Quad with Flint and company. She likes me now, ever since I banished you from my presence."

"Just don't make a habit of it."

"I won't, Nick. I've gotten used to having you around."

Nick smiled again. Laura did also, endearingly.

"You did want me to get the feminist angle."

"Better you than me," said Nick. "I'll be safer among the Guevarans."

Laura chuckled, then frowned.

"How bad do you think it will get tonight?"

"Pretty bad," said Nick. "Those baseball bats aren't for little leaguers."

"Should Lassiter bear some of the blame?"

"Not in my book, which is the Constitution. She has the right to speak."

"Even hate speech."

"Especially hate speech," said Nick. "What lefties brand any opinion they dislike. If you're pro-life, you're anti-woman. For traditional marriage, you're anti-gay. For securing the border, you're anti-immigrant. Pro-Second Amendment, you want schoolkids to die! Your side has gotten away with that canard for years. But not tonight."

"I suppose you're going to stop it."

"We are, Laura. You and me. We'll report the facts and let the chips fall where they may."

"You forget I'm a liberal."

"A classic liberal."

"What's the difference?"

"Would you ban *To Kill a Mockingbird*?"

"'Course not. It's brilliant."

"A school district in Virginia did this year," Nick said.

"Because of its realistic depiction of Depression-era racism."

"Even though the book condemns it. How 'bout *Huckleberry Finn*?"

"'Never," said Laura. "That's another anti-racism masterpiece."

"Banned. And not only in Virginia."

"I know. It hurts me. I love books. Their power to describe a universe, even an evil one, full of ugly words. I'd hate to see literature censored into disclarity."

"You see? You respect the men who made Western Civilization, warts and all."

"It was an exclusive club back then."

"Founded by a gay guy and a Jew."

"Socrates and Jesus," said Laura.

"And the last best hope for preserving their ideas, like it or not, is this country."

"It could use some political correction."

"But not destruction, like so many of your allies want," said Nick.

"That's a mad conspiracy theory."

"Is it? They take down our monuments, starting with the easy ones—Robert E. Lee, Stonewall Jackson, Jeb Stuart. But why stop there? Our founding fathers were slave owners—Washington, Jefferson, Franklin, the whole gang. Sure, they wrote the greatest governmental document of all time, but they were slave owners, so that tears it. And if the Constitution's no good, then the Bill of Rights is moot, and you can make up the laws as you go along, like any banana republic. Which is what we'll be if they get their way—another Venezuela."

"There's something in what you say," said Laura.

"Hey, I like the sound of that."

"A broken cuckoo clock is right twice a day, Nick."

They finished their breakfast and went out. Pausing outside the theater building, they stood very close and face to face, Laura's brown eyes focused on Nick.

"If you stay alive, I may marry you," she said.

Nick grinned. "Then tonight I'll be Superman."

"Superman's a toxic male."

"Good thing I love my kryptonite," said Nick, moving in on Laura.

They kissed passionately. After half a minute, Laura drew back, looking worried.

"Nick, are you sure about this?"

"Sure," said Nick, giving Laura a warm smile. "It's a mystery."

"Call me when you're out of danger."

Laura turned around and walked away. Nick watched her disappear amid the moving student bodies. At that moment, he felt younger than all of them, in fact, giddy as a schoolboy. He started back toward the Delta house, pondering his near future.

His past before Laura seemed a fog, so fully had she become the most important and exciting part of his life. He looked forward to making their relationship permanent, official, sacred. By next year, he could be a Washington Post reporter, able to support a wife—and kid. Should the Post not hire him, another news outlet certainly would, based on his clips. Laura could work also, if she wanted to, until a new life entered her. And if for some unpredictable reason his journalism options dried up, Nick had a Plan B, the family tradition, a stint in the United States Marine Corps. Though his bride to be would certainly disapprove of it.

34

The student demonstrators on the Quad now numbered over a hundred, making a wider turn around the Daniel Carroll statue. Tension ran high, like an electric current through faulty wiring, with the target of the protest just eight hours away. Laura marched beside Flint, behind Goatee—real name Dennis, she now knew—and ahead of Flint's two handmaidens, Brenda and Michelle. Laura again carried the *Stop hate! Stop Lassiter!* sign.

Flint did seem to have warmed to her after her feigned rebuke of Nick, appearing to hold no grudge about her romantic displacement with Professor Ballard. On her part, Laura appreciated Flint's passion for the same causes she believed in: sexual, racial, and economic "equality," a better word than the loaded "justice." In Laura's view, for instance, the two white women who invested in a burrito stand should be celebrated for female empowerment, not damned for cultural appropriation. She feared that her side had begun to devour its own, providing more ammunition to astute opponents, such as her "fiancé."

She gulped at her own casual definition of Nick. Being his wife would be absurd, given his expectations of a woman's role—basically housewifery. Images of herself flashed through her mind. In a bathrobe at the door of a white-fenced cottage, kissing the business-suited Nick goodbye. At the cottage's kitchen table, feeding spoonsful of baby food to an adorable infant in a high chair while a cute girl of three played with a bowl of Cheerios. In sweat clothes, vacuuming the cozy living room. In a slinky blue dress, handing a martini to the coatless Nick. In a child's bedroom doorway, smiling at Nick reading to the little girl *The Little Mermaid*.

Laura tried to frown at the last image but couldn't. Instead, the identical smile came to her in the present. It dawned on her that the last ten days had been the headiest she'd ever known, and with, yes, the best sex. Could wedlock to Nick continue the rite of passion for years to come?

"Laura."

She snapped out of her reverie, turning to Flint on her left.

"You're spacing out. Wanna take a break?"

"I'm all right," said Laura.

"It's hard work, isn't it? Protesting injustice."

"Certainly is."

"I know it's a new thing for you ..."

"This physical, for sure," said Laura. "Up to now I've been more passive aggressive."

In front of the two women, Dennis perked up, clearly listening to their conversation.

"You were pretty open yesterday," Flint said. "Blowing off your significant other."

"He deserved it."

"Yeah, he was a patriarchal jerk."

"But he had a sweet side," said Laura, feeling the strange obligation to defend Nick.

"Yeah, that's how they get you—good-looking boys like your ex. They come on all nice and warm, then once you hook up with 'em, they turn into possessive dicks. I had my fill of them in my teens, when I didn't know any better."

Laura turned on her mental recorder, lacking a digital one.

"Tell me about it, Flint."

"I was a waitress at a biker bar in Glen Echo. Thought I was hot stuff for hooking up with the gang leader. Till he got me pregnant, me and another girl. He wanted a bunch of kids just to show off his male prowess to the gang. When I aborted mine, he went nuts, beat me up bad. At the women's shelter I went to, I read shit I never learned in high school. How white male privilege oppresses women and minorities. So I decided to fight it. Made myself harder, smarter. Even changed my name to reflect the tough, gender-neutral me. And I got into this school."

"What's your birth name?"

"Margaret—Hale."

"But you still have relations with white men, like Professor Ballard?"

"Only woke white men, who blast their own kind."

"I'm woke," said Dennis, looking hopefully back at Flint and Laura. "I hate white men."

"Sorry, Dennis," said Flint.

Nick walked by the elliptical running track toward the workout bars just outside its north end. He had on a grey sweat shirt and pants, black wool gloves, and a navy blue ski cap to ward off the cold noon wind. His iPod earbuds played stirring film music, at this moment the theme from *The Year of Living Dangerously*. The movie, about foreign correspondent Mel Gibson finding danger and romance in revolutionary Indonesia, had inspired his newspaper vocation. Now he faced danger and romance in revolutionary America.

He reached the workout station, consisting of a pullup bar and waist-high parallel bars. Dropping to the grass, he did forty full-extension pushups. He walked around the station for two minutes, his iPod switching to *Genesis Countdown* from *Star Trek II: the Wrath of Khan*. He grabbed the pullup bar, hands two feet apart, and did twenty pullups, full extension. After a two-minute walkabout, he started doing twenty full-extension dips on the parallel bars. A comely coed in short gym shorts ran by him on the track, to his disappointment, without slowing down to admire his form.

On his next walkabout, he listened to more *Genesis Countdown*. Returning to the pullup bar, he reversed the handhold and did twenty chin-ups. He concluded the upper-body workout with thirty-five more pushups.

He began powerwalking clockwise on the track, listening to *Promontory* from *The Last of the Mohicans*, until the cute runner overtook him. When she got fifteen yards ahead, Nick broke into a jog at her pace. Something nice to look at while he ran, he thought. In two hours, he'd be facing an uglier sight, the Guevarans.

35

Ned O'Rourke's Ford Explorer was parallel parked eight cars back from the shuttered Sports Bowl building on Main Street. The now unmarked warehouse took up the western quarter of a downtown Clifton block. O'Rourke had the engine running, heat on, and panel lights lit, the dashboard clock marking 6:17 PM. His long-lensed Nikon camera lay between him and Nick, wearing his white Irish fisherman's sweater and black jeans. Both men sipped coffee from the coffee house across the street.

"Maybe they called it off," said O'Rourke.

"Part of me hopes so," Nick said. "It would mean no violence tonight."

"And the other part?"

"Wants a real donnybrook, with lots of action to write about," said Nick.

"I remember that feeling. Got my fill of it in Iraq."

"And a Pulitzer."

"That was nothing compared to a Purple Heart," O'Rourke

said solemnly. "I've shot a bunch of those being given out. Too many to next of kin."

"God bless our heroes."

"Amen. Speaking of—I read your piece on that wounded sergeant. Good stuff."

"Thanks, Ned. Thirty bat-wielding cretins aren't worth one of him. I still need to find out what makes 'em tick—besides hatred of America."

"If they show up."

"They'll show up. UPS truck dropped off three boxes round noon."

"You've been here since then?"

"No," said Nick, pointing up. "Street surveillance camera. Friend of mine's monitoring it."

"Might go black soon, if you're right about the university brass supporting the protest."

"Good point. Clifton's a college town. Couple dozen armed masked men parading up Main Street would make an embarrassing video."

"That's why I'm here," said O'Rourke, tapping his Nikon.

The street lights came on, illuminating the shops-filled sidewalk.

"Time to earn your pay," said Nick, pointing to the windshield.

In front of the Sports Bowl, four thirtyish, hirsute men in coats and jeans got out of a grey Toyota Yaris, and approached the warehouse. Their apparent leader was a Van Dyke-bearded man dangling a set of keys. The Toyota drove away.

O'Rourke grabbed his camera and went out the Explorer driver's door. He popped up beside Nick's passenger window, snapping pictures of the Sports Bowl quartet. Nick lowered the car window as Van Dyke unlocked the store's front door.

"Those guys are too old to be students," said Nick.

"Alumni?"

"Soviet U."

Two actual collegiate types crossed the street toward the building. O'Rourke photographed them all the way to the Sports Bowl door. One of them knocked hard three times. The door opened to admit him and his companion. Soon, three older men neared the same door, also covered by O'Rourke's camera. The lead man knocked three times, and went inside with the rest.

"Three knocks must be the passcode," said Nick.

"Clever."

Nick's deduction proved correct. Every other man or group made the same three-knock announcement. By full dark, Nick counted twenty-three men inside, just eight of them likely Daniel Carroll University students. He stepped out of the car next to O'Rourke.

"Here's hoping they don't all know each other," said Nick.

"Be careful in there."

O'Rourke pointed his Nikon lens at Nick and clicked off a shot.

"What's that for?" asked Nick.

"A 'before' picture, in case we have to reconstruct the 'after'."

"Gallows humor isn't funny," Nick said. "Be seeing you."

He started toward the Sports Bowl entrance. Reaching the door, he knocked hard three times. The door opened, held by one of the first crew to enter, an overweight young man with straggly brown hair. He stared at Nick.

"Who sent you?"

"The Washington Post," Nick almost said.

"Doctor Ballard."

Straggly continued to evaluate him.

"Nick Jar ..."

"No last names," Straggly interrupted Nick. "If any of us get arrested, we won't be able to ID the others."

"Smart."

Straggly let Nick in and closed the door. Van Dyke stood a few feet away to their right, talking through a cellphone headset. Nick nodded at him and he nodded back, focusing on his phone communication.

"Drop your phone in there," said Straggly.

He indicated a deep plastic tray by the door with about twenty cellphones inside. Nick deliberated quickly under Straggly's watchful eye. He took out his Post digital recorder — about the same size and shape of a cellphone — and dropped it in the tray, satisfying Straggly. Nick hoped there wouldn't be an inspection of the tray's contents anytime soon. He moved further back into the warehouse.

The concrete room was cold, dim, dusty and bare, except for the twenty-plus men sitting on the floor at the back right corner, and the three open cardboard boxes to their left. Nick took a seat between the men and the boxes — after noticing the wooden baseball bats in the closest box.

He sat down beside a peach fuzzed young man in a green sweatshirt, looking curiously at him. Nick noted the minimal conversation among the rest of the group, limited to men who had come in together. The others just sat, having no phones to occupy their time and minds. Nick suddenly sweated the thought of his own phone ringing. He reached into his back right pocket to mute it. He noticed Peach Fuzz still looking at him, and stuck out his hand.

"Nick," he said.

Peach Fuzz hesitated a moment then shook Nick's hand.

"Alan."

"Where you from, Alan?"

"Baltimore. You?"

"Philadelphia. How long you been in this group?"

"Few months."

"Me too," said Nick. "What's your story?"

"Fucking corporations, hogging the wealth, screwing the rest of us."

Nick thought of the mega-corporation that owned the Washington Post, and the owner's ideological leaning.

"Some of them are on our side," he said. "They might hire you."

"They want robots working for 'em, not creative types like me."

Straggly opened the front door for a pair of tough-looking men in their late thirties, one in a green cap, the other huskier with a reddish face.

"What do you do?" asked Nick.

"I'm a screenwriter."

"Wow. Written anything I might've seen?"

"I wish," said Alan. "The system's rigged. Corporations run Hollywood. They make all their money in China. It's why they keep putting out the same FX-loaded comic-book crap, and reject original ideas."

"Like what?"

"Like—a coked-up, ass-kicking detective goes after a serial killer of African-American millionaires."

"That is original," said Nick, suppressing an eye roll.

"Get this. The detective's an African-American woman! Think Oprah."

"Wow. I can't believe you haven't sold that one."

"I know, right? Like I said, the system's rigged."

"So how do you get by?"

"I don't really. I live at my parents' house. Been stuck there two years. Ever since I came home from Ithaca College with a worthless Film degree."

"And your folks let you hang out? Mine wouldn't."

"Dad gripes, but mom backs me up. She knows how dedicated I am to my craft."

The two new arrivals headed toward them.

"How'd you end up here?" Nick asked. "The Lassiter dame has no connection to Hollywood."

"Dwight Melnick does. He's this huge A-list director. Does all the Star Force films…"

"There's a new one out now."

"Yeah, 'Star Force Three—Earth Fights Back'," said Alan. "Melnick's the head of the Resistance in Hollywood. Right after the election, he started this group, PHAT …"

"Fat…" said Nick.

"P-H-A-T. Progressive Hollywood Action Time."

Green Cap and Red Face sat down on Nick's right, Green Cap right beside him. Nick could see Red Face's visage was the result of some faded rash. He also recognized the logo on Green Cap's cap—two hands shaking in front of a globe—as that of the International Public Service Union (IPSU). It explained the five physically formidable older men in the room. These union thugs would cause the most mayhem tonight, Nick figured, not softies like Alan.

"What does PHAT do?" Nick asked.

"Mostly dis the President. But *not* belonging to it makes breaking into the biz even harder than it normally is."

"Wait, are you telling me you got to be a member of PHAT to sell a screenplay?"

"Pretty much."

"That's incredible," said Nick, a new story idea popping in his head.

"I could either send 'em ten bucks a month, or earn brownie points doing work for 'em."

"Social justice jobs?"

"Whatever their youth group tells me to do."

"The Tomorrow Students Society," said Nick.

"That's them."

"So getting arrested tonight could make you a star, especially on an anti-Lassiter play."

"It would give me street cred in Hollywood."

"Brilliant," said Nick.

He looked at Van Dyke, by the entrance next to Straggly. He still had his headset on and seemed nervous. Nick turned to Green Cap on his right. The man nodded slightly at him. Nick pointed at his cap.

"My uncle's I-P-S-U."

"Yeah?" replied Green Cap. "Where?"

"Philly. Ambulance drivers' union. What's your turf?"

"Catering—Ohio public schools."

"I read the new Education Secretary just gutted the school

lunch menu," Nick said. "Scrapping the last First Lady's health food plan."

"Yeah. Three friends of mine lost their jobs 'cause of that bitch, and her asshole boss."

"The President. You're not a fan, huh."

"His Supreme Court voted down mandatory dues for non-union leeches, almost killing our union," said Green Cap. "I'll pretend I'm smashing his skull in tonight."

"Stopping Lassiter isn't enough for you?"

"Just between you and me, I agree with her girly man bathroom stand."

"How many in your crew?"

"Four besides me. Can't count on these college pussies. Though you look like you can swing a bat."

"I played some ball in my youth. I'm Nick."

"Ed."

The two shook hands. Ed had a strong grip. Van Dyke and Straggly approached the sitting group. Everyone looked up expectantly at the pair.

"Guevarans," said Van Dyke in a high-pitched voice.

Nick pulled his cellphone up to his spine, and turned on the voice record function.

"Alice Lassiter just left her Shady Grove hotel. She'll be at the university in half an hour. Both campus entrances will be blocked by student protesters, so she won't get far before we get to her. But silencing one vile speaker isn't enough. All fascists, from the President on down, must be taught a lesson. That their efforts to pollute young minds with old and decadent ideas will be met by force. We are that force! And tonight, the Resistance will become the Offensive!"

"Right on," Alan said to Nick.

"Most of us will go in the West Gate, where Lassiter will be," said Van Dyke. "A small group will cover the East Gate and create general chaos, led by Robert."

He pointed to Straggly.

"Everyone, make your presence known. Start by breaking objects rather than people. The campus police won't interfere. But if the Young Conservatives try to stop you ... well, those little Nazis deserve every broken bone they get. When I give the word, drop your bats, remove your masks, and blend in with the student demonstrators. They won't turn you in."

Van Dyke looked at Ed, next to Nick.

"You union men will be on my team."

Ed nodded.

"All right, grab your tools."

The Guevarans stood up, and approached the three boxes, as did Nick. They took baseball bats out of the first two and black ski masks from the third box.

"Leave the masks off till I tell you," said Van Dyke. "We'll be going out the back door in five minutes."

Nick saw Alan feebly clutch his bat, and felt sympathy for him, clearly in over his head.

"Passion is needed for any great work," said Van Dyke. "And for a revolution, passion and audacity are required in big doses."

Nick recognized the quote by Che, and Van Dyke as another fanatic. Ed appeared beside him with four other brawny men, made more intimidating by the bats they held.

"You're with us," Ed said, looking in no mood for disagreement.

"Okay," Nick said. "I need to go to the bathroom first."

"What's'a matter, punk?" said Red Face. "You getting scared?"

"Yeah," said Nick. "But I'll feel better once you put your mask on."

Ed chuckled. Red Face looked even redder and meaner.

"Go on, kid," said Ed. "We won't start without you."

Nick walked to the two bathrooms at the rear left corner, and went into the men's room. Four Guevarans stood before the two urinals, both toilet stalls also occupied. A student exited the closest stall. Nick entered it. He took out his cellphone, dropped his pants, and sat down on the toilet seat. He began typing a text.

26 Guevarans exiting rear of SB. Target 2 DCU gates. IPSU men + me to east gate. Expect violence.

He sent a group text to Laura, O'Rourke, Lee, and University Police Chief Tracy Bosco. Bosco might disregard it but she couldn't ignore it, even if she threw in with President Tamara Harris. Either way, Nick feared there would be blood. Noticing impatient, possibly suspicious, feet under the stall door in front of him, he flushed the toilet. He stood up, pocketed his phone, and opened the portal on a nervous young Guevaran.

"I wouldn't go in there just yet," said Nick, waving off an imaginary bad odor.

Ned O'Rourke read Nick's text in the driver's seat of his Explorer. He pulled out of the parking space as fast as he could without bumping the vehicles on either end. He drove thirty yards past the Sports Bowl to the street corner and turned right. He made a second right at the first back street, and stopped near the rear door of the Sports Bowl. A garbage dumpster behind the adjoining restaurant appeared suitable for his purpose.

O'Rourke grabbed his camera and jumped out of his car. Just as he reached the dumpster, the Sports Bowl's back door opened.

A stream of bat-carrying men filed out of it. O'Rourke snapped them moving past his dumpster cover. Six big guys stood out among the group, Nick one of them. He looked left, and appeared to focus on O'Rourke's position before reaching the street with the others. The nearly thirty men turned right in the direction of the university. O'Rourke ran back to his Explorer and jumped in. Headlights off, he began to follow the group. He had a lot more work to do that night.

36

Laura anxiously read Nick's text, then resumed videotaping the campus scene below with her phone. She stood on the sixth-floor balcony of the Daniel Carroll University Visitor's Center overlooking the university's West Gate. It was a posh, glassy, on-campus hotel for rich alumni, wealthy parents, and VIP speakers, Alice Lassiter excluded. Evan Ballard had rented the top-floor suite to savor his night of triumph, and well-earned prize—Laura.

Close to a hundred angry students clustered on both sides of the gateway road, many holding signs denouncing Lassiter. They were being kept back from the road by two beefy young campus policemen, a black and a white, on opposite sidewalks. Between them moved a slow train of cars, and student pedestrians of a decidedly cleaner cut than the demonstrators.

A gaggle of mostly television reporters and their camera-men occupied a grass patch on the north side of the road. Laura recognized dapper Craig Yellen from the Post National Desk among them. Yellen had twice hit on her in the newsroom, but subtly enough to deny any harassment claim she could level. He appeared more alert than his colleagues, as if he'd also read Nick's text.

Two male protestors on the south lawn gave the black cop a wide berth, and crossed the sidewalk to the road. The closest car to them stopped hard, as did the one behind it. Black Cop blew a loud whistle at the scofflaws. Then the dam burst. A dozen more protestors stepped onto the road from both sides, blocking both incoming and walkthrough traffic. The cars began to honk, the noise further disturbing Laura on the balcony.

She heard a closer sound behind her, the suite's glass door sliding shut. She put her phone on voice record and tucked it in her right coat pocket. Ballard approached Laura with his own phone in hand, relishing the sight of her. She looked so desirable in her red coat, grey wool skirt and green tights showcasing her amazing legs. Nature certainly made gender neutrality a challenge, Ballard thought. He moved to Laura's left, shoulders touching.

"It's starting," Laura said, nodding at the commotion below.

"This is only the prelude. My Greek chorus setting the stage for the main players, who are already on the march."

"The Guevarans?"

"Yes," said Ballard, then frowned. "How do you know their name?"

Laura thought fast. "Flint told me."

"The jealous fool. She knows better than to link me to them."

Laura strategically changed the subject. "Flint, jealous?"

"Of you, Laura. She longed to be the one up here instead. But I wanted you — to share this victory with me."

Ballard put his arm around Laura's right shoulder. She left it there, knowing he'd record better that way.

"What you see unfolding down below is occurring at the West Gate even as we speak. Lassiter will be repelled, as will her master's voice. It's the beginning of the end of the white patriarchy. Soon, we will fundamentally transform America into a true people's republic."

"By silencing one conservative gay woman?" Laura asked.

Below them, the two campus policemen confronted the road blockers. Black Cop furiously gestured at the crowd to withdraw, his partner barking into a hand radio. Laura doubted they would get any backup, after Nick's account of his police paramour's dilemma. The horn blasting got louder. Ballard spoke over it.

"Alice Lassiter's a Trojan Horse. A traitor to her gender and sexual orientation, and a pawn of the Christian Right. Repulsing her will show the regressive fools that Judgment Day has come early. Not from their mythical God, but from their anti-Christ—we diabolical progressives. Everything they hold sacred in this country will be remade in our image—black, brown, female, poor, and queer. America will be Hell on Earth for conservatives. Isn't it wonderful?"

"Yes," said Laura.

"And you'll have a front row seat at my side."

Ballard moved his mouth toward Laura's. She stopped him with her palms on his chest.

"Let's celebrate when this is over, shall we," she said.

Ballard looked upset. Laura knew she'd broken character by being too assertive, and noticeably softened.

"Forgive me, Evan," she said pouting. "I'm just so afraid that something will go wrong."

Ballard recovered his ego. "Impossible. I've planned this out too well."

They heard a loudening group chant from below.

"Hey hey, ho ho! Lassiter has got to go! Hey hey, ho ho! Lassiter has got to go!"

The two cops could now only stand by, watching the hostile takeover of the campus road.

"You see," Ballard said. "The old enemy is impotent before our revolt."

"He may still have some tricks up his sleeve," said Laura.

Nick and eighteen Guevarans walked across Clifton's main street, heading toward the university's West Gate, a quarter mile uphill. Nick travelled in the three-man second row, between Alan and an IPSU gorilla, just behind Ed, Red Face, and Van Dyke. Cross-street cars braked, giving wide space to the bat-wielding men sweeping by before them. Seven more had continued on the back road, intending to enter the campus East Gate half a mile farther.

Team One reached the southeast corner sidewalk of the university approach road, causing new traffic hazards on their left as drivers rubbernecked at the sight of them. Two coeds walking downhill toward town saw them, jumped off the sidewalk, and almost got hit by a swerving, horn-blasting SUV.

Ned O'Rourke dashed down the sidewalk from the West Gate, toting his camera and cursing Nick Jarrett. Ever since he met that kid, he'd done more running on the job than he had in years. He had to admit it was worth it. Thanks to Nick's text, he had gotten the jump on his rivals, still waiting disinterestedly on campus for something eventful to happen. But he'd dutifully informed his Post colleague Craig Yellen of the imminent threat.

O'Rourke stopped ten yards in front of the oncoming Guevarans, and Nick, thirty yards from the West Gate road behind him. He began shooting the bat-armed men while retreating at their approach speed, an old news photographer's skill.

"We're being photographed," Ed said.

"Masks on!" shouted Van Dyke to the men behind him.

Nick and the Guevarans quickly put on their black ski-masks. Beyond Ned, Nick saw a long line of cars being prevented from accessing the gateway. Alice Lassiter's audience, he presumed, with the lady herself somewhere in that logjam. He saw no sign of the campus cops, so assumed Chief Bosco had made her choice — obey the stand down order and keep her job. He should have expected it. All the films noir he'd seen and he'd still counted on a dame. The closer his group got to the West Gateway, the louder a chanting became.

"Hey hey, ho ho! Lassiter has got to go! Hey hey, ho ho! Lassiter has got to go!"

Van Dyke pulled out his cellphone and read the screen.

"Listen to me!" he said over his shoulder, loud enough for all his men to hear.

"Lassiter's in the back seat of a white Honda Civic, license plate T-A-U-two-one-seven! It's trapped right inside the gate! Let's welcome her Guevaran style!"

Nick cringed at the efficiency of Guevaran data gathering, paid for by Gregory Lanos. His team closed on the gateway, now fifteen yards ahead. The vehicles there didn't, couldn't move. Ned O'Rourke did, to the other side of the car line. He got behind the hood of a yellow Mustang and pointed his camera at the oncoming troublemakers.

Nick stepped aside from the moving group and stopped. The

other men swept by him toward the car line. He could make out the scared young faces in the cars as the armed men came closer.

"These people came to hear Lassiter speak!" shouted Van Dyke, pointing his bat at the car line. "Make them regret that!"

The four IPSU men moved forward. The non-union Guevarans hesitated.

"Do it, Gus!" said Ed.

Red Face, Gus, swung his bat against an SUV's windshield, causing a massive spider crack on it. A girl inside the car screamed. Horrified pedestrians backed away from the vehicles, leaving the occupants to their fate. Gus moved left to a Chevrolet Cruze. He bashed the hood, leaving a huge dent. The other union men started smashing car windows and parts to more screams. The younger Guevarans joined in the assault and battery.

"Get to Lassiter's car!" Van Dyke shouted.

The marauders made their way toward the West Gate, bashing every car before it. On the opposite side of the car line, O'Rourke moved parallel to them, shooting their path of destruction.

Nick became aware of someone behind him on the sidewalk. He turned to see another bat-holding Guevaran, only with revulsion in the eyes behind the mask, and recognized Alan. Nick put his free hand on Alan's bat, and effortlessly took it from him.

"Go home, Alan," he said.

Alan started backpedaling from Nick. He took off his ski-mask, and threw it onto a shrub.

"Forget serial killers," said Nick. "Write a script about nice people. PHAT may not like it, but an audience might."

Alan spun around and hurried down the hill. Nick turned to

the West Gate, the Guevarans almost at it, walloping cars like piñatas. He tossed Alan's bat, and clutched his own.

"Play ball," he said, and started running toward the gate.

"Lassiter," said Ballard, pointing his forefinger over the balcony railing.

Laura looked down to where he pointed — a white Honda Civic trapped several cars inside the gate. A horde of protesters raged against the car, only kept at bay by the two campus policemen on each side of it, wielding their extension batons. More protestors confronted them. The news cameramen were hard at work photographing the chaos. While the reporters hung back, awaiting a safer opportunity to interview participants.

Or survivors, Laura fretted. From her sixth-story height, she saw what the two cops couldn't yet. More than a dozen black-masked men storming in through the gate on the right side of the car line, bashing vehicles with baseball bats. Even the student protesters backed away as their destructive allies made their way toward them.

"Evan, stop this!" Laura cried. "People are going to get hurt."

"Casualties of the Revolution," said Ballard, his eyes glazed like a pyromaniac's witnessing a fire. "A necessary first step."

"Madness," Laura said.

She watched the Guevarans get closer to the Honda, their bats sparing none of the cars behind it. Only three unbroken vehicles remained between a hulking man and Lassiter's transport. The two cops, now aware of the more violent threat, prepared to confront him, batons ready.

Then another ski-masked man rushed in through the gate,

bat in hand. Seeing his black jeans and white Irish Fisherman's sweater, Laura gasped. The new man approached a large Guevaran, who was bashing the trunk of a black Chevrolet Equinox. Irish Fisherman's bat struck his right upper arm, causing him to drop his bat and clutch his shoulder in pain.

"What?!" Ballard said on Laura's left, having also witnessed the surprise attack.

Irish Fisherman ran past two more small masked men toward the next stocky one, hammering the roof of a Dodge Charger. He batted the man's right shoulder. The Guevaran fell to the ground, writhing and rolling. Irish Fisherman kept running to the front of the car line.

"What!?" cried Ballard nonplussed.

Laura ignored him, transfixed by the action below. Irish Fisherman bypassed three more unimposing Guevarans to close on the third large one, busy smashing an SUV's left taillight. On his left, a fourth broad Guevaran had become aware of the turnabout intruder, and shouted a warning to his comrade. The man reacted too late, as Irish Fisherman bashed his right elbow. The man screamed, dropping his bat.

Ballard appeared choleric. "That bastard is ruining everything! Who the hell is he?!"

Irish Fisherman pulled of his black ski mask.

"My boyfriend," said Laura with a slight smile.

Ed confronted Nick with bat raised, ready to do damage. Behind him, the oblivious Gus demolished a Saab sedan just one car behind the white Honda, still being protected by the two campus cops. Nick gripped the bat in his right hand, facing Ed.

"I knew there was something wrong with you," Ed said through his mask.

"You call this right?" cried Nick, nodding at the smashed car line. "Destroying property? Terrorizing innocent people? How'd you sink so low?"

"I'm protecting our union."

"Union men built those cars!" declared Nick. "They still got their pride! Shame on you, Ed!"

"They asked for this! They voted against their own interests! The whole state of Michigan did!"

"You're better than this, all of you. You guys lived. Raised families. Made the country work. Look at you now—creepy masked thugs!"

"We got paid to do a job!" Ed snapped.

"By a sick billionaire who hates Americ and hopes to weaken it. But it's a lot stronger than Lanos thinks. Too bad you weren't."

Gus had finished his destruction of the Saab and was approaching the white Honda. The two campus policemen braced to stop him. Black Cop unfastened the strap on his pistol holster and glanced at his partner. White Cop shook his head, gripping his baton. Black Cop nodded and refastened his gun strap. They would take on the threat the hard way.

"Gus!" yelled Ed.

Gus turned to Ed, and saw him confronting the unmasked Nick. Ed pointed at Nick.

"Hurt 'im, Gus!"

Nick could almost see Gus grinning through his ski-mask. The union gorilla came at him, circling his bat. As a kid, Nick had lost every stick duel to his older brother, Scott, but he'd learned some neat moves in the process. He hoped he could remember some of them. A thick bat would hurt a lot worse than bamboo.

Gus swung his bat at Nick's left collarbone with shattering force. Nick's bat rose to block it, faster than his conscious command. His arms trembled from the blow. He had no time to recover as Gus swung the bat at his right collarbone. Nick's bat intercepted it. The two bats crashed loudly, the impact knocking Nick to one knee.

Watching Nick go down, Laura held her breath. A train of thought rushed through her mind. Her Arthurian romance with Nick had turned into a nightmare. She stood on an evil lord's palace tower, watching her champion on one knee, a bestial black knight about to smite him. Nick had drawn her into this feudal fantasy. Now he was about to perish in it. And her return to modern womanhood would be sadder without him.

"Do it!" Ballard said through gritted teeth.

Gus's bat swung down at Nick's skull. It clanged against Nick's suddenly upraised one. Gus drew his bat behind his right shoulder for the ultimate power strike. Nick didn't wait for it. In one quick fluid motion, he swung his bat leftward over his head then hard into Gus's ribcage. Gus howled, gripping his struck side with his left hand, his right still holding the bat. Nick sprang up and bashed Gus's right wrist. The bat fell from Gus's hand. He dropped to his knees, left hand clutching his wrist. Nick kicked the bat out of his reach.

"Fucker!" Ballard exclaimed.

Laura exhaled, and slapped Ballard hard on his right cheek. He looked at her tragically, rubbing his crimson cheek, eyes moistening.

"Laura?"

"I know thee not, old man," said Laura.

She strutted away from him, and through the glass door.

Nick looked up at Ed, now joined by Van Dyke.

"Who are you?!" Van Dyke asked.

"Your worst nightmare," Nick snarled, then added in a normal tone. "I waited my whole life to say that."

"Get rid of him!" Van Dyke said to Ed.

Ed advanced on Nick with his bat, more warily than Gus had. Suddenly, he convulsed and dropped the bat, clutching his chest like from a stroke. Van Dyke seemed to be looking past Nick through his mask.

"No," he cried.

Nick turned around, and smiled. Seven young university cops in riot gear—black vests and helmets with dark plastic faceguards—marched toward the gateway, led by Chief Tracy Bosco. She wore no protection herself, and carried a small megaphone. The blonde surfer cop beside her had his Glock pistol out, having just shot Ed with a non-lethal bullet. The other cops rapidly formed into a line on Chief Bosco's right. She raised the megaphone to her mouth.

"This is the University Police!" she said in an amplified voice. "Drop your weapons!"

Nick tossed his bat. The student demonstrators froze. The

fallen union men stayed down. Only the upright smaller Guevarans, their backs to the police, continued bashing cars. Except for Van Dyke, who snuck away from the line of vehicles, slipping off his ski mask.

"I said drop your weapons, now!" said Chief Bosco's augmented voice.

The younger Guevarans ignored her, smashing more auto glass and metal. Chief Bosco lowered the megaphone.

"Pistols," she said in an unenhanced voice.

Down the line, her officers drew their Glocks.

"Fire one round."

The cops fired. Rubber bullets pelted the standing Guevarans. They contorted, shrieked, and collapsed, placing their now empty hands on their "wounds." Chief Bosco spoke again through the megaphone.

"You demonstrators! You have three minutes to clear the area, or you will be arrested!"

The protesters looked at each other as if searching for guidance. Finding none, they began to disperse away from the gateway entrance road. The reporters sprang into action, chasing down students with their digital recorders and cellphones. Their cameramen tried to make them look good. O'Rourke joined Craig Yellen. Most car occupants remained inside their vehicles, including the white Honda. Chief Bosco indicated the collapsed Guevarans.

"Cuff 'em," she said. "Then make sure everyone's okay."

Her young cops approached the Guevarans, simultaneously unclipping their handcuffs. Nick spotted the unmasked Van Dyke sneaking away among a trio of student protesters.

"Oh no you don't," said Nick.

He ran up behind Van Dyke and tackled him to the ground. Sitting on his back, Nick noticed a pair of shapely legs in green tights on his left. He looked up the legs to the grey skirt to the red coat to Laura's exquisite face. Her expression of relief vanished, replaced by reproach.

"What are you doing, Nick? Beating up a peaceful protestor?"

"This guy's a dangerous radical," Nick said.

"I see you used your standard debating technique on him."

Chief Bosco approached the pair, her surfer cop sidekick in tow. Nick stood up next to Laura, pointing at the downed Van Dyke.

"He's the leader of the local Guevarans," said Nick.

Chief Bosco indicated Van Dyke to her adjutant. Surfer Cop helped the man up, cuffed his hands behind his back, and led him away.

"What took you so long?" Nick asked.

"Maryland State Police," said Chief Bosco. "They were slow to lend us their riot gear. Took me a while to convince them."

"How did you?" asked Laura.

Chief Bosco looked curiously at her.

"My partner," Nick said.

"Not in crime," said Laura.

"Daniel Carroll's a state school," said Chief Bosco. "I told the captain he'd catch heat from the Governor for any damage done here."

"You mean like that?" said Nick.

He pointed to the line of smashed cars, the cops aiding shaken people out of them.

"Yeah," said Chief Bosco. "But I'm still giving the staties

high marks. I'll be hitting 'em up for a desk job after President Harris fires me."

"I got a hunch it's Harris who'll be looking for a job," Nick said.

"What makes you say that?" Chief Bosco asked hopefully.

"Read tomorrow's Washington Post," said Laura.

"The Post?" said Chief Bosco, turning to Nick. "I thought you were with the Daily Bobcat?"

"I graduated," said Nick.

Chief Bosco approached the white Honda, the original two-cop team standing beside it. White Cop opened the rear left passenger door, and helped a short woman with limp brown hair and glasses exit the car. Two well-dressed students, a boy and a girl, came out of both front doors. They joined the woman and, along with the officers, escorted her away on the sidewalk.

"Looks like Alice Lassiter's speech is still on," said Nick.

"You want to attend it?" Laura asked.

"Not me. She's nuts."

37

Nick and Laura returned to their respective Greek housing to pack up and say goodbye. In the Delta House, Lee accompanied Nick to the foyer.

"I'm sorry I missed Ben," said Nick.

"He's introducing Lassiter's speech."

"Beats delivering her eulogy."

"Yeah, I saw it got pretty rough out there," said Lee. "And you smoothed things out with a baseball bat."

"Couldn't've done it without you, Lee."

"Just don't name me in your story."

"Or else you'll have to kill me," Nick said.

They chuckled.

"Hey, speaking of your secret life," said Nick. "I have another mission for you — if you choose to accept it."

"Who's my target this time?"

"Dwight Melnick," said Nick.

"The 'Star Force' guy?"

"The PHAT guy."

"What's his weight got to do with anything?"

"It's how he throws it around," said Nick. "PHAT, P–H–A–T, is his Progressive Hollywood Action Time. Showbiz hopefuls gotta join it if they want to move up to the big time."

"Why, that's un-American."

"Downright McCarthyite I'd say. Funny. Hollywood keeps making movies about the horrors of the Blacklist, and yet they've created another one. Shut out conservative writers, actors, producers, and keep the industry leftwing."

"More Clooneys, fewer Eastwoods,"

"PC Harry," said Nick.

"I'll see what I can dig up," said Lee.

"Thanks, man. Be seeing you."

Nick went out the door. Approaching Laura's sorority house, he spotted her on the porch, individually embracing her "sisters," Liz, Cathy, Jenny, and Trina. She scooped up her tote bag and joined Nick. Caroline's Dodge Challenger pulled up beside them, Peter at the wheel, a radiant Caroline beside him. Nick opened the right rear door for Laura, who no longer balked at his old school etiquette, and got in on the opposite side.

On the way to the Shady Grove Metro Station, Laura invited the younger pair to visit them in DC. "A couples' thing," Nick thought, actually enjoying his new status. At the station drop-off spot, the women exited the car's two right doors, and Nick the rear left one. He approached the driver's window. Peter lowered it.

"How's your no-sex life?" Nick asked.

"I'm going through withdrawals," said Peter.

Nick smiled. "Love is a high, not a rush. It's supposed to last a while — maybe forever."

"I'd like to score some time before then."

"You will, but with strings attached."

"I'll take 'em."

"That's the general idea," said Nick, and shook Peter's hand through the car window. "Good luck, Pete."

"Thank you," Caroline said to Laura.

"You'd better invite me to the pinning ceremony," said Laura. "After all, we're sisters."

They hugged. Nick joined them. Caroline kissed him on the lips, and got back in the car. Nick and Laura approached the metro station entrance.

"Think they'll make it?" asked Laura.

"Stranger things have happened."

"You and I are proof of that."

They went in through the turnstile and approached the upward escalator.

"We do make a pretty good team," Laura said.

"Let's climb the ladder of success together," said Nick.

They stepped on the same escalator step and rode it up to the outdoor platform. In the nearly empty southbound train, they took the middle right seats, Nick the window side. They pulled out their cellphones, earphones, and notebook computers, and began writing the story while on the nine-station ride to Van Ness.

They walked north from Van Ness Station to Nick's building. Inside the apartment, Laura sat on the left side of the sofa, typing. Nick placed two open bottles of Dos Equis, the box of leftover pizza, and a roll of paper towels on the coffee table in front of her. He sat down on her right with his laptop, and started to type. They wrote, ate, and drank in silence.

Laura finished first, and sent Nick what she wrote. She sat back while he integrated it into one long feature. Snuggled against him, she read the start of it aloud. The more she read, the more excited she became.

"A violent riot shook Daniel Carroll University Wednesday night, when more than twenty men wearing ski masks and swinging baseball bats smashed cars and menaced people to protest a conservative speaker. It was an attack not just against transgender-rights critic Alice Lassiter, and her audience, but on the First Amendment. But even more sinister was the direct participation of an esteemed faculty member in the attack, and his stated motivation for it.

"'Alice Lassiter's a Trojan Horse,' said Evan Ballard, Professor of Social Justice at Daniel Carroll. 'A traitor to her gender and sexual orientation, and a pawn of the Christian right. Repulsing her will show the regressive fools that Judgment Day has come early.'"

"You're great, Nick," Laura said, no longer reading.

"Thank you—but what about my writing?"

"That's what I meant," said Laura with a smile.

"Oh."

"You do have another fine talent."

"I thought you'd get around to that," said Nick, pulling on his imaginary tie.

"Inflaming liberals."

"Ha. I only wanna light one liberal's fire."

Nick gave Laura a forceful kiss, to which she similarly responded. After half a minute, they drew apart.

"I'm getting warmer already," said Laura.

Nick smiled. He wrote a two-line email to Frank Russell at

Washington Post, attached the story to it, and put his finger over the laptop execute key.

"Send?" he asked.

"Send," said Laura.

Nick did. He and Laura sprang to their feet and rushed into the closet bedroom.

38

At six twenty-three in the morning, Nick lay on the futon in grey briefs, holding his cellphone above his head, a naked, wide awake Laura pressed against his right side. The phone screen glowed in the darkness, illuminating Laura's gorgeous face while she eagerly stared up at it.

"Is it up?"

"We'll know soon enough," said Nick, forefinger tapping the phone screen.

Laura held his forearm as he linked to the Washington Post homepage. Under the masthead appeared a color picture of two black-masked Guevarans bashing a pair of cars, looking like wraiths in the lamplight. The photo caption read, *Activists smash cars at Daniel Carroll University campus to protest Alice Lassiter speech (Ned O'Rourke, Washington Post Staff Photographer)*. Laura squeezed Nick's arm.

"Good on Ned," Nick said.

"Blast Ned," said Laura. "Where are we?"

Nick scrolled down to the headline, *Daniel Carroll Univer-*

sity protest turns violent, then the sub-headline, *Outside agitators held responsible,* then the byline, *By Craig Yellen, Washington Post Staff Writer, and Nick Jarrett and Laura London, Special to the Washington Post.*

"What?!" Laura exclaimed. "No separate feature for us — 'Behind the Protest?'"

"Looks like they dumped us into Yellen's piece," said Nick, continuing to scroll.

They read the article together, getting increasingly upset. Some of their more newsworthy findings and quotes remained, only diluted by meandering wordage. The story still inculpated Doctor Ballard, faulted President Harris, and praised Chief Bosco. But it obscured the militant leftist thread that Nick and Laura had exposed — Laura commendably against her own side. She let go of Nick's arm.

"They killed our baby, Nick."

"Certainly split it," said Nick. "It names the Guevarans, but not the commie billionaire behind them, Gregory Lanos. It quotes Ballard channeling Gandalf, but leaves out his anti-Christian rant on the balcony. And it practically blames Lassiter for starting the riot."

"I detest her views but she's in no way responsible."

"Welcome to Media Bias One-O-One. Now you know what us conservatives have put up with all these years."

Laura sighed. "No one will know what our contribution was. And what we went through to get it."

"Russell and Henley will know. They're bound to reassign us in the future."

"Great."

"Okay, so we're not overnight sensations. And it's back to

the copyaide station for now. You coming in with me or an hour later?"

"Later," Laura said. "I've some things to do first."

"Like tell Phil you're moving in with me."

Laura squirmed. "He thinks I spent last night at Sarah's. I intended to."

Nick was unpleasantly surprised. "Why?"

"I've decided I need to separate our personal and professional relationship."

"A little late for that, isn't it?" said Nick, irritated.

"It all happened so fast, Nick. I was just getting used to us being lovers. Next thing I know, we're partners on a major story."

"One thing led to the other."

"Precisely. It's as if I slept my way to a career upgrade. Something I swore I'd never do."

"But you did," said Nick.

Laura looked bitterly at him.

"With two qualifiers," Nick said. "One, you're good enough to handle the job."

"What's the other?"

"I love you," said Nick.

Laura's face softened. "I may love you too, Nick."

"That leaves room for doubt," said Nick.

Dawn light streamed through the closet door shutters.

"I just need to spend some time apart from you to sort it out," said Laura. "You want me to be sure of us, don't you?"

"You're sure, Laura. You're just scared."

"Of you?" asked Laura, trying to sound dismissive.

"No. You know damn well I'd never hurt you. Of losing your religion."

"I'm an atheist."

"*That's* your religion," said Nick. "The key to the progressive kingdom. And I'm the heretic who can make you question your devotion to it. Then what would become of your crusade?"

Laura looked uncomfortable. She stood up on the futon, and walked into the bathroom. Nick watched her bare ass, thinking he would never tire of that privilege. Hearing the shower start, he closed his eyes. He reopened them eighteen minutes later, to see a fully-dressed Laura kneeling beside him on the futon. She smelled enticingly of pine, his shampoo an aphrodisiac on her. She kissed him sweetly on the mouth.

"See you in three hours," she said, and backed out of his sight.

Nick heard the front door close behind her. He didn't like the sound of it.

Part Three

The Compliance Decree

39

When Nick walked into the copyaide station, Mike and Warren greeted him like a brother, abandoning the full mail crate on the table.

"Nick!" Mike said. "Are we glad to see you."

"We missed you," said Warren.

"Cut the crap, guys," Nick said. "I know you wanna get back to your cushy desk jobs."

"Why, Nick, the thought hadn't occurred to us," said Mike. "I'm outa here."

He started for the newsroom exit.

"Hold up, Mike," Nick said.

Mike stopped and turned to Nick.

"What're you guys doing after work?" Nick asked.

"Mixing songs for Tammy's Halloween bash tomorrow night," said Warren. "Superheroes and villains theme. You two are invited—against my advice."

"What's Tammy's gonna be?" Mike asked.

"Cougar Woman."

"I'm there!" said Mike.

"Hey," Warren said reproachfully.

Mike and Nick laughed.

"Gym night for me," Mike said, then to Nick. "Wanna join?"

"I'll skip this session," Nick said, rubbing his right bicep. "Had a little too much batting practice last night."

"Yeah, we read your college story," said Warren. "Great job by you and Laura."

"You got a better idea for tonight?" Mike asked Nick.

"'Star Force Three — Earth Fights Back'."

"Saw it yesterday," Warren said. "But I'll go again."

"And defy Tammy?" asked Nick.

"I'm my own man," said Warren, sheepishly adding, "For a few more hours."

"Didn't take you for a Star Force geek," Mike said.

"I'm not," said Nick. "I'm interested in the director of it for a story idea."

"Dwight Melnick," said Warren.

"Seeing as you clearly have the nose for a good story, I'm in," Mike said. "Where and when?"

"Uptown Theater, five forty-five."

"I'll beam over," said Mike.

"Wrong franchise," Warren said. "The Forcers would 'vap' you."

"Geez," said Mike. "I better go before I grow pointed ears."

"Antennae," Warren said.

"Wrong franchise," said Nick.

Mike shook his head and left through the open doorway. Nick and Warren attacked the mail crate on the table. Hugh came in just before ten, bearing another full crate of mail. He smiled to see Nick.

"Welcome back."

"Thanks, Hugh."

"The lovely Miss London here too?"

"Any minute."

"See you guys tonight, if not before," said Warren, exiting toward the newsroom.

Hugh looked questioningly at Nick.

"'Star Force Three'," Nick said. "And you're drafted."

"Great. I'll have a force field against girls all day."

Nick laughed. He and Hugh began sorting the mail.

"So, three hot nights with Laura," said Hugh. "Discuss."

"Did you read our story?"

"Yeah. Now I want to hear it," said Hugh. "The good part—you and Miss London."

"Totally professional."

"Oh, come on."

"Okay, not totally," said Nick.

"Ha. You're my hero."

"Because of my journalistic prowess."

"And your carnalistic one."

"No more of that talk, Hugh."

"Oh man. You *are* in love with her."

Nick nodded. He and Hugh concentrated on the mail. Laura strode into the station.

"It's the Rat Pack together again," she said.

"What's she talking about, Dino?" asked Hugh.

"Search me, Frankie," Nick said. "I don't speak doll talk."

"And they told me the Post was a woke workplace," said Laura.

"Not this rabbit hole," said Hugh.

"Good thing you two can't breed," said Laura.

"But we can marry," Nick said.

"Except you let *her* come between us," Hugh said overdramatically, nodding at Laura.

"She went to a finer school than you," said Nick.

Hugh made a wounded face. Laura smiled. The three of them sorted mail. Susan Machado emerged from her office.

"Thank God, my 'A' team is back. Miss London, Mr. Jarrett, kudos on your nice article."

"Thank you, Susan," said Nick and Laura.

"Keep it up, and I may have two openings to fill, sooner than expected."

Nick and Laura beamed.

"Why not three?" asked Hugh.

"Are you planning to leave us, Mr. Sinclair?"

"No. I just thought I might be promoted in the near future."

"Let's make it 'the' future," said Susan.

Hugh moped exaggeratedly. Susan turned to Laura.

"Laura, they need assistance on the Foreign Desk, till ten at night. Can you take it?"

"Bien sur, madame," Laura said in a perfect French accent.

"Good, you can start now. I'll note your extra hours."

Susan retreated into her office.

"Au revoir, paysans," Laura said, moving toward the open doorway.

She stopped and spun around, raising her right fist. "Vive la Revolucion!"

Nick and Hugh watched her depart.

"Mount Holyoake," Nick said.

"All women," said Hugh.

They both nodded.

Nick took the internal mail run at eleven. Approaching the Metro Desk, he saw Frank Russell editing a story. Nick wished the writer of it better luck than he and Laura had. He paused beside Russell. The editor turned to him.

"Jarrett."

Nick waited.

"You're wondering what happened to your special feature," Russell said.

Nick looked at him.

"It was good," said Russell. "You and London did a great job. Henley thought so too. We wanted to run it just like you wrote it."

Nick raised his eyebrows to express, "Why didn't you?"

"Politics, kid," said Russell. "Newsroom politics. Craig Yellen is National Desk. National News drives the digital edition of the Post. And the digital edition ..."

"Keeps us in business," said Nick.

"Yep. As Snyder lets us know every chance he gets."

Russell pointed over his shoulder at the National Desk. Nick glanced that way. National Chief Editor Paul Snyder sat talking into his desk phone. He was a thirty-something dandy with black mop hair, wearing a blue pinstriped shirt, red tie, and tortoise shell glasses.

"I figure when he read your story, he saw it was better than his golden boy, Yellen's. And for a supposedly soft feature, harder hitting. He couldn't let that stand."

"So he just stomped it," said Nick.

"Like I said, I fought for your version. Henley was on our side. He just didn't think it was worth pissing off Snyder for."

Russell leaned closer to Nick, and spoke low.

"Between you and me, Snyder was on the Lassiter protest train. His section leans that way. Someday, I'd like to wipe the smirk off his yuppie face."

"Thanks for the support anyway," said Nick.

"Well, I owe you one. People here know how good you are, and London too. There'll be another shot for you two."

Nick finished his mail run at the Foreign Desk. Laura smiled at him, although somewhat reservedly. Whatever was bothering her still loomed, he thought. They could address it tonight. Nick gave Laura Russell's postmortem on their collaboration, including the few rays of sunshine.

"So we're still a team," Nick said.

"Theoretically."

Nick thought he caught a double meaning in that but let it go.

"Lunch?" he asked.

"I can't. We're waiting on a big Euro conference in Berlin, with the Secretary of State. Vasquez will be reporting from there round that time."

"Foreign correspondent, how romantic," said Nick. "Mel Gibson in *The Year of Living Dangerously*. Something to aim for, eh?"

"The only country you'd fit in, Nick, is Saudi Arabia."

"It's getting too liberal for me. Women can drive there now." Laura snorted.

"I'll drop by at ten to take you home," Nick said.

"You don't have to do that."

"Sure I do. Supposed to snow tonight. And you're my lookout now."

"What if I decide to go to Sara's?" Laura probed.

Nick hesitated for just a moment.

"Then I'll see you to your ride, and end my watch on you."

Laura understood. As long as she was with Nick, he would protect her with his life. The absence of any danger hardly mattered, only their bond did, and only she could break it. If or when she did, Nick would shut her out, no matter how much it hurt him. She'd read about such men in books, like Denys Finch Hatton in *Out of Africa*, but never known any. Now one loved her, and perhaps she did him, against her ideological grain. She was in a classic head-versus-heart dilemma, her body clearly on the heart side.

"See you here," said Laura.

Nick started for the copyaide station, feeling a slight chill in his spine.

40

Laura performed superbly during the Berlin conference, fielding unrelated calls while Foreign Desk Editor Victor Hopkins — a lean, soldierly Englishman with a trim beard and Oxford accent — dealt with the main event. At five o'clock, Hopkins gave Laura a half hour "tea" break. She ducked into the copyaide station to see if Nick could join her but found it vacant. She went out through the back door, and turned right into Editorial.

The Editorial Department comprised of a broad, comfortable reception room with an open corridor entrance at the center, reflecting a more serene and intellectual atmosphere than the newsroom. The orange-carpeted corridor ran fifty feet to four offices on each side. Passage into the corridor was past the right of a red wood desk with two plush brown armchairs facing it. Sarah Woronov sat behind the desk, looking at the sleek desktop monitor. She brightened on seeing Laura.

"Laura London. It's been years."

"Three days."

"An eternity here without you, and chauvinist pigs all around."

"I'll bet," smiled Laura. "Wanna go for coffee? I have half an hour."

Sarah pointed to a fancy coffee machine by the left wall. "Editorial's a prestigious outfit. Have a seat. I'll make you a cappuccino."

Laura sat down in the right visitor's chair as Sarah walked to the coffee machine. She stood a Styrofoam cup under the spigot and pressed two buttons. In less than a minute, the cup filled up. Sarah handed it to Laura and retook her desk chair.

"I got your text last night," said Sarah. "Short and direct. 'Can't make it tonight. Sorry.'"

"I meant to call you but didn't have the chance."

"Phil did, four times."

"Four," Laura repeated with unease.

"He knew you were due back from your college thing last night. Nice story by the way, even with Nick sharing it."

"Phil tried to get a hold of me too. I'd turned my phone off. Needed to clear my head."

"Why? Where were you last night?"

"Promise you won't yell at me?"

"Oh no ..."

"I was with Nick."

"No!" balked Sarah. "No, no, no! At the university too?!"

"Since the night of my party."

"Jesus Christ, Laura!"

"I know, I know. But he's very sweet once you cut through the veneer."

"You need a blowtorch."

"And he makes me laugh. I hadn't done that for a long time."

"With good reason. Men like Nick."

"He's in love with me," said Laura.

"Who isn't?"

"Aw, Sarah. It'd be so much easier with you."

"Are you in love with *him*?"

"I ... I think so."

"God! Listen to you. How can you do this to me?"

"I'm still with you, Sarah."

"You're sleeping with the enemy! He'll have you turned around before you know it."

"You're wrong," said Laura. "I've been softening *him* up. Making him more tolerant."

"You think so, huh. Let me show you how that's working out."

Sarah started typing on her keyboard.

"Here's an Op-Ed we're running next week. Rick Spencer sent it to Lowenstein. She thinks it's satire."

"And what is it?" asked Laura.

"Enemy propaganda," said Sarah.

She began reading aloud from the screen. "The New Man—formerly known as 'wimp'—has been around since Genesis. Adam could have stayed in Eden after his girlfriend took a bite of the apple. Instead, he took the Fall for her, and got booted out of Paradise. Today, women are still driving men out—of their minds. That could be their mistress plan. Make men crazy enough, so they'll be able to understand women ..."

"My God," said Laura, seething. "Who wrote that?"

"Take a guess."

Laura gasped. "Nick?"

Sarah nodded and read more. "'The New Man Test'—by Nick Jarrett. Catchy title, huh? That's how he thinks, Laura. It's who he is. And he's very close to being a staff writer here. Once he's in the club, he'll be a real threat. A new Sean Hannity, only wittier. He'll damage us."

Laura felt like she was falling, and grabbed her chair's armrests for support.

"But he's been really good to me," she said, and regretted it the moment she did.

"Christ, listen to yourself," said Sarah. "A week ago you were mocking Nick. Now you're under him, in every sense. He's the poster boy for white male privilege, yet 'he's been really good to you.' You can't be a part of that, Laura. Part of him."

"You're right," said Laura. "I can't be."

"You've got to hit him, Laura, hard. It's the only way to stop him, and regain your power."

Laura nodded grimly, her eyes moistening.

41

The Uptown Theater on Connecticut Avenue in Cleveland Park is one of the last of the old movie palaces. Its seventy feet long, forty feet high, curved single screen ranks among the best in the country, making it the favorite DC showcase for epic motion pictures since the theater opened in 1936. Films that premiered there include *Spartacus*, *West Side Story*, *Lawrence of Arabia*, *2001: A Space Odyssey*, *The Shining*, *Apocalypse Now*, and *Full Metal Jacket*. It was currently showing *Star Force 3: Earth Fights Back*. Approaching the neon-bright marquee with Hugh, Nick fully expected to be let down by the latest title.

As a classic movie fan, he'd grown increasingly bored by the infantile, pyrotechnical, antiseptic entertainment fare aimed at his age group and younger. He'd seen whole cities wiped out on screen, always with less thrill than a single swipe of Toshiro Mifune's sword, or Keir Dullea blasting himself from a space pod to the mother ship without a space helmet.

It was another cold night, the air thick with an imminent preseason snowfall that Washington media had been warning about like Armageddon. Nick wore his aviator coat and Irish tweed cap, Hugh his double-breasted faux-fur cashmere. A short line of moviegoers stood to the left of the old-fashioned ticket booth. Most were iGen males, except for a pretty, thirty-ish, high-cheekboned brunette in a navy blue down coat near the back of the line with a boy of around ten. Hugh smiled suavely at the woman as he and Nick went by to take their place in line.

"Those clowns better be saving us good seats," Hugh said.

"In the Earth bleachers," said Nick. "We don't wanna get 'vapped' for cheering on the home team."

Hugh stared at the brunette's backside two places ahead. He left his spot next to Nick and walked up to her.

"Excuse me, miss," said Hugh, pulling out his wallet from his back pocket.

The woman turned pleasantly to him. Hugh showed her his Washington Post press card.

"Hugh Sinclair, Washington Post. I'm doing a story on family-friendly entertainment, like this movie."

Nick shook his head.

"Is your kid brother a Star Force fan?"

"He's my son," said the young mother.

Hugh looked incredulous. "What? No way. You look like you should be sweating midterms at G-U."

The mother smiled fetchingly.

"Billy's nine," she said, as if to validate Hugh's opinion of her youthfulness.

"I'll be ten next month," said Billy, appearing ready to protect his mother from Hugh.

Hugh drew an unofficial Washington Post business card from his wallet and handed it to the woman.

"Being a single man myself," he said suggestively. "I could use more input on this assignment—if and when you have the time."

"Sure," said the mother, pocketing the card.

The line moved forward. Hugh stepped beside Nick, no longer the last in line. Nick looked disapprovingly at him.

"What?" Hugh asked.

"She's a mom, Hugh."

"Right, so she's perfect for me. She'll want a break from sexual monotony but can't risk her setup by cramping my style."

"What if her husband finds out?"

"Then he'll know his wife's a slut, and that he's been living a lie. I'd be doing him a favor, man to man."

"There's a logic to that that disturbs me," said Nick.

"Or she could be a divorcee."

"A DILF."

"Who can't jeopardize her alimony," said Hugh. "Either way, it's a win-win for me."

"Not if Susan catches you handing out unofficial Post cards. She'll fire your ass."

"Hey, I'm gonna end up in Harvard Law anyway. The Post is just my resume enhancer."

Moving forward, they saw Mike crossing the street to join them.

"What the hell," Hugh said. "You're supposed to be inside with Warren, saving us seats."

"Warren's gone," said Mike. "That's why I'm late."

"What do you mean 'gone'?" asked Nick.

"I waited for him in Sports like we agreed. He didn't show. Went by Style. Nelson said he took off with Tammy. I called and texted him...no response."

"Tammy must've cracked the whip," said Nick.

"Tammy with a whip..." Hugh said reflectively.

"And stiletto boots..." said Mike on Hugh's wavelength.

"I'm sitting by myself," Nick said.

From the movie theater, they walked into the outdoor section of Maggie's Pizzeria, shielded from the chill by a transparent plastic tarp.

"Man, that was lame," Mike said.

"Part threes always suck," said Nick. "It's like a rule. You got Die Hard Three, Terminator Three, Alien Three, Godfather Three –"

"College Vixens Three," said Hugh.

Nick and Mike turned to him.

"So I've heard," said Hugh, clearing his throat.

"Well look who's there," Mike said.

Directly ahead, Warren sat alone at a four-place table, looking miserable and unsteady, a half-empty beer mug in hand.

"And not looking too good," said Nick.

The three friends sat down at Warren's table. He barely acknowledged them through reddish eyes.

"Hey, Warren," Mike said. "Been here long?"

"At least two of those," said Hugh, nodding at the quarter-full beer mug.

"I have not yet begun to drink," Warren said, slurring his words.

"I know what this is," said Hugh. "I know the signs. Chick trouble."

"Where's Tammy?" asked Nick.

"Preparing for her party...without me," Warren said, then added with a tragic expression. "She dumped me."

Hugh gave Nick a knowing glance.

"When?" asked Nick.

"Why?" asked Mike.

"Like three hours ago," Warren said. "I don't *know* why."

"Sorry, dude," said Mike.

"Look on the bright side," Hugh said. "One week with Tammy could be a record."

"Shut up," said Warren.

Nick shot Hugh a disapproving look.

"What happened, War?" Nick asked.

"I spent last night with her. It was awesome. Cheesy word, I know, but I can't describe it any better, what it feels like being with Tammy. We came to work together. Around five o'clock, I'm getting ready to meet you guys, and she asks me to come to the Post Pub. Then she let me have it. She really likes me, she said, but only as a friend."

"The F-word," said Hugh and Mike almost in unison.

"What'd I do wrong?!" cried Warren. "What didn't I do?"

A busty, brown ponytailed waitress appeared beside the table with an order checklist. Hugh visually approved.

"Hello, boys."

"We're not boys, we're newspapermen," said Hugh, flashing the waitress his press card. "Hugh Sinclair, Washington Post."

"Wow, cool."

"I'm doing a story on DC's hottest waitresses, and you more than qualify."

"Really?" gushed the waitress.

"Absolutely."

Hugh handed the waitress one of his illicit Post business cards. She looked at it while he read her nametag. Nick shook his head.

"Call me for an interview—Sharon," Hugh said. "Dinner on the Post."

"Will do that, Hugh. Thanks."

"Okay if we order now?" Mike asked Hugh.

"What can I get you guys?" said Sharon.

"Large pepperoni with mushrooms, pitcher of beer."

Sharon cheerfully departed. Warren gulped down the last of his beer.

"You should switch to coffee," said Nick.

Warren looked ghoulishly at his friends.

"You guys are so damn smart," he said. "How do I get Tammy back?"

The other three exchanged uncertain looks.

"You got one chance," said Hugh. "But you're not gonna like it."

"Tell me."

"Cut out the friend act. You both know it's bullshit."

Nick nodded.

"Act like she means nothing to you," said Hugh. "Just another chick you banged."

"I can't do that," Warren said.

"I know," said Nick.

"Hey," said Mike, looking out the tarp's plastic window. "Thar she blows."

Nick and Hugh followed his gaze to see snow falling fast

and thick on Connecticut Avenue. Nick shivered slightly despite the toasty heat inside the tarp. Mike noticed it.

"You okay, Nick?"

"So fair and foul a day I have not seen," said Nick broodily.

"Something's wrong," Hugh said. "He's quoting English lit again."

"Macbeth," said Nick. "You know, Shakespeare was the Spielberg of his age. A writer-director himself, he used Nature to foreshadow trouble for his characters. I got a bad feeling about this snow."

Everyone but Warren stared at the snow.

42

Nick stepped out of McPherson Square Metro Station into a downtown winter wonderland lit by soft streetlamps. He turned left toward Franklin Park, snow white instead of green. He crossed Fourteenth Street to the park's southwest corner, walked south to K Street, and made a right. He stopped directly across from the Washington Post building, on the very spot he'd stood two weeks ago for the first time.

How his life had changed in such a short time, he thought, and for the better. Three bylines in the Post, a journalism career within reach, and an incomparably spirited, smart beauty for a girlfriend, partner, and, God willing, future bride. He gazed proudly at the seventh-floor newsroom lights glowing through the snowfall, believing himself to be a part of something fateful. For the first time, he appreciated the Post motto he'd once mocked as pretentious: *Democracy dies in darkness.*

Laura emerged from the front door, her maroon coat complimented by a grey French beret she could have modeled in Paris. Nick smiled at her. She frowned at him. It was the same expression she had often given him early in their acquaintance, before she found him lovable. He started toward her, but slowed halfway across the street, the snowfall feeling heavier somehow. Laura waited for him like an ice sculpture. His trademark half-moon wave failed to thaw her.

"I'm not coming with you, Nick," Laura said, her frosty tone chilling Nick more than the weather.

"What's wrong?" he asked, abandoning all playfulness.

"The New Man Test."

It took Nick a moment to grasp Laura's meaning, and identify the source of it.

"Sarah."

"You should be quite pleased with yourself," said Laura. "They're running it in Outlook, courtesy of your rising status at the Post. You'll forgive me if I don't congratulate you, much less kiss you, for it."

"Laura, listen to me. I wrote that the night of your party, before you came over. Remember how it was? Phil and your friends tried to fumigate me like a rodent. And you were right in there with 'em. I was hurt. But my piece was meant to be funny."

"The joke was on me, and women like me. But you left out one cliché. It's a woman's prerogative to change her mind. Or in my case, return to sanity. And I have, Nick, about you."

"Laura, please. We can talk about this back at my—"

"Let me finish. I fell for you in a moment of weakness. It will never happen again. I'm going back to Phil, and our lost causes. When I see you at work, I'll be cordial. But know this, Nick, I'd prefer never to see you again."

"I can't believe that," said Nick.

"You will eventually."

"Didn't our time together mean something to you?"

"It did. A huge mistake."

"I love you."

"That's your problem," said Laura.

Nick winced. But Laura wasn't done with him.

"Has it ever occurred to you, Nick, that the thing you're proudest of is what you should be most ashamed of—your maleness?"

Nick shuddered. Laura noticed it.

"Are you all right?"

"For a moment there, I thought I felt a sledgehammer," said Nick.

Dim headlight beams illuminated the falling snow around them. A beige Toyota Camry came to a stop nearby. Nick made out Sarah's dark form behind the wheel. He couldn't be sure, but she seemed to be smirking.

"Goodbye, Nick," Laura said, and climbed into the passenger seat.

He watched the Camry pull away, and fade into the snowfall. He stood on the sidewalk, feeling gut-punched for another minute. Then he began to walk, mindlessly, aimlessly, like a shell-shocked soldier in the Ardennes. He turned left on Fourteenth Street, heading south. He passed his McPherson Square Metro transportation point and kept walking.

Some incalculable time later, he found himself in the National Mall near the Washington Monument. For the first time, he was left cold by its magnificence. He made a right on the north path, keeping the tall obelisk on his left. The only other pedestrian in sight was a purple-scarfed old bulldog walker heading his way. Nick approached the Lincoln Memorial Reflecting Pool, reflecting now lighter snow. The glowing Greek temple at the far end beckoned him like a beacon in his darkness. He passed between the center two Ionic columns and went inside.

The interior was deserted apart from the Jovian marble giant on his throne. Nick stopped far back enough from the ten-foot-high pedestal to take in the sixteenth President of the United States. He had written his junior-year term paper on the Civil War, and postulated a controversial idea, even for the University of Wyoming. He remembered his introductory sentence. *Since the very founding of the country, God has blessed America with the finest men at precisely the worst crises in its history.* But for the figure towering before him, Nick thought, the United States today would now be two separate Soviet satellites.

"Hello, Abe," said Nick. "You helped Mr. Smith come to Washington. How 'bout me? Though I'm not really a Frank Capra guy. More Howard Hawks. My trouble's pretty silly when compared to all of yours…Okay, it's a girl. The most aggravating, wonderful girl I ever met. I know. You had an easier time abolishing slavery than dealing with your woman. Maybe that's my destiny too—putting down sedition over love. In your day, it was North against South. Today, it's Left versus Right—with Laura on the wrong side. But unlike your troops, I can't just shoot the enemy, unless…Maybe I can. Maybe Lord Lytton was right, that the pen is mightier than the sword. Then my laptop would be even mightier…Yes, by God! This will be my Sherman's March! They drew first blood—taking Laura from me. Now it's my turn. I'll slaughter every one of their sacred cows! The show must go on!…Um, sorry, Abe. I guess you're not too fond of shows."

43

It was barely snowing as Nick walked north on 23d Street toward the Foggy Bottom Metro Station, now with renewed purpose. The spectral stillness around him matched his mood. Just before midnight, his cellphone rang. Nick hoped it might be Laura, calling for his forgiveness. It was Lee Kwan, his indispensable ally on the Alice Lassiter protest story.

"Hey, Lee. How's school?"

"A lot quieter since you left."

"Yeah, that was a riot," said Nick.

"I've got something for you."

"You on a secure line?"

"That's not such a joke," said Lee. "Because there is a conspiracy—of politics and art."

"You turned up PHAT."

"Progressive Hollywood Action Time. The more I looked into them, the creepier it gets."

"Spill it," said Nick, interest overcoming his funk.

"You were right about them. They have their boot on the entire movie business. I took a look at their server. It was pretty well encrypted. It's no surprise why. Every current actor, producer, and director you've ever heard of—and a hundred you haven't -- is a contributing member of PHAT, dedicated to one main goal."

"Bringing down the President."

"Yes. And not just politically. Some of their communications are pretty bloodthirsty."

"I can imagine," said Nick.

"Of course PHAT funds a bunch of leftwing Democrats."

"That's a redundancy."

"But they have a more subversive agenda," said Lee. "I gleaned it from one of their emails—to the top literary agencies in LA and New York. I'm sending it to you."

"Can you read it to me? I'm walking in the snow."

"Okay, here's the gist," Lee said, then read aloud. 'Any screenplay submission to a PHAT signee that has been recommended for production will be vetted by our Compliance Department ...'"

"Compliance Department?! That sounds like the House of Un-American Activities Committee."

"'For adherence to the following Compliance Decree ...'"

"Decree," said Nick. "As in Manifesto?"

"There are ten rules listed. Wanna hear 'em?"

"I'm almost afraid to. Shoot."

"One—three or more heteronormative relationships must be counterbalanced by at least one LGBT one."

"Pretty good ratio for four percent of the population," said Nick.

"Two—one or more villains of a racial minority must be counterbalanced by at least one white male."

"A bad guy diversity program."

"Three—one or more Muslim villains must be counterbalanced by at least one positive Muslim character."

"I got no problem with that one," said Nick.

"Four—overtly conservative characters, including police and military, must be shown in a neutral or negative light, so as not to appear as role models."

"Mama, don't let your babies grow up to be cowboys."

"Five—overtly Christian characters must be shown in a neutral or negative light, so as not to appear as role models."

"Or altar boys."

"Six—female sexuality must be de-emphasized."

"Any Meryl Streep picture will do that," said Nick.

"Seven—female domesticity must be de-emphasized."

"Stay-at-work moms only."

"Eight—a male hero must not display any salacious interest in a woman based on her physical appearance."

"Goodbye, Mr. Bond," said Nick.

"Nine—a heroine in combat must be as formidable as any male counterpart, including against male combatants."

"Hello, *Ms.* Bond."

"Ten—a heroine in peril must extricate herself from danger with no male assistance."

"Back off, Batman, she's got this."

Lee read more. "Submissions that comply with this Decree may be greenlit for production. Noncompliance will reflect negatively on the submitting agency."

"That sounds like a threat," Nick said excitedly, Laura's betrayal momentarily forgotten.

"Signed—Dwight Melnick, Chairman, Progressive Hollywood Action Time."

"We got 'em, Lee!" exclaimed Nick.

"Wait, you can't use this. It was clandestinely acquired."

"I know, with top secret equipment," said Nick impatiently. "There's got to be a way around that. Some kind of Metro News angle."

"I'm way ahead of you. Local author Stuart Harrow. He had a book-to-movie deal with Titan Pictures. The PHAT Compliance Department seems to have put a sudden end to it."

"Stuart Harrow," said Nick. "Name rings a bell."

"Mystery writer."

"Oh yeah. I read a review of his first novel, around a year ago. *The Redeemer*, I think it was called. Private eye stuff, with a twist. I meant to read it. You have his contact info?"

"I'll text it to you. He lives in Richmond, Virginia."

"How appropriate," said Nick.

"Why?"

"Confederate capital, Civil War."

"I don't follow."

"'He is trampling out the vintage where the grapes of wrath are stored.'"

"You've lost me."

"Never mind. Thanks, Lee, for everything."

"Don't mention it. And I mean don't mention it."

Nick smiled.

"Later," Lee said, and hung up.

"All right, Laura," Nick said aloud. "You started this war.

Now I'm gonna wage it. And my first target will be your side's cultural and financial base—Hollywood."

He sped up his pace, a new spring in his step.

Frank Russell had little trouble sleeping at night. Fielding Metro stories on deadline took a physical toll, even sitting on his butt all day. He recalled having had more energy as a Baltimore Sun police reporter, scurrying to crime scenes, drinking with the cops, then playing with his young son and daughter at home, and afterward his wife. But that youth was long gone. Of course, he and Jessica being empty nesters made his home life a lot more restful. He could never make it through the Conan O'Brien show each night without dozing off.

In the master bedroom of his two-story Logan Circle townhouse, Russell got down to his boxer shorts. Jessica lay asleep on the left side of the bed, night table lamp on, her latest black romance paperback open spine up on her stomach. Russell tenderly lifted the book, put it on her night table, and turned off the lamp.

Moving to the bed's right side, he got under the covers and switched off his lamp. He was dead asleep when the phone rang. News emergency, he instantly thought, groping for the phone. Looking at the caller ID, he could hardly believe the name—Nick Jarrett.

"You better have found a dead body," Russell snarled, low enough to not wake up Jessica.

"No, sir," said Nick. "But a story nonetheless."

"Can't it wait till tomorrow?"

"I'll be chasing it tomorrow, and need cover with Susan. You did say you owed me one."

"What are you after?"

"A new Hollywood blacklist, only this time against conservatives."

"That would be for the National Desk," said Russell. "And they don't like you."

"There's a local author—well, Richmond. But his book is DC-set. Stuart Harrow. He's agreed to talk to me, on the record, but only in person. I'm taking the morning train tomorrow."

"Hmm," said Russell with increased interest. "You need me to cover London too?"

"No, she's…otherwise engaged."

Russell heard the pain in Nick's voice, and understood. The personal had ruined the professional, not for the first or last time.

"Sorry to hear it. You guys are good together."

"Yeah, we were," said Nick.

"All right, Jarrett. I'll make it an official Metro assignment."

"Thank you, sir."

"I guess Hollywood deserves a good smackdown."

"For its rampant sexual abuse?"

"No for making crappy movies."

44

The Richmond-bound Amtrak train exited the Union Station tunnel early Friday morning. It was rather empty, reminding Nick that Washington was the magnet for northern Virginia. The bloating of the federal government under the previous Administration had infused DC's southern suburb with excess liberals, turning a once dependable red state almost solidly blue. A shame, Nick thought, revering the limited-government demigods who came from there, led by George Washington and Thomas Jefferson. Both would be appalled at the intrusive behemoth their handiwork had mutated into.

He sat in a rear right window seat, iPod earbuds on, down-loading the audiobook of Stuart Harrow's novel, *The Redeemer*. His laptop case, bombardier coat, and Irish tweed cap lay on the vacant seat beside him. Nick thought he would need the warm wear. Although rain now sprinkled the window, more snow was forecast. Having never been to Richmond, he wanted to enjoy the scenery instead of book print for the three-hour train ride. And listening to one would better keep his mind from Laura—he hoped.

He'd had a rotten night once the adrenaline surge for the new story came down. Lying alone on his futon had loosened the depressing thought that he would never again be intimate with Laura. It was bad enough to be dumped by the only woman he'd ever loved, let alone be damned by her for his beliefs. This had led to his overnight questioning of them, if perhaps to get her back.

It would be so easy to be a liberal, he thought. Just pretend that terminating unborn life isn't killing babies but a woman's right. That blacks are helpless victims, repressed by past slavery and modern racism rather than the absence of fathers in the home and needing government welfare to subsist. That there's no physical difference between men and women, who can switch genders like socks. That guns commit murder of their own volition yet are opposed to saving lives for some reason. That America abolishing its nuclear arsenal will inspire worldwide disarmament. That taxing carbon emissions will cool any climate other than the economic one. That capitalism is unfair, but socialism utopianist—never mind Cuba, Venezuela, North Korea, and everywhere it's been tried. After several sleepless hours, Nick had reached the same conclusion. His convictions built western civilization, Laura's would collapse it. And yet he almost longed to be on the road to chaos with her.

The book narration commenced, read by the deep, manly voice of actor Richard Salkind.

> I approached the Gentlemen's Delight Club wearing the right look for the joint: white tennis shoes, dark blue jeans, light yellow jacket over a blue-grey sweatshirt, and a guilty expression on my thirty-one-year-old face.

The one-story building stood alone in a small industrial block, so the tall sign showing the golden silhouette of a curvaceous nude female could shine proudly over the half-full parking lot. Outside the entrance, a bald bouncer stretching out a black t-shirt stared slightly down at me despite my six-foot height. He seemed underdressed for the chilly night, but a coat would have lessened the muscleman effect. He let me pass.

It was a rather upscale place for the titillation trade. A concrete corridor ran thirty yards to the back wall. Along the right side, from the entrance forward, were two bathroom doors, a swinging kitchen door, a long bar — manned by a white-shirted Latino and a black looker in pink off-shoulder blouse and beige yoga pants — and an office door beyond it. Three far-apart arches demarked the left wall, a red glow and percussive music emanating from within. I bypassed the Latino to stand before the sexy bartendress.

"What can I getcha?" she asked automatically.

"Scotch and water, and a little information," I said.

"One's nine bucks, the other maybe more."

I put a twenty-dollar bill on the bar. It was out of pocket, like every job I did for Cork, who always hid behind his vow of poverty. Bartendress turned to the Scotch bottles, showing me her admirable behind. She filled the proper glass and set it in front of me. She punched up the sleek cash register, lay my twenty in the drawer, and took out two bills.

"Keep it," I said.

"Don't you want it for the dancers?"

"I'd rather watch you with clothes on."

Bartendress smiled. She stuck the money in her tip glass, appraising me with intelligent brown eyes.

"You don't look like the stripper type," she said.

"You haven't seen me work a pole."

Bartendress laughed.

"How do they look?" I asked, hoping to blend in with the crowd.

"Kind'a sad. Even the rich guys. They dress nice, throw money around, and act all macho... but they're here for a fantasy, and can't hide the real loneliness inside."

"Maybe I can," I said.

Bartendress shook her head. "Too confident. I'm Cassie."

"Dan."

A brunette waitress in gold hot pants, black tank top, and grey tights came out the swinging kitchen door, carrying a tray with two hamburger platters. I sideways watched her stop at the right end of the bar. Latino Bartender plopped two beer bottles on the counter. The waitress put them on her tray, and passed behind me toward the middle arch. I turned back to a smiling Cassie.

"Where were we?" I asked.

"You're Dan."

"Oh yeah."

We exchanged smiles.

"What do you wanna know?"

I pulled out my phone, and found the photo of Heather Camp in her Whitman High cheerleader outfit, once more struck by the lovely, sweet, yet subtly haunted face between thick curtains of dark blonde hair. I showed Cassie the picture. She stared at it for a long moment, then let out a sigh.

"God, it's Erica."

"Erica…" I said reflectively.

"When was this taken?"

"Last year. Walt Whitman High School. Her real name's Heather Camp. Just turned eighteen."

"I knew she wasn't twenty-one," Cassie said, then suspiciously added, "Why are you looking for her? You her old man?"

"Nope. A friend of mine's worried about her. Asked me to help."

"Is he trustworthy?"

"He's a priest."

"I repeat the question," said Cassie.

I nodded. "He's a good man. I've known him a long time."

"And who are you?"

I showed Cassie my official District of Columbia Confidential Investigator's license, with a comforting picture of myself. It was a duller ID than "Dan Burnside, Private Eye," but Cassie seemed satisfied about my pure intentions.

"Center stage," she said. "She should be on soon."

"Thanks, Cassie."

"Something you should know. The boss is kind'a hot for her. He won't like losing her if it comes to that."

"*Guzman?*"

"Yeah."

I knew Red Guzman owned the place, and had some underworld connections. That made us even. I had some law enforcement ones.

"He'll live," I said. "Hopefully not for long."

"Get her out of here, Dan."

"Can I buy you a drink sometime … somewhere else?"

Cassie wrote down a phone number on a cocktail napkin and handed it to me.

"Be calling you," I said, and headed for the middle arch.

In the archway, I stepped aside for the exiting waitress, who gave me a tired smile. I entered the red-light district, actually a purplish illumination flooding the long oval stage and, more dimly, the broad spectator lounge. Wine-red chairs furnished the room, three around each small table, all facing the stage.

A third of the chairs were occupied by men between thirty and sixty, a rare mix of blue collar and white collar, some eating, all drinking and watching the stage. A fit brown stripper of indeterminate age, with dyed blonde hair and bare silicone breasts, was being imaginative on the left pole. About a dozen spectators stood near the stage, encouraging her with thrown bills. I took an empty chair set some twenty yards from the show, and waited for Heather Camp, AKA Erica, to appear.

She strutted out in a green knee-length kimono and spike heel shoes to Uprising by Muse. It took even my trained detective eye a moment to recognize her. No trace of the sweet, cute blonde high school girl remained in the erotic, crimson-lipped, thick-haired redhead gyrating on stage. Every *other man gaped lustfully at her. I might have too if I hadn't known her background. Yet when the kimono came off to reveal her voluptuous body busting out of a brown mesh bodysuit, I had to suppress my more primitive urges.*

Her strong cheerleader's legs dominated the right pole. Replanting both feet on the floor, she flung off her bodysuit to expose firm breasts and buttocks in black thong panties. Paper money flew at her. I got up and joined the men standing by the stage. When Erica crawled our way on all fours, I waved a hundred-dollar bill at her. Her long-lashes blinked twice in acknowledgement. I tossed her a twenty, and started back toward my seat.

I spotted two men watching me from the archway. One was another musclebound black t-shirted bouncer with shaggy blonde hair, the other a heavyset fiftyish guy with his grey-black hair combed back and a gold shirt open to mid-chest. Red Guzman, I ascertained, keeping tabs on his prize possession. Guzman said something to Blonde Bouncer, who nodded slightly, eying me like a hearty meal.

I nursed my drink in the chair, half watching a lanky Asian dancer writhe to David Bowie's China Girl. *How politically incorrect, I thought — as if strippers weren't. Then Erica appeared beside me, wearing her see-through bodysuit and a seductive smile. I took a deep breath to remind myself of the spiritual being inside that carnal face and desirable body.*

"Hi," she said huskily, sounding nothing like a teenager. "I'm Erica. What's your name?"

"Dan."

"You want a lap dance, Dan?" she asked, as if aroused by the thought.

"Sure."

Erica led me toward a green curtained section near the right wall. We passed several faces looking wistfully at her, and enviously at me. She parted the curtain for me, then closed it behind her.

We were in a space the size of an upscale changing room, only with a soft armchair instead of a bench. A small music player lay atop the single shelf on the left wall. Erica maneuvered me into the chair, then leaned her striking face and blatant breasts close to me.

"I'm gonna make you feel real good, baby."

Actually, I felt very uncomfortable, having left out sexual attraction from my mission planning. Erica took a mini-remote control off the shelf and clicked it. Low, sultry instrumental music began to play, nothing like the pounding rhythm from the stage. Erica swayed to it as in an erotic dream. Looking lasciviously at me, she straddled my legs. I'd heard lap dancers weren't allowed to touch customers, but she skirted that rule with her hands on my knees. She again moved her red lips close to mine, deceptively inviting me to kiss her.

"Heather," I said softly.

That shattered the spell. She recoiled from me, her face no longer desirous but afraid. She stared accusingly at me.

"Father Cork sent me," I said.

"He broke his vow!" Heather cried, her voice now that of a young girl. "He broke his vow!"

I shook my head.

"He didn't say a word. Just sent me a picture. I had

to work out the rest. It's an arrangement we got, so he doesn't violate the seal of the confessional."

"What'd you work out?" Heather asked meekly, as if fearful of the answer.

"That you left home for good reason, and that you need help, Father Cork's, but right now, mine."

"What's yours?"

"Let's say it's more physical than spiritual."

Heather looked torn for a moment, then made the wrong decision.

"You better go."

I had to talk fast, being almost out of lap-dance time, as no doubt clocked by Guzman.

"Heather, if you stay here, you'll be in the hands of scum, who want just one thing from you—your body. Your mind, your soul, are extra baggage to be ransacked. Till all that's left of you is a beautiful shell where a good Catholic girl used to be. When that cracks—and it will sooner than you think -- you'll be thrown out to the street like a broken doll. I've seen it, kid, and it's ugly ... Or you can come with me, now, to people who'll take care of you."

"Like daddy," she said, almost spitting the words.

"No," I said with feeling. "He'll never touch you again."

Tears appeared in Heather's eyes. "You know?"

I shrugged.

"Comes with the job," I said.

"He won't let me leave."

"Guzman? I'm sure he will."

Heather nodded. I stood up, took off my jacket and

held it open for her. She slipped into it, and pulled up the zipper.

"Been a while since I zipped up instead of down in here," she said.

"Good girl," I said, smiling. "Stay behind me."

I parted the green curtains and went out, followed closely by Heather. We started for the arch. Blonde Bouncer still stood under it, grinning at me in anticipation. He stepped forward, clenching his right fist. I got within his arm range, eyes at his chin level, and saw him pull back his fist. My UNC boxing coach, Jake Phillips, would have cursed him for telegraphing a punch. I did worse to him. I fired two left jabs at his jaw, rocking his head back, then threw a right punch to his stomach. It was gym hard, not ring hard. He grunted in pain, left hand on his belly, and took a wild right swing at me. I ducked it easily, and launched a right cross at his chin. He spun right, legs buckling, and fell against an empty chair.

Bald Bouncer appeared in the archway, not smiling like his pal had been. He approached me warily, his flat hands circling karate style. I knew this was a feint even before the roundhouse kick flew at my right rib. I blocked it with my right forearm. It hurt but did no damage. He followed with a left kick. I leapt right, creating a gap too far for his sweep, and trapped his spent leg under my left arm. I shot my right elbow into his knee pit and heard him shriek. Still holding the leg, I shoved his chest with my left palm and dropped him on his back. I rained hard blows on his chest and jaw. He stayed down, groaning.

Heather stepped around him and took my right hand. We walked out through the arch. Guzman stood in the corridor with his back to the bar, staring daggers at me. Behind the bar, Cassie looked on in approval, Latino Bartender with interest.

"Erica," Guzman said. "Where do you think you're going?

"Erica's already left," I said. "Now it's Heather's turn."

Guzman spat on the floor.

"Hey, asshole," he said. "Do you know who I am?!"

"Yeah. You're Moe Green. You made your bones when I was going out with cheerleaders."

Latino Bartender chuckled silently so the boss wouldn't hear him. Guzman seethed, and took a step toward me.

"Think twice," I said.

Guzman halted in mid-second step, raging. I led Heather by the hand out the front door.

Chapter two…

Nick paused the audiobook to analyze what he'd just heard. It was well enough written, if deliberately Chandleresque, like so many mystery writers tried to be. The hook was original—a moral hero acting as the worldly knight for a priest bound by the seal of the confessional. But more to the point, in just the first chapter, *The Redeemer* defied five of the ten guidelines in the PHAT Compliance Decree.

Nick checked the Decree on his cellphone. Number four—no sympathetic conservative character. Well the hero, Dan Burnside, certainly is just that. Number five—no sympathetic

Christian character. Father Patrick Cork certainly qualifies as that, if only by reference so far. Six—no overt female sexuality. It takes place in a strip club full of hot women. Eight—no ogling by the hero. Burnside ogles all the women, including the young girl he rescues, which also violates number ten—that a heroine must rescue herself.

Nick thoroughly approved of the forbidden sensibilities, but he could see how woke Hollywood might have a problem. Yet the book had sold decently, and been bought for six figures by Titan Pictures. It seemed to be the Hollywood dream—until PHAT entered the picture and turned it into a nightmare. Exactly how they did this was what Nick hoped to expose. He restarted the audiobook on Chapter Two.

45

Stuart Harrow lived in a cottage-style house near the James River in Woodland Heights. The blue ground floor had black window frames and a black front door. A second floor lurked somewhere within the in-slanted grey roof, discernible by two white gull windows telescoping outward. A rose brick path split the tiny lawn. Nick walked it in a drizzle from his Uber to the front door, seeing no sign of a six-figure windfall from *The Redeemer*.

He rang the doorbell. Awaiting a response, he read the words on the brown welcome mat: *Christ is the head of this house*. But He don't have much clout in Hollywood, Nick thought, beginning to comprehend Harrow's alienation. The door was opened by an attractive, slender, fortyish woman with short grey hair. She wore a light blue sweater and a long green wool skirt.

"I hope you're Nick from the Washington Post," she said with a cheerful smile.

"Yes, ma'am."

"Call me Janet. I have to say, you look young enough to be delivering the paper instead of writing for it."

"If I don't come up with a good story, I probably will be," Nick said.

Janet laughed and opened wide the door. "Come on in."

Nick entered a wood-floored foyer with a staircase just four feet across from the right of the door. A wooden coat rack further narrowed the right passageway. It led away from the small Americana-decored living room to dead end at a closed white door. Janet indicated the coat rack, on which hung a yellow ski jacket.

"It wants your cap and coat," she said.

Nick started to hang up both after removing the digital recorder from his coat pocket.

"Tea or coffee?"

"Coffee, please. Cream and sugar."

Janet pointed to the white door and spoke conspiratorially.

"My husband's having a productive writing day, so it's safe to go in there now."

Nick smiled and walked the few paces right to the door. He knocked lightly.

"Come in," said a male voice.

Nick stepped into a cozy study that made full use of its tight space. The right wall had two tall packed bookshelves. The wet rear window showed a sliver of yard and the wood fence beyond. A metal desk hugged the back left corner. A large Apple monitor screen shared the desk with two standing photos, one of a hiking, robust Janet, the other of a handsome boy and girl in their late teens. The computer keyboard lay on a pullout slab. Stuart Harrow tucked it in before swiveling his chair to face Nick.

He was in his late fifties, slim and pale, with grey-streaked red hair, white facial stubble, and sharp blue eyes unblunted by square black glasses. A grey sweatshirt and sweatpants seemed to offer him long-term sitting comfort. He stood up and shook Nick's hand.

"Stuart Harrow."

"Nick Jarrett."

Janet entered gracefully, despite the Ikea-style dining chair she carried.

"I could have brought that," said Nick, grabbing the front of the chair.

"It's not heavy," said Janet, setting down the chair beside Nick. "Coffee and tea coming right up."

She exited even more lithely. Harrow indicated the guest chair.

"Have a seat," he said, sitting down himself.

Nick did, and turned on the digital recorder on his lap.

"So you want to know about my brush with show business," said Harrow. "The lights, the glamor, the beautiful women, the whirring cameras ..."

"Sounds exciting," said Nick.

"Yes, did to me too. 'Course I never experienced any of that—well, maybe the beautiful assistant at Titan Pictures, but the only thing she gave me was bottled water."

"Beats tap."

"Do you know my book, 'The Redeemer'?"

"I listened to about half of it on the way down. It's really good."

"Thanks."

"I read a lot of mysteries," said Nick. "Yours has a very original hook—a private eye aiding a priest who's bound by the seal of the confessional, and who can only nudge him in the right direction."

"That hook is known as a 'high concept' in the 'biz—or as we 'insiders' call it, 'the Industry'. Anyway, 'The Redeemer', the novel, did rather well. Sold about fifty-thousand copies, so far."

"You got a good review in 'Cloak and Dagger'," said Nick.

"But nothing in the New York Times, USA Today, NPR, or your paper, which limited its sales."

"I wonder why."

"Do you really?"

"Let me see," said Nick. "Christian male hero, damsels in distress, sultry femmes fatale, old school morals—pretty traditionalist stuff. So how'd you get a movie deal? Hollywood's PC land."

"My New York agent, Charles Owen, is a closet Republican. He knows Sam Weinberg, one of the three heads of Titan, and sold him on my book."

"Success."

"Short-lived," said Harrow.

Janet came in bearing a silver tray with two steaming coffee mugs. She lowered it between the men, who took their cups. She floated away with the tray. Harrow may have fallen short in Hollywood, Nick thought, but he scored big in life with Janet—unlike him with Laura. Focus on the story, he commanded himself.

"It was an 'option' not a sale," said Harrow. "More Industry jargon. Titan paid me two-hundred-thousand dollars to secure the movie rights for a year, against one million by first day of production. I'd get first shot at writing the screenplay, and a year to do it. I was high as a kite. I imagined a whole Dan Burnside film series. Weinberg threw out names at me — Damon, Affleck, Gyllenhaal, Pratt. He was going to be bigger than Bond. Then I ran into SPECTRE ..."

"Better known as PHAT," said Nick.

"Specifically their Compliance Department. A real Ministry of Love."

"'Nineteen-Eighty-Four'."

"Very good," Harrow said, impressed. "But so much more subtle. I found out about their interference too late. Weinberg finally admitted it to Charles, who told me."

"Now you're telling me, and the world."

"I used the option money to pay my kids' college tuition, believing there'd be plenty more where that came from. Janet and I moved into the Beverly Hills Hotel for the writing job."

"Beverly Hills," said Nick.

"I know. I went the full cliché, minus the boozing and womanizing. I was disciplined, boy. I devoured screenwriting books. They were great on format directions, but they left out one valuable lesson."

"What not to write."

"Exactly," Harrow said appreciatively. "So I plunged right in. Cranked out the great American screenplay in under three months. Then sat back to await the notes for the second draft, as per my contract. A month later, I was still waiting. I couldn't get ahold of Weinberg. He was always at a meeting, and would call me back."

"Said his beautiful assistant."

"Gina," Harrow said sourly. "After five weeks of no word, Charles called Weinberg. Who admitted, in confidence, that

PHAT's Compliance Unit was reviewing my script. And his two partners at Titan would not produce the film without its seal of approval. Turned out they're both members of PHAT in good standing."

"Jesus."

"Finally, six weeks after submitting the thing, I got the script notes."

"Must've been pretty extensive after all that time."

"Try offensive. Beginning with my hero, Dan Burnside. 'Too masculine, and objectifying of women,' said the notes."

"Needs to be in touch with his feminine side," said Nick. "Unlike the female characters?"

"You said it. So did they. 'Your women are too sexual. No name actress will play one.'"

"Kim Basinger, Sharon Stone, and Kathleen Turner would have, in their film-noir heyday. They were all strong yet sexy women on screen, and great actresses. Kim won an Oscar for *LA Confidential*."

"Playing a hooker," Sinclair said in a mock outraged tone. "Women no longer use their wiles, Nick, just their brains."

"And muscles. So there's no need for Burnside to save Heather, or Sherry."

"Another criticism of my script."

"Based on the book they paid for," said Nick.

"Welcome to Hollywood. To be fair, that was before the Compliance Department got a hold of it."

"Did Titan still give you a shot at the rewrite?"

"Contractually they had to. But they demanded a few changes."

"What, other than a metrosexual hero and asexual dames?"

"The priest."

"What's wrong with Father Cork?" said Nick. "As if I didn't know."

"'Too devout', they said."

"As in too religious."

"'Must have a special motivation for being a priest.'"

"Um, God?"

"That's crazy talk," said Harrow.

"I lost my head."

"They wanted something darker, out of Cork's past, that put the Church in a questionable light. Such as ..."

"Don't tell me ..."

"He was molested by a priest as a child," said Harrow.

Nick groaned.

"My sentiments exactly. That's why he's fighting evil, outside and inside the Church."

"Which neutralizes the Christian message. Did you make the changes?"

Harrow rubbed his chin. "I was tempted to. The thought of seeing my hero on the big screen kept dancing in my head. But deep down, I knew it wouldn't be *my* hero up there, only a eunuch version of him. I wrote 'The Redeemer' as a counter to the mainstream culture and its full frontal assault on basic truths and faith. In real life, men are dogs and women sexually alluring. That doesn't mean girls can't be smart, or tough, or physically strong, to a point, only that their sexuality is immutable. As for Christianity, it's been a positive force in the world for two-thousand years, and not divisive, except to secular progressives. I couldn't betray my artistic vision for stardom. So I killed the deal. PHAT would have anyway. They don't want my story told. And I have more of them to tell..."

He pointed at the monitor screen, where shone a Word document with dialogue.

"Novel two," said Harrow. "The new Burnside and Cork mystery."

"I'll try to get it reviewed in the Post," said Nick. "Maybe I can do it myself. That is if I'm still there when the book comes out. I suggest you hurry up and finish it."

46

Duke's Bar and Grill was a traditional American restaurant on Main Street, two blocks east of the old Richmond Train Station. It had a checkerboard floor and wood dining furniture, except for a row of green-cushioned booths alongside the front window. Nick sat in the last booth with his back to the wall, for maximum quiet amid the dwindling lunch crowd. He alternated between a hot turkey lunch, a cold Heineken Dark, and reading his phone screen. He was scrolling through any notes from Alice Goodwin, Story Editor at Titan Pictures, to Stuart Harrow that smacked of the PHAT Compliance Decree.

They were even worse than Harrow had said—a total leftist redirection of book to screenplay. But to expose PHAT's agenda, Nick needed a 'smoking gun'. He had the Compliance Decree, but couldn't use it, as it had been illicitly attained by Lee. He required something on the record, and had only one lead, with three hours left before boarding the 5:30 train to DC. Turkey eaten, Nick put on his wireless earphones, and called a phone number in west Los Angeles.

An effete male voice answered. "Titan Pictures."

"Sam Weinberg," said Nick.

"Please hold."

Nick heard the lines switch.

"Sam Weinberg's office," said a woman's appealing voice.

Gina, Nick guessed.

"This is Nick Jarrett of the Washington Post. I'd like to speak to Mr. Weinberg."

"Just a moment, please."

Nick waited on hold for thirty seconds, then Gina came back on the line.

"I'm sorry. Mr, Weinberg's in a meeting right now. May he call you back?"

"Sure," said Nick. "Tell him I'm doing a story on Titan Pictures and Progressive Hollywood Action Time, about how they're censoring conservative writers. He's got an hour to comment before my deadline. My editor's name is Frank Russell. Thank you very much."

Nick hung up. It was pure bluff. There would be no story without Weinberg's input. When questioned, Frank Russell would either back him or fire him. Nick strangely didn't dread the second choice. He couldn't work next to Laura every day from then on and not be intimate with her, and he hated the thought that she could with him. He drank his beer while looking out the window at Main Street. The rain had turned to sleet. An umbrella-bearing salesman rushed to his parked car. Nick's cellphone rang. He glanced at the caller ID—Titan Pictures. He answered it.

"Nick Jarrett."

"This is Sam Weinberg," said a middle-aged male voice, sounding slightly nervous.

Russell had backed his play, Nick knew. He turned on the record app on his phone.

"Thanks for calling back, Mr. Weinberg."

"I was told you're writing a story about my company and, ah, the Progressive Hollywood Action Time?"

"Yes, sir. Regarding the blacklisting of conservative writers. I've got three on the record so far."

If you're going to lie, lie big, Nick thought.

"Oh? Who are they?"

"You'll find out when you read the piece," said Nick. "But two of them named Titan as a repeat offender."

"There is no artistic censorship at Titan."

"That's demonstrably false, sir. Your business partners, Cary Schulman and Max Fleming, are both Premium Members of PHAT, fully committed to its Compliance Decree, which I have a copy of."

An invalid copy, Nick didn't say. There was a long silence. Nick guessed Weinberg was calculating the financial damage of a conservative backlash against their upcoming slate of films.

"'Fraid your company's gonna come off looking pretty bad in this story. You could provide some balance for it."

"How?" asked Weinberg.

"Headline. 'Heroic movie producer stands up for artistic merit across the political divide—even against his own partners.' Could soften the commercial blow, don't you think?"

Another stretch of silence followed, then Weinberg spoke again, sounding deflated.

"I told Max and Cary joining Melnick's team would bite us in the ass. But the new President made them go nuts. Fuck both of 'em! What do you want from me, Mr. Jarrett?"

"Besides your side of the story," Nick said, containing his excitement. "A list of Compliance Decree signees."

"Not exactly Hamilton and Jefferson."

"But your Declaration of Independence — from Hollywood groupthink," said Nick.

"So my next film will be made in Bollywood. What's your email?"

"Jarrett N at Wash Post dot com," Nick said smiling.

"Hold a minute, please."

Nick mini-pumped his fist. More than a minute later, Weinberg came back on the line.

"My assistant Gina is sending you the list. Got any more questions for me?"

"Tell me about PHAT."

"It started right after the Election," said Weinberg. "Almost as therapy. You have no idea how traumatized people out here were, like the Big One had just hit. Beverly Hills and Malibu were Zombieland. Secretly, I thought we deserved it for being so contemptuous of the opposition."

"Most of middle America."

"Yeah. I kept my thoughts to myself. But Dwight — he took it personally."

"Melnick."

"He'd been injecting progressive content into all his pictures for some time, even his popcorn fare."

"Venus Squadron in 'Star Force Three'," Nick said.

"You caught that, huh."

"A team of alien warrior women who rescue the enslaved men? Pretty obvious."

"Not to kids."

"No, to them it's indoctrination," said Nick. "Then there's Star Force's archenemy, the Gorlons. Cannibalistic mutants led by the mad high priest to a dead god, whom he claims will come again. Subtle."

"Dwight abandoned subtlety after the elections. He swore conservative entertainment was seeping into the Industry, rousing the ignorant masses, which accounted for their vote. So he decided to expunge it."

"Politics is downstream from culture," said Nick. "Andrew Breitbart."

"That was Dwight's motivation for creating PHAT. He was wrong about one thing though. He thought it would take a while to catch on. But the floodgates opened right away. Money and pledges poured in. In less than a year, PHAT grew into a powerhouse."

"Followed by the Compliance Department, and Decree."

"There was mass hysteria in our community," said Weinberg. "I tried to fight it in my own small way."

"You optioned 'The Redeemer'."

"Good book. Could've been a hit movie, and franchise. But because of its sensibilities, PHAT shot it down."

"Which leads to my next question," said Nick. "One I've always wanted to ask a Hollywood bigshot."

"Go ahead. I'm in enough trouble already."

"Why?...Why are the richest, prettiest, most privileged people in the country such leftwing zealots? Don't you realize in the kind of world you're pushing for, you guys'll be the first to go?"

"Probably right. Maybe because we live outside the rules — of morality and tradition. So we pretend that that's the key to happiness, even though very few out here are happy. A lot are empty inside, and resentful of those who believe in something greater than themselves. But you can't match something with nothing. So they latch on to every new idea that comes along."

"And keep preaching to the choir," said Nick. "Most of the country between California and New York voted for the President. Yet all you do is bash him. Think there may be a disconnection?"

"More like an echo chamber. We hear the same progressive chatter over and over again, until outside voices are just noise pollution."

"Your box office numbers are way down. Why do you keep making movies that turn off mainstream Americans when it's so clearly bad for business?"

"Because the fools have to be woken," said Weinberg. "That's the general idea here."

"But who the hell are you people? You're entertainers — jesters. What gives you the intellectual or moral weight to tell hardworking, churchgoing, child-raising folks how to live and think?"

"To understand that, you'd have to be one of us. Every day, we're told how wonderful we are by wannabes and never-weres clinging to our ladder of success. But in our gut, we know that there but for the grace of God — if we believed in God — go we. The more insecure we get, the more virtue signaling we do."

"What would happen," said Nick, "if you ignored PHAT's

Compliance Decree? Say turned a popular romance novel into a film. There's one on the New York Times Best Seller List every week, all with similar covers. A lovely lass fleeing from a castle, with a well-built handsome devil in amorous pursuit. A lot of women must still be eating up those books."

"They are. I look at the sales figures."

"But they never make it to the screen, even with a guaranteed female audience. Only more Jennifer Lawrence-Jessica Chastain 'take on the Patrimony' films, most of which flop. What would happen if you made a good old-fashioned bodice ripper?"

"I'd make a boatload of money," said Weinberg. "Assuming I could get the project past my partners without a Lawrence or Chastain, who'd never do it. Although any unknown starlet would jump at it. But then I'd be ostracized at the golf club by my peers, beginning with Dwight Melnick."

"Are you saying that social status is more important than commercial success?"

"Out here they're co-dependent," said Weinberg.

Nick relocated to the nearest Starbucks. Nursing a large coffee, he began to write.

Dan Burnside could be bigger than James Bond or Jason Bourne. The fictional Washington private eye is less carnal than the first, less paranoid than the second, and as tough as both. But he has two fatal flaws for a screen future. He's a devout Christian and he rescues damsels in distress. To modern Hollywood, that makes him more repugnant than Hannibal Lector, who'll get another movie shot before Burnside. And yet last year, a major production company actually bit. Titan Pictures optioned the first Dan Burnside novel, The Redeemer, *from Richmond, Virginia author Stuart Harrow, even hiring Harrow to write the screenplay. What killed the deal was a clandes-*

tine leftwing group with tentacles throughout the entertainment in-
dustry, Progressive Hollywood Action Time. How PHAT committed
cine-cide, and continues to this day, is a story more intriguing than
any recent thriller, which it will never, ever be ...

Nick finished the article at a little past five. He emailed it
to the Metro Desk with the attached Compliance Decree and a
list of PHAT Prime Members, numbering close to a thousand.
They included almost everyone alive in Hollywood, and someone Nick actually knew. He'd put Lee Kwan on to him, and
gotten back some useful information, which he sent to Russell
in a separate email. Nick gathered up his belongings and walked
out into the sleet.

He dashed the block and a half to the train station, too cold
and wet to appreciate the historic brown brick, orange roofed,
cathedral-like building until inside its modern warm interior.
He caught the Washington train with twenty minutes to spare.

On the ride north, he listened to the second half of *The Re-*
deemer, trying not to think about Laura or his now uncertain
future at the Post. But looking out the window, an hour from
DC, he noticed the rain had turned to snow. The image of Laura
outside the Post building, letting him have it, reentered his head.

"Now is the winter of our discontent," he said, sinking into
melancholy.

47

In his Metro Desk hot seat, Frank Russell edited Nick's story with apprehension. It was crisply written and quite incisive on an increasingly shrill and monotonous community since the last election. What it wasn't, he worried, was a contained Metro story. Its scope went far beyond the local angle into National, Style, even Financial territory. The attached list of PHAT bigwigs made it a neutron bomb. One name flagged by Nick struck very close to home, and Russell was keeping it under wraps. To cover his butt, he'd forwarded the piece to Henley. So he was not surprised when at six-nineteen, Nancy Shea told him the Managing Editor wanted to see him.

He was equally unsurprised to see Paul Snyder plopped in the farther visitor's chair of Henley's glass office, his bespectacled boyish face even smugger than usual.

"Jeff, Elliot," Russell said, entering the office.

"Hey, Frank," Henley said somberly.

Snyder just nodded at him. Russell sat down in the vacant chair.

"I sent Elliot the Jarrett kid's story to look at," Henley said. "He has some concerns."

"Such as?"

"To begin with, tone," said Snyder. "It's a vicious slap at Hollywood, without a hook."

"That local author, Harrow, is the hook," Russell said, more to Henley than Snyder. "He got reamed by the Hollywood secret police, this PHAT group."

Snyder snorted, really annoying Russell.

"The novel's more than a year old," Snyder said. "And was only a minor success. The writer was lucky it even got optioned."

"You seem pretty up on what the movie crowd's looking for," said Russell.

The National Editor smirked before replying, "I read the trades."

"The trades?"

"Variety and the Hollywood Reporter," said Snyder, as if to a child.

"Sounds like inside jargon to me," Russell said.

"What films and television people are watching reflects the National mood."

"This story's about what people *aren't* seeing," said Russell. "'Cause a progressive Mafia is killing traditional entertainment. Shouldn't matter which side of the field you're on. A rigged game is bad news. And we're still in the news business."

"Elliot?" inquired Henley.

"Continuing Frank's Mob metaphor," Snyder said smarmily. "We don't want to launch a 'vendetta' against an entire industry, without providing more balance. One embittered writer and a vetoed film producer hardly represent the full picture. Tell you what, Jeff. I'll send Gallup to LA tomorrow. She's a UCLA grad, and knows a lot of Hollywood players. She can talk to some A-Listers and get the full story on this eee-vil leftwing conspiracy."

"A-listers?" asked Russell.

"The top tier of actors, producers, and directors," Snyder said impatiently.

"Are you in that club, Elliot?"

"Me?" Snyder replied, suddenly uncomfortable. "Why would I be?"

"Oh, I don't know" said Russell. "Maybe 'DC Beat', coming next spring on NBC."

Snyder froze in his chair. Russell pulled out his phone and read aloud from the screen.

"'DC Beat'. Drama. Jim Harding and Carol Williams play hard charging reporters for the Washington Herald—keeping the powerful in check, and politicians answering to the People.'"

"Sounds exciting," Russell added.

Snyder squirmed in his chair like a worm on a hook. Russell continued reading.

"The series depicts the realities of life in and around a major Washington newspaper."

"What's that got to do with Elliot?" Henley asked.

"Oh, didn't he mention it? He's going to be Executive Consultant on the show. To make sure it depicts the realities of life at a major Washington newspaper."

Henley glared at Snyder. "Is this true?"

"We've had some negotiations …." Snyder stammered.

"They must'a gone pretty well," said Russell. "You've been cited in the 'trades'. And all it cost you were two annual donations to PHAT of five-thousand bucks apiece...Oh, and signing that Compliance Decree."

Snyder shrank.

"This is no good, Elliot," Henley said.

"It's only an advisory position," Snyder said. "It won't interfere with my job here."

"It already has," said Henley. "What you do outside this newsroom is your business. But you just now tried to influence a story that you're a part of—while hiding your involvement."

"To protect your other boss, Dwight Melnick," said Russell. "Yes, he's Executive Producer of the show."

"That's unethical, and unacceptable," Henley said. "Frank, we'll run Jarrett's piece on Tuesday. Send O'Rourke down to Richmond to get pictures of that author. Elliot, you take next week off. I'll talk to Doug about any weeks after that."

Snyder stood up shakily, and slunk out of the office. Russell suppressed a smile. Henley looked at him.

"You're pleased with yourself, aren't you?"

"I could light up a cigar," said Russell.

"How'd you know about Elliot?"

"He's on the PHAT donors' list Jarrett turned up. Five grand a year. You've been paying him too much. Jarrett also made the TV show link, or his source did."

"Who's his source?"

"Some computer geek. Jarrett won't reveal him."

"Christ, not again," said Henley. "Do they meet in a parking garage?"

Russell smiled.

48

Zorro picked up Nick in front of Union Station, his Subaru roadster's headlights showcasing the flying snowflakes. He sat behind the wheel, wearing a black sombrero, mask, and male ballet tights but minus the rapier. Nick got into the passenger seat and put his laptop case on the floor. The heater and windshield wipers were doing their job well.

"Zorro," said Nick. "The Robin Hood of Spanish California. Where's your sword?"

"It's hidden on my person. But I hope to unsheath it tonight."

He drove past the massive white marble, multi-arched train station worthy of the Nation's Capital.

"You realize that costume is cultural appropriation," said Nick.

"Good thing we're going to Tammy's party and not Laura's."

Nick winced. Hugh saw it as he turned right onto Massachusetts Avenue, westbound.

"Sorry about you and Miss London."

Nick nodded.

"You and Warren shot down the same night .... It's a bad month for men."

"Go ahead and say it. 'I told you so. Don't fish where you swim.'"

"In your case, I'd hoped I was wrong," said Hugh. "You and Laura were made for each other. We all felt it."

"You got any more old sayings?"

"Plenty more fish in the sea?"

"Not with those gills," said Nick, adding in a hardboiled tone, "'Women are the most numerous creatures on earth — next to insects.'"

"Bogie?"

"Glenn Ford in *Gilda*. He was a tough guy, about Rita Hayworth no less. Unlike me. Little Laura kicked my guts in worse than Chuck Norris."

"You gave her that power over you."

"I know. Like you told Warren, you can't afford to care. That's how they get you."

"But there's always one, isn't there, who cuts right through, straight to the heart."

"What do you do about it?" brooded Nick.

"I guess ... fly on automatic pilot a while. Hope at some point you can take back control."

"You sound pretty expert. Have you met your one?"

"Not yet," said Hugh. "But I know she's out there, the Herminator, targeting me, to abort my future fun with other girls."

"I wish Laura was 'out there' instead of at the Post. I'm gonna have to face her every day at work. Not sure I can handle it."

"Look on the bright side. You'll be able to stalk her on the clock."

"The hell with that," said Nick. "Last night, I swore my career comes first. I plan to blow past Comrade Laura. She wants war? Meet General Jarrett. I'm gonna burn down her Left Field. I'll make feminists cry 'mommy', and gun grabbers blow their brains out. The New Man? He's a dead man."

"Yikes. Now you're scaring *me*."

They approached the enormous Dupont Circle, white with snow.

"Think I'll skip the party," said Nick. "Let me out at the metro."

"Come on, man. You have got to come. You're wearing the perfect Halloween disguise."

"What disguise?"

"The Wounded Lover."

"It's the real me."

"Even better," said Hugh. "Chicks will line up to mend your broken heart, but they'll have to get to you through me."

"What a pal."

"I am. But I might as well get something else out of it."

"In that case," said Nick. "How can I refuse?"

Hugh drove around Dupont Circle, exiting southwest on New Hampshire Avenue. Despite the slippery streets, his Subaru entered Georgetown in under twenty minutes. Hugh parallel-parked almost a block past Tammy's row house on R Street. He and Nick got out and started walking in the direction they'd come. Hugh wore nothing over his Zorro costume to maximize the dashing hero look. Nick left his flight jacket in the car, believing his Irish Fisherman's sweater warm enough for the short walk. The snowfall had thinned but still stuck. Hugh vigorously rubbed his arms and chest as they walked.

"Zorro didn't have to contend with this cold in old California."

"Only unfair taxes and an oppressive government," said Nick. "Come to think of it, that state hasn't changed at all."

"Please, no politics at Tammy's. Some of those babes are libs. And I plan to, ah, share their pain."

"I won't start anything," said Nick.

"Any chance *she'll* be there?"

"Among a bunch of fantasy-costumed girls just wanning to have fun? Doubt it."

"Lucky for you. Though I'd love to see Laura underdressed as Batgirl."

"Bat Woman," said Nick.

They approached a narrow alley entrance just before Tammy's row. It was one of the many old alleys crisscrossing Georgetown since its founding as a tobacco river port in 1751, predating Washington by forty years. Soft rock music emanated from Tammy's place three houses beyond.

"Anyway," said Hugh, "I'm hoping for a very politically incorrect welcome from the chicks who are there."

"Well, if Tammy's housemates are anything like her, the odds are in your fav—"

The sound of smashing glass interrupted Nick. It came from somewhere in the alley. Nick and Hugh stepped up to the alley entrance and looked left. The alley was bordered on each side by a high wooden fence protecting the two row-house ends. Some twenty yards in, Warren Jones, in his black duster-like coat, leaned back against the left fence, guzzling a bottle of Budweiser. A six-pack carrier stood at his feet, minus two bottles. Shattered glass from one bottle lay at the base of the right fence.

"Warren!" Nick said.

Warren turned to him and Hugh.

"What the hell are you doing?!" exclaimed Hugh.

Warren gulped down the rest of the beer. Before Nick and Hugh could say more, he flung it against the right fence, shattering it. He pulled a third bottle from the six-pack, twisted off the top, and began to drink.

"Dude, are you crazy?!" shouted Hugh. "This is Georgetown, not skid row!"

"Come with us before the cops show up," said Nick.

"Let 'em take me," said Warren, and guzzled more beer.

"We're talking DC jail," Nick said.

"It's full of killers, crackheads and..." Hugh added with a shudder, "Politicians."

"I don't give a shit," said Warren.

"Come on, Warren, let's join the party," said Nick.

"I was just in there. A good time being had by all. Especially the lovely hostess!"

Warren chugged more of the beer in hand. Nick and Hugh exchanged anxious looks.

"It's freezing cold out here!" Hugh said. "Let's talk inside."

"I'm all talked out," said Warren. "I told her how much I love her..."

"How much I need her!" he yelled over the right fence in the direction of Tammy's place, adding in a mournful voice, "She doesn't wanna hear it."

He drained the beer bottle and wound back his arm to fling it at the fence.

"Don't!" Nick and Hugh said in unison.

Warren threw the bottle. It shattered like the others, creating a pile of dark broken glass.

"Good arm," Hugh said to Nick, then off his friend's frown. "Cut it out, Warren!"

Warren opened the fourth beer bottle. Nick tried to think of something, and did.

"Tell you what, Warren. Let me talk to Tammy. Find out what her story is."

Hugh spoke low in Nick's ear, "Bad idea."

Warren turned to Nick with a hopeful expression, taking the bottleneck out of his mouth.

"You'd do that for me?"

"Sure," said Nick. "I just got dumped myself."

"No shit! By Laura?"

"Yeah, but at least I know why."

"That would help," said Warren. "If I knew what the problem was, maybe I could fix it."

"The problem is there is no problem," Hugh said to Nick.

"I'll do anything to get her back," said Warren.

"Okay, first… retire that pitching arm," said Nick.

"All right."

"Second," said Hugh. "Get the hell out of there."

"I'll walk around a while," Warren said. "Give you some time alone with Tammy."

"This won't end well," Hugh said to Nick.

Warren began walking away toward the opposite end of the alley. Nick and Hugh watched him for a minute

"If I ever get like that," Nick said. "Shoot me."

"It would be my duty," said Hugh.

49

Laura and Sarah entered Laura's apartment, their headwear wet from melted snow. Sarah held a bag of leftover Thai noodles from the Siam Palace in Union Station. Both living room lamps were on, lighting the gold mattress loveseat, brown leather armchair, and round silver coffee table. A blank sheet of copy paper lay flat on the tabletop. More light emanated from beneath the slightly ajar study door.

"Phil?" Laura called out, to no answer.

"That's odd," she said. "He always turns off the study light when he goes out."

"Saves carbon-based energy," said Sarah.

"Even with halogen bulbs."

Laura removed her beret and coat and hung them in the closet. She took Sarah's food bag so her friend could get out of her hooded green ski jacket. Laura admired Sarah's tall, athletic form, as shown off by her purple sweatpants and yellow crew-neck blouse. Sarah basked in her friend's appreciation, trying to downplay her excitement as Laura hung up her coat.

"I wonder where he is," said Laura, closing the closet door. "He said he'd be home half an hour ago. I've sent two texts since, with no answer."

"Relax. I'll get us some wine."

"Wineglasses just left of the fridge."

Sarah disappeared into the kitchen. Laura sat down on the loveseat, ignoring the blank sheet on the coffee table. She spoke loudly toward the kitchen.

"To think how close I came to leaving Phil for Nick. I should be burned at the stake."

"Instead you burned Nick," Sarah answered from the kitchen. "You're my heroine."

"He took it better than I thought. So much for damaging him like we said."

Sarah exited the kitchen carrying an open chardonnay bottle in one hand, two wineglasses in the other.

"Don't worry," she said. "It'll eat away at him. Seeing you at work the whole time. So close, and not being able to touch you… I, ah, know the feeling…"

Laura nodded. Sarah put down the wineglasses on the white sheet atop the coffee table and filled them both. She sat down on Laura's right, their legs touching. They clinked glasses.

"You planning to tell Phil about Nick?" Sarah asked, sipping her wine.

"Never. It would crush him."

"What — another man — or that man?"

"Both. But accent on that man."

"How would he feel about another woman?" Sarah asked, looking intently at Laura.

"He'd probably be more forgiving," said Laura, aware of Sarah's more serious tone.

Sarah started caressing Laura's cheek, sensuously, tenderly. She had a nice touch, thought Laura. She took another sip of wine, as if steeling herself for something inevitable. Sarah moved her hand strokes down Laura's neck to inside her blouse.

Sarah cooed in Laura's ear. "Did you enjoy doing it with Nick?"

"Yes, damn me. He was totally focused on me, as if my pleasure was his own."

"I can relate to that," said Sarah, caressing Laura's breasts.

"You're nice, Sarah."

"I can be much, much nicer."

Sarah took Laura's wineglass and set both glasses down on the blank sheet of paper. Laura knew what was coming next but said nothing. Sarah gently turned Laura's beautiful face toward hers, and kissed her passionately on the mouth. Laura let the kiss linger, without contributing to it.

"Sarah," she said softly.

"Shhh," said Sarah, and kissed Laura again, more fervently, her right hand massaging Laura's breasts.

"I have a confession to make," said Laura.

Sarah again kissed her, putting everything into it, this time with a tinge of desperation.

"It's very embarrassing," said Laura. "Tormented me all through college ..."

"Tell me, darling," Sarah said.

"I'm straight," said Laura.

Sarah ceased her physical seduction of Laura, looking glum. Laura gazed kindly at her.

"It isn't you, Sarah. You're marvelous. In fact, if I ever see the light…we have a date."

Sarah smiled sadly. Laura picked up the two half-full wine-glasses and handed Sarah hers.

"Friends?" asked Laura.

"Sisters," said Sarah.

Laura noticed two red wine rings on the blank paper. She picked up the sheet and turned it over. It displayed a cat-eared, ultra-leggy, voluptuous Tammy Perkins in a grey eye mask, bust-ing out of a skimpy feline costume with see-through tights and thigh-high boots, poised like a sensuous predator. Bold letters above the picture proclaimed: *HALLOWEEN PARTY! SUPER-HEROES AND SUPERVILLAINS ONLY! FRIDAY, OCTO-BER 30, 9PM to ??? 3000 R Street, NW.* And in smaller letters below that: *Your hotesses — Tammy Perkins, Rachel DePaul, Jill White.* Followed by: *Lowly copyaides welcome.*

"Oh no!" Laura gasped, alarming Sarah.

"What is it?"

"This invitation to Tammy's party. Phil must have printed it out — from my email. Not the shy, insecure portrait of Tammy I gave him. If I'm right, that's where he's gone, to find out where I've been all week."

"Instead he'll find Nick."

"Who, thanks to me, will have plenty to say to him."

"I'll drive," said Sarah.

They sprang to their feet and rushed over to the coat closet, Laura clutching the invitation.

50

The Halloween party was in full swing when Nick and Hugh joined it. Over fifty young professionals, evenly split by gender, mingled in the living room. Most of the women, and many of the men, wore comic-themed costumes, the female outfits naturally provocative. Self-control had to be a superhero's secret power, thought Nick. Almost everyone held a beer bottle from the two coolers by the right wall. Father John Misty's *Real Love Baby* played on the stereo. No doubt selected by Warren before his ouster by Tammy, Nick assumed.

He noted two Wonder Women—one in the star-spangled hot pants he favored, the other the bland movie incarnation. He also spied Batgirl, Black Widow, a black Catwoman, Poison Ivy, Harley Quinn, Lara Croft and the Scarlet Witch, among less familiar *Game of Thrones* vixens. Only subsequently did he notice unimposing versions of Superman, Captain America, Doctor Strange, the Flash, a bowless Green Arrow, Nick Fury, and, he assumed, *Game of Thrones* men. A muscular black Batman stood by the fireplace trysting with the shapely black Catwoman. Nick recognized the pair as Mike and his law student girlfriend, Natalie.

"Well," said Hugh, admiring Poison Ivy's green foliaged rear. "I can see I'm going to get laid tonight."

He and Nick approached the coolers. They extracted two beers, and joined Batman and Catwoman by the fireplace.

"Batman, fraternizing with the enemy," said Hugh, adding with a wink at Catwoman. "And I don't blame you."

"Guys," said Mike.

"Hi, Nick," said Natalie, smiling much too sweetly for a super-villainess.

"You top Halle Berry in that outfit," Nick said.

"Ha."

"Hugh, this is my girl, Natalie," said Mike.

"That's odd," said Hugh. "On the phone at work you called her Stefa…Oh."

"Hello, Natalie," he added in mock embarrassment.

Natalie and Mike smiled.

"We reached a decision, Nick," Natalie said.

"Oh?"

"Actually she did," Mike said. "We're getting married."

"Congratulations," said Hugh, flashing a secret horrified look at Nick.

"After I graduate from Howard Law next year," Natalie said.

"That's fantastic," said Nick. "So you resolved your income disparity issue."

"We extended it," Mike said.

"I don't need to make six figures right away," said Natalie. "They have small law firms everywhere. Where Mike goes, I'll go. It'll just take longer to pay off my loan."

"And the pediatrician," Mike said. "When the time comes."

"A loving mom and dad is worth more than money in the bank," said Nick.

"Yeah, you can save on dates and still score," said Hugh.

Everyone smiled. Hugh looked to his left past Nick's head. His look changed to a gawk.

"Yowser."

Nick turned to see an erotic vision of Tammy Perkins, filling her scanty Cougar Woman costume better than any comic illustration. She was gradually making her way toward his group, pausing to chat with salacious male guests along the way.

"No wonder Warren's in pain," Hugh said. "With bait like that, I'll take the hook."

"She's smoking hot all right," said Nick. "But I've already been burned to a crisp."

Tammy finally reached Nick's group, and gave the two new arrivals a dazzling smile.

"Nick, Hugh, thanks for coming," she said.

"I had to prove my theory," said Hugh. "That beauty attracts beauty."

"And beasts," said Tammy. "Go easy on my friends, okay?"

Hugh winked, and moved off toward Poison Ivy and Scarlet Witch. Mike and Natalie also withdrew, leaving Nick alone with Tammy. She looked poignantly at him, despite the cougar ears atop her thick blonde hair.

"You look haggard, Nick."

"I had a bad dream."

"Not about me."

"No, a meaner girl," said Nick.

Tammy nodded sympathetically. "I invited Laura. Don't know if she's coming or..."

"Not."

"I see," said Tammy. "If you wanna talk, I'm all yours."

Her striking blue eyes seemed to give the cliche extra meaning.

"Now that you mention it, there is someone we should talk about."

Tammy sighed.

"Warren," she said.

"He's out there now, freezing his ass off 'cause of you. He deserves to know why he got iced."

"It's my problem, not his."

"But he's the one who's hurting."

"All right," said Tammy. "I wanted to talk to you anyway."

She glanced around the boisterous crowd.

"Not here," she said. "In private."

She led Nick to the staircase, and up the steps. Following her, Nick couldn't help noticing her firm buttocks and great legs showcased by the skimpy Cougar Woman bodysuit, tights and boots. Tanita Tikaram's *Twist in my Sobriety* began playing on the music system. Down in the living room, facing Poison Ivy and Scarlet Witch, Hugh watched Nick climb the steps behind Tammy. He shook his head, and resumed amusing the two super vixens.

Tammy turned left at the top of the stairs, Nick behind her. They approached the end of a dim old hallway, the sensual song from downstairs still audible. Tammy stopped before the last bedroom door on the right. She opened it, releasing more light into the hall. She held the door open for Nick then stepped in after him, closing the door behind her.

Tammy's bedroom was not the seductive mantrap Nick had imagined on a couple of feisty nights, but a small, modest yellow-walled boudoir. A long brown rug with gold abstract shapes covered most of the wood-panel floor. The carpet terminated on the left at a vintage accordion radiator hissing under the rear window. A queen-size bed with a dark wood headboard and yellow comforter took up the left back corner, its head just right of the window. Above the bed hung the poster of a flattop mountain overlooking a vast American forest. Tammy indicated the edge of the bed.

"Have a seat, Nick."

Nick glanced around for less compromising seating, but saw only an uncomfortable vanity desk stool on his right. Tammy followed his look, and read his mind.

"Contrary to popular belief, I don't bring a lot of men in here."

Nick nodded semi-guiltily.

"I'm honored," he said.

He started toward the bed, but paused to look at the poster on the wall above it.

"That's spectacular," he said. "West Virginia?"

"Uh huh. North Fork Mountain. We used to go hiking up there — me, my brothers, and our folks till they got too old for it."

"But still with you?"

"My dad is," said Tammy. "Though I wouldn't want 'im to see me in this outfit."

She struck a naturally sexy pose as if to dare parental disapproval, and got the opposite result from Nick. He sat down on the edge of the bed, near the window, the falling snow visible outside it. Tammy stood provocatively in front of him.

"Look at me, Nick. What do you see?"

"Cougar Woman."

"Besides the costume."

"A babe," said Nick.

"What else?"

"A hot babe."

"What else?"

Nick couldn't come up with anything right away. Tammy nodded morosely, and sat down on Nick's right, her shapely left leg pressing his jeans.

"That's my curse," she said. "I'm smart. Maybe not like your Laura, or them other Wellesley snobs at the Post. But I got mostly 'A's through high school and college. So what if I don't give a hoot about politics, or some angry Indian singer ..."

"You're looking better," said Nick.

"Ever since middle school, people have been judging me on my looks. So I played up to that. I mean being pretty's a plus, isn't it?"

"You bet."

"Does that make me a bimbo?"

"Hey, bimbos get bad press," said Nick. "It's feminist misogyny. But you're not one, Tammy. You got way too much class."

Tammy looked gratefully at Nick. "You mean it?"

"Hundred percent."

"Thank you, Nick," said Tammy, placing her left hand on his knee. "Means a lot coming from you."

Nick thought her hand on his knee might confuse matters, but it felt good so he left it there. The nearby radiator continued its hissing. Nick felt the warmth from both sides of him.

"Can you turn down the heat?" Nick asked, aware of his double meaning.

Tammy's sultry expression suggested that she caught it too.

"Sorry, I got no control over it. Why don't you take off your sweater?"

Having committed himself, Nick removed his Irish Fisherman's sweater, exposing an olive-green t-shirt. He refocused on his purpose.

"Let's talk about Warren."

"Warren..." Tammy said melancholically. "You see how the other copygirls shun me — Sarah pretty blatantly. Laura's always polite to me, but I can sense her disapproval. She can't control it. I'd love to hang out with her outside work. Can't say the reverse is true."

"Sisterhood has its limits."

"But you guys made me feel welcome. And you're so comfortable round each other, unlike us girls."

"Laura holds that against us," said Nick. "Male bonding."

"Well I like it, and being with you all. But there was only one way I could fit in."

"You'll never be one of the boys."

"Yeah," said Tammy. "Only as a kind of cheerleader."

"You got the right attributes."

"I know. I was cheerleader captain at UNC."

"No wonder they won the ACC last year," said Nick.

"There's a little sex in every cheer. You can't separate the two, or cheer for any one player on the team. 'Fraid Warren caught the full wallop. I like Warren, just not that way."

"But you slept with him."

"That I did," said Tammy. "He was sooh hot for me, Nick,

like a puppy. Guess I got carried away. I didn't have too much to say to him, so I let my body do the talking."

"And you didn't like what it said."

"It's why I cut it off…I know I hurt Warren. It was the last thing I intended. You probably think I'm a slut."

"No, Tammy," said Nick. "But till tonight, I never figured you for lonely."

Tammy gazed at Nick, her blue eyes now opaque.

"You're the first boy to ever see that. Most don't look past my face and this." Tammy indicated her impressive costumed physique. "But you kept on doing just that, even when I got right in front of you. You're the one I was cheering for, Nick, the whole time. I wanted you since our first day in the copyaide station. But you only had eyes for Laura."

"And she nearly poked 'em out," Nick said, evading Tammy's confession.

"I can make you forget her."

"Take one helluva cheer," said Nick.

Tammy moved her stunning face closer to his, her hand from his knee to his groin, and rubbed it through the jeans. Nick felt mentally troubled, yet physically aroused. He made a weak vocal protest.

"Tammy, don't. Warren's my friend."

"Ooh, sweetheart," Tammy cooed. "Be selfish for once. Can friendship do this for you?"

She pulled down Nick's fly zipper, and put a hand through the open flap. She began stroking him. Nick stifled a moan of pleasure, finding it hard to think. A girl most men could only fantasize about was seducing him, and he was trying to resist her—not just out of loyalty to Warren, but to the only woman he'd ever loved, who'd pierced him through the heart.

"This?"

Tammy started licking his ear, her wild tongue stimulating pleasure points he didn't know he had.

"Stop," he thought but did not say.

"This?"

Tammy pressed her gelatinous lips against Nick's mouth. Her tongue snaked into his throat, charming him like a cobra. He mindlessly responded, causing her to moan with delight. After a series of intense, rousing kisses, she pushed his torso down on the bed, his head on the pillow, her face just above his groin. She unclasped the single button on his jeans, and pulled down his underwear, clutching what arose from it.

"This?"

She brought her mouth down to his most intimate part. He groaned in ecstasy. His eyes rolled right, catching sight of the window and the falling snow beyond it. Falling, Nick knew, on the friend he'd just betrayed.

51

Sarah parked her blue 2014 Toyota Prius in a vacant space one block short of Tammy's house. She and Laura got out, and continued their approach on foot, Laura scouring the snow-topped vehicles around them.

"I don't see Phil's car. That's a good sign."

Several row houses from their destination, they spotted a familiar figure nervously pacing the sidewalk ahead of them.

"Is that Warren?" Sarah asked.

"Either him or the Phantom of the Opera."

"Wonder why he's not enjoying Tammy's male fantasy party."

"I'm guessing his party's over," said Laura.

Warren reached the turnaround point and pivoted, catching sight of his female colleagues.

"Hi, Warren," said Sarah.

"Sarah, Laura," Warren said gloomily. "Didn't expect to see you two here."

"We're feminist police," Laura said.

"We heard women are degrading themselves in there," said Sarah.

"No, only me," said Warren.

"Are you coming or going?" asked Laura.

"Neither. I'm waiting on Nick."

"Nick," Laura said anxiously. "Is he in there?"

"Yeah."

"Is he leaving soon?"

"No, he's talking to Tammy for me. We, ah, had a falling out. Heard you and Nick did too."

Laura frowned. "Does the whole world know about us?"

"Just his friends," said Warren. "And we know something else."

"What?"

"He's in love with you."

"He said that?" Laura asked softly.

"He didn't have to," said Warren. "But thanks to you, he got what I'm going through. Why he offered to help."

Laura appeared wistful. Sarah noticed, and changed the subject.

"Has there been any trouble at the party?" Sarah asked.

"Yeah," said Warren. "Two Sam Smith singles."

"It could get uglier," Laura said. "I have to find Nick before Phil does."

"Who are you protecting?" Warren asked.

"Me," said Laura.

"I'll take you to him," said Warren.

He led Laura and Sarah to Tammy's house. They went up the porch steps then through the door, failing to see Phil's silver

BMW cruise by in search of parking.

In the festive living room, Zorro was entertaining Poison Ivy and Scarlet Witch.

"There I was, surrounded by ISIS soldiers. Their guns pointing at my head. So I said to their leader, 'You can kill me if you want, but my story's already on the wire!"

"Wow," said Poison Ivy.

"What'd they do to you?" asked Scarlet Witch.

"They ..." Hugh began to elaborate but balked at a sight near the entrance. "Shot me."

The two superwomen looked curiously at him. Hugh watched Warren, Laura, and Sarah wade into the party. Batman Mike and Catwoman Natalie went over to greet them. Warren said something to Mike, who pointed at the staircase. The three newcomers started toward it.

"Oh oh!" said Hugh.

He dashed to the foot of the stairs, reaching it before his coworkers. He bounded up two steps then spun to look down on them. They stared up at Hugh, thea beer in his hand, clearly blocking their ascent.

"Warren, what are you doing?" Hugh asked. "Nick's still rapping with your chick. Or are you planning a threesome?"

He gave Laura and Sarah a nod. Sarah grimaced.

"I have to see Nick, Hugh," said Laura.

"Why, so you can hurt 'im again?"

"I just need to talk to him."

"He'll be down shortly," Hugh said.

"What are you, his Press Secretary?" asked Sarah.

"Good one, Sarah," said Hugh. "Did I ever tell you my lesbo fantasy? There are these two hot dykes dancing real close to each other. I cut in, and one of 'em grabs me by the nuts, while the other one..."

"Get out of the way, Hugh," said Warren, suddenly nervous.

"You don't wanna go up there right now," Hugh said.

"Step aside."

"Wait right there," said Hugh, raising his left hand, a beer in his right. "I'll get Nick."

He rushed up the steps. Reaching the upstairs hallway, he looked frantically in both directions, unsure of which closed door to approach. He went right, to the first door on the left.

"Nick!" he said in a low voice near the door.

He saw Warren rise from the staircase and turn left, away from him, toward the last door on the right. Hugh froze, like someone witnessing an imminent car wreck.

Naked on top of him, Tammy looked even more incredible. She was the most naturally beautiful woman Nick had known, let alone made love to, including Laura. Her luxurious blonde hair, gorgeous face, large firm breasts and lithe body combined to give him guilty pleasure. Only her extreme desirability could have provoked a physical response in him despite his broken heart. It was like being ravished by Sharon Stone in *Basic Instinct*. Nick almost welcomed the icepick. But what came next hurt also.

The bedroom door flew open. Warren stood in the doorway, looking sick. Nick and Tammy turned to him, Nick's face racked by shame. Warren stumbled backward and out the door. And where he had stood, Laura materialized. Her expressions ran the gamut from hurt to sad to angry.

"So much for the Code, Nick," she said and vanished.

Nick dropped his head back on the pillow, feeling ill. Tammy rolled off him to his left side, and lay beside him. She stroked his leg, more supportively than sexually. Then a third visitation appeared in the doorway, Zorro, observing the couple in bed.

"I just remembered another old saying," said Hugh. "Never rains but it pours."

Hugh dissapeared into the hall. Nick rolled off the bed to his feet. He began to dress quickly, Tammy studying him from the bed.

"I guess one more ride's out of the question," she said.

Near the foot of the staircase, Mike and Natalie watched a despondent Warren almost tumble down the steps, clutching the handrail all the way down.

"Your friend looks older coming down than he did going up," Natalie said.

"He looks like I felt when my leg blew out, a dream shattered."

"And a new one now begun."

"Yeah," said Mike, with an affectionate smile at Natalie.

Warren moved unseeingly through the partiers and toward the front door. The entering Phil Cartwright had to step aside to avoid him. Phil looked quite upset himself, even in a stylish icaramel overcoat with false fur lapel. He scanned the revelers, getting turned off more than on by the scantily clad superwomen, while searching for one woman in particular.

Sarah appeared beside him. He spoke tersely to her. She led

him past Mike and Natalie to the staircase, just as Laura slowly descended it, looking distraught.

"Whatever's going on up there has got to be pretty traumatic," Natalie said to Mike.

Mike nodded, watching the soap opera continue to unfold.

"Laura!" Phil exclaimed.

Laura looked downstairs at Phil, and struggled to refocus on him, her mind clearly elsewhere.

"Phil," she said dully, reaching the lower steps.

Phil grabbed her hand like a drowning man would a life saver. His tight grip and troubled face brought Laura out of her fog.

"What's wrong?" she asked.

Phil whispered in Laura's ear, making her frown. She let him pull her toward the front door. Sarah watched it close behind Laura, and on her. She saw Hugh coming down the stairs. He gave her a friendly shrug, then joined Mike and Natalie.

"Warren?" he asked.

"Ran out of here like he'd seen a ghost," Mike said.

"Here comes Casper now," said Hugh, nodding at the staircase.

Nick came bounding down the stairs fully dressed. He stopped at the foot of them, glancing all around. He looked inquiringly at Hugh, Mike, and Natalie. Mike pointed to the front door.

"She went that-a-way, with Phil."

"Loan me your car," Nick said to Hugh.

Hugh took a Subaru remote key from the waist strap of his ballet tights, and tossed it to Nick. Nick caught it and ran out the door. Mike and Natalie stared inquisitively at Hugh.

"Don't ask," said Hugh.

Sarah joined them, looking unusually vulnerable. She appraised Hugh's costume.

"Zorro."

"At your service, Senorita," said Hugh, doing a bad Ricardo Montalban impression.

Sarah seemed about to zing him but caught herself.

"Buy you a drink?" Hugh asked in his normal voice.

"Why the hell not," said Sarah.

She and Hugh started toward the coolers. Sarah put her arm through his, pleasantly surprising Hugh.

"About your lesbian fantasy," she said. "Tell me more."

52

Stepping off Tammy's porch, Nick looked left. It had stopped snowing but a fallen portion covered the cars and pavement. He looked right, then froze. Near the end of the long block, Phil appeared to be shoving Laura forward, his hand on her back. Nick recalled Laura saying Phil had hit her once, and intimating that he might again. *As you're by now aware, he has a temper.*

Nick wondered if his promise to protect Laura superseded her cruel breakup with him. His instincts answered for him. He started jogging after the pair. Halfway there, he saw Phil open the passenger door of his BMW, then seem to force Laura into it. Nick broke into a sprint, but the car took off before he reached its former spot.

He frantically glanced around for Hugh's black Subaru while clutching the key remote. He double pressed the unlock button. Three cars behind him, a snow-topped vehicle beeped and flashed its lights. Nick ran to it and got behind the wheel.

He pulled out of the space quickly, just missing the front car's rear bumper. Gaining speed, he ran the stop sign at the end of the block. Halfway down the next block, he spotted the BMW, slowing down for the subsequent stop sign. Nick reduced speed a good way back from it. When the other car crossed the street, Nick followed it.

"Bond," he said in a Sean Connery accent. "James Bond."

The BMW continued west, away from Capitol Hill. Phil wasn't taking Laura home, Nick realized. Both cars made a left on Wisconsin Avenue, Georgetown's main street. Sparse traffic allowed Nick to keep the BMW in sight from a discreet distance. Many of the shops, restaurants, and bars were still open at midnight on a snowy Saturday. Small business was booming under the new President, Nick knew, with record low unemployment, despite the apocalyptic shrieks from Laura's crowd. When Phil turned right on "M" Street, so did Nick.

They approached Key Bridge on the left, its sand-colored concrete arches spanning over the Potomac River. Nick wondered if Phil would turn and take it to Virginia. The BMW continued straight toward the west end of the city, Nick two cars behind it.

On the right rose the steep, narrow stone steps made famous by the film, *The Exorcist*, climbing up to Georgetown University. Nick's cellphone rang on the passenger seat, the screen indicating *Sinclair, Hugh*. Nick put the phone to his left ear, steering with one hand, eyes on the BMW merging onto Canal Road.

"Your car's still in one piece," he said.

"Where are you?"

"Heading west on Canal Road. I'm following Laura and her boyfriend. No, I'm not stalking her. I just want to make sure she's okay. Phil seemed pretty pushy with her back there."

"So what are you going to do when you catch up to them?"

"Don't know yet. Maybe fly to her rescue like Superman. 'Course Laura hates Superman. She prefers New Man Clark Kent. Anyway, I'll think of something. Have it out with them I guess. Talk to you soon, Hugh."

Nick hung up and tossed the phone back on the passenger seat. A mile farther, Phil veered right, heading northwest on Foxhall Road, Washington's toniest street. The mansions on both sides of the rising road were so grand, you could barely glimpse them behind their castle-like garden walls. They reminded Nick of a line from his favorite Western, *Rio Bravo*. Dean Martin asks John Wayne if he thinks Ricky Nelson is as good with a gun as some think. Wayne answers, "I'd say he is. I'd say he's so good, he doesn't feel he has to prove it." Substitute "rich" for "good," and it describes most Foxhall Road residents.

The two cars climbed the hill road for a quarter mile. Phil made a sudden right into a wide driveway. It was blocked five yards in by a black iron gate interrupting a high cobblestone wall.

Nick drove past the driveway, frustrated by the zero parking options. Instead of a sidewalk, an unbroken row of tall shrubs by the street made stopping impossible. Nick got the message—sightseers not welcome. He thought about abandoning his likely unwelcome rescue of Laura and leaving her to her chosen fate. But when a narrow side street appeared ahead on the right, he took it.

He pulled onto a patch of frosted grass between the street and the corner wall. Expecting floodlights and armed guards at any moment, he jumped out of the Subaru. He ran back to Foxhall Road, then left on the downhill street. A set of headlights came fast at him. He darted left off the street and into the nearest shrub, grabbing on to its stems. He heard and felt the car whisk by his rear. He hoped nobody in it would report a man in a white sweater making love to a bush.

Back on the street, Nick ran down to the driveway Phil had entered. Reaching it, he crossed to a silver mailbox on the opposite side, and read the name inscription: *Hawthorne*. Senator Wayne Hawthorne, mused Nick. Champion of the little people. But not in his neighborhood. No riff raff allowed around here.

Another pair of headlights came fast up the hill. Nick ducked behind the nearest shrub. The car shot past him. Standing up, Nick turned to the black iron gate. Again he thought about bolting. Laura, Phil, and Senator Hawthorne deserved each other. He would only get in trouble by intruding on them. But he couldn't shake the dread that something was wrong inside. It was a mystery that involved, possibly imperiled, the only girl he'd ever loved, whom he deep down believed still loved him. In his book, that called for some cheap heroics.

He knew better than to breach the gate. It was probably wired to a security alarm, if not high-voltage electricity. He'd read enough thrillers. He moved right along the cobblestone wall for twenty feet and stopped. He took hold of a head-high cobblestone, put one foot on a lower one, and began to climb the wall. It was like the obstacle course at Fort Piedmont, except DC cops would fire at him with real bullets.

"Okay, Jarrett," said Nick, halfway up the wall. "You like having your name in the paper. Here's another chance to make the Metro Page. 'Prowler Shot Dead on Senator's Property.'"

He became aware of headlights approaching from the left. He flattened himself against the wall, certain the next light he saw would be flashing red. But the car went by, leaving him in the dark. He reached the top of the wall, and surveilled the grounds: Large yard with cedar trees. Grey Tudor mansion, a few window lights, circular driveway in front, Phil's BMW parked outside the front door, engine still on, behind a silver Mercedes sedan.

As he watched, both BMW doors opened. Phil and Laura got out. They must have been talking in the car for a long time, Nick thought, or fighting. Phil circled the hood and joined Laura on the passenger side. Nick couldn't make out their too distant faces but her body language suggested reluctance, his extreme anxiety. They approached the mansion's front door. The automatic porch light came on. Phil opened the door without knocking. He let Laura enter first, as if not trusting her to go in second. He closed the door. After a moment, the porch went dark.

Nick rolled over the wall. He hung down from it for a second, then dropped to the ground. He rushed through the snowy yard to the cedar tree nearest the house, and hid behind it. Knowing the porch light would turn on before the door reopened, he advanced on the two cars. He kept low while inspecting the Mercedes. It had a District of Columbia license plate with the medical symbol on the left—two serpents on a winged staff—and letters that read *GOLF MD*. The porch light came on.

Nick got back to his cedar tree just as the front door opened. Laura stepped out with an expression of disgust marring her lovely face. She appeared unhurt, Nick saw, at least physically. She went to the BMW, and leaned into it, both palms against the passenger window. Phil exited, looking upset. He moved to Laura's right, and stood anxiously beside her. She turned to him.

"I can't do this, Phil. It's rape."

Nick heard her clearly behind the cedar.

"No," Phil said in a shaky voice. "It was consensual. She seduced him."

"How, by shaking her pom-poms at him? For God's sake, she's just a kid!"

Phil winced. "He'll stop, Laura. I'll make him stop."

"You can't. *He* can't. He's sick."

"Goddamit!" exclaimed Phil, losing control. "We've worked too hard for this. It's not about private behavior. It's about a cause, our cause, Laura. And Hawthone's an irreplaceable leader in it. Think about all the good he can do as Vice President. Think of the alternative!"

Laura looked torn. From the mansion emerged a balding, fiftyish man in a blue tracksuit with fanny belt, supporting an unsteady, pretty teenager with long thick brown hair. The girl wore a blue ski jacket over her knee-length beige skirt. Phil and Laura turned to look at her.

"How's she doing, Doc?" Phil asked.

"She'll be okay," Doc said, then kindly to the girl. "Just a little further, Cindy."

Cindy appeared at a loss. The doctor moved her closer to the BMW passenger door being blocked by Laura. Behind the cedar, Nick pulled his cellphone out of his jeans' back pocket. Left hand obscuring the screen light, he found the video function. He began to film the nocturnal activity. Doc, still holding Cindy, looked questioningly at Laura. Phil joined him.

"Just take her back to her parents' house, Laura," said Doc.

Laura didn't respond or move. Phil seemed to get more desperate.

"Please, Laura," he said. "We need this."

Laura said nothing for a moment, then turned to Phil.

"All right. But for that girl's sake, Phil, not for you, or Hawthorne. I want her the hell away from here for good."

"Thank you," Phil said with relief.

"Don't thank me. Or call me. I won't be home tonight, if ever."

Phil handed her the key remote. She circled to the front of the car, and got into the driver's seat. Phil opened the passenger door for Cindy. Doc gently placed her on the seat and withdrew. Phil closed the door.

Laura drove the BMW around the Mercedes. Phil and Doc watched it approach the gate. Phil's reserve air of authority completely abandoned him, leaving him a jittery mess. Doc took out a pack of cigarettes from his fanny pack and offered him one. Phil accepted it, then a light, and took a drag.

"That was close, Doc," he said. "Naomi and their daughter will be here early morning."

"I could almost hear little Emily on finding Cindy there. 'Daddy, do you need a babysitter too?'"

"Afraid he does," said Phil. "Me."

They reentered the mansion. Nick dashed toward the closing front gate, and got out just before it shut.

53

At one-thirty in the morning, the Washington Post newsroom resembled a ghost ship. The busy dayside desks of Financial, Investigative and Sports were vacant and dark. The Foreign Desk had a single occupant—the cordial thirty-something Indian-American Editor. The National Desk had two—the fortyish, auburn-haired female Editor and a boyish millennial reporter. The Metro Desk had three—heavyset, bearded Editor Joe Baroni, haggard middle-aged Police Reporter John Hogan, and Nick Jarrett.

Nick sat at a cubicle typing on the desktop computer. It was a faster, smarter machine than his laptop, as demonstrated by the rapid matching of the two names he input: *Senator Wayne Hawthorne* and *Cindy*. The *Washingtonian* magazine photo came up in three seconds. It was the same teenager Nick saw at Senator Hawthorne's house, maybe a year younger and more childlike, walking hand in hand with a cute little girl in a private school uniform—white blouse and long blue skirt. The photo caption read: *Public School Champion, Private School Parent*. A blurb underneath disclosed more: *Senator Wayne Hawthorne's (D-Connecticut) daughter, Emily, 9, leaves Stone Ridge Elementary with babysitter Cindy Immergut. Hawthorne voted against private school vouchers for low-income children, but enrolled Emily in the exclusive academy rather than the local public school.*

Not his worst hypocrisy, Nick knew. He leaned back in the chair, rubbing his jaw. This was a career-making story, and in Hawthorne's case, a career-breaking one. Nick looked from the monitor screen to Joe Baroni talking on the desk phone. Should he give him the scoop, start the ball rolling right away?

He turned to the National Desk, where Night Editor Audrey Woods sat reading her computer screen. Hawthorne was a United States Senator and Democratic stalwart, which meant national impact. He, Nick, would blast off with a National Desk shockwave. And then there was the personal angle, the life blow he would deliver to the woman who hurt him. He had a hold of dynamite and he had to figure out how best to explode it. But he needed a little more data.

He walked over to John Hogan's chair. Hogan looked up at him with reddish eyes. Nick noted his bulbous Irish face, prematurely disfigured by booze and too many gruesome sights.

"No murders tonight, Jim?"

"Couple," Hogan said solemnly. "Gang drive-by in Anacostia. Not worth my personal appearance. You seen one shot-up twelve-year-old kid, you seen 'em all."

Nick swallowed. Could he someday be that jaded?

"If they offer you the police beat, Nick, say no. It's soul killing. I oughta know."

"You got a great book out of it," said Nick. "*Dead Men Tell.*"

"Yeah, sixteen years ago. When I thought there was a point

to crime and punishment, and that killers had a conscience. Maybe they used to. Not the new breed. They don't feel a thing. And they're getting younger every day."

Nick had nothing to add to that so he kept silent.

"You want something from me?"

"Got a license plate on a story I'm working on," said Nick. "Would like to know whose car it is. If only I had a contact with the Metro Police ..."

"Or knew someone who did," said Hogan.

Nick grinned sheepishly.

"Whatcha got?"

"Mercedes, maybe twenty-sixteen. Belongs to a doctor. Vanity plate. Caduceus ..."

"Caduceus?"

"Medical insignia," Nick said. "Two snakes on a winged staff."

"Is that what that thing's called, college boy? What's the plate number?"

"All letters, 'Golf MD'."

"Golf Doctor. What an asshole. I'll send you the dope on 'im."

"Thanks, John."

Nick walked away, pulling out his cellphone. He punched in Laura's number. It rang once and stopped. A message appeared on the screen: *Blocked call*. He nodded.

"All right, Laura," Nick said aloud. "See if you can block my next move."

He headed for the elevators.

54

Nick sat at his dinette table breakfasting on Special K and coffee. His cellphone lay next to the cereal bowl, displaying the video he took of Cindy Immergut and Dr. Jerome Sadler in Senator Hawthorne's driveway. Hogan had sent him the physician's name and data, after his police contact ran the Mercedes license plate. Exhausted by his long, eventful Friday night, Nick had slept past ten. But he'd woken up knowing how he would proceed, professionally and personally. Both would have irreversible consequences.

He put in the hands-free earphone and phoned Laura's cellular. Again he got the blocked call message. Between cereal bites, he found Sarah Woronov's number in the copyaide directory, and called her. Sarah answered on the third ring with an unfriendly tone.

"Hello."

"Good morning, Sarah," Nick said with false cheer. "How are you today?"

"What do you want?"

"To speak to Laura."

There was a brief pause. As if Sarah had to consult someone, Nick thought.

"She's not here," Sarah said.

"It's important."

"I said she's not here."

Nick heard the cut-off click. What he hadn't heard was Sarah telling him to call Laura. Because she knew Laura had blocked him. Nick took a sip of coffee, and pressed the phone redial button. The line rang four times then Sarah's voicemail came on.

"This is Sarah Woronov. Leave your message at the tone. I'll call you back."

Nick waited for the beep, and said two words. "Cindy Immergut."

He hung up. He ate more Special K and sipped more coffee. His cellphone rang. He ignored it, finishing his cereal. The phone rang three more times. Nick looked at the screen. The caller ID read *London, Laura.* Call unblocked, thought Nick. He took it.

"Jarrett residence," he said, sounding like a cartoon English butler.

"What about Cindy Immergut?" asked Laura, trying a bit too hard to sound defiant.

Nick clicked on the video of Cindy on Hawthorne's driveway.

"I can't confirm her age," he said. "Is she an old sixteen or a young seventeen? Maybe I should ask Doctor Sadler."

There was a long silence. When Laura next spoke, it was with no trace of bravado, only uncertainty.

"Where are you?"

"In my bunker."

"Wait there for me," Laura said, then almost gagged on the next word. "Please."

She hung up. Nick took the empty cereal bowl and coffee mug into the kitchen. He rinsed one and refilled the other. He carried the cup into his quasi-living room, and sat down in the chair facing the door, feet on the coffee table.

"Alexa, play 'Sunset Boulevard' by Crimson Ensemble."

"'Sunset Boulevard' by Crimson Ensemble," said Alexa.

The title theme to Andrew Lloyd Webber's *Sunset Boulevard* began playing on the device. Only film-noir aficionados recognized it as originally the theme from *Gumshoe*, the unsung 1971 gem directed by Stephen Frears and scored by Lloyd Webber. Nick drank his coffee, eyed the door, and had Alexa keep repeating the song. On the fifth play, the door opened.

Laura stood in the doorway in her red coat and green skirt. She looked as beautiful and powerful as when he first saw her. Her fierce brown eyes, beneath and between her rich raven hair, focused accusingly on him.

"Hello, Laura," said Nick. "Change your mind again?"

Laura closed the door, and advanced to the backrest of the sofa. Her eyes never left Nick, like a gunfighter's before the draw.

"You followed me last night," she said.

"Only the first leg."

"Why?"

"It was an irresistible combo," said Nick. "Your perfume, my nose for news."

"And what did you learn?"

"Senator Hawthorne's really working the youth vote."

"You're a pig, Nick."

"Maybe," said Nick. "But you're the one covered in slime."

"You can't prove it."

Nick held up his cellphone with a picture of Cindy and Dr. Sadler on the screen. Laura's brown eyes went to it and flashed.

"I got a press card, and I know how to use it," said Nick.

The intimidation power drained out of Laura. She took off her coat, revealing her formidable chest in a gold cashmere sweater, and threw it on the backrest. She circled to the front of the sofa and sat down.

"What do you want from me?" she asked.

"What we both want. A reporter job at the Post. We've proven we make a good team. On this story, I got the bull by the horns, and you're riding it."

Laura looked incredulously at Nick. "You want me to help you expose Senator Hawthorne?"

"He's going down anyway, baby, so you might as well get something out of it, like a career. As for your boy, Phil—he can write a book. Sex scandal and politics. Guaranteed bestseller. He'll be a CNN star."

"You're sick."

"I was," said Nick. "You cured me, cold turkey. I would've done anything for you. Kissed off the scoop of a lifetime. Not any more, sweetheart. Hawthorne's going down, and it's my gravy train running him over. I'm giving you the chance to climb aboard."

Laura tried to glare at Nick. But her eyes began to moisten, her lips to quiver. Nick looked at her in surprise and, against his will, sympathy.

"Hold on now…"

Laura's steel dam broke. She started crying, completely, femininely. Nick had to restrain himself from going to her.

"It's all my fault!" she said. "I did this to you! I didn't know how to handle you! It was so hard holding everything together! My beliefs! My desires!"

"Stop that, will you. It's dirty pool."

"I fell for you too, Nick. For all the stupid reasons you said. You're smart, funny, and, God help me, prime husband material—circa Fred Flintstone."

"And you, Lara Croft," said Nick. "A swell pair we are."

He stood up and walked to the sofa. He sat down next to Laura without touching her. She nodded, grateful for his closeness and detachment. Her crying stopped.

"Your New Man piece set me off," she said. "I got scared. I had to break us up, slow you down. I hit you with everything I had, and you barely flinched."

"I was crying on the inside."

"I couldn't get past your disdain for my beliefs."

"Not for you, Laura. Never for you. I'd love you no matter how many communist meetings you went to."

"Well, you're a better man than I am, Gunga Din."

"Thank God for that," Nick said, nodding at Laura's chest. "I can appreciate your finer points."

Laura glanced down at her bosom.

"They're no match for Tammy's," she said, saddened by a thought. "Are you and she ..."

"No. That was a perfect storm you threw me into. It'll never happen again. Besides, I'm a brains man—in the right body of course, yours."

"The left brain rules."

"No, it just dictates," said Nick. "Try working out the right sometime."

"I'd need a good trainer. Want the job?"

"What will I get out of it?"

"All of me," said Laura, leaning back on the sofa.

Nick kissed her passionately. Laura responded full force. Their chemistry reignited, their bodies interlocking everywhere. They made love for lost time. They finished sitting half naked on the sofa, Nick's arm around Laura's bare shoulders.

"I love you, Nick," she said softly.

"You know where I stand."

Laura smiled. Nick broached a touchy subject.

"About the story…"

"We'll write a new one!" said Laura. "Leave Hawthorne to Phil. He won't have me anymore. You will."

"Hawthorne's no good. The people have a right to know."

"He'll self-destruct. Please, darling, we need a clean slate, apart from this. Promise me you won't write the story."

She gave Nick a deep wet kiss. "Promise me."

"I promise I won't write the story," said Nick.

"You'll never regret it."

Laura stood up, and started dressing. Nick watched her, amazed by the eroticism of it.

"I'll be needing a new place to stay," said Laura. "Can I come home with you Monday?"

Nick nodded. Laura dressed, bent down, and kissed him.

"See you soon, darling."

Laura grabbed her coat off the sofa backrest, and left. Nick leaned back, a troubled expression on his face. *Sunset Boulevard* played on.

55

Nick rode his Cervelo bicycle northeast on Western Avenue from Chevy Chase Circle at a steady nineteen miles per hour. His hooded purple University of Wyoming sweat jacket, green backpack, wool gloves, sweatpants, bike shoes, and vigorous pedaling kept him warm on the cold Saturday afternoon. His iPod was playing *Genesis Countdown* from the soundtrack to *Star Trek II: the Wrath of Kahn*.

He reached Beach Drive in under ten minutes, then turned right into Rock Creek Park. The weekend blockade of cars made cycling through the park a scenic pleasure. Or it would have been to Nick if not for his concern about the daunting task ahead of him.

He made a left on Sherrill Drive, and soon went over the rocky creek that gave the park its name. On the east side, the trail ended at 16th Street. Nick flew across the four-lane highway and continued straight on Aspen Street. He rode the two miles to Georgia Avenue, then two more into Takoma Park village.

The picturesque old town was evolving from the progressive roots that dubbed it "Berkeley West," due to hippies dying out and millennials moving in. But the counterculture influence had preserved the town's Norman Rockwell appearance, even with the intrusion of corporate chains like Starbucks and Target.

Nick made a left on Fourth Street and slowed to a cooldown cruise. He rode two blocks up the tree-rich residential road, scanning the addresses on the quaint two-story wood and mortar houses to his right.

He dismounted before a pale blue home with an elevated porch and a wide window on the right, its venetian blinds downturned. He leaned his bike against a slender sidewalk tree and solemnly approached the house, pulling off his earbuds. Climbing to the porch, his tension rose, as did the deathrock song inside.

He rang the front doorbell. The song volume dropped. The door opened, held by a red-eyed, stubble-jawed Warren in a black sweatshirt and blue jeans. He looked at Nick with disbelief, then slammed the door in his face. A moment later, the deathrock got loud again.

Nick returned to his Cervelo. He took off his backpack, gloves, and sweat jacket, leaving on the sweat-damp grey T-shirt. The cold struck him right away. He sat down on the ground in the lotus position, his back against the bike's down tube. The faint music from the house switched to an equally grim new song. A shivering Nick saw the middle blind in the right window bend up for three seconds, then straighten.

Sometime later, he heard another creepy song. It matched his mood as he froze to death. At least his name would make the Post one last time—the Obituary page. Under his breath, he recited his favorite poem by John Keats, *The Eve of St. Agnes*, deeming it an appropriate sendoff.

"Saint Agnes' Eve—Ah, bitter chill it was/The owl for all its feathers was a-cold/ The hare limped trembling through the frozen grass/And silent was the flock in wooly fold/Numb were the Beadsman's fingers, while he told/His rosary, and while his frosted breath/Like pious incense from a censer old/Seemed taking flight for Heaven, without a death ..."

Nick saw the middle blind rise for a moment, then fall again. He forgot the rest of the Keats poem, but recalled another, *Ode to a Grecian Urn*. Ode to Laura's ass, he thought. He would miss seeing it again, let alone feeling it. He smiled bitterly, knowing what Laura would say if she could read his mind.

"Even his last thought of me was sexist."

God, she's wonderful, Nick reflected sadly. He realized he could no longer feel his fingers, and wiggled them without sensation. Warren's front door opened. He emerged glumly on the porch in a brown down jacket. He stopped in front of Nick, looking down at him.

"You turning Japanese?"

"I really think so," Nick said, teeth chattering. "Need a sword to do it right."

"Try the knife you stuck in my back."

"I'm s-sorry, Warren."

"I trusted you!"

Nick nodded. "N-not my finest hour. For what it's worth, I won't forgive myself. "

Warren's stare softened slightly. "Why are you here?"

"I got something for you," said Nick. "Will prove more durable than Tammy."

"What?"

Nick blew on his hands, and unzipped his backpack with some effort. He extracted a document-size manila envelope, and held it up to Warren. Warren took it.

"What's this?"

"The stuff careers are made of," said Nick.

He stood up, and donned his sweat jacket, backpack, and gloves. He mounted his bike, and rode off toward the Takoma Park Metrorail Station, two blocks away.

Warren carried the envelope back into the house. The living room had cheap yet serviceable furniture. A brown bearded young man with round glasses, yellow sweat pants and a blue flannel shirt occupied one of the chairs, blasting zombies on his laptop. He didn't look up when Warren entered and sat down on the love seat with the manila envelope.

Warren opened the envelope, and took out four sheets of paper: the *Washingtonian* magazine photo of Cindy Immergut and Senator Hawthorne's daughter, a photo of a middle-aged man in a track suit supporting a dazed, unsteady Cindy before a fancy mansion, information on the man in the track suit as some kind of doctor, and typed bullet points under the heading, *Senate Sex Scandal*. Reading the last paper, Warren's eyes widened.

Todd Armstrong had a pretty good poker hand. Less than an hour into the Saturday night ritual at his cherished Fairfax home game room, he was down two hundred dollars, most of it to Cuban cigar-smoking blowhard Art Billingham. With his cruise line thriving since the last election, Billingham didn't need his money. This deal was Armstrong's chance to win it back, and more. He took a sip of his Hennessy cognac and placed four chips in the large pot.

"Raise you two," he said.

Three of the other four men around the green felt table did nothing. The fourth, Billingham, puffed on his Montecristo and threw down four chips.

"I call."

At that moment, Armstrong's cellphone rang.

"Really?" said investment banker David Epstein on his left.

"Could be work, guys," said Armstrong, checking the phone screen without recognition.

"Hope it means the President's resigning," said attorney Bob Strezinski on his right.

"In that case, I'll need this pot," Billingham said.

"Hello," Armstrong said into the phone. "Speaking...Oh yeah, I know you, Warren. You're one of Susan's kids. What can I do for you?"

He listened for a minute, stiffening the entire time.

"Jesus! Okay, you meet me at the Post. My desk, twenty minutes. See you there."

He sprang to his feet.

"I gotta go," he said. "Make yourselves at home."

"Show your hand first," said Billingham.

Armstrong turned over his cards, showing three kings. Billingham displayed three aces, and began gathering the pot.

"That's okay," said Armstrong. "It could still be my lucky night."

He dashed out of the game room.

56

Nick plopped the Monday morning edition of the Washington Post on the mailroom table. He had come in early to absorb what he'd wrought. The headline, plus the color photo of a coated Senator Hawthorne trying to ward off the camera with one hand, said it all: *TEEN GIRL ODs IN ALLEGED SEX RELATIONS WITH U.S. SENATOR.* The sub-headline delved deeper: *Girl, 17, had to be revived by doctor.* The double byline followed: *By Ted Armstrong, Washington Post Investigative Reporter, and Warren Jones, Special to the Washington Post.*

The die is cast, thought Nick. Sticking to his Julius Caesar comparison, all that remained for him was getting stabbed to death, and he knew by whose hand. He turned toward the Editorial side door. The clock above it marked 9:47. On its left, the muted TV showed a grim CNN anchorwoman, with a still shot of Senator Hawthorne off her left shoulder. The chyron at screen bottom read: *Senator Hawthorne Denies Sexual Relation with Minor.* Nick found the TV remote and unmuted the sound, keeping it low.

"A high school student who worked as the babysitter for Connecticut Senator Wayne Hawthorne overdosed on Ecstasy Friday, following a sexual encounter with the Senator — according to a story in today's Washington Post. Hawthorne is calling the report a 'right wing lie'. The unnamed minor's parents are refusing comment. But the Post quotes a doctor who allegedly saved the girl's life — Hawthorne family physician Jerome Sandler. Senator Hawthorne was recently named the perfect running mate by two frontrunners for the Democratic Presidential nomination. We'll have more on this story throughout the day."

The image switched to post-hurricane recuperation efforts in Fort Lauderdale.

"South Florida residents may be singing 'Bye, Bye Bertha' as Hurricane Bertha dissipates off the mid-state coast. The Category Four storm left an estimated eighty-million dollars in damage costs from Key West to Tampa. Rescue efforts are ongo..."

Nick muted the volume, just in time to hear Hugh's singing on the approach.

"Oh-ho the Wells Fargo Wagon is a-comin' down the street, oh please let it be for me. Oh-ho the Wells Fargo Wagon is a-comin' down the street, I wish, I wish I could know what it could be..."

Hugh entered through the open doorway and smiled at the sight of Nick.

"Well, I'm surprised to see you here," he said. "I thought you'd be halfway to Afghanistan by now. You'd be safer facing down the Taliban than a mad Miss London."

"I know. Her bullet has my name on it," said Nick.

"You could tell her Warren broke the story on his own."

"Nah. This frigging nightmare is all mine."

"You gave up the girl, and you gave up the story. What the hell were you thinking?"

"A man's gotta do what a man's gotta do?"

"Try, 'There's a sucker born every minute.'"

"P.T. Barnum," said Nick. "He was wrong about one thing. Laura and me, *we* were the Greatest Show on Earth."

Laura appeared in the open doorway, staring daggers at Nick. Nick felt them but neutrally returned her stare. Hugh couldn't take the crosscurrent.

"I forgot the copy paper," he said.

He scurried out past Laura. She remained staring at Nick. Susan Machado walked in behind Laura then went around her, not noticing anything amiss.

"Good morning, kids," she said. "Miss London, I need you on the National Desk pronto. Their phones are ringing off the hook over this Hawthorne scandal."

Nick winced.

"Yes, Susan," said Laura.

"Nick, Mr. Sinclair will be on the Financial Desk today, so you'll be alone."

"Again," Nick said softly.

"Pardon me?"

"No problem."

Susan entered her office and shut the door. Laura turned back to Nick, her brown eyes still piercing.

"I misjudged you, Nick. You're a cold, hard bastard. You promised me!"

"That I wouldn't write the story. I kept my promise. As you see ..." Nick tapped the newspaper on the mail table. "Ted Armstrong did, with a little help from Warren."

"Was nailing Hawthorne so important that you could do this to me?" said Laura.

"I did it for you, and for our country."

"Since when are we two on the same page in your book."

"You both have my Pledge of Allegiance."

Laura groaned.

"Listen to me, Laura. Wayne Hawthorne may be Senator New Man. But he's a freak. He's not fit to be Senator, let alone Vice-President. You've known that the whole time, but you were too close to it to kick his ass."

"So you spared me the decision. Me being a girl!"

"My girl."

"I could've been," said Laura. "I was ready to live with you."

"Sure, till the story got old. No thanks, Joan of Arc. I'd rather not have you at all than as a martyr for the Cause. You wanna fight for something important? Start with the Truth, wherever it leads. You see, that's the difference between you and me. I'd nail Mike Pence in a minute if he did to any kid what Hawthorne did to Cindy. Maybe that's the feminist in me."

Laura shook slightly, and walked out to the newsroom. Nick gloomily began unloading the supply cart.

57

Nick entered the Style department carrying two parcels misdelivered to the newsroom. Handing them off to cheerful, gay, always well-coiffed Style aide Tom Nelson, he noticed a small crowd around the Music Desk. Moving closer to it, Nick made out Rick Masetti and six other Style people congratulating Warren, a rare smile on his face.

Glancing at the Fashion Desk, Nick saw Tammy also appraising Warren, or reappraising him. She looked typically beautiful in a pink cashmere sweater, green slit skirt and grey tights. As if reaching a decision, Tammy stood up, and slinked toward the Music Desk. She stopped beside Warren, and leaned over his desk with a fetching smile. Nick almost heard Warren gasp from twenty feet away. Watching him melt all over again, Nick shook his head, and started back toward the newsroom.

On the noon internal mail run, Nick approached the Financial Desk with a full basket. Hugh sat in the assistant's cubicle, talking on the desk phone like a stockbroker. Nick put the Financial mail in the 'In' tray, and waved an Asian-stamped post-card next to Hugh's face. It showed a Japanese model wearing only a pink Asahi T-shirt while holding an Asahi beer bottle. The printed text on the card said: *ASAHI—38% Market Share!* A handwritten note beneath that read: *To Alex. Look forward to seeing you in person at Asahi US Tennis Tour, March 16. Love, Akiko.* Hugh took the postcard from Nick's hand.

"It's for my stamp collection," he said.

He opened the top right drawer of his cubicle desk. Nick spied three other postcards from Europe and Asia with exotic models promoting their national products, all with personal notes to Hugh. Nick continued toward the National Desk. Halfway there, he stopped short, and took a deep breath.

Despite minimal momentum, the National Desk radiated energy. Instead of Paul Snyder, a forty-something brown-haired man Nick didn't know sat in the Editor's chair, eying CNN on the mounted TV monitor, a landline telephone receiver at his ear. Craig Yellen, headset on, was typing furiously. The two Copy Editors, a young husband-and-wife team, the Hedisons, scanned their screens. Lanky young National News Aide Ray Attanasio, also wearing a headset, scribbled in a reporter's note-book. He cast wistful glances at the cubicle next to him, where Laura London worked the phone lines with utmost poise.

Nick moved into her line of sight. Laura didn't acknowledge him as he placed a parcel in the 'In' mail desk tray. He would have preferred a smirk or scowl. He resumed his delivery route. Only as he walked away did Laura look at him, and sighed.

She worked diligently all afternoon and early evening, fielding calls, taking and transferring messages. At six o'clock, she saw officially temporary, but possibly permanent, National Editor Jack Schaeffer sit upright in his chair while staring at the television monitor.

"This is it, people," he said.

Everyone on the National Desk turned to the TV screen. It showed Senator Hawthorne's Foxhall Road mansion, the front door open and floodlit, a standing microphone right outside it. Reporters and news crews clustered in the driveway, on which Laura wished she'd never set foot. She gulped when Phil came out, followed by Senator Hawthorne in his long black overcoat, and his plump, elegant wife Ellen, the two holding hands like newlyweds. Camera lights flashed. Phil approached the microphone.

"Good evening," he said grimly. "The Senator will be giving a very brief statement. And he will not take any questions afterward. Senator..."

Hawthorne stepped up to the microphone. His wrinkles appeared more prominent under the perfectly combed hair. He spoke reproachfully more than regretfully.

"I have only one thing to say. The charges against me are damnable lies, trumped up by my rightwing enemies, and by this corrupt Administration. I did not have immoral or illicit relations with the young girl in question..."

Laura stiffened.

"The truth is my wife and I were planning to dismiss her for two reasons. First, we felt she was becoming overly familiar with me to an inappropriate degree. Also, because we suspected her, sadly, of using narcotics."

Laura stiffened in her seat.

"That's a lie!" she blurted almost entirely under her breath, but not quite.

The clearly infatuated Raymond turned to her.

"What was that, Laura?" he whispered.

Laura shook her head, indicating "never mind."

"Now I'm going to go back to my wonderful wife and family, to keep working for the fine people of Connecticut and America, and fighting the right-wing purveyors of this lie. Thank you."

Hawthorne turned away from the mike. He, Ellen, and Phil started back toward the house, ignoring shouted questions from reporters.

"Senator! How do you explain Doctor Sadler's statement?!"

"Who's the other unnamed witness?!"

The Hawthornes and Phil reentered the house, and the door closed after them.

Laura felt queasy. Someone tapped her right shoulder. She looked up to see prim black nightside News Aide Nicole Haggis smiling down at her. Laura surrendered her seat. She glanced at the clock, reading 6:17. A sudden panic seized her, seemingly out of nowhere. Yet she somehow knew the source of it, and the reason. She started toward the copyaide station, her speed increasing with each step, until she practically ran in through the open doorway.

The station's only visible occupant, Hugh, was locking the supply cabinet. Laura looked left into the alcove then anxiously back at Hugh.

"He's gone," said Hugh.

"Home?" Laura asked, aware of the frantic note in her voice.

"After a brief stop."

"Where?"

"The closest Marine Corps recruiting station."

"What?!" Laura said, very afraid.

"That's right. He said the French Foreign Legion's no longer in fashion."

"No," Laura said, having trouble breathing.

Hugh studied her.

"Are you going to be nice to him?" he asked.

Laura looked at Hugh with a glimmer of hope.

"Yes," she said. "Oh yes."

"Tenth and K. If you hurry, you can catch him."

Laura rushed out of the copyaide station. She snatched her scarlet cloak out of the closet and hurried to the elevators. She pressed the down button several times, willing any elevator door to open. The left one finally did. Laura donned her coat on the way down.

She exited the Post building and ran left on K Street. She scoured the backs of pedestrians under the streetlights, looking for Nick's flight jacket and Irish cap. Seeing neither on the Post block, she hurried across Thirteenth Street. She came up empty on the next block also.

The Twelfth Street light turned red. Laura dashed into the moving traffic. Cars on both sides of her braked hard. None of them blasted their horns as she hurried by in front of them. She wondered if not getting honked at was sexual discrimination, then dismissed the thought. Nick was right, she realized. Her side had gone too far.

She saw him crossing the street half a block ahead. She ran across Eleventh Street, and caught up to him. He was three office fronts away from a high American flag, fluttering above the door of the US Marines Recruiting Station. Laura grabbed Nick's right arm, halting him. He turned to her. A pleased yet inquisitive expression dawned on his face.

"Laura," he said.

"Are you going to get yourself killed just to haunt me, Nick?"

"Fair is fair," said Nick. "You'll haunt *me* forever."

"I can do a better job of it in the flesh."

"Forever?"

"Forever," said Laura.

Nick smiled. So did Laura. The American flag snapped loudly in the breeze, distracting Nick. He looked reverently up at it. Laura gulped with concern. Nick turned back to her.

"I suppose I can fight here at home," he said.

"Especially our home."

"No," said Nick. "You and I will make love, not war."

He took Laura in his arms and prepared to kiss her, but paused to look at her contented beautiful face.

"Well, maybe a few skirmishes," he said.

"Even those will be fun," said Laura, with an impish smile.

Nick kissed her, and she eagerly responded. They kept kissing in the middle of the sidewalk as pedestrians walked around them, moving left and right.

Acknowledgements

To the wild bright kids at the Washington Post controlled—or not—by the angelic Nancy Brucker: George Clifford, Ned Corrigan, Sarah Isaac, Sean Kelly, Nina Killham, Danny Klaidman, Laura Lafay, Bob O'Harrow, Bill O'Leary, Kevin Spear, Dave Ungrady and the rest, who inspired my characters

To the mighty Washington Post editors and writers who took time to help guide an ambitious but naïve young writer back in the day.

To Alix and Christina Barrett for invaluable insight into college sorority life.

About the Author

Lou Aguilar was born in Cuba and lived there until age six, when his anti-Castro scholar father flew the family to America, one step ahead of a firing squad (for his dad, not Lou). He attended the University of Maryland, where he majored in English, minored in film, and found both to be dependent on great writing. He became a journalist for The Washington Post and USA Today, then a produced screenwriter, and, in 2016, a published novelist with *Jake for Mayor*. Lou has had three independent movies made, including the cult science-fiction film, "Electra" (33rd on Maxim magazine's list of "The 50 Coolest 'B' Films of All Time"). He presently writes only "A" scripts. His last short story, "The Mirror Cracked," was published in the prestigious horror anthology, Kolchak: the Night Stalker Chronicles, which was nominated for a Bram Stoker Award.

www.ingramcontent.com/pod-product-compliance
Lightning Source LLC
Chambersburg PA
CBHW030553020726
47494CB00005B/1590